Please return / renew by date shown.
You can renew it at:
norlink.norfolk.gov.uk
or by telephone: 0344 800 8006
Please have your library card & PIN ready

D0298921

NORFOLK LIBRARY
AND INFORMATION SERVICE

NORFOLK ITEM

30129 071 251 376

Also by V. M Whitworth

The Bone Thief

THE TRAITORS' PIT

V. M. WHITWORTH

EBURY
PRESS

1 3 5 7 9 10 8 6 4 2

Published in the UK in 2013 by Ebury Press, an imprint of Ebury Publishing
A Random House Group Company

The Random House Group Limited Reg. No. 954009

Addresses for companies within the Random House Group can be found at:
www.randomhouse.co.uk

A CIP catalogue record for this book is
available from the British Library

The Random House Group Limited supports The Forest Stewardship Council®
(FSC®), the leading international forest-certification organisation. Our books
carrying the FSC label are printed on FSC® -certified paper. FSC is the only forest-
certification scheme supported by the leading environmental organisations, including
Greenpeace. Our paper procurement policy can be found at:
www.randomhouse.co.uk/environment

MIX
Paper from
responsible sources
FSC® C016897

Printed and bound by CPI Group (UK) Ltd, Croydon, CR0 4YY

ISBN 9780091947200

To buy books by your favourite authors and register for offers visit:
www.randomhouse.co.uk

ACKNOWLEDGEMENTS

I am very grateful to all the friends, colleagues, family and readers who have asked me for a sequel to *The Bone Thief*, and who have helped me to produce one. In particular, I must thank my colleagues at the Centre for Nordic Studies in Orkney and Shetland, who have been a tremendous support and given me a peaceful haven in which to write creatively as well as academically: Donna Heddle, Ragnhild Ljosland, Alex Sanmark, Lynn Campbell, Andrew Jennings and Silke Reeploeg. It's great being part of the team.

It's tricky for any York graduate to lay claim to a particular view of a past incarnation of the city, and some readers will recognise how very heavily my fiction relies on the researches of Julian D. Richards, Rosemary Cramp, Martin Carver, Peter Addyman, the late Richard Hall, Christopher Norton, and many, many others. I am particularly grateful to the York Archaeological Trust for making so many of their publications freely available on-line. I have cobbled together details from the work of all these scholars to construct my fictional *Jórvík*: should any of you read *The Traitors' Pit*, please remember that it *is* fiction, and be kind.

I am also deeply appreciative of the many colleagues elsewhere who have offered helpful comments, advice and companionship, especially John Blair, Katherine Lewis, Joanna Huntington, Sarah Semple, David Petts, Sam Turner, Steve Ashby and Helen Gittos. Other friends whose support and feedback I particularly cherish include Jessica Haydon, Sophie Holroyd, Susie Holden, Janni Howker, Becky Ford, Kiersty Tams-Grey, Anna Elmy and Lucy Blackburn. Thanks also to the staff at the Jorvik Viking Centre, and especially Jane Stockdale. My sister Kate has also been wonderful (other family members will have to settle for my collective, and heart-felt, thanks). My agent at MBA, Laura Longrigg, and my editor at Ebury, Gillian Green, have both been full of constructive suggestions, and extremely patient with me.

But above all it's been my husband Ben who, despite his own writing commitments, has backed this project all the way, and has dedicated so much time to looking after our daughter, Stella.

DEDICATION

For Ben

Look at the stars! look, look up at the skies!
O look at all the fire-folk sitting in the air!
The bright boroughs, the circle-citadels there!
—Gerard Manley Hopkins

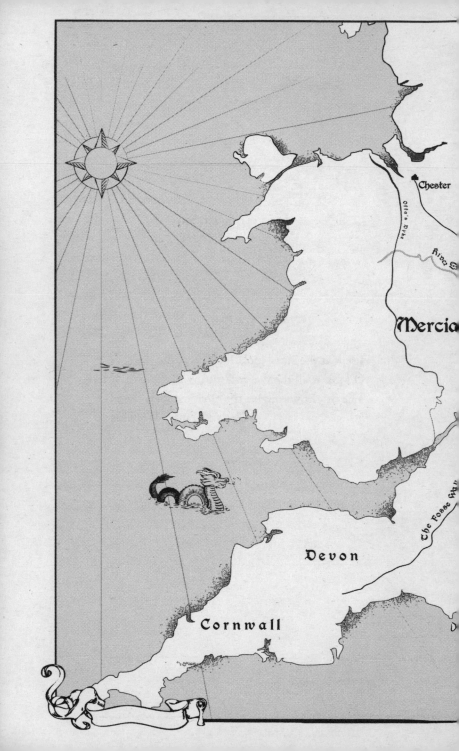

CAST OF CHARACTERS
in Order of Appearance

NB Historical characters are marked with an asterisk; characters who first appeared in *The Bone Thief* are marked with an obelisk.

†**Wulfgar** first of Meon, then of Winchester, now of wherever the Lady of the Mercians happens to be. Known to some as 'Litter-runt' and others as 'Soft-Hands', but his friends call him Wuffa (Little Wolf/Wolf Cub).

*†**Athelfled (Fleda), Lady of the Mercians** Eldest child of King Alfred (the Great) of Wessex, and married in her early teens to Athelred, Lord of the Mercians.

Alda, Reeve (Estate Manager) of Meon A family servant who has known both Wulfgar and his brother Wystan since they were born.

Wystan of Meon Wulfgar's older half-brother – they share a father but not a mother – and now owner of the extensive family estates.

Judith, Wystan's wife Younger daughter of Sigewulf, Eldorman of Kent: of rather higher birth than her husband and she has never forgotten it.

*†Edward, King of Wessex and old school-fellow of Wulfgar's. Eldest son of King Alfred, and younger brother of the Lady of the Mercians. He is known to historians as 'Edward the Elder' as there was another King Edward later in the tenth century, but obviously this did not apply in his life-time.

*†Denewulf, Bishop of Winchester Legend has it that he was the swineherd in whose hut King Alfred burnt the cakes, and who later entered the Church. But it's only a legend.

Cwenhild, Wulfgar's half- and Wystan's full sister A nun, formerly at Shaftesbury and now at the new nunnery in Winchester, the Nunnaminster.

Oswin, Reeve of the Palace King Edward's senior official, who has known Wulfgar since he was seven.

Alnoth of Brading A West Saxon thane, with lands on the Isle of Wight.

Edric of Amport A West Saxon thane, with lands in what is now called Hampshire.

†Garmund 'Polecat', Wulfgar's slave-born half-brother, and close associate of King Edward.

Beornwulf of Winchester, Wulfgar's maternal uncle and Archdeacon of Winchester.

*Athelstan, young son of King Edward.

Helmstan, Wystan and Judith's baby son.

*†Werferth, Bishop of Worcester Werferth was Bishop of Worcester from 873 onwards. He was a close friend of King Alfred, a scholar and translator, and godfather to Fleda. If he really did have only one eye, no chronicle ever bothered to record it.

*†Kenelm the Deacon, the Bishop's nephew. He counts as a semi-historical character, as charters record a Kenelm the Deacon in Worcester in 897 and (separately) a kinsman of Bishop Werferth's of that name, who was an abbot in the early tenth century. It is possible that the two Kenelms are the same man.

Thorbjorn of York Loyal hearth-man-of King Knut of York.

*†Athelred, Lord of the Mercians Husband of the Lady Athelfled, old war-leader, now incapacitated by a stroke.

†Ketil Grimsson 'Scar', Jarl of Leicester and younger brother of the late Hakon Grimsson Toad, who seized control of Leicester when the Norse Great Army conquered eastern Mercia in the 870s.

†Gunnvor 'Cat's-Eyes' Bolladottir, whose father came over from Norway to join the Great Army. Only she knows where her father's hoards of silver are buried.

Gerd Thorbjornsdottir Young woman of York, eldest daughter of King Knut's house-carl Thorbjorn.

*Lothward, Archbishop of York Another character who counts as semi-historical. There are two archbishops attested in the years around 900, but they have names (Athelbald and Wulfhere) that are too similar to those of other major characters in my story. So I made one up.

*†Athelwald Seiriol, Atheling of Wessex His father was Alfred the Great's older brother and predecessor as King of Wessex. Denied the throne on his uncle's death, he rebelled against his cousin Edward, the new King. Almost nothing is known about his mother: I have taken the liberty of deciding she was Welsh in order to round out his background a little, and give him a second, Welsh, name in order to distinguish him from the other Athel-somethings in the story.

Elfled of Wilton A nun from Wimborne. First cousin once removed of King Edward, Athelwald Seiriol and the Lady of the Mercians.

*Knut, King of York Only known from his coins, which imply a fascinating and complex character.

†Father Ronan of St Margaret's Kirk, Leicester Son of a Canon of Leicester Cathedral and his house-keeper, an Irish slave-woman.

†Toli Silkbeard Hrafnsson, Jarl of Lincoln.

Alwin, son of Alnoth of Brading A fifteen-year-old boy in the service of Athelwald Seiriol.

†Uhtsang, a harp that once belonged to St Cuthwin of Leicester Some people might not think of a harp as a person, but Wulfgar and Ronan certainly do.

†**Hakon Grimsson Toad, the late Jarl of Leicester** Although he was dead before the story started, he is very present to Wulfgar.

†**Kevin** Father Ronan's son and altar-boy.

†**Conan** Kevin's dog.

***Grimbald of St Bertin, first Abbot of the New Minster, Winchester** A French Benedictine monk, he was head-hunted by King Alfred, and became a pre-eminent figure in the late ninth-century revival of learning.

CHAPTER ONE

Gloucester

Wulfgar had been working the summer-long day in his cluttered little writing room attached to the royal palace of Kingsholm, a short walk from the gates and walls of Gloucester. The light was fading at last from the single window set high in the wall, and he was leaning back on his stool, rubbing the cramps out of his right hand and wrist. The King of the York Danes had suggested this treaty, but his Lady had agreed to it and ordered it drawn up, despite the fierce opposition of her council. Wulfgar felt he owed it to her to frame every clause in terms as rewarding to the Mercians as possible. While her Lord lay ill, the Lady of Mercia needed every advantage she could get.

He bent forward and was about to dip his quill once more when he realised what the ebbing daylight meant: time to head to the palace chapel for the restorative calm of Vespers. Just him, and the Lady's chaplain; there should be no false notes in the singing this evening. He reached for a square of ink-stained linen to wipe the quill clean. But, in his haste, he picked up the wrong scrap of fabric among all the odds and ends on his desk, and a little gilt-enamel brooch tumbled out of its wrappings and clattered onto the floor. Heaving a sigh, he went down on his hands and knees, wondering as he did so what could have prompted him to buy it two days earlier.

It had been St John the Baptist's birthday. He had emerged from the gloom of St Peter's Minster in Gloucester after a deeply satisfactory Mass, still singing. '*Nesciens labem, nivei pudoris, prepotens martyr, heremique cultor...*' Now, that would go nicely into English. 'Innocent of evil', he chanted under his breath, groping after the right rise and fall, 'unblemished as snow, most – no – mightiest of martyrs...' Still mulling over the right English word to convey all the nuances of *cultor*, he had stumbled against the corner of something hard.

'Watch out, you fool!'

Wulfgar found himself clutching the edge of a trestle table, a stall, in the middle of Gloucester's annual Johnsmas market. The stallholder, grabbing the board and preventing his stock from disaster, was looking at him with exasperation.

'You nearly had the whole lot over.'

'I'm so sorry.' Appalled at the prospect of tipping all those expensive trinkets into the mud and litter of the market, Wulfgar stammered his apology. 'I'm really, really sorry.'

Flustered, he sought to make amends. One little brooch winked up at him, the swirl of red and green enamel in its silver setting reminding him of someone, against his will.

'How – how much is that?'

It had been a furtive transaction: he didn't want anyone to wonder why an ambitious young cleric might be investing in such an obviously feminine knick-knack. He had rebuked himself for it all the way home and he was berating himself now as he scrabbled under his desk. The brooch, hardly larger than his thumbnail, had rolled into a dusty corner and he was more than half-minded to leave it where it lay. After all, the woman who had prompted its purchase lived in Leicester, more than a hundred miles away over the far side of the border with the Danish badlands.

And God and His Holy Mother only knew when – or even if – Wulfgar would ever set eyes on her again.

What a fool he was.

As though she would thank him for a trumpery trinket like this. He still owed her more money than it was worth.

Anyway, buying brooches for beautiful women belonged to another kind of life, a life on which the door had been closed when he himself had been too young to have a say in the matter.

If only he had been his father's heir...

He closed his eyes, ashamed of the thought. It was almost tantamount to wishing his older brother dead. He would have to tell his confessor about it, brooch and all.

The knock on the door was so unexpected that he jumped, cracking his head hard on the underside of the desk. Stifling a curse, he grabbed the brooch, shoved it into the soft leather pocket he wore on a thong round his neck, and struggled to his feet.

'Come in.'

A diffident slave poked his head around the door. 'The Lady is calling for you.'

'Why?'

He shuffled his feet. 'She didn't say why.'

'Look at me,' Wulfgar said. 'I'm in no state to enter her presence.' Apart from the new coating of grime on his knees, he was ink-stained from fingertip to elbow; his head was buzzing and his eyes sore, and he didn't need to look down to know that he needed to retie his sagging leggings.

'But she said to fetch you right away,' the boy insisted, wide-eyed and anxious.

'Very well.'

He cast a last look at his disordered desk, and reminded himself that he wasn't a child any longer; that no oblate-master would beat him for the untrimmed pens and uncapped inkwells. 'I'm coming.' Yawning, rubbing his sore head, he followed the slave boy across the cobbled courtyard, noisy with roosting starlings, to where his Lady was waiting for him in her private bower. The guard stepped aside as he approached, acknowledging him with a nod.

The crowded little room almost dazzled him with colour; he had to blink for a moment to make sense of what he was seeing. The Lady, in her chair. Two of her women flanking her, sitting on low stools. A bolt of linen several ells wide was spread across the laps of all three, and rainbows of silk threads spilled out of the basket that one of the women was holding, while the other was reeling up gilt filaments that scattered the light of a dozen candles. Their honey fragrance vied with the rosemary strewn across the floorboards.

It looked as though the Lady and her women had been working on the altar cloth she had vowed to her new church of St Oswald. He knew she spent hours there on her knees, haggling with Heaven over the healing of Mercia's Lord.

'My Lady?' Did she want to consult him again about the theology of her choice of embroidery motifs? If so, wherein the urgency?

'Wulfgar.' Her neat, oval face looked grim. She glanced beyond him, over his left shoulder. 'Tell him.'

Wulfgar turned, bewildered, to find he was not the only man in the room. In the shadows to one side there stood a scruffy, harrowed-looking figure, singularly out of place. He was staring fixedly at Wulfgar, his expression strained and eager. Wulfgar found himself smoothing the hair around his tonsure. What was the man staring at? Had he ink on his face as well as his hands?

When the stranger spoke, his voice was rough-edged with weariness. 'Master, your brother...' he stopped and swallowed. 'Your brother has been arrested for treason.' A broad, West Saxon accent, mouthing words that made no sense.

'What?' Wulfgar could feel the muscles between his brows twitching, the skin of his face growing red and stiff with embarrassment and anger. 'But he's King Edward's man.' His mouth had dried, but he managed to add, 'And, please, don't call that man my brother. He may be my father's son, but he's not my brother.'

'Not your brother?' The messenger was shaking his head like a dog with a flea in its ear. 'King Edward's man? Acourse he's King Edward's man. How would it be treason, else?'

Why, Wulfgar wondered, had this man come here, to him? *I am not my brother's keeper.* He squinted at the exhausted-looking newcomer. There was something familiar about him and his deeply furrowed brow, though the sparse grey hair was strange. One of the Lady's slaves was bringing the man a palm-cup of ale and he nodded his thanks before draining it at a swallow.

'I know you,' Wulfgar said.

The man nodded sombrely. 'That you do, young master, though it's many years since we saw you last at Meon.'

Recognition came late, but it came at last.

Meon.

His late father's estates in the undulating chalklands east of Winchester in distant Wessex. And this man had been his father's reeve.

'Alda. Forgive me. I don't know what I was thinking. I just never thought to see you here.' The man bowed. 'And why on earth should you come to me, with news of – Wulfgar's mouth twisted, despite his best efforts – 'of Garmund?'

'*Garmund?*' Alda blinked, incredulous. 'Garmund Polecat? That slave-born—' His lips clamped shut, remembering he was in the Lady's presence. Then he said, 'I wouldn't bring you a message from him, not to save his life, not if it meant damnation otherwise.'

Wulfgar thought he must have misunderstood the reeve's message, though it had seemed clear enough. Surely the words *treason* and *brother* in the same breath could only refer to his father's son, his old enemy, the man whose name he could hardly bear to say?

He became aware that the Lady had been leaning forward, intent on their every word. She reached out to him, putting a hand on his sleeve and drawing him closer to her.

'Wulfgar, I understand why you might assume a message of treachery must refer to Garmund.' The hand tightened. He looked down at it in surprise. 'Nothing that that man might do would surprise you, or me.' He shifted his gaze to her face, and found that, while a complicit little smile hovered about her lips, he could see only worry in her eyes. 'But it's not about Garmund,' she swallowed. 'Not this time.'

'Not…?' An anxious tic tugged his eyelid. 'Not Garmund?'

'You have another brother, master,' the reeve broke in.

'Another—?' And Wulfgar staggered, as though a great buffet of cold wind had hit him from the rear. He put his hands to his ears. His lips parted, framing a name, soundless.

From a great distance, he heard Alda say, 'Aye, it's my own master I mean. Your eldest brother. Wystan of Meon.'

Wulfgar found his knees buckling. At the Lady's nod one of her waiting-women brought up a faldstool, onto which he subsided, head in hands, and closed his eyes.

Wystan's snub-nosed, ruddy, cheerful face danced in the darkness behind his eyelids.

That face, a traitor's mask?

Wulfgar found his head spinning like the beechwood top Wystan had whittled for him once. He forced himself to breathe deeply, and raised his eyes to meet the reeve's.

Alda had worked for their family since his brother Wystan was in tail-clouts, over thirty years ago. Alda would know.

'Tell me. Tell me everything.'

CHAPTER TWO

'They claim he'd planned to overthrow the King.' Alda sounded as though the words were being dragged from him with flesh-hooks. 'Plotted to put the King's cousin' – he glanced at the Lady – 'your cousin, Lady, on the throne instead.'

Wulfgar felt, rather than heard, the Lady's sharp intake of breath. 'Which? Which cousin?'

The royal line of Wessex was over-endowed with cousins. But Wulfgar thought he knew the answer, and from his Lady's taut, nervy face he guessed that she had reached the same conclusion.

'Athelwald Seiriol, Lady,' Alda said, confirming their suspicions. 'The Atheling. Your brother's heir.'

'Overthrow?' she said. 'What does that mean? Tell me the exact terms of the accusation.' She was sitting upright as a statue now, her hands curled hard round the ends of her armrests. Wulfgar looked at her face, her cold, grey eyes, and even though he was still seated he felt another sudden, giddy lurch, as though he were staring over the edge of an abyss. The room had filled with an unspeakable suggestion.

'To kill him. To kill the King,' Alda said. And then, a note of growing desperation in his voice, 'He's not alone. There's two other thanes been taken up. What's the day? Tuesday?'

Wulfgar nodded jerkily.

'It was Sunday they came. Your brother and his lady and their household were on their way to Mass.'

Wulfgar was hanging on his every word. He could imagine each limewashed stone of Meon Minster, church and churchyard hallowed by ten generations of his family's dead.

'They came whooping through the borough-gate, King Edward's hearth-men. More than a dozen, to take one unarmed man.' Alda's face convulsed. 'They bound him fast and put him up on a spare mount they'd brought along with them. They – they weren't gentle. To treat a man like that, in front of his own slaves …' Alda's angry face darkened still further. 'And Garmund Polecat was at their head.'

'I can't believe it,' Wulfgar said. His lips had gone numb, as though he'd drunk some vile poison. He might not be able to believe it, but he could see the image the reeve painted with agonising clarity, right down to the triumphant smile on Garmund's gloating face. 'It's all wrong.' He groped after some way of expressing the impossible nature of this news. 'It – it's not *logical*.'

'I wouldn't know about that, master.' The reeve shook his head. 'They had it all down pat. They said that your brother and the others planned to meet the King coming back from the hunt – one of the other thanes taken with him, see, it's his family's right to give the King his stirrup cup? That he would pull the King out of his saddle, and then they would all pile in with their belt-knives ...' He closed his eyes, his shoulders slumping. 'I can't believe it of my master, neither. But they said the Atheling had promised him great things.' A faint wailing note had entered his voice. 'What's going to become of him? What's going to become of *us*?'

Wulfgar tried to fight his way through the cloud of numbness to some kind of understanding. Had such an accusation been made against any other man, he could have credited it. As he himself had excellent cause to know, Athelwald Seiriol, Atheling of Wessex, could have suborned one of God's own chosen disciples.

But surely not Wystan. Dull, plodding, sturdy Wystan?

He was suddenly aware of his heart, fluttering wildly within his ribs like a newly caged bird.

'No doubt the King my brother will let me know of this matter,' the Lady said. Her voice stayed calm, but even in the flattering glow of the candlelight Wulfgar could see that her face was drained of all colour. Her breathing was shallow and rapid. 'It is evident, Wulfgar, that you cannot believe this of your brother. For that matter, I cannot believe it of my dear cousin Seiriol.' She paused for a moment, looking down so that her face was hidden behind a swathe of fine white lawn. From behind that sheltering veil, she said, 'Seiriol has been the greatest consolation and support to me since my Lord fell ill at Easter. I know it was a blow to him, when the councillors of the West Saxon Witan passed over his claim to the crown in favour of Edward. But that it would lead him to murder?' She tipped her head back and breathed in deeply, pulling her shoulders back. 'This whole thing must be a terrible mistake. A misunderstanding. Or' – and her face lit up with a brief flicker of hope – 'someone is trying to blacken the name of innocent men.'

Alda was shaking his head, and rubbing his brow as though trying to eradicate the furrows the years had ploughed there.

'I wish you may be right, Lady. I wish you may.'

'How does my cousin Seiriol answer these charges?'

'He doesn't,' Alda said. His voice had a new bitterness to it. 'He's gone to earth at his Wimborne estate, they say, Lady. Wherever that may be.'

'Dorset,' she said, under her breath. 'To his father's grave.'

Alda was nodding. 'The King has sent men to summon him to Winchester, and to bring him bound, too, if he won't come willingly.'

'Oh, my dear God.' Her hand was covering her mouth. 'Edward resents Seiriol. He always has. But *this*...'

The reeve shifted, eyes on the floorboards, visibly uncomfortable. Wulfgar agreed: some thoughts were best left locked away. He was painfully aware of the alert women pausing in their folding and sorting of linen and thread to exchange whispers and significant glances.

Alda said, 'The King wants an excuse to keep them imprisoned. He's summoned the Witan. It won't be a full session at such short notice, though.' He glanced at Wulfgar. 'It was your brother's wife sent me here. She needs oath-swearers to the master's good character. As many as she can muster.'

Wulfgar nodded. He had a sudden, vivid memory of Judith, his sister-in-law, at the wedding: her sallow, narrow-lipped face incongruous in a smother of gauzy veils and wreaths of wilting hedge-roses.

'You'll come then?'

11

'Of course I will!' He felt a sudden spurt of indignation that Alda should feel he had to ask. 'This has to be resolved.' He turned to the Lady. 'With your permission, of course, my Lady—'

The expression on her face stopped him in his tracks.

'The embassy,' she said. 'The York ambassadors. The treaty.'

They stared at each other for a long moment.

'They're due any day,' she said.

He couldn't utter a word that might be read as a challenge, not with Alda's avid face so close at hand, not with her women so busily pretending indifference.

'What if they don't speak English?' She put out her hand to him again. 'I haven't got another Danish-speaker I can trust.'

Again, a long meeting of eyes. Wulfgar had to look away first from that reproachful grey gaze. He took a long, deep breath.

'My Lady, could we talk in private?'

He didn't want witnesses. He was worried by the thought of what she might reveal.

She jerked her head at the reeve.

'Be so good as to wait outside.' She swivelled to stare at her suddenly busy women. 'You, too. All of you.'

'My Lady,' he said, as soon as they were alone, 'the treaty is all done. As tight and tidy as I could make it. If I go back to my desk now, I can finish the fair copies tonight.' It would mean working through the night, but they were only a week past the solstice and dawn would come early.

'No,' she said. 'You have to be here when the Danes arrive.'

'King Knut's letter was in Latin,' he reminded her. 'Poor Latin, but Latin all the same. These aren't the barbarians of our prejudice, my Lady. And the Bishop of Worcester will be with you in a day or two.'

She shook her head again, looking so weary and fragile that Wulfgar began to wonder whether she was ill. 'I should have known you'd let me down, too, in the end.'

'My Lady!' He couldn't keep the outrage from his voice. 'The Queen of Heaven knows, I don't want to go back to Winchester. I haven't been there since your father died, and there's no welcome there for me now. But I have to do this, don't you see?' In his agitation, he stood up, fighting the urge to grasp her shoulders, stare into her eyes, *make* her understand. 'For my brother, yes, but not only for him. What about your cousin the Atheling, my Lady?' He was well aware now that he was walking on eggshells, but he couldn't stop himself. 'If King Edward gets the chance to destroy him, he will. But if we can save Wystan, then perhaps we can save him, too.'

13

CHAPTER THREE

Winchester

Winchester basked below them in midsummer noontide sun. Wulfgar's horse tugged hard at the reins, wanting to get at the lush new grass. Distracted by the prospect spread out before him, Wulfgar let the leather straps drop.

She had let him go, in the end. But he had known from the set of her chin, from the tightening and deepening of the fine lines about her mouth, that she hadn't liked it. Only his repeated assurances that he would sort out this muddle and return in a matter of days had won him his Lady's leave. And he knew, in his heart of hearts, that she didn't care one way or the other about his brother Wystan. It was the threat to her cousin Seiriol that had made her nod her head at last.

The painfully familiar clanging of the cathedral bells was borne upon a soft southerly breeze, ringing his onetime colleagues in to the noonday service of Sext. The feast of St Peter today, he remembered with a start, and the first anniversary of his ordination as subdeacon, in that very cathedral. It just went to show how preoccupied he was, that he should have forgotten the date. He closed his eyes against a swarm of memories, persistent as biting gnats.

'Master?' Alda's voice, tentative behind him.

Wulfgar knuckled his eyes. 'Yes, I know. We should get on.' He fumbled for the reins and hauled his horse's head back to the blinding white of the road. Not an exile, nor a failure, nor an outcast from the charmed circle, he told himself. Secretary to the Lord and Lady of the Mercians. As ripe a plum as ever fell into the lap of a mere subdeacon.

And besides, what did it matter, how he himself was feeling? Extraordinary as it still seemed even after a day and a night on the road, it was Wystan he had to worry about. He took a deep breath and thumped his heels into the horse's sides, goading him into a reluctant, bone-jarring trot.

For all his attempts to cheer himself up, he still ducked reflexively as they passed through Winchester's west gate.

Nothing happened. No thunderclap, no earth-shudder.

Busy, familiar Cheap-Street wound down and away, the gable-ends of thatched houses flanking the market place, and the roofs of cathedral and palace over away in the distance, on his right. Nothing seemed to have changed in the three seasons since he had seen the place last, except that he had left in sad, smoky autumn, and here he was returning in all the glory of high summer. He inhaled sharply, unsure whether what he smelt was real or compounded of many layers of memory. That lush, green scent was drifting up from the water meadows, fed by the chalk-streams rich in cress and trout; and that heady, almost yeasty, aroma was the sun-baked wheat-straw of the thatch. Even the tainted whiff of tannery drifting in on the breeze was welcome and familiar: coming on that southerly air, it had to be the stink of the cathedral's own vellum workshop. He had served some of his scribe's training there, soaking the calfskins in the vats of piss until the fat and hair could be scraped away, his eyes endlessly watering, his mouth and nose burning with the reek of it...

He brought himself forcibly back to the present.

'Where should we go?' he said to Alda. 'Godbegot, or do we go straight to the palace? Where is Wystan being held, anyway?'

'Palace, aye. But best go to Godbegot, master. Hear if there be any news.'

So, before they reached the great walls that enclosed both palace and cathedral, they turned instead down an alleyway that ran north away from Cheap-Street, along the long narrow plot of Godbegot, the family town house, and under the great gateway that led into the courtyard. The plump little housekeeper came clattering down the stairs from the hall as they dismounted, screeching over her shoulder for hot water and towels. Wulfgar submitted to her embrace, half-expecting to have his cheeks pinched, to hear her exclaim how he had grown, to ask whether he had been eating properly. He was horrified when she burst into tears and clung to him.

'Come now,' he said ineffectually. 'Calm down.' He patted her shoulder. But it was Alda who grasped her elbow firmly and steered her towards the mounting block where she subsided, pulling her apron up to wipe her face.

'Oh, master,' she said, scrubbing one eye then the other, 'I'm that sorry.' She shook her head. 'The mistress will be so glad you've come. They've brought the hearing forward, you see.'

'So when is it?'

'Tomorrow, master.'

16

'*Tomorrow?*' The news came like a punch in the gut. 'How can Edward summon the men of the Witan in time?' But if the West Saxon councillors were meeting tomorrow, then he might be able to ride back to Gloucester the day after. He pushed the thought away. While he was in Winchester, there was only one matter to attend to. The Lady's business with the York treaty would just have to wait. 'Is Judith here?' Wulfgar's eyes flickered up to the carved door, but the housekeeper shook her head.

'Still out at Meon, master.'

Wulfgar frowned. 'I'd have thought she'd want to be in Winchester.'

'Did you think you were the only one who might swear to your brother's virtue?' Alda's tone was dry. 'She's sending round to all the folk whose lands abut ours, begging support.'

Of course.

'No, you fool, the wheat bread,' the housekeeper snapped at a flinching slave bearing a basket. 'Master, forgive me.' She got to her feet, still wiping her red-rimmed eyes. 'They can't manage a moment without me overseeing them. You'll get muck full of chaff only fit for the swine, else.'

But she didn't move, and after a moment Wulfgar realised she was waiting for him to grant her leave to go. It was an unfamiliar feeling, being lord here in his brother's absence. Unfamiliar, and deeply unsettling. Although their father had bought Godbegot long before he had been born, Wulfgar had never lived here, although he had visited often enough over the sixteen years that he had spent at Winchester Cathedral. Now that the housekeeper had relinquished her hold on his attention, he realised that the house was looking neglected. The red and yellow pigment was weathering away from the carvings round the door, the thatch was grey and sagging, and mats of goosegrass and chickweed were spreading over the cobbles.

When the housekeeper, pink-eyed still and sniffing, returned with her tray, she told them that no new tidings, good or ill, had reached the Godbegot household. Under her watchful eye, he dutifully downed a beaker of ale and a hunk of her best bread, which might as well have been ash and straw for all the pleasure he could find in it. When at last she was satisfied she could do nothing more for him, Wulfgar pulled the rough, comforting brown wool of his cloak back around his shoulders.

'We'd best be going to the palace then.'

Wulfgar ached from his crown to the soles of his feet, and it wasn't only the result of his day and a half in the saddle. Reluctant as he was to see Wystan a prisoner, he was even less eager at the prospect of going back to his old home, behind the encircling palisade.

He felt as though he had changed so much over the last nine months, since he had last emerged from behind that wall: he had seen and done so many new things. And all the while life at Winchester Cathedral would have been carrying on as usual. Little short of the death of a king had ever been allowed to intrude upon the beauty and order of its round of song and prayer. He could see and hear and smell it all so clearly; it had been haunting him with a passionate nostalgia ever since he had left for Mercia: the long, low timber and thatch of the oblates' dorter where he had slept for ten years; their tiny chapel; the well-worn path to the north door of the cathedral; the little stone house in the corner of the close where his old Latin tutor, Grimbald, had taken up residence in retirement.

They came through the gate.

And Wulfgar stopped dead.

Alda glanced at him. 'Aye, it's been all come-and-go since you were here last.'

No oblates' dorter.

No chapel.

Nothing, in fact, remained of the tight huddle of ancillary buildings that had packed the north quarter of the cathedral close, though stacks of timber and stone to one side suggested the fate of some of them. In their place was a rough, claggy wasteland, crossed and re-crossed with surveyors' strings and trenches, and men digging out a broad, shallow rectangular pit a few feet from the cathedral's north door. Only old Grimbald's little stone house was still standing, looking exposed and isolated.

'What's happened?' His jaw felt tight and painful.

'The King's new church,' Alda said.

'*Here?*'

The reeve nodded. 'They say it's what his father wanted.'

'*No*,' Wulfgar said violently. 'A new church, yes, but not here.' He and the old King must have planned their new minster twenty times or more: the apse, the towers, the walls adorned with images of the saints, the library...But this was all wrong. He stared at the trenches. 'Are those for the foundations?'

Alda nodded.

'But then there won't be room for a cat to squeeze between the two churches.' His eyes ranged this way and that, trying to make sense of the chaotic scene. 'What in the name of Heaven does the Bishop have to say about it?'

Alda shrugged. 'None too pleased, from what I hear, master. The King's granted cathedral lands to the new church, they say.'

'*What?*'

'Aye, and made that foreigner, that Grimbald, the new abbot.'

'But he's withdrawn from an active life. He must be all of seventy.' Had King Edward forgiven all that schoolroom sarcasm, then?

'And there's more.'

'Go on.'

'They're planning on digging up the old King's body out of the cathedral to rebury him in the new minster. Him, aye, and all his kin besides.' The reeve gave a tight little smile. 'No, the Bishop of Winchester's not pleased, folk say. The Bishop's not pleased at all.'

Wulfgar was aware of Alda watching him, his face almost greedy for a reaction. He felt himself blink once or twice, and forced himself to breathe slowly and deeply. He couldn't waste time getting upset about this.

His brother was waiting.

CHAPTER FOUR

'Wuffa. Thank God.'

Wulfgar's distressed eyes took in the bruised and filthy face, the black eye and swollen lower lip. In the last few moments before the guards had escorted his brother into the little enclosed yard behind the King's stables, he had been trying to recall when he had last seen Wystan.

Nearly a year ago, it must have been.

At the old King's funeral? He couldn't really remember. Those days had been such a frightening whirl of grief, and then he had left for Mercia and the Lady's service.

His brother looked older and somehow smaller than he remembered, shrunken and fragile for all his height and bulk. When had that shabby grey appeared in the rich russet of his beard?

'You came then,' Wystan was saying. 'Judith got word to you.'

'How could I do anything else?' Moved by a sudden warm impulse, he stepped forward to grasp his brother's hands.

He stopped mid-pace, mortified.

Wystan was shackled, and Wulfgar hadn't even noticed. His brother's hands were weighed down with thick iron cuffs and chain, his wrists red and wet where blisters had formed and burst.

'I thought the King might stop you seeing me,' Wystan said.

'I haven't been to the King. I went straight to Oswin.' He noticed his brother's frown. 'The palace reeve – he's always been kind to me. I hoped he might let me in to see you on the quiet.' Alda had been left kicking his heels in the guardhouse: Oswin's kindness hadn't stretched that far, to Wulfgar's secret, guilty relief. He said, 'I owe him now, for not making me go crawling to Edward, begging to see you.' He shivered. 'Are you all right?' What a stupid question.

Wystan shrugged. 'Backache, toothache. That old knee of mine. Nothing that wasn't troubling me a week ago.' He caught Wulfgar's glance at his wrists and shrugged again, with a wry twist of the mouth.

Suddenly, his expression changed. He glanced from side to side as though there might be spies concealed in the very stakes of the palisade and dropped his voice, although they stood a dozen feet or more from the guards loitering by the only exit.

'Wuffa, it's a plot.'

'What, that you're accused of? Alda told me—'

But Wystan was shaking his head.

'Not that. A plot against *me*. They want my land.' He paused, looking hard at Wulfgar. 'Our land. Godbegot. Meon, and my other estates. Everything.'

'They? Who's *they*?'

'The King, of course. He wants to reward that – that son of a slave. He hates our family, you know that.' Wulfgar found he had taken an unexpected pace backwards, wrong-footed by his

22

brother's intensity. 'Look at the way he used to bully you, before you went to work for your Lady. Now he wants to take everything we have, and give it to Garmund.' Wystan turned his head and spat, and then tried to lift his hands to wipe his mouth. The shackles clanked. In a stuttering, ragged voice, he said, 'Wuffa, I don't care what happens to me. I've had a grand life. If they want to kill me, let them. But you know the law. None better. Don't let them take the land. We have to keep it safe for Helmstan.'

'Your son,' Wulfgar said gently.

'Hard to credit you've never seen him.' He blinked, squeezing his bloodshot eyes furiously, but failing to keep the moisture at bay. 'Such a brave lad. Eight teeth now. And walking, almost.'

Wulfgar was unnerved by the unprecedented sight of his brother's tears.

'I can imagine,' he said, anxious to reassure, to claim fellowship. 'I've a little fosterling myself now, an orphan. Half a year old, or thereabouts. Electus, he's called. He's with a wet nurse in Gloucester.'

'Really? That's good. You understand, then. We've got to look after our children. They're all that matters, in the end.' He managed a smile then, or half a one. 'I've been worrying about you. You were always such a lonely little boy. I should have done more for you.'

Wulfgar found himself staring at the beaten earth of the yard, at the dusty toes of his own leather shoes, at Wystan's bare, grimy feet. 'I'm not lonely now,' he heard himself saying.

'A girl?'

'*No*,' more forcefully than he had intended.

Wystan nodded sagely. 'I didn't really think there would be. You'll end up a bishop yet, for all Edward's efforts.'

'Come on.' Wulfgar was aware suddenly of the guards in the gateway, shifting restlessly, hawking and spitting, sending them long, sideways glances. 'Tell me what you need from me. We don't have long.'

'What I need?' That smile, never very convincing, had fallen away entirely from his brother's face. 'Keep the estates safe for my boy.' Wystan's shackled hands had grabbed his arm and were gripping it tenaciously, his dirty face with its bloodshot eyes uncomfortably close. 'It's all bookland, you know.' The grip tightened further. 'Given to us in writing, and for ever. I've got the charters the old King gave Father, safely stowed in my chest, and copies at Meon Minster. There must be a way to keep the land, if they hang me. You can inherit, if my boy can't. Hold the estates in trust. *Something.*'

Wulfgar put his hand over his brother's where they were clutching at his sleeve, pressed them gently, then pushed them away. He couldn't think with that oppressive presence crowding in on him.

'But if you're innocent, you won't be hanged.'

'Haven't you been listening?' Wystan shook his head angrily. 'They won't find me innocent. It's all been fixed.'

'The court, you mean? The verdict? That can't be right.' Wulfgar could feel his brow tightening. 'You must have misunderstood. West Saxon justice is scrupulous.'

'*Was* scrupulous, maybe.'

Wulfgar pressed his fingers to his temples, trying to fight the sensation of pressure. 'That's a very serious claim,' he said slowly. 'Are you suggesting the King's witnesses will be lying on oath? If so, then surely we can disprove their statements.'

'There's no time.' Wystan clenched his shackled hands. 'They'll

24

find me guilty tomorrow. And then they'll hang me. But I'm counting on you.' He bared his teeth in a hideous parody of his earlier smile. 'They say no one knows the law better than you, little brother.'

Wulfgar felt an awful pit opening up at his feet, full of nameless horrors.

'But Wystan, the minimum penalty for treason is confiscation of all property. I can't change that. If they find you guilty and for some reason the Witan decides against execution or exile, they'll still take your lands. If – *if* – they find you guilty.'

'I don't believe you.' Wystan closed his eyes. 'God damn it!' he shouted suddenly. 'What gives that little upstart the right to do this?'

Wulfgar felt a sudden and desperate longing for the old, banal, fraternal relationship: *How's the little wolf-cub today? Learning your* hic haec hoc, *eh, Wuffa? Never my strong point, Latin! Ha ha!*

Words that had made him wince at the time, and seemed now like a lost dream of innocence.

Wulfgar forced himself to concentrate. He seemed to have learned nothing useful so far in this conversation. There was one question he had to ask.

'But are you?'

'Am I what?'

'Are you guilty?'

Wystan pressed his lips together and lowered his head, putting Wulfgar in mind of a scarred old bull, baited beyond endurance.

For the first time since hearing Alda's tidings, Wulfgar felt a shiver of doubt crawl across his nape and up his scalp.

'Alda told me about the plot. You and two other thanes, and a

plan to kill the King. Put Seiriol – the Atheling – on the throne.'
There, he had put the awful thing into words.

Silence.

That spidery frisson of doubt spread further through his veins,
try as he might to push it back.

'Wystan, don't you see? If I'm to give you good legal advice, I
have to know everything. Is this true? Who are the other thanes?
Are they being tried tomorrow too?'

Wystan lifted his head then, his eyes blood-threaded and
pouchy.

'I'm in a trap, Wuffa. Why can't you understand what I'm
saying? It doesn't matter whether I'm guilty or innocent. The King
wants me dead.'

'How do you know?'

'He told me—' Wystan's mouth snapped closed then, his lips
compressing till they whitened.

'Told you what? Who told you?' Wulfgar could not keep the
frustration from his voice.

His brother shook his head.

'Wystan, I will do everything I can.' Wulfgar's heart felt as
though it were cracking in his chest. 'But if your lands are
confiscated, the King can grant them wherever he likes.'

'But surely not to Garmund? In defiance of our father's will?'

'If it please him, then yes.'

They stood in shared stillness for a long moment.
Somewhere far above the squalid little yard, invisible in the
depths of the summer sky, an oblivious lark was singing its
heart out. Wulfgar contemplated his brother's weary face.
What was he concealing behind that honest, stupid, sun-
weathered mask?

26

'Are you ready to swear your oath tomorrow?' Wulfgar asked at last.

'What?'

'Your oath of innocence.' Wulfgar tensed, his mind racing suddenly.

'What does it matter what I swear? The King's made his decision.'

Wulfgar bit the tip of his tongue, trying to stay calm. When he did speak, he picked his words carefully.

'Wystan, if you refuse to plead, we may be able to buy some time.'

Time to find out what he wasn't being told. Time to talk to people, to find out what had really been going on between his brother and the Atheling. His ribs were tight with anxiety and he was painfully aware of the guards at the gate looking in their direction.

Time, that commodity beyond price, was slipping through their fingers.

'How?'

Wulfgar glanced at the approaching guard.

'There are two paths we could take,' he said quickly. 'First, if you don't admit guilt, the King will need the support of the Witan to condemn you to death. But there's not been nearly enough time to summon everyone. So, if they sentence you' – he swallowed hard – 'to death but there are too few men in attendance, the law allows us to ask for your case to be deferred until the full session of the court.'

'And what's the use of that?' The bitterness was back in Wystan's voice.

'It gives us time to undermine their story. To prove your innocence.'

Wystan stared at the ground, his breathing harsh and ragged.

Eventually he said, 'And the second thing?'

'It's just a thought, but' – Wulfgar plucked up his courage – 'if you refuse to plead, the Witan will then have to refer the case to the Church court.' He swallowed, nervous again. 'They'll – they'll put you to the ordeal.'

'No!' Wystan swung away.

'Please, listen to me.' Wulfgar put out a hand, beseeching. 'It'll get you out of Edward's clutches. And, if you are innocent, the ordeal will proclaim it. Beyond all doubt. There's no possibility of corruption in that verdict.'

'The ordeal,' Wystan said slowly. He was frowning, staring down at his shackled hands. His whole body shuddered suddenly. 'I can't.' He lifted his head again. 'Wuffa, I couldn't do that.' There was no doubting the sincerity of the horror that gripped him.

'Time to go,' the guard said, loud in Wulfgar's ear.

'A moment,' Wulfgar pleaded. He turned back to his brother. 'Would you rather be hanged?'

Wystan said nothing, but the rapid flicker of his eyes betrayed his fear.

'Who's your confessor at Meon now?'

'What?'

'He will need to be part of this, if they do send you to the ordeal.' Wulfgar was concerned by his brother's frown, his hunched, defensive stance, and he put out a tentative, reassuring hand again. 'It's terrifying, I know. Putting your hand into boiling water or picking up a bar of red-hot iron.' His own flesh flinched in sympathy. 'But it's better than being hanged.'

Wystan was silent for another long moment. He opened his mouth once or twice. Wulfgar saw his throat working. At last he said, 'And if the ordeal finds me guilty?'

Wulfgar stared at him. 'Then no one can save you.'

28

CHAPTER FIVE

There had been little chance of sleep that night at Godbegot, despite the little housekeeper's best efforts at making him comfortable. Wulfgar and Alda had sat up late into the night, chewing over the law. Now Wulfgar's eyes were sore, his back aching and his heart heavy. Yesterday's sunshine had been usurped by grey skies and a keen east wind.

He heard Judith's stifled gasp as her husband entered the courtyard. Wystan was still shackled, the welts on his wrists sore and angry. Had he been left like that since Wulfgar had seen him the previous day? The guards were marching him briskly into the cleared space before the rostrum.

'Incline our hearts, O Lord, to justice tempered with mercy, and preserve our realm in peace...' Wulfgar's old superior, Denewulf, Bishop of Winchester, was opening the extraordinary session of the Witan. He had risen ponderously to his feet, next to the still-seated King, while all Wulfgar's attention had been on his brother.

Wulfgar joined in the ragged *Amen*. As he had hoped there were many empty places on the tiered benches. Most of those who had come at such short notice were cathedral clerics or those thanes who lived within an easy day's ride of Winchester. Wulfgar glanced at the seated figure on the dais, but Edward was wearing a light horn-plated helm with silver-gilt trim: the nose- and brow-guards hid just enough of his face to make his thoughts inscrutable. With so few of his council present, what could the King legally do?

Nor were all those who *were* present eligible to do more than observe. Wulfgar identified Athelstan, the King's acknowledged son, all of eight years old, sitting a few yards away with a gaggle of other lads. None of them would be entitled to speak or vote, any more than the nuns who stood in a little flock at the back of the court. As they caught his eye one of the veiled shapes raised her hand in stealthy acknowledgement.

Cwenhild, his eldest sibling and only sister.

He sent back a swift but heartfelt smile before returning his eyes to the front.

Oswin, the reeve of the palace, was reciting the charges. '. . . that Wystan of Meon did wilfully and feloniously plot the death of his sworn lord and true King. . .' Oswin's familiar, sharp-nosed face was uncharacteristically sombre, as though he could hardly believe the words coming out of his own mouth.

Wulfgar listened closely, but there were no surprises in his speech: it all tallied with the tale he had heard already.

And then, 'Will you swear your innocence?'

Wulfgar stiffened.

Wystan had been standing with his head lowered and his shoulders hunched, his whole body expressing mulish resistance. He didn't move.

'Wystan of Meon,' the palace reeve repeated, 'will you swear?'
But Wystan stood mute as stone.

'Wystan of Meon—' Oswin began for the third time, with exaggerated patience.

But he wasn't allowed to finish.

'Call his witnesses!' It was King Edward, on his feet. Behind the shelter of his helm, Wulfgar could see now that his usually pale face was flushed and his eyes bright. 'Let's hear their testimony first. He can swear us his oath afterwards, if he's so minded.'

A stir went rippling this way and that along the benches. Wulfgar could feel it as a shiver across his shoulder blades.

Oswin said, 'It's hardly conventional, my Lord King.'

'We've invited him to defend himself. He may be shackled, but he's not gagged.' Edward waved a gloved and glittering hand. 'Read the list of his oath-helpers.'

The palace reeve glanced at Wulfgar and the men massed behind him. A little fretful muttering came from the benches, but no one rose to challenge the King's command. Wystan's other oath-helpers were all familiar to Wulfgar: tenants from Meon, neighbours from the valleys around, many connected to the family in some way. Well over a dozen of them, all prosperous and reputable, each striding or shuffling up in his turn, swearing his oath and making his deposition. Every man of them prepared to share in Wystan's shame and penalty if the verdict went against them.

All the depostions were very much the same. What was there to say, after all?

Wystan was trusty, they attested.

Reliable. Loyal. Conscientious.

Not even when tongues were drink-loosened at sheep-shearing or bride-ale had he ever been heard to criticise the King.

No, not this King.

No, nor the last one either.

The present King of Wessex and his Bishop sat on their rostrum and listened. Edward was seen occasionally to drum his fingers on the arm of his chair.

Wulfgar, youngest and last in line, stood with Judith while he waited to be called. She had ridden into Winchester from Meon, exhausted, at midnight, and they'd had no time than do more than exchange strained, nervous greetings.

'Why can't a woman testify?' she muttered to Wulfgar.

She looked drained to the dregs, pale cheeks, pointed red nose, pink-rimmed eyes.

'Who knows him better than I do?' his sister-in-law continued. 'And I'm an eldorman's daughter: I outrank them all.' She jerked her chin towards the gaggle of witnesses.

'It's not done in Wessex.'

She bit her lip and scowled. 'I should have brought my son to show the court. The King has a son of his own.' She glanced over her shoulder at precocious, bright-faced Athelstan, and said loudly, 'Guilty or innocent, he couldn't condemn a man with a little son.'

Couldn't he? Wulfgar felt desperately sorry for her. He lowered his own voice. 'Do you know anything more about this business? Why do they think he's guilty?'

She shrugged, her shoulders trembling. 'I don't know anything. Wystan's never shown any interest in court matters. Not even when I've told him again and again I want to spend more time in Winchester. Did you see the state he's let Godbegot get into?

There's never a man free for that, but if a new field needs ploughing, oh, it's a different story then!' He heard the whine of habitual bad temper in her voice and guessed she'd said all this before. 'I'm an aldorman's daughter,' she repeated. 'It's my right to attend the royal ladies.' She cast a baleful look at her husband. 'And now look at me.' She took a deep breath. 'What were you asking? Oh, he's always done what the King asks, of course – kept the bridges in repair, sent men to the levy – but no more. And now this, out of a clear sky.' She closed her eyes.

Wulfgar found his brother's other oath-swearers had little to add to Judith's unofficial testimony. Detail by detail, they embroidered a picture of a peaceful, bucolic life, edged by the watersheds of the river Meon. Wulfgar could have walked the boundaries of his brother's world with his eyes closed: from the thorn clump down to the sedge pool, from the sedge pool up to the bullock field, from the bullock field along to the ash grove ...never, it seemed, had there been a less likely traitor. Wystan was a man whose overt ambitions went no further than adding another hide of land here, another flock of sheep there.

Was there really nothing more to him?

Wulfgar shook his head. A suspicious mind might find the picture too consistent. Was any living soul really content with so little? Would the court believe that this wealthy, respected man, whose father had been a King's thane at the heart of West Saxon political affairs, had never had a shred of worldly ambition?

'Wulfgar of Meon?'

Oswin was beckoning him forward, his familiar face severe and formal.

'I do solemnly swear...'

Here he was again, up before the bantam-cock and the old bellwether, state and church, hand in glove. Two men who had known him since early childhood. He and Edward had learned rhetoric together from old Grimbald. Time to put those lessons into practice. It wasn't his place to engage with the accusation, only to put hand on heart and swear by his hopes of eternal salvation that Wystan had never uttered treachery in his hearing. How could he make them listen to his testimonial when King Edward loathed him, the Bishop was afraid of the King and he had nothing new to say, anyway?

'Men of Wessex,' he began. As he spoke, he scanned the benches. Too few men present. That was where their true hope lay, not in his words. He had their attention though, and he wanted to use it well. 'A terrible mistake is being made here. Look at my brother. Yes, you see a man guarded and in shackles. Any one of us would look guilty in Wystan's circumstances.'

He paused. Were they agreeing with him? It was impossible to tell from those shrewd, withdrawn expressions.

'But that is not the true Wystan of Meon, and in your hearts you know it.' He hesitated, trying to find the words that would go true to their target. 'We've heard from friends and neighbours. Wystan is loyal. Wystan is faithful. His word is his bond. Has any of you ever seen or heard anything to make you doubt the truth of this? How many of you have bought cattle from him? Sold land to him? Not one of you – and I know this is the truth – can remember a single occasion when Wystan's honesty and fair-dealing have been called into question.' He tried to smile. 'If anything, you'll have gone away from your bargaining shaking your head and wondering how such a simple, straight-forward man can prosper in this wicked world of ours.' He caught Judith's eye, and remembered

34

her complaint of a moment ago. 'If Wystan has a fault, it is lack of ambition, not excess of it.'

The court heard him out in silence. He saw a few heads nodding.

Oswin raised his eyebrows, but Wulfgar shook his head. He had done his best.

He was returning to his stand when the King spoke. 'Discount his testimony. He serves Mercia now.'

Wulfgar whirled, outraged, open-mouthed.

'My Lord!' Oswin sounded every bit as pained. 'The law does not distinguish—' The rest of his words were drowned out by the growing mutter from the benches.

The Bishop of Winchester was holding up his hands, waiting for calm. Several thanes had got to their feet, shouting in protest, and the Bishop's usually amiable, ovine expression was becoming increasingly annoyed.

At last Oswin bellowed, '*Silence!*'

The Bishop cleared his throat. 'I fear we cannot disallow Wulfgar's testimony on that account, my Lord. He is in good standing; his oath is valid.'

Edward looked from one side to the other. 'Is this the verdict of the court?'

A growl of assent.

'Then I bow to your wisdom.' Which he did, with an elegant inclination of his neck. He smiled. 'Let his words stand, even if his loyalties lie elsewhere.'

Wulfgar walked hot-faced and seething back to his place. What had all that been about? Had Edward been testing what they would let him get away with? The King must have known that that line of attack would get him nowhere. It wasn't even as though Wulfgar had said anything controversial or added anything useful to the powerful evidence in Wystan's favour.

'Seventeen oaths,' he realised Judith was saying to him. '*Seventeen*. All oath-worthy men, Two of them King's thanes, and you the King's own sister's secretary. It must count for something.'

CHAPTER SIX

Seventeen names for the defence.

And only two called for the prosecution.

But Wulfgar felt Judith stiffen like a ewe who smells wolf in the wind.

'What? What is it?'

'Those men.' She had put her fingers to her temples, deep lines suddenly raked between her eyebrows. A shivery note of panic had entered her voice. 'I don't understand! How can they be called?'

'What?' Wulfgar felt like shaking her. 'What do you mean?'

'They're the men who were arrested with him. For the same crime, I mean. The other thanes accused of plotting to' she swallowed audibly – 'plotting against the King.'

And the first of these witnesses was already speaking.

Alnoth of Brading, a dark-haired, slightly built man of forty or so, was the thane from the Isle of Wight, the one whose family claimed the right to bring the King his stirrup cup on his return from hunting. He had started his account of their murderous plan in a dull mutter, facing the King and the Bishop, until the reeve told him to turn round.

'Address the Witan too. They need to hear everything.'

The man swung round, stumbling slightly, and began again. 'We planned to strike on All Hallows' Day coming.' The details of the plot he outlined were almost childish in their simplicity. 'I was to bring my Lord and King the cup as he rode through the gate, but instead of giving it to him I – I was to throw the wine in his face, grasp his hand while he was blinded and topple him from the saddle. Edric of Amport was to be hard by with his belt-knife. He was to kill... when my Lord and King was on the ground I was to pull my own knife and help to finish him off. Wystan' – he half-turned towards Wulfgar's brother, standing flanked by armed men at the side of the rostrum – 'Wystan of Meon was to be ready with three horses, outside the gate, for us to make good our escape and ride for the coast. If need be, he was going to help us with the – the murder. We were going to hide over on the Island, on my estates. The Atheling said he would send us word when he'd been proclaimed King.'

The man was crying now, apparently heedless of any embarrassment.

'I was mad, my Lords. Mad.'

Still crying, he stumbled to one side, framed between his guards.

Broad-shouldered, fair-haired Edric was sworn-in in his turn. And the story he told corroborated Alnoth's in every particular, as detailed as it was damning. Wystan's character witnesses might swear that he was an unlikely traitor till the trumpets sounded for the Last Judgement, but Edric and Alnoth, grubby and bruised, exhausted and shackled as they were, gave evidence of treachery that seemed irrefutable.

The Witan sat in uneasy silence while each man spoke in turn, but as soon as Edric fell silent uproar broke out. Man after man rose to his feet, trying to catch the eye of the palace reeve, waving and yelling. Only with difficulty did Oswin restore a semblance of peace and, at the King's nod, invite the first question.

Wulfgar knew the face – a rosy-cheeked, guileless-looking thane with round eyes and a lamb-white beard – but couldn't recall the man's name.

'Who instigated this, you or the Atheling?'

Edric and Alnoth looked at each other, their eyes shifty and flickering. It was Alnoth who spoke at last.

'He flattered me, my Lords. He always remembered the names of my wife, my children. Honoured me with gifts. He offered my son a place among his hearth-companions. It was a privilege – or so I thought.' He looked as though he were gagging on his own words. 'He gave the boy a silver-hilted dagger – you should have seen his face.' Tears were welling up again.

'The Atheling gave me a bolt of silk for my wife.' Edric's mouth was working as though he had tasted a bitter draught. 'He sorted out a long-standing dispute between me and my neighbour over grazing rights.'

'And Wystan of Meon?' The white-bearded thane turned towards the third prisoner. 'What did the Atheling give you?'

Wystan shook his head and muttered something below his breath.

Oswin said, 'Speak up.'

Wystan threw his head back. 'Nothing,' he shouted at the sky. 'He gave me nothing!'

'The Atheling poisoned our minds,' Alnoth said. 'He told us

lies about the King, like a serpent dripping its slow venom.' His voice was trembling.

'Lies?' Edward said, his head on one side.

Alnoth swung towards the King. 'That you were weak, my Lord. That you had no true claim to your father's kingdom. That you took sides.' He was evidently on the verge of hysteria. 'That you overlooked the talents of good men, like us. That if we killed you, all Wessex would thank us...' His voice tailed away at the sight of the King's tight-lipped expression.

Wulfgar wondered how King Edward was feeling, hearing all this come out in such a public forum.

And something else was nagging at him.

These men were admitting their own guilt as well as accusing Wystan, condemning themselves out of their own mouths.

But they had not been tried.

No oath-swearers had been summoned to speak for them.

What exactly was going on? Why were they falling over each other in their eagerness to incriminate themselves? Not merely to confess, but to confess to the most heinous part of the crime?

Another thane was interrogating them now.

'But why? Why did you include Wystan, of all men, in your devilish intrigues?'

'Why?' Edric looked astonished to be asked such a foolish question. 'Because no one would ever have expected treachery of him, of course.'

'No, I mean, why approach him?' The thane was frowning. 'Why not me, or any other of the King's men? What made you think he would listen?'

It was Alnoth who answered. 'It was the Atheling's idea. He said' – Alnoth swallowed audibly – 'he said that Wystan hated

King Edward because Edward had always been so unkind to his little brother.' He looked directly at Wulfgar.

It was all Wulfgar could do not to stagger. He felt the eyes of the whole assembly turn on him. It was one thing having spent his childhood ducking and weaving to escape Edward's malice, but it was quite another to have it public knowledge. He felt obscurely, irrationally, ashamed, as though someone had rummaged through his chest and pulled out his soiled linen.

The interrogation moved on, though at first Wulfgar found it hard to concentrate again. Names and places and dates: the two men's stories, as they wound in and out of one another, agreed in all but the occasional, tiny, detail. If it were all a lie, it was an astonishingly well-rehearsed and plausible one, rendered all the more believable by the way Edric and Alnoth evidently loathed one another.

Wulfgar wondered whether the thirty or so thanes and clerics behind him were convinced by it. Without turning round, he could sense them, chunnering and growling in a bass rumble that he could feel in his diaphragm. It made him queasy. Wystan of Meon was known to every man present, well known to some. They had to see that this was inconceivable.

King Edward put his head on first one side, then the other, eyeing the witnesses coldly before turning to Bishop Denewulf on his left, and saying something in an undertone. Denewulf nodded, pink jowls gently quivering, his hands nervously pleating the delicate green silk of his chasuble.

The Bishop and the King were still murmuring to one another. Edward's eyes, shadowed under the rim of his helm, were darting from Wystan to the other two accused thanes. Although he was no more than four yards away from the dais, Wulfgar couldn't make out a single word. Then the King beckoned and spoke quietly to his palace reeve, who nodded, and turned, and cleared his throat.

'Wystan of Meon,' Oswin said, 'the court has been very patient with you. You have heard all the evidence. This is your last chance. Will you swear to your innocence?'

Flanked by his guards, Wystan stepped forward. He seemed to have recovered something of his old vigour, boosted, perhaps, by hearing all the solid testimony in his favour from his old friends and neighbours. Wulfgar wondered whether his brother could find the telling phrase at last, the evidence that would demolish this house of straw.

'Call this justice?' Wystan's voice bounced around the palace yard. 'If I'm guilty, so are they.' He gestured, two-handed and clanking, towards Edric and Alnoth. 'Why aren't they on trial along with me?'

The King's lips tightened. Then he said, 'Edric has confessed already, in private. And so has Alnoth. We have come to an understanding. They will be punished appropriately. There has been no need for a trial.'

Wulfgar felt his brow tightening. *No need for a trial?* A private understanding? This wasn't any law of Wessex that he knew. Such a private settlement might be appropriate for a dispute over a stolen bridle, but not for a plot against the King's very life.

Wystan was shaking his head in evident disbelief. Then he threw it back, tossing his matted hair out of his eyes. 'Where is your cousin, my Lord King? Why isn't Athelwald Seiriol here before you' – he brandished his jangling wrists – 'in chains?'

'My cousin has not yet been detained.' For the first time during this process Edward looked discomfited. 'I have sent men to Wimborne to arrest him.'

'I'm a scapegoat, then?' Wystan's voice was hoarse. 'Hang me because you can't hang him, is that it?' He swung round to face the benches. 'Don't you see? It's me today, because he wants my land. It'll be you next, or you. Any of you. Anyone who's got something he wants.'

Wystan fell silent at last, but his words could not be unsaid: Wulfgar could hear them still, echoing round the court.

Edward got to his feet. Slight as the King was, he looked truly regal, from the silver-gilt sheen of his helm to the glitter of the braid on his buskins.

'Men of Wessex, we live in difficult days.' He paused, and when he spoke again his voice was richer and more resonant. 'The oldest among us has known nothing but menace on our borders. Now we face an inner enemy as well, an enemy like a noxious worm that eats at the heart of our nation.' The King lifted the helm from his head and tucked it carefully under one arm. A new earnestness entered his voice. 'Treason is like the dock-weed; you think you have dug it all out, but if you leave a single scrap of taproot in the soil it returns and drives out the nourishing crop.' His voice hardened. 'Traitors must be eradicated; rendered powerless at the very least. The laws of Wessex have recognised this for two hundred years, and they give us the means we need.' Wulfgar could sense the nods of agreement from the men behind him. No one made a sound. The King looked at Edric. 'Confiscation.' He turned to Alnoth, his face grim. 'Exile.' Then, very quietly to Wystan, 'Death.'

CHAPTER SEVEN

'He's good, isn't he?' A voice in Wulfgar's ear.

Wulfgar's head snapped round.

The man whom of all men he least wanted to see was standing at his shoulder, exuding affability, the sharp white teeth and wet red mouth gleaming in his dark beard.

Polecat.

'Don't worry, Litter-runt,' Garmund said. 'I'm not going to hit you.'

Wulfgar knew he hadn't flinched at the sight of his half-brother, but there would be no profit in arguing. The bigger man was holding up a hand in mock-solemn reproof, sliding his dark eyes towards the King and shaking his head.

'My father made us strong,' the King was saying. 'It has fallen to me to keep us that way. Does a doctor recoil when he has to suck poison from a wound or sever a rotting limb?' He shook his head sagely, looking at the faces of his audience as he did so. Even Wulfgar caught a flicker of eye contact. The King took an audible breath, exhaled through his nostrils, and stood straighter. 'Men of Wessex, what should we do with this traitor?'

Traitor? But there had been no judgement yet. Wulfgar found his nails digging into his palms.

'Hang him! Damn it, hang all three!'

Wulfgar turned to see the thane with that deceptively soft white beard looming over him.

'My Lord King, I'm an old man and I've seen a few things in my time.' He lowered his voice a little. 'You're young, full of dreams about mercy. But you can't go chopping and changing the law to suit your dreams. Think of your father, my Lord. He was fair. But he was hard, too. Hard times demand a hard king. We chose this man last year' – he swung round to address the benches – 'we swore him our oaths just a fortnight since, at Pentecost. Let's show him we meant what we swore!'

The King nodded sombrely. 'Alnoth and Edric have confessed to me and, as I have told the court, we have reached an agreement. For Edric, confiscation and his family deprived of all title. For Alnoth, confiscation and exile on pain of death should he ever return to Wessex. Hardly a light sentence.' He glanced at all three prisoners. 'But Wystan of Meon has refused to admit his guilt, and therefore his life is forfeit.'

Wulfgar felt as though the air had been sucked from his lungs. There was a tremendous roaring, and for a moment he thought it was the blood in his ears. Moments later he realised it was punctuated by stamping, and shouting. The Witan had risen to its feet.

He scanned the faces, looking for support, for someone to challenge the King.

Nothing. Almost to a man they were bellowing for his brother's blood. Even some of Wystan's oath-swearers seemed to have been overborne now, and were shouting with the rest, though Wulfgar found it incredible that they could have been swayed by this farrago of truth mashed with lies. Judith was hanging on so hard to his right arm that he was losing all feeling in his hand.

The Bishop of Winchester was saying something to Oswin, indicating towards the benches. The reeve stepped forward, gesturing for the crowd to fall silent, thumping the ferrule of his staff on the planking of the rostrum again and again, until at last there was grumble rather than roar. He used his staff to point to another man, halfway back. As the new speaker pulled himself to his feet, Wulfgar recognised the silvery tonsure and beaky nose of his uncle.

'Archdeacon, please.' Oswin held up his hand for quiet once more. 'Beornwulf, Archdeacon of Winchester.'

Wulfgar felt a swirl of relief rush through his veins. Now, at last, the assembly would hear the voice of reason and experience.

'Men of Wessex,' the old man said, stifling a cough. 'As many of you know, I have an interest here. When Wystan's mother died, my sister married his father. He may not be my nephew by blood, but I have called him kin for some thirty winters, and he has always seemed an honest man.' Another surge of hope welled in Wulfgar's heart. But the old man was going on. '*Seemed*, I say.'

Wulfgar put his fingers to the furrowed space between his brows, trying to rub away his confusion.

'But now,' and the old Archdeacon, both hands planted on his walking-stick, loomed forward like an eagle scanning for prey, '*now*, he brings shame on us all. Blood-kin, marriage-kin, no matter: all Wessex is tainted by association. You've heard this disgusting story. You've seen the contempt with which he treats the highest court in the land. I agree: what can you do but hang him? Hang them all.'

He sat down to renewed bellows of approval.

Edward was leaning back in his chair, turning his light helm round and round in his hands. When the old canon had finished, he looked up, lips pressed together, and waited for the hubbub to die down. When he spoke, it was without getting to his feet. 'Is this, then, the considered verdict of the Witan?' His voice was quiet: Wulfgar had to strain to hear him. 'Will you force me to revise my judgement? Break my promise? Hang all three? Edric of Amport, Alnoth of Brading and Wystan of Meon?'

A roar of assent came in on the heels of each name.

That white-bearded thane was on his feet again. 'One more thing!' At a nod from the King's reeve, he said, 'Hang them today, my Lord King, not tomorrow. It's a bad thing, to hang a man on Sunday.'

And Wulfgar turned and watched as man after man stood up. Some were tardier hauling themselves to their feet, looking first along the rows of their peers, waiting to be sure of the general mood, but in the end, as far as Wulfgar could see, the support for death was unanimous. Judith was still leaning hard against his right arm, and he could feel her beginning to shake. He was vaguely aware of an aura of satisfaction emanating from Garmund, still standing offensively close to him. Edward's glance went left then right along the lines of men: the King didn't need Oswin's hasty tally to tell him the verdict of the court. Slowly, grim-mouthed, he nodded.

'My Lord, you promised!' Edric's voice was hoarse with fear.

Wulfgar felt a cold fury possessing him. Casting all caution to the four winds, he stepped forwards, up to the rostrum.

The palace reeve glanced down at him.

'Oswin,' he said, putting all the calm urgency he could into his voice. 'Old friend. You've got to let me speak.'

Oswin sent an edgy glance back over his shoulder at the King.

'I have to speak,' Wulfgar said again. 'I'm an oath-swearer. You can't stop me.'

Oswin stared at him for a long moment. At long last he nodded. 'Wulfgar of Meon.' Bang, bang, bang, with his ferrule.

A restless quiet fell at last.

Wulfgar could feel the furious blood in his face. 'My Lords,' he said, his voice catching despite all his care. He swallowed, and began again. 'My Lord King. My Lord Bishop. Men of Wessex. Look along these benches. How few there are of you here today.' He caught a glimpse of Garmund's dark, brooding face and moved quickly on, scanning the benches until he found his uncle, still scowling impenetrably. He had to send every word true to its target. Looking the old canon in the eye, he said, 'Since when was it the law in Winchester that a mere handful of you could condemn a man to death, who had not previously condemned himself out of his own mouth? Wystan has offered no plea—'

'The words of Alnoth and Edric condemn him,' the King snapped.

Wulfgar opened his mouth – *The words of self-confessed traitors* – but he was forestalled, and from a most unexpected quarter.

'He's right, Father.' The clear, carrying voice of a child. It was Athelstan, on his feet, evidently being egged on by his older companions. 'Wulfgar's right. Had you forgotten?'

So, *someone* knew the law.

Out of the mouth of infants and of sucklings Thou hast perfected praise…

Wulfgar took a long slow breath, fighting back the whoop of hysterical laughter that threatened to break from him. The world, which had seemed so chaotic and lawless a moment ago, began to settle back around him in its familiar, ordered patterns. When Oswin called on him again, he would tell – no, *remind* – the Witan that a defendant who didn't plead would need to be referred to the cathedral's court for the ordeal.

But he wasn't given the chance.

Edward pushed his chair back and got up slowly. When he spoke, his voice was quiet and controlled. 'In that case, very well. Let no one say I am above the law. For Wystan of Meon, I will wait for the sitting of the whole Witan, at the harvest even-nights. He will remain in custody until then. As for those two' – he gestured at Edric and Alnoth before swinging back to his audience – 'condemned, as you say, Wulfgar, out of their own mouths...' he paused for a moment, his eyes narrowing. 'Do as you think fit, men of Wessex. Take them up to Harestock, to the gallows and the pit, if that's how you read the law. The King is but the voice of the Witan, after all.'

Edward paused again, and looked first at Oswin, then along the benches, his expressionless gaze resting for a long moment on his son, and at last he stared straight at Wulfgar, his blue eyes giving nothing away.

Their eyes locked.

'Come September, I will demonstrate to the whole court that your brother' – Edward pointed his accusing finger at Wystan – 'meant to kill me. And then we will hang him, by the book. Are you satisfied, Wulfgar? Is this the action of a king?'

The court was silent for several long heartbeats.

'My Lord! My King...' Alnoth of Brading's voice cracked on the last word.

Edward turned back to Oswin. 'What are you waiting for?'

CHAPTER EIGHT

King Edward had been as good – or as bad – as his word.

Edric of Amport and Alnoth of Brading, still shouting the King's name in violent protest, were bundled away through the gateway. Wystan had been marched back to his prison. Wulfgar's furious demands to talk to his brother again had fallen on closed ears.

'You heard my Lord King,' Oswin said. 'You have three months, nearly, till the full court convenes.' He paused then, and softened a little, bending forwards and lowering his voice. 'I'll see he's no worse treated than he has been. Now' – and he had glanced up at the sun – 'if you'll forgive me, Wulfgar, I've a gallows to ready.'

Wulfgar watched him hurry away. His own thoughts were still in an uproar. He sat down on the nearest bench as the yard emptied, setting his elbows on his knees and his head in his hands and staring at the beaten earth.

Three months.

Where did he start?

Talk to Wystan, if he could, find out what evidence there was against him other than the unsubstantiated words of Edric and Alnoth...

Talk to Edric and Alnoth.

That had to come first.

He scrambled to his feet and hurried out of the yard.

There was no difficulty in finding them. The crowd was gathering mass as he pushed his way through the narrow defile of Cheap-Street and out onto the road to Andover, the same road that he and Alda had ridden down only the previous day. They must have trotted right past the hanging-place at Harestock, only a league or so from Winchester, and he had been so caught up in his own petty anxieties about coming back to Winchester that he had never even noticed.

No difficulty in finding them, but no possibility of getting near, even once he had caught up with the heart of the sorry little procession. Alnoth of Brading and Edric of Amport, their hands tied behind their backs, were being marched up the chalky way, closely guarded by more spear-men who jabbed at their legs and buttocks to keep them moving as though they were bullocks reluctant to meet the butcher. Two other men were carrying a long, unwieldy ladder, and a third had a heavy-looking coil of hairy rope slung over his shoulder.

They had trudged the whole three miles to the hanging-place, and still Wulfgar had had no chance to get close enough to speak to either of the condemned men, when they turned off the road. There were sheep in the field and the grass was close-cropped, studded with golden blooms where vetch grew among the grass. Blue butterflies flickered over the turf. The thin east wind was dropping, the sun was threatening to come out, that chilly grey day succumbing to summer at last. Wulfgar felt it as a last, poignant irony.

The gallows stood at the top of the rise, its uprights and lintel like the doorway to a vast invisible hall. The two men lugging the ladder shouted and shouldered their way through the mob of onlookers. There was no getting past those self-important spearmen. Wulfgar weighed up his options and pushed his way through the crowd to where Oswin was standing at the foot of one of the two gallows posts.

'These'll need renewing soon,' Oswin was saying to the men steadying the ladder. He kicked the base of one of the posts. 'The wet's got in. All that bit's rotting, look at it.' He looked up. 'Wulfgar.'

'Oswin, let me talk to them. They haven't seen a confessor.'

'No more they have. They never do. Does it matter? They're going in the pit so they're damned anyway.'

'But they weren't expecting to die!' Wulfgar could hear his voice rising. He relaxed his fingers and breathed deeply, trying to calm himself. 'You were at the trial; you saw what happened. They've had no chance to make their peace with God.'

'You've had two favours from me already.' Oswin shook his head. 'And they're not allowed a priest.' He ruminated for a moment. 'But then again, you're not a priest yet, are you?'

Wulfgar shook his head. 'Still only a subdeacon, but' – he looked around him one more time – 'I'm all that's here.'

Oswin's shrewd, pointed face softened. 'Go on. You'll not have long though. The King's waiting for the news.' He patted Wulfgar's shoulder. 'Come with me.'

The guards parted at the reeve's approach, and stood away a little.

'Be quick, remember,' Oswin said as he turned back to the gallows.

'Wystan's little brother, isn't it?' Edric of Amport said. His tone was bitter.

'I can't absolve you,' Wulfgar said rapidly, 'but I can pray with you. And if there is anything you want to confess, if you entrust me with it, I can take the matter to a priest.' It was hardly orthodox practice, but surely God, whose own Son had been hanged on a tree, would understand their plight. He shot a look at the guards. 'Was all that true, what you said in front of the Witan?'

'He promised us our lives,' Alnoth of Brading said. 'We weren't expecting...' with a shudder, he glanced over at the gallows.

'I have confessed,' Edric said. 'I confessed to the King, and he absolved me and pardoned me and thanked me for having had the courage to bring him the news.' His voice shook. 'He promised me my life.'

'Is that how Edward found out about the plot?' Wulfgar asked. 'You told him? And was it true?'

'He lost his nerve.' Alnoth of Brading threw the other man a look of contempt, his sallow, fine-featured face taut and twisted. 'Why? You must have known what would happen!' As his voice grew louder, the guards moved a little closer.

'I trusted the King.' Edric's chin was shaking like a schoolboy trying to hold back tears. 'You confessed too, remember.'

'You fool, Edric.' But Alnoth had control of himself again. He was looking past Wulfgar, at the gallows. 'Come on then, little subdeacon. We've not got long.' He dropped awkwardly to his knees, his bound hands behind him. 'Do what you have to do.'

Edric, his face sullen, copied his fellow-prisoner.

Wulfgar looked at the two heads of the men kneeling in front of him, one sandy, the other dark and sleek as an otter's fur. What secrets did they have locked away in there? And he still wasn't sure whether they believed what they had said about his brother. What was more important, these men's immortal souls or the faint hope of learning something that might exonerate Wystan?

'And Wystan?' There wasn't much time. 'Was all that true, what you said about him?'

Oswin was at his shoulder. 'Come on, lads. Let's get this over and done with.'

'Just a little longer?' Wulfgar gestured wildly. 'We haven't finished yet.' How could he let them climb the gallows with those lies on their consciences?

'I've given you all the time I can.' Oswin's face was set and grim.

Wulfgar, desperate to find words of comfort and resolution, could think of nothing better to do than to recite the general confession. *I have sinned greatly in my thoughts and in my words, in what I have done and in what I have failed to do...*

He could hear them joining in, muttering along with his Latin. *Mea culpa, mea culpa, mea maxima culpa...*

The guards were prodding Alnoth and Edric to their feet with the tips of their spears. The man with the rope was looking expectant. The sun had come out at last, just before it set, to send a warm yellow light over the long summer grasses. The elongated shadow of the gallows reached almost to where they were standing.

Suddenly, Alnoth was stumbling at his side. 'Thank you, little subdeacon.' His face lit up briefly. 'That helped.'

For the first time, Wulfgar caught a glimpse of what this man might have been like before his world had come crashing down about his ears. But there was no time for him to respond. He watched the two of them being marched to the killing-place, a lump forming in his own throat. His liberating anger had quite ebbed away.

One man was up the ladder, throwing the lengths of rope, already looped and knotted, over and over the cross beam. Another was at the foot, pushing those knotted loops over the two men's heads and prodding them towards the ladder. Two more, with others setting down their spears and coming to join them, were grabbing the loose ends, ready to hold fast till neck-bones cracked and windpipes were crushed at last.

Wulfgar looked down at his feet. The grass was damp, and the soft leather uppers of his shoes were soaked. The sun had sunk a little, and the shadow of the gallows-lintel fell across his feet. He stepped back nervously. The meadow flowers were still full of bees, gathering their last nectar before the night fell, and he watched one enormous white-tailed bumble-bee, the little bags on its legs bulging with its golden hoard, stagger out of a gentian blossom and launch itself humming into the air. He shut his ears to any more distressing sounds, concentrating instead on the industrious bee-chant and the song of a single evening blackbird coming from a nearby thicket of ash trees.

He smote himself hard on the breastbone in the gesture of repentance.

My fault, my fault, my most grievous fault…

Thump.

And again, thump.

CHAPTER NINE

'Three months,' Judith was saying now, as she had a dozen times already. They were in the upper hall at Godbegot. It was midnight, but no one wanted to sleep. She had her spinning in her hands but her usual deftness had deserted her: the fibres of her spun yarn were parting every few moments, letting the spindle go clattering onto the floorboards. She had bent over and over again to pick it up, but this time she left it where it had fallen, to roll back and forth in diminishing arcs.

Chubby little Helmstan set off after it on all fours.

'Not in your mouth,' Cwenhild chided, pulling the boy back.

'What use is the summer to us? We've tried everything already.' Whey-faced and weary, Judith looked around the hall as though she were seeing the faded hangings and the smoke-darkened beams for the first time.

'A lot of use,' Wulfgar said, trying to imbue his tone with confidence. 'We can recruit more oath-swearers, for one.'

'What difference will *that* make? We had more than the law requires today, and see how much it helped!'

'I can think of one who will make a difference,' he said quietly.

Cwenhild was stooping to pick up her nephew and try to settle him, wriggling and protesting, on her hip. 'So can I,' she said. She looked at Wulfgar, her usually cheerful, round face worn and weary.

He nodded.

'What can you mean?' Judith asked. She huddled herself into her veils.

Wulfgar could hardly bring himself to say the name.

Cwenhild cut in.

'The Atheling. Athelwald Seiriol, that's whom you mean, Wuffa. Isn't it? If we could only get *him* to swear to Wystan's innocence...'

Helmstan, sensing her attention was elsewhere, slithered bonelessly out of her arms and set off on his explorations again.

'Wystan wouldn't tell me much,' Wulfgar said, 'and what he did say was' – he wondered how to phrase it – 'cryptic at best. Now that we're not allowed to see him, there's only one other man living who knows the truth of it. We have to find him.'

'What good could it do?' Judith sounded exhausted. 'I should just take Helmstan and go home to Kent.'

'Dear sister-in-law.' A hand pulled back the door-curtain with a rattle of rings. 'Please, don't go running back to Kent on my account.'

Wulfgar braced himself.

Garmund Polecat strolled in, smiling at them. 'Here we all are,' he said. 'The happy family, for the first time since your wedding.' He inclined his head courteously at Judith, then looked around in a derisive pose of surprise. 'Oh, forgive me. Not quite all. Where is the master of the house?'

'Get out,' Wulfgar said, hardly able to speak through his fury.

Garmund looked at him, long and level, before turning to Judith. 'They haven't hanged him. Yet.' He bared his teeth. 'Unlike his fellow-sinners.' He shook his head. 'Not pretty deaths. Not pretty at all. Wulfgar can endorse that, can't you, Wuffa?'

No one responded.

Wulfgar looked at Garmund steadily, noting with some dispassionate part of his mind how prosperous he was looking, the quality of his double-dyed dark-blue linen visible even in the lamplight that glinted off the massive gilt brooch at his neck. Still shoulder-to-shoulder with Edward, then, as he had been for the best part of twenty years.

A cheerful burble from the floor seized Wulfgar's attention, and he and the women watched nervously as Helmstan made his single-minded way towards his half-uncle, whose leggings were fastened at the knee with gleaming silver tags.

Helmstan chortled in appreciation and reached out with his grubby fist.

'Not those, young man,' Garmund said. He bent to scoop up the child, oblivious to the cries of protest from Helmstan's mother and aunt. 'What else can I find you to play with? Oh, look, what have I got in my hand?'

He held it up.

A ring. A chunky, gold ring.

Helmstan reached for it with a cry of joy, only to have it withdrawn beyond his reach. 'Then again, perhaps not,' Garmund said, his voice creamy with amusement. 'Your mother wouldn't like it if you swallowed it and I had to fillet you with my belt-knife to get it back.'

Cwenhild barged forward, her face a study in silent fury, to wrestle the boy out of the crook of Garmund's arm.

'Don't tease us,' Judith said, her voice uncertain. 'You shouldn't say things like that, even as a joke.'

Garmund ignored her. He was holding the ring between thumb and forefinger, angling it to catch the little light from the lamp.

'Let me see that,' she said, her voice wavering even further.

Garmund tossed it up carelessly and caught it again. 'But it's mine, dear lady. For the time being. Just as' – and for the briefest moment Wulfgar saw the fury beneath the insouciant mask – 'it was my father's before me.'

And then Wulfgar knew.

It was Wystan's ring.

Belatedly he realised that Wystan hadn't been wearing it the day before. He had a sudden memory – almost as tangible as the real thing – of his brother's hands, the wrists red and weeping and weighed down with manacles, the grubby knuckles and broken nails, clutching at his own.

The ring that went with being master of Meon formed no part of that picture.

He chose his words carefully. 'Has the King confiscated his lands, then, even without a verdict?'

'No, alas. But someone needs to oversee the land for the season, till we do manage to hang him. It's a busy time of year. Late lambing. Hay harvest. Who better than me?'

'Me, perhaps,' Judith spat.

Garmund smiled at her. 'The King has graciously allowed you and your son to remain in residence here for the summer, dear lady – unless you go running home to Kent, of course. But to let a traitor's wife administer his estates? No, you must see that would never do.'

'He's not a traitor,' Cwenhild muttered.

Wulfgar stood very still, trying to think coherently. Everything that Garmund had said and done since he entered the hall served to confirm Wystan's wildest-seeming accusations: that he had been caught in a trap; that the real plotters were Edward and Garmund; that this was a ruse to deprive the rightful heir of the Meon estates and give them to this slave-born cuckoo in their nest. He felt fury blaze up inside him like a freshly stoked bonfire.

'He's dead already, really,' Garmund was saying, his tone light, almost playful. 'Just like Alnoth and Edric. There's no virtue in fighting it.' He pulled Wystan's heavy carved chair – the only chair in the room – away from the table and settled himself down ostentatiously. 'Chilly for June tonight,' he said amiably. 'Cwenhild, tell one of our slaves to stoke that brazier.'

Cwenhild looked mutinous, her mouth clamped shut.

Wulfgar took a step towards him. 'Don't get too comfortable.'

Garmund stretched one leg, then the other, and settled back on the cushion. 'No, I mustn't. You're quite right. The King's expecting me.' At some point he had slipped the ring onto the middle finger of his right hand and he extended his hand and turned it this way and that admiringly. The chased and inlaid surface of the gold, patterned with little animals, broke up the light. Wulfgar, a couple of yards away, didn't need to approach any closer to recognise the ornament: he could have picked that ring out of thousands. A dog chasing a hare, a falcon swooping after a swan, two little crosses, and his brother's name where he'd had it re-engraved after their father's death: ✠WYSTAN✠.

It felt sickeningly like a memorial.

'Make the most of it,' Wulfgar said. 'It won't last. He's innocent, you know.'

'Really, Litter-runt?'

'Don't call him that,' Cwenhild snapped. She had moved to Wulfgar's side, the struggling child still in her arms. Wulfgar shot her a grateful look, struck by how much she looked like Wystan and how much they both looked like their late father with their ruddy, solid, open faces. So unlike him.

'Oh, Cwenhild.' Garmund looked up at her, still smiling. 'Are you going to put me over your knee and spank me? It must be twenty years since we last had the pleasure.'

Cwenhild stiffened visibly but tightened her lips.

Judith had retrieved her spindle and was pulling the spun yarn off it with short, angry movements. Shreds and tufts of ill-spun wool flickered to the floor between her fingers.

'He's innocent,' Wulfgar repeated. He turned to Judith, desperate to reassure her. 'And I'm going to prove it.'

CHAPTER TEN

Gloucester

Brave words.

But empty ones.

Riding steadily down into the vale of the river Severn, Wulfgar thought back to his last view of Godbegot before he had heaved his horse's head round and clopped under the gateway and out into the road.

'The Lady asks your forgiveness, but she needs you, after all,' the agitated horseman had said. He had accepted a cup of ale but he hadn't dismounted from his sweating steed, brushing away the invitation to stay and eat with a 'There's scant time for that.'

Wulfgar had looked around the courtyard at Godbegot with a sensation of doom. He had been half-expecting this, he realised, ever since Garmund had walked into their hall in that proprietary fashion, only two nights earlier. Another bolt-hole, another escape route for Wystan, was being stopped up. The Lady might not know it but she was doing Edward's and Garmund's dirty work for them. He unfastened Helmstan's fat little hands from his tunic and passed him into Cwenhild's arms.

Judith had come down the stairs to see who the visitor might be.

'Can't it wait, whatever it is?' Cwenhild was saying. 'Send this man back with a message. When she knows what's happened, Fleda will understand. Even a few days could make the difference.'

His sister's use of the Lady's given name took Wulfgar aback for a moment, but then he remembered they had been girls together. And Cwenhild the elder of the two.

He shook his head, though his heart felt about to break. 'I have to go,' he said. 'I'm sworn to her.'

'But we're your family,' Judith said furiously. 'We need you too.'

The messenger cleared his throat.

'The Lady is waiting.'

'It's the York embassy.' Wulfgar tried to explain to his kinswomen. 'She wouldn't summon me like this if it weren't important.' The look on his sister-in-law's face silenced him. How could anything, her eyes said, be more important than proving Wystan's innocence? And the trouble was, in his heart of hearts, he agreed with her.

'But you *promised*.' Judith bit off the end of the last word, lifting her chin and swallowing hard.

Wulfgar heard her unwitting echo of Edric of Amport's last words to his King, and he felt a terrible pang.

'I only promised I would try.' He looked at her tight-lipped expression. 'I'm sworn to the Lady, Judith. If I don't go, if I break my oath—'

'What? She'll find another secretary?' She spat out the words as though they were bitter on her tongue.

It was Cwenhild who had come to his rescue. Putting her free hand on Judith's shoulder, she said, 'Judith, she's his Lady. Don't you see? He can't defy her, and he won't. No more than I could disobey the Lady Abbess at the Nunnaminster, or you would break your marriage vows.'

Judith muttered something, and turned away.

But Wulfgar still felt like a traitor to his kin, even as he told the housekeeper to see his bags were packed, and waited for the ostler to bring him his horse. He looked around, at the carved wood of the gables and the massive oak planks of the external stair. A stable boy had brought up a bag of feed for the weary horse. As it bent its head to the nosebag the sparrows squabbled round its hooves for discarded flakes of barley. Warm, savoury smells came drifting from the kitchen.

Nine days ago, his brother had been uncontested master of this little world.

'I know she's your Lady. But you mustn't let her...' Cwenhild paused, looking at him with concern. A shadow passed across her broad-cheeked, snub-nosed countenance. 'Oh, never mind.'

Wulfgar stepped up onto the mounting block at the foot of the stair and heaved himself into the saddle, feeling as though leaden weights were attached to his ankles.

It had been a weary ride back to Gloucester, and he was relieved now, at last, to see the gilded shingles of the palace at Kingsholm gleaming in the distance.

She was waiting for him.

'Don't let them know you speak Danish,' the Lady said to him, even as he was making his bow.

She was pale to the point of translucence, her head held very high. The hollows beneath her cheekbones were surely more shadowed than they had been a week ago.

'I want to know what they're saying behind their hands. They think I'm weak.' Her lips tightened. 'They wouldn't even condescend to treat with me at first; they demanded to see my Lord. So I took them to see him.' She smiled then, a taut parody of mirth. 'It was one of his bad days. He couldn't even sit up, never mind speak. That sobered them. But now they think they can tear up the treaty you drafted. I've heard them muttering to each other – *thralls*, I heard them say, and *geld* – but I don't understand much of it.'

'I see, my Lady.' And he did.

He really did. But all through that relentless ride back to Gloucester Judith's face had been haunting him. That baffled, betrayed look in her eyes.

Yes: the treaty with York needed to be agreed and ratified and written up but it surely needn't take more than a few days. Then he could ask the Lady for permission to go straight back to Winchester. He hadn't had a moment yet to tell her what had happened there, and she hadn't asked. When she knew what was at stake, she would understand.

She was leading the way into the hall and indicated that he should sit on a stool by her chair at one end of the long table that had been set up for the meeting. He sat obediently and tried to muster his thoughts.

'What have you discussed with them so far, my Lady?'

'Nothing solid.' She gnawed her lower lip in that poignantly familiar way. 'We've been sparring, testing each other's resolve, probing for vulnerability...' She smiled. 'I can do it, you know. It seems I haven't sat by all these years and watched my Lord at work for nothing.'

He was sure she was right: little had ever escaped that cool, grey gaze of hers.

'But they're hard men.' She swallowed. 'I almost think it would be worth it – paying geld, I mean. My father did it, after all. If it would guarantee their support...'

'A dangerous precedent, my Lady.'

'Yes. Perhaps that's why the Bishop is fighting me at every step.' She glanced furtively around her, though the hall was still empty of anyone but her ever-present attendant women. 'They think I'm weak, Wulfgar,' she said again. 'They all do. But not you.'

He shook his head vehemently.

'I can rely on you,' she said. She gave him a long appraising look, her eyes narrowed. 'There's something I should—'

There was a bustle at the door, and they both stiffened.

The guards stood back to admit the Bishop of Worcester with his clerics. Wulfgar got to his feet. He recognised the Bishop's nephew, Kenelm, as the third of the tonsured young men in attendance: impossible to miss his gangly height, topped with that pink face and hair like sun-bleached straw.

'My Lady.'

She inclined her head. With her elegant burden of linen veil she reminded Wulfgar of a swan. The Bishop, magnificent in full vestments, nodded briefly to him, and they all sat. Three of Mercia's senior thanes had entered in their wake, and there was more nodding, and settling, and muttering.

Wulfgar found his eyes drawn ineluctably to the door. It was a hot day, and the shutters high in the roof were open but admitting hardly a breath of air. He could feel dampness gathering in the small of his back and under his arms. The table had been moved down from the dais and set up parallel to the long walls, with the Lady seated at one narrow end in her Lord's carved chair. Wulfgar was on her right, sitting on his low stool with his tablets on his knee, and then to his own right, on one end of the long bench, was Werferth, Worcester's Bishop, fully vested in his gold-trimmed mitre and martyr-red chasuble. Wulfgar glanced nervously at the old man, but he was seated on the Bishop's blind side and there was no reading that grim profile with its empty eye-socket. The thanes, a trio whom he knew by sight and by solid, loyal reputation, were talking in low voices among themselves. Beyond them a silent-footed slave was lighting the oil lamps on stands along the wall.

A clattering at the door, the movement of shadows, and loud voices. Their visitors were removing their weapons. Wulfgar's blood was pounding now, and he put his wax tablets down on the white linen to wipe his palms surreptitiously on the fine wool of his leggings.

The steward banged his staff on the floorboards, and everyone – even the Lady – rose. No, Wulfgar realised after a heartbeat, not everyone. The Bishop of Worcester had not stirred from his seat.

'Thorbjorn of York,' the Lady said, her hands extended, ignoring the Bishop's discourtesy. 'Welcome back to my table.'

The leader of the Danish party nodded, unsmiling, and growled a response from somewhere deep in his grizzled beard. He was a massive man, with a thick, reddened face, the skin flaking from some eczemous condition. The sight of him made Wulfgar's own skin crawl. There were only four men in the Danish party, but somehow they seemed to take up as much space as all the Mercians combined, including the guards at the door and the Lady's attendant women, hovering by the embroidered hanging at the hall's far end.

The Bishop led the prayers. He bowed his head over his folded hands, but he had lifted it again to stare down the table even before the last *Amen* had died away.

'Your demands are out of the question,' he said. 'Mercia has never dealt with Northumbria on those terms, and it never will.' He leant back from the table in a shimmer of red silk and gold thread, his lips compressed.

Thorbjorn's face had been expressionless while the Bishop was speaking. Then, 'The past is over. You are an old man and your time is over.' He stabbed his thick index finger at the Bishop. 'We are not *Northumbria*. We are York. This is something new. Your old sagas mean nothing to us.'

He and the Bishop were staring each other down like a pair of sparring tom-cats.

'Gentlemen. Why is this proving so difficult?' The Lady's voice was as emollient as warm milk. 'Your King is a Christian, Thorbjorn.' She picked up the letter the ambassadors had brought, which Wulfgar had barely had the chance to scan, and held it out. '*One of the holy fraternity of Christian Kings* – his own words to me and my Lord. Baptised and confirmed in Frankia; and anointed and crowned in York's minster, by the Archbishop himself on the Feast of Our Lord's Nativity.' She sounded properly impressed. 'And he now he bids us join hands across the pagan divide.'

Despite the oppressive warmth, Wulfgar felt his nape prickle.

'*Já*,' Thorbjorn said, as though reading his mind. 'You' – that stabbing finger again – 'agree to fight Ketil Scar of Leicester, and little Toli Silkbeard of Lincoln, and the rest of them, for us.'

Wulfgar tried to cover his jerk of recognition and fear, shifting ostentatiously on his rickety little stool and flexing the cramped fingers of his writing hand. *Lincoln*, he wrote. *Leicester*. His pulse had quickened.

'Exactly.' The Lady was nodding. 'And, of course, you do the same for us.'

There was a long moment of silence. If ever he were going to speak, surely this was his opportunity. He cleared his throat.

'Wulfgar? Do you want to comment?' His Lady was looking down at him from the height of her chair.

Now the Danes were looking at him with puzzled and speculative expressions. He swallowed again.

'I – I was just wondering... I thought perhaps our honoured guests might have more recent news than we have? Of Lincoln.'

Leicester. As ever, the name of that city evoked recent memories, some welcome, some less so: a flash of red silk, the exotic whiff of pepper and cinnamon, a mocking jarl with a terrifying, scarred visage. He couldn't even frame the word.

His Lady did it for him.

'Leicester and Lincoln and the rest of the Five Boroughs. Quite right, Wulfgar. Thorbjorn, do you have any recent reports of events?'

Thorbjorn snorted.

'Young Toli of Lincoln claims the ties of friendship with our King, but he's less than half the man his father was. And Leicester?' He grinned his gap-toothed smile. 'Things are hard in Leicester. Ketil Scar has raised the *gjald* payments for merchants, and he's fallen out with all his late brother's friends. Word is, he won't hold Leicester without mending his ways.'

'All his late brother's friends?'

Wulfgar felt like a fool, repeating Thorbjorn's words apparently mindlessly. He hadn't meant to ask the question, but he could feel that little brooch in the pouch round his neck weighing him down as though it were a quernstone. He guessed what the answer would be, but he had to ask anyway.

'All Jarl Hakon's friends? What about Gunnvor Bolladottir?'

69

CHAPTER ELEVEN

'Bolladottir? That hatchet-faced bitch? Hakon's woman?' Thorbjorn grunted with laughter. '*Já, já*, her too. Last I heard, she'd been stripped of some of the goodies Hakon had given her, like toll rights. But they say she's still the richest woman in the Five Boroughs!' He eyed Wulfgar curiously. 'I wouldn't have had her marked as a friend of yours, little churchman.'

Wulfgar closed his eyes briefly, wishing he'd never asked the question.

He should never have thrown the door open for Thorbjorn to walk in and wipe his filthy boots all over her name.

'I wouldn't presume to call her a friend. She helped me once.' She had bought him out of the hands of a slave-dealer who wanted him dead, for the bargain price of five øre. What sort of basis was that for friendship? He had never told the full story to his Lady.

'Well, that's all very interesting,' she said now. 'Are we agreed, then?' She couldn't quite keep the hope out of her voice. 'Can we shake hands on this?'

'What about the *gjald*?' Thorbjorn said.

The Lady's eyes flickered towards the Bishop.

'We are not your tributaries,' he growled.

The Lady said, 'King Knut's letter says nothing of geld, in silver or in kind.' But there was a tremor in her voice.

Kind was a euphemism for slaves, Wulfgar guessed. He was scratching their words down on his wax tablets, concentrating on the task in hand and trying not to worry about his Lady, caught between these two unyielding men.

'We did not know then how weak you Mercians are,' Thorbjorn said bluntly. 'Your old man is as bad as dead.' His eyes gleamed. 'You need us more than we need you. Far, far more.'

'This will be a treaty of equals, or it will be no treaty.'

'*Equals*, Fleda?' the Bishop said. 'Have you forgotten what these men did to Mercia?'

'My Lord Bishop,' she said, and paused to take a measuring breath, 'with all due respect, I was hardly weaned when Mercia fell. We have to deal with the world as it is.'

'We never fought Mercia,' Thorbjorn said, indicating his henchmen, who nodded in agreement. He paused for a long moment, long enough for the assembly to think he had finished, before adding, 'My half-brother did, though!' He roared with laughter. 'And *his* father' – he jerked a thumb at one of the other Danes – 'and his! And his old uncle, he was at Repton when your King was driven out howling to the Pope with his tail between his legs!'

Wulfgar could feel his cheeks reddening in sympathy with the Lady's humiliation.

Thorbjorn leaned back on his stool, sucking his surviving teeth and looking pleased at the effect of his words.

The Lady was fingering the little gold cross that hung at her throat.

'Unless you accept me as the ruler of Mercia, there can be no treaty. You are commanded by your King to make this treaty. I can see you are enjoying your position of strength; I acknowledge it. But we need to look beyond the moment.' She lifted her chin, looking hard at Thorbjorn. 'We are agreed that Ketil of Leicester and Toli of Lincoln represent threats to both Mercia and York. Neither of us trusts them. We both need this treaty.'

She stood up, and gestured the other Mercians to their feet.

'But,' she paused and swallowed, 'we are to be equals, or nothing.'

There was a long silence.

Thorbjorn didn't move so much as an eyelid for a long moment.

At last, 'Sit down, lass.'

She stayed on her feet.

Wulfgar looked askance at his Lady. She had changed in the last few months, and perhaps in the last few days, too.

'You have the right of it,' Thorbjorn said at last. 'We need each other.'

He slapped his massive hand down on the parchment containing Wulfgar's scrupulously worded clauses.

'This treaty can stand for a season,' he said. 'Till harvest, when men stand down their spears for the year. A summer and winter and then we can come back to the table in the spring' – he grinned – 'thee and me.'

The Lady nodded cautiously. Wulfgar thought that only he was close enough to her to see the tiny beads of perspiration that dotted her upper lip.

'Sit thyself down,' Thorbjorn said again, almost paternal, and this time she obeyed.

Wulfgar perched himself back on his stool, relief flooding his veins. He scratched in his wax: *renew treaty next year?*

'We're nearly done then—' she started to say.

'*Done?*' And Wulfgar realised that the Bishop of Worcester was still on his feet, crackling with fury, his hands balled into fists. 'You're doing a West Saxon's work here, Fleda, whether you know it or not. This is treachery. You're putting Mercia in peril.' He swung round, stabbing a bony finger at Thorbjorn and the others. 'Do you trust these Danes? Really? Do you believe them? Then you're a fool, girl. They'll come in the guise of friends and then attack us themselves, and then – dear God – we'll have to beg Wessex for help—' He stopped, and looked away. 'What a fool I've been myself,' he muttered. He beckoned abruptly as he moved towards the door, his hesitant clerics starting to follow.

'Godfather,' the Lady said, her voice cool and hard.

He went on walking.

'Godfather, if you leave this hall now you will no longer be part of my council.'

The door curtain swung back in the Bishop's wake.

Thorbjorn was chuckling deep in his beard. 'If you think that old priest of yours makes trouble then you should see the quarrels my master has with his Archbishop!'

'I thought they were friends?' Her voice was cool. She indicated the letter on the table in front of her, a faint frown creasing the smooth skin between her eyebrows. Wulfgar suspected she was close to tears.

'Oh, *já, já*. They call each other friend to their faces. But they fall out often enough to keep matters lively in Jórvík.' He settled his broad rump more comfortably and grinned his gap-toothed smile. 'Now, our pledges?'

'Pledges?'

'*Gíslar*. Hostages, lass. I told you.'

'I know that.' Still cool, tight, controlled.

'We've those two nephews of our King, to leave with thee till *hairst*.' He paused. 'Harvest, that is.'

She nodded again.

'Whom shall we take home in return? Hast decided? Two of thine own bairns?'

One of the attendant women gasped, her hand flying to her mouth.

The Lady lifted her chin, her eyes brighter than ever. 'Surely even in York it is known that my Lord and I have not yet been blessed with children?'

'Not *yet*, eh?' Thorbjorn leaned back and muttered something in an inaudible undertone to his neighbour, who sniggered. The words might have been muffled but the sense was blatant.

The Lady's cheeks had gone a hot pink.

'Come on, Lady,' Thorbjorn said. 'Two of thy folk to come north with us while the treaty holds. Bad faith, and all four lose their eyes and ears.'

'I cannot accept that.'

He shrugged. 'Hands and feet, better?'

She sat very still, her clenched hands resting on the white linen in front of her, staring, expressionless.

'It is the custom of Mercia, they tell me.' Thorbjorn leaned back, looking at her levelly.

She jerked her head in a nod. At last, she said, 'If there is bad faith, then the hostages will be killed.'

'Killed, eh?' Wulfgar thought the burly Dane was looking at her with more respect, but her words were a cold trickle down his own spine.

Oh yes.

She had changed.

'Nor are they to be hanged,' she went on, her voice growing stronger as she spoke. 'Killed cleanly, yes. With a priest in attendance.' She looked Thorbjorn in the eye. 'Without torture.'

'Over-nesh, lass,' he said, shaking his head. 'Tha'll have to toughen up to stay in this game.' But he was grinning. 'So, if no bairns of thine own, who then?'

The Lady's eyes flickered to her left, to where the Mercian thanes had huddled, talking together in low, urgent voices, darting hostile looks at the Danes. Not one of them was responding to the naked plea in her face. Wulfgar couldn't imagine they would have reacted to her husband with such sluggish loyalty. If Mercia's Lord had been presiding they would have been competing with each other to offer their sons, their cousins, their younger brothers. He could read every thought in her face, every flicker of uncertainty and fear, and he was sure he wasn't the only one to do so.

She looked at him then, an odd, wary glance. Her lips framed a silent question. Reading it as a plea for support, he gave her a little nod. She raised her eyebrows, her eyes wide, her head slightly tilted, still questioning, and in that moment a sudden, chilling certainty came over him. She needed someone to put himself, body and soul, at her disposal.

She was asking him.

And he couldn't possibly do what she wanted him to.

He opened his mouth, but the words wouldn't come.

His Lady took a deep breath, and turned back to the table.

'Wulfgar will go.'

CHAPTER TWELVE

'Who is this *Wulfgar*?' Thorbjorn's voice was sceptical. 'This boy – does he rank with a king's nephew?'

Wulfgar burned under the collective gaze of the Danish embassy. But even while his cheeks reddened in the face of their scrutiny he could feel the cold of shock creeping over him as the meaning of the Lady's words sank in.

Go to York? Till *hairst*, Thorbjorn had said. Harvest. But that was when the West Saxon Witan would be meeting...

Impossible.

He couldn't challenge her, not in public, not when she was so weak already. But he had to go back to Winchester, and as soon as he could. Save Wystan's life. Stop Garmund. Find the Atheling. Find the truth.

He glanced down at the abbreviated scribbles in his wax. Was *this* why she had stipulated the clause about no torture? Realisation sank slowly in, like silt settling at the bottom of a pond.

She had had him in mind as a hostage from the start.

And how could he blame her? There were few other members of her family or her retinue she could have nominated in his stead.

Few? None that came readily to mind.

And while he could think only of his brother's fate, he knew that the fate of all the folk of Mercia lay in his Lady's hands.

'Wulfgar is my secretary,' she was saying. 'He is the son of a noble West Saxon house. I value him highly.'

'And his death would be regretted, eh?' Thorbjorn's grin was positively wolf-like. He rubbed his hands together and cracked his knuckles loudly. 'Who for thy second, then? Our King fair dotes on his nephews.'

'We will let you know.'

She stood up again, and this time it was clear that the meeting was over. The Danish envoys made their bows and clattered out and the Mercian thanes started to follow.

The Lady held up her hand. 'Wait.'

She paused, and Wulfgar suspected she was hoping one of them would offer himself as the second hostage, or at least put forward a fruitful suggestion.

Obediently, they waited.

At last, and a little lamely, she said, 'Discuss this among yourselves. I will be interested to hear your thoughts, later.'

They bowed, and backed out.

'You will go, won't you, Wulfgar?'

He jumped. 'I am yours to command, my Lady.' He could hear how stiff, how unfamiliar, his own voice sounded. 'Is this why you summoned' – he had nearly said *dragged* – 'me back from Winchester?'

She tried a smile then, strained and beseeching. 'You've done so well before. You speak Danish. I trust you. I couldn't think whom else I could ask.'

And he had misled her with his stupid nods and smiles. He was complicit in this. Oh, Queen of Heaven. He was sworn to her, head and hand. He closed his eyes briefly, and Wystan's grubby, bearded face danced before him in the darkness, as if bobbing from a rope.

'My Lady,' he said, tentative and dry-mouthed, 'can this wait a little? Say three months?' He could hear how outrageous his suggestion sounded. 'Six weeks, even?'

'*What?*' She shook her head at him, a flurry of white lawn and gold. 'Wait? Of course not. What are you saying?'

'The King your brother has given me the summer to disprove the charges against Wystan.' He felt guilty and soiled, just saying the words, when she already had so much to burden her. 'Or he hangs him when the full Witan convenes in September.'

'I see.' She looked away from him, over to the far side of the hall, her lips pressed tightly together. 'Oh, my dear God.'

He waited.

'You won't go? Is that what you're telling me?'

'Of course I'll go. You've ordered me to go. In front of witnesses.'

He tried to keep the bitterness out of his voice. It would be Wystan's death sentence, but it wasn't her fault. He stared at her remote, absent profile, willing her to turn and look at him, and at long last she did.

'Do everything you can for my brother,' he said. His mind was racing. 'And if I don't come back, pray for me. And look after my godson.'

'You'd better come back.' He could see that relief and anxiety were battling for supremacy in her expression. She put out a hand and grasped his wrist. Her fingers were corpse-cold. 'I'll talk to my brother about Wystan. Ask for a reprieve. More time. Something. I promise I will.'

'Thank you, my Lady.' Would Edward ever reprieve a man he'd publicly called *traitor*, just because his elder sister asked him for a favour? He doubted it. 'And, my Lady, I do understand why you're asking me to do this. It will seal the Danish treaty, which gives Mercia a summer of security, *Deo volente.*'

'Security,' she said thoughtfully. 'Is there such a thing in our sublunary world?'

She turned his hand over and clasped it in her own. He longed to chafe some warmth into those chilly fingers.

'Even my women' – she dropped her voice to a murmur as her glance flickered towards the door and those expectant, waiting figures – 'they spy on me, you know. They're all from thanely families. Everything I do goes straight back to their fathers and brothers.'

Their eyes met for a long moment.

'Enough of this.' She pulled away. 'We have to find a companion for you, and quickly. Whom shall we send? Someone with whom you feel comfortable.'

'Someone near at hand,' Wulfgar said drily. He hesitated for a moment. 'There is one obvious person, my Lady. I don't know if we would ever get the Bishop to agree though.'

'The Bishop of Worcester is not the Regent of Mercia.' Her eyes narrowed. 'Whom do you have in mind?'

'I'm thinking of Kenelm, my Lady. The Deacon.'

'The Bishop's own nephew,' she said slowly. 'You're right. He won't like it.' She frowned suddenly. 'But, are you and Kenelm friends?'

'He was hoping to get my job.' Wulfgar sighed. Kenelm had not been the only Mercian cleric to be disappointed when a West Saxon, and a mere subdeacon at that, had leap-frogged into the secretary's post, right over his head. 'Kenelm's quite talented,' he went on slowly, 'and the Bishop keeps him down. I don't know why. He was made a deacon very young, but he's not been given responsibilities to match.'

'The Bishop's shadow is long,' the Lady said drily, 'and not many young plants flourish in it. You could be right: this might be the making of Kenelm.'

'It would mean a lot to him, being chosen. And I think we could work well together.'

CHAPTER THIRTEEN

The feasting was over. The oaths had been sworn. Masses had been sung. Bags were being packed.

The Danish hostages, lively, bright-eyed imps of five and seven, had fallen in with a gang of the palace children, and Wulfgar was watching a shrieking game of Kite, Hen and Chicks on the grass to the north of the Kingsholm chapel.

He hadn't expected them to be so young. That alone guaranteed their safety, surely. The Lady would never execute children. Not such little ones. But a shiver tightened his spine.

'My uncle's livid, you know. About me going to York, I mean.'

Wulfgar turned slowly. 'I'm sorry.' If Kenelm's eyes were any paler, they'd be white. That lightest blue, the sky where it meets the horizon.

Kenelm shrugged.

'Have you packed?'

The other man nodded. 'You?'

'Yes. I have to go and say goodbye to Electus, though, and his wet nurse.'

'Who? Oh, that Danish brat you brought back with you after Easter? Your godson?'

Wulfgar nodded, keeping his thoughts to himself, and turned his attention back to the children. Their game had now changed to Grandmother's Footsteps. He had been wondering if the new arrivals from York spoke English, and whether it would help if he went over to them and offered to interpret, but it appeared that childhood had its own language. They were already part of the rabble, shaking with muffled giggles, creeping up on the one boy who had his back turned.

That must be what it was like for the Lady: endless machinations going on just beyond the edge of vision, plots to bring her down; hearing things, catching furtive glimpses...

And yet, when she turned to face her terrors full on, there was nothing moving, and everyone was smiling at her.

He shivered.

Word had come that morning from Wessex that when King Edward's men had arrived in Wimborne, sweat-lathered and swords drawn, they had found the Atheling's manor deserted. The messenger had brought some tale of scandal among the little house of nuns there, too; but once Wulfgar had heard that Edward's men had failed to flush their quarry into their nets, he had been unable to pay proper attention to any other gossip.

He hadn't realised how much he had been relying on the Atheling being arrested and scotching this ridiculous story of Wystan's supposed treachery.

Now that avenue of escape was also closed.

And no one had any clue, it seemed, as to where the Atheling had gone to ground.

A fugitive prince with a price on his head.

Where are you, Athelwald Seiriol?

'Wulfgar?'

He realised his name had been spoken more than once.

One of the Lord's young retainers was standing in front of him. He and Kenelm were both staring at him, perplexed expressions on their faces.

'Didn't you hear me? The Lady wants you, at once.'

'I'm sorry. I was lost in thought.' He began to walk away. 'Thank you,' he said over his shoulder.

'She's not in her bower,' the boy said. 'She's with her Lord.'

'Was I sent for, too?' Kenelm sounded as though he had already guessed the answer, and the boy was shaking his head.

Kenelm shrugged, trying to mask his chagrin. 'It's time I went to the chapel, anyway.' He cast an unfathomable look at Wulfgar. 'I'll take your apologies to my uncle.'

She dismissed her women as soon as she saw him darken the doorway. The healer was lingering by the bed.

'You too,' she snapped. 'Out!'

The air in the little room was close and heavy with the smell of a sickroom, rendered even more nauseating by the incense smouldering in its bronze pot.

'Wulfgar, you leave today?' She passed a fine-boned hand over her forehead.

'As you know, my Lady.' Wulfgar found it hard to keep his eyes away from the supine figure in the bed, whose every breath sounded like the death rattle. The Mercians hadn't seen their Lord in public for weeks.

'I summoned you here because I want my Lord to hear what we say. He understands more than you might think, though today is not one of his good days.' There was a silver needle-case hanging from her girdle and she was toying with it, pulling it up on its little chain and running the links though her fingers, over and over again.

'I want you to swear me an oath,' she said.

'But I'm already oath-sworn to you.' *Hand and heart and hope of Heaven.*

'A new oath.'

She sat down on a low stool by the bed, and held out a hand.

Baffled, he knelt, releasing the cloying almond scent of the meadowsweet blossoms as his knees crushed them against the floor. He lifted his clasped hands and let her fold her own around them as he rested his forehead on the smooth blue linen covering her lap.

'Repeat after me.' There was a long silence. He fought the urge to rub his cheek, cat-like, against her knee. 'If I divulge what my Lady tells me, may I burn eternally in the pit of Hell with Lucifer, Judas and Arius, and all the other traitors.'

He lifted his head to stare up at her, but she was gazing beyond him, grey eyes wide and unfocused. He spoke instead to the draped linen, the blue of flax-blossom, '...*what my Lady tells me...*' Queen of Heaven, what could she be going to say to him? '...*the pit of Hell...*' He had a sudden vision of those doomed men in Winchester, going off to the gallows and the pit. 'Amen,' he concluded, dry-mouthed, and realised as he did so that she had forgotten to ask him to say it.

He felt her hand rest on his hair, a little caress of her thumb over the soft, moleskin stubble of his tonsure, and he closed his eyes, not wanting the moment to end. He couldn't remember a time when he hadn't longed for her approval.

'Yes,' she said, and took her hand away. 'You meant that. I could tell.'

He sat back reluctantly on his heels and looked up at her again. 'My Lady, has this to do with York?' It patently had nothing to do with Wystan, and York was the only other matter of which he could think.

She was gnawing at her bottom lip again. As he spoke she glanced over at her unconscious husband.

Wulfgar's eyes followed hers. The old man lay motionless apart from his sporadic, laboured breathing; his eyes were closed, and a snail's trail of saliva was working its way down from the corner of his mouth.

'York?' She blinked and seemed to come back from a very long way away. 'I – York. Of course. Yes.' She clasped her hands across her lap as though trapping one with other. 'You'll be Knut's hostage, but I want you to get close to the Archbishop.'

Wulfgar had the impression that she had wanted to talk to him about something quite different, but he was willing, as ever, to follow where she led him. 'It's still Archbishop Lothward, isn't it, my Lady? I met him once.'

'His consecration?'

Wulfgar nodded. 'I was an altar-server. Five years ago?'

'Six, it must be. So, you know him?'

Wulfgar tried to think. He remembered clearly a rose cope, so stiff with gold that it would have stood on its own, but the man inside it? He shook his head. 'I hardly spoke to him, except when I poured the water for him to wash his hands.' He smiled. 'I was so nervous and the silver ewer was so heavy, I nearly caused a flood.'

'Lothward wants Leicester,' she said. 'Or so I am led to suspect.'

'*Leicester*?' His heart was beating a little faster. 'But he's got York. Leicester's a ruin – a beautiful one – but there's no cathedral community left. And little prospect of change, now that Ketil Scar is Leicester's Jarl. And Leicester's in the see of Canterbury, anyway.'

She let him ramble to the end.

'Quite. But for all that, there are rumours…' She massaged her temples briefly. 'Think of where Leicester is. If you hold Leicester, you hold the Fosse Way and Watling Street.' Her fingers sketched a saltire cross in the air. 'If you have an army based in Leicester, you can take it anywhere. How did Mercia become so powerful, think you, once upon a time?'

'But why would the *Archbishop*—' he began.

'I don't know!' She stood up abruptly, shoving the chair back with a protesting screech of wood on wood. 'But while you're in York you're my eyes and ears. Anything you hear, anything you can find out, has to come back to me. I don't know what they're up to, in the north. They say they want to be my friends. I don't believe a word of it.' She turned and stared down at her insensate husband. 'Can you hear us, my Lord? Why don't you open your eyes?' She swung back to Wulfgar, her fists tightly clenched. 'How could he do this to me?'

'You want me to be your eyes and ears?' He got to his feet reluctantly.

'Find out everything you can. I don't care how you do it.' Her breathing was ragged. 'I have people who send me news, but it takes too long, and it's not reliable.'

'You want me to spy for you.'

'Yes. Listen at doors. Go through document chests. Bribe. Steal. Lie. For the love of God, Wulfgar, how explicit do I have to be?

If anyone is going to take Leicester, it will be Mercia. It will be me.
It has to be.'

He nodded, thinking hard, deeply troubled by her words.

'Don't stand there blinking like a cornered hare. What more do
you want? If I – if *we* – that glance at the bed again – 'get Leicester
back, there'll be something in it for you, I promise you that. It'll
mean a vacant bishopric. Leicester Cathedral. Think about it.'

Her words were sweeping over him, pummelling his senses like
a river in spate. He found he had lifted his hands as though to
fend her off. 'My Lady. You don't need to bribe me. You should
know that.'

A revived bishopric, though…

Her words had to imply that she was offering him the mitre.

He was too young. Much too young. But if an old man were
appointed, to keep the *cathedra* warm, and he himself were put
into a post close to the incumbent…

He could be Bishop of Leicester, perhaps five or six years hence.
The prize was in sight. His head swam.

'Is this what you mean that oath to cover, my Lady?'

'That oath? No … no, it wasn't that.' She turned away from him
and took a few moments to settle herself again on the low stool,
smoothing her veils and disposing her skirts. 'It wasn't that at all.'
She looked down at her intertwined fingers, dominated by the
massy gold of her ring, and then up at him again. She paused then,
long enough for his mind to drift back to the dizzying images
those few words of hers had conjured. It wouldn't be an easy post,
Bishop of Leicester, but…

'And after all, God knows, Mercia is overdue an heir.' She threw
another quick glance at her comatose husband.

'An heir?' Wulfgar could guess what she meant. Not an easy

decision, but one she had been long expected to make. 'Whom have you chosen, my Lady?'

'What?' Her voice had sharpened again.

'Is it Athelstan?' He had a sudden vision of that bright, solemn eight-year-old, laying down the law in Winchester. 'That would be a wise choice. I haven't had the chance to tell you, my Lady, but it's largely thanks to him that Wystan hasn't been hanged already—'

'What are you talking about?'

'Young Athelstan, of course. Your brother's son. He seems to be the only person left in Wessex who knows the law—'

'Athelstan,' she said, as though she'd never heard the name before. 'Yes. Of course. Edward wants me to foster him here, did you know? Athelstan, and the rest of his base-born brood. Edward wants him raised as the next Lord of the Mercians.' She looked down at her hands, clasped demurely across her lap. *'Athelstan.'*

'My Lady, we pray hourly in every church in Gloucester for your Lord to recover. But it will make your thanes happier, knowing that you – and he – have nominated an heir.' He forced a smile, trying to lighten her mood. 'The more children about, the better. Those little Danish boys are settling right in; there are some riotous games going on outside your chapel.'

Had she even heard him?

Was she ill, too?

It was so out of character, this vagueness, her hunched and huddled pose.

He waited, for what seemed a long time.

At last she said, 'You have my leave to go. Get word to me from York, when you can.' She sighed deeply, closing her eyes. 'Send me my women.'

CHAPTER FOURTEEN

Charnwood

'Come on, Wulfgar, who's tupping that ewe-lamb of thine?'

Wulfgar stared between his horse's ears, gritting his teeth, seeing nothing.

'Ewe-lamb? Nay, lad,' another man shouted. 'She'll not see thirty again.'

'And no get from that knackered old tup she's shackled to, to boot,' a third called across. 'I'd see her well-raddled, and I lay she'd thank me for it.'

Wulfgar silently added their names to his litany of loathing. At that moment, even Garmund came lower down the list. It was a hot evening, and he was sweaty and filthy and chafed. His only consolation was that Kenelm, with his ungainly height, looked even more incongruous on a horse than he did. Wulfgar was wearing lay dress – his lightest tunic and sturdiest leggings – but Kenelm had clung to his robe as more befitting his diaconal status, and had been riding with the extra yard of fabric bunched clumsily around his knees, and his bare bony ankles on display.

Wulfgar's only consolation, but a meagre one.

He hated Thorbjorn for the endless succession of coarse jokes about the Lady, and he hated him even more because they had ridden the Fosse Way north-east for a day and a half, heading straight towards Leicester. He had daydreamed, for a day and a half, about visiting the cathedral again and viewing it with a new, proprietorial eye. About wandering round it with his dear friend Father Ronan, of St Margaret's Kirk in the Gallowtree-gate, and talking about restoring the smoke-damaged window-surrounds, and whether those cracks in the plaster hinted at more serious damage.

He hadn't told Kenelm any of that. Nor had he shared with his colleague his hectic fancy of going to a Leicester ale-house, and asking whether its proprietrix might be in town. *Yes, that's right*, he could hear himself saying. *The late Jarl's mistress...*

I owe her some money...

He had been almost feverish with excitement, for a day and a half. The nervousness that went with being a hostage was small beer by comparison.

And then, without warning, Thorbjorn had jerked his horse's head round and they had gone off the Fosse, heading north towards steep, rocky Charnwood. They weren't going to Leicester at all.

'What, lad? Hankering after Leicester?' Thorbjorn, catching a glimpse of his unguarded face, rocked in his saddle with laughter. 'Treaty or no treaty, old Scarface Ketil has no love for men of York. There are a few old grudges not yet scabbed over. Happen Leicester might bring rough justice for some of us.' He jerked his head sideways and mimed a rope, gagging loudly and lolling his tongue. Then he laughed again, when Wulfgar winced and looked away.

'We'll have to stop soon,' Kenelm muttered from his other side. 'I'm numb from the waist down.'

'Aye, we'll stop soon,' Thorbjorn agreed. 'We don't want to be benighted in a place not of our choosing.'

Wulfgar was about to reply, but Thorbjorn held up a repressive hand.

'Quiet!'

The whole troop stood as still as half-a-dozen horsemen can. Hands were taut on reins, but the horses tugged and snorted, and their harness fittings jingled faintly. They were in a narrow pass. Above the crags the sun still shone, but down here dusk was gathering.

'What is it now?' Kenelm muttered crossly, but he quailed when Thorbjorn turned on him with a silent, gap-toothed snarl.

Then they all heard it: the steady pound of hooves coming up behind them, fast.

Thorbjorn lifted his head and sniffed the wind. Then he relaxed. 'Blades ready.'

It was clearly a familiar order. The others were wheeling their horses to face back down the track, left hands on their reins, right hands on their pommels, prepared to ease their long knives – and in Thorbjorn's case, a sword – from their sheaths.

Their pursuers were in sight now, and Wulfgar realised why Thorbjorn's tension had lessened. There were only three of them.

A hundred yards away.

Fifty.

Twenty.

They weren't slowing down.

Wulfgar hauled on his reins, trying to urge the obdurate animal off the track, and when he realised that Kenelm wasn't moving he shoved his reins into his own left hand and leaned over to drag at Kenelm's with his right.

'Come *on*!'

But there was nowhere to go. The track was fringed with spiky sloe, hawthorn and gorse, and the horses flinched back.

Their attackers were on them now, screaming wildly. Wulfgar recoiled from the thundering onslaught, only to be met by another wild ululation from above. He twisted, startled, in his saddle, to see another dozen figures on foot pounding down through the bracken and the thorns. A dark shape launched itself at him and together they hurtled to the ground.

Confusion of noise and crashing and trampling hooves.

Someone was hauling him up by the wrists. He fought wildly for a moment before he was kicked hard on the ankle-bone. His arms were gripped behind his back. He was sick and dizzy and dazed, but he couldn't feel any broken bones.

There was Kenelm, hood fallen back and shaven crown gleaming, his face shocked, his mouth a black O.

And Thorbjorn, only a couple of yards away, roaring and lunging, with four men to restrain him. He was bleeding from a gash on one temple, and shaking his head this way and that to keep the blood from running down into his eyes.

'*Hvar frá*? Where from?' The leader of their attackers was poised in front of Thorbjorn, knife in one hand. 'Winchester?' He was young, slim, light on his feet, long, dark hair gathered away from his face.

'*Winchester*?' Thorbjorn spat at the other man's feet and went on in Danish, 'Do I sound like a shit-eating West Saxon?'

'Maybe. West Saxons speak Danish, some of them.'

Wulfgar was shocked into sudden clarity. He fought back his

shivers, straining to understand, snatching at familiar words as they flew past his ears.

'Who wants to know?' Thorbjorn said. 'Are you Ketil Scar's men?'

'I'm asking the questions.'

Wulfgar watched the two men sizing each other up like a brace of fighting cocks. He could almost see the little jumps, the flapping wings and flash of sharpened spurs. Their followers – on both sides – had closed in a rough circle. And suddenly Wulfgar realised that the dark-haired leader of the gang looked familiar. Something about the way he moved, his stance…

'Very well, *já*, we are Knut's men. I am Thorbjorn Thorsteinsson. And – friends or no friends – York has a treaty with Leicester. So, let us go our way.'

The other man nodded and growled something, knife still jutting, but he had registered Thorbjorn's name with a little nod of recognition, even respect. The mood in the gang – in both gangs – had shifted. Captors were stepping away from the men they had been holding, both sides still wary, but there was an easing of the tension, the exchange of a few bantering words that stopped short of apology. Wulfgar rubbed his throbbing wrists.

The leader of the Leicester men said, 'There have been West Saxons riding through here. Avoiding Leicester, just like you boys.' He barked with laughter. 'A big party in the last couple of days, but we heard about them too late to deal with them. When our scout brought news of you we thought it was more of the same.'

Thorbjorn was mopping his gory forehead with his sleeve. 'We should thank thy lads, eh, for doing us a favour? Letting us talk before they kill us? Is that what tha'rt saying?'

But the leader of the Leicester men was laughing, raising his hands, taking a step back.

'*Já*, we could cut your throats and leave you in the waste for the buzzards and the wolves. But why should we blunt our knives on you?' He paused and glanced left and right. In response, his men closed in around the York embassy and their hostages. 'When, instead, we can ask you to take a message for us.'

Thorbjorn nodded. He wadded up the bloody rag and threw it to the ground at the other man's feet.

'I understand. I will be your errand-boy. I will even forgive you that blow. Now,' he gestured back down the track, 'let us be. We need to make our camp.'

'Camp?' The dark-haired young man sounded appalled. 'Our honoured guests? No, my friend, you're coming to Leicester tonight. You can make your promise to Ketil Scar himself,' he paused, '*errand-boy*.'

Ketil Scar's man still looked naggingly familiar to Wulfgar. Had he seen the man in the Jarl of Leicester's entourage, back in April?

Something like that, but not quite.

The man was nodding now. He jerked his chin at his followers, and snapped his fingers for his horse.

'Bring them in. I'll go ahead, let our Jarl know to order the feast.'

As he mounted, he gave a curious little double bounce on the balls of his feet before vaulting into the saddle, and the elusive memory darted shining into Wulfgar's mind like a shaft of sunlight.

This was one of the men who had waylaid him last spring. None too far from here, collecting the toll due at High Cross, where the Fosse Way met Watling Street. If the circumstances hadn't been so similar Wulfgar doubted he would ever have recognised him again.

Gunnvor's man, he had been then.

Ketil's man now.

What did that mean?

'Stop!' His voice was a croak. He tried again. 'Wait, please!' Panting, he found himself at the man's stirrup. 'Gunnvor, Bolli's daughter, whom men call Cat's-Eyes?'

'*Bolladottir*?' Had that been a cough, or a laugh? 'What of her?'

Wulfgar scrabbled after his Danish. 'You were her retainer, weren't you? *Felagi*?' Was that the wrong word? '*Vinr hennar*? Her friend?'

It was definitely a laugh this time.

'Friend? A wise man's only friend is himself.'

He clapped his heels to his horse's ribs, wheeled, and was gone.

CHAPTER FIFTEEN

Leicester

They clattered over and splashed through what seemed like an endless series of little plank-bridges and shallow fords until they reached the narrow strip of land that divided the river from the walls. Their cavalcade turned to the left, following the line of the walls and ditch round a great curved corner, until a roof bowed like an upturned boat came into view, a dark shadow against the last trails of sunset in the north-eastern sky.

'Jarl Ketil's house,' said the man riding on the right, and Wulfgar caught a flash of white teeth in the dusk. A brief glance to the other side showed him that Kenelm had shrunk down into his cloak, sitting hunched over his reins as though he wanted to render himself invisible. Wulfgar could well remember what a first encounter with the Jarl of Leicester was like, but he himself felt alert, curious and wary rather than afraid. Thorbjorn, who was riding just beyond Kenelm, was scowling, his shoulders braced with bad temper.

They dismounted in the courtyard and Ketil Scar's man told

them to wait outside while he had a word with the guard at the door in one of the narrow ends of the longhouse. And then they waited again after the guard laughed and went inside.

The horses shifted and stamped. There was a sudden frantic quacking of ducks from one of the little streams as a child ran past with a stick, trying to round them up for the night. The air was thick with hearth-smoke, and Wulfgar was suddenly, powerfully hungry.

At last the guard returned. He jerked his head at Thorbjorn. *'Thu. Ok English-mathar.'*

You. And the Englishmen.

Wulfgar curled his fingers into fists, resisting the urge to step forward and betray that he had understood. He fielded a nervous, sideways look from Kenelm.

'What did he say?'

He was given no time to reply. They were already being beckoned forward, ducking their heads under the lowering lintel, coming into a packed, smoky space in which most of the light came from a long, rectangular hearth whose smouldering logs glowed so brightly that Wulfgar found his dark-adjusted eyes watering painfully.

There was a seated figure, a grim, looming blur, beyond the orange brightness of the hearth, and Wulfgar heard a guttural, mocking boom: *'Hej! Litill Englis-mathr!'*

Wulfgar was vaguely aware of people sitting on the deep benches flanking the long hearth, of fascinated eyes, bodies shifting themselves out of his way as he stumbled between the pillars towards that peremptory voice. He knew Ketil Scar spoke perfectly adequate English: he was not going to let himself be bullied and intimidated, not this time.

But it seemed Ketil Scar was not in a games-playing mood, either. He gestured Wulfgar to a low three-legged stool by the hearth, ignoring Kenelm and Thorbjorn who lingered in his wake. Wulfgar shook the stinging tears from his eyes and forced himself to look up at Ketil's face.

It had grown no easier on the eye for being a season older.

Wulfgar had so steeled himself not to flinch from the blinded eye, the truncated nose, the twisted mouth thick with alternately red and livid scar tissue, that it took him a heartbeat to realise that the Jarl of Leicester was reaching out a richly be-ringed hand.

'Greetings, little friend,' he said in English.

Wulfgar returned the clasp, wincing. Ketil's joints might be sore and swollen but his grip still felt powerful enough to squeeze blood from a stone, the thick metal shanks of his rings grinding against Wulfgar's very finger-bones.

'*Sjá thetta?*' Ketil was saying.

Wulfgar, fighting the urge to massage his throbbing hand, looked as instructed at the still-extended paw. It took him a moment to realise that Ketil was indicating one ring in particular: a massive gold hoop set with a gleaming carnelian the colour of fresh blood. Ketil was laughing.

'See? I'm still wearing your ring, little one,' he said, in English this time. 'No man need fear me while I yet wear his gift.'

He turned his head and added something loudly in Danish to the man standing beside him. Wulfgar understood, though: *When I take the ring off, then let him worry!* He kept his polite smile with considerable effort. The Bishop of Worcester was still formidably angry about that ring – his precious relic-ring – having been bestowed upon a Danish Jarl, even a baptised one. Offering it as a gift had probably saved Wulfgar's life, but that fact did not seem to have mollified the Bishop.

For all that, Wulfgar was relieved beyond words to see his pledge still on the Jarl's forefinger.

Ketil Scar was indicating back beyond the fire. 'You,' he said in English. 'Here.' The finger stabbed towards the floor, next to Wulfgar. Wulfgar started to get to his feet, but a chopping gesture from Ketil Scar stopped him as Kenelm picked his tentative way forward.

'Another churchman?' Ketil Scar said. 'Or are you a woman? Shall I give you to my house-carls, to find out?'

Loud laughter from the men standing around Ketil Scar's chair.

'Do you have a name, man-woman?'

Kenelm looked too terrified to reply. Wulfgar wasn't even sure his colleague had understood the question. He said, 'This is Kenelm, my Lord. Deacon of the Church of Worcester and nephew to the Bishop.'

'Not a woman, then, for all his long skirts and smooth chin!' Ketil Scar reached forward to jab at Kenelm's groin. 'Gelding?' He leaned down to Wulfgar. 'Geldings for your God, the pair of you?' Another guffaw of tainted breath and a thump on the shoulder. 'Up you get, little Englishman. You're safe under my roof, but don't go wandering off in the dark. You don't know who might pounce.'

Limp with relief, Wulfgar scrambled to his feet as Ketil Scar bellowed, 'Now, Thorbjorn Thorsteinsson! You old scoundrel! Sit yourself down and tell me what tricks you've been getting up to with the lovely Lady of Mercia.'

Wulfgar backed away, stumbling against the edge of the hearth-stones, bowing to Ketil as he took Kenelm's arm. 'Come on.'

Now that he had survived the encounter, he realised with agonising clarity that it hadn't been the prospect of seeing Ketil Scar that had made him anticipate Leicester with fear and trembling.

She might be less than a mile away.

Oh, Queen of Heaven...

Don't go wandering off in the dark...

Had Ketil read his mind?

He could leave Ketil's longhouse and turn left, and just by keeping the walls on his right he could navigate the reeky maze of the Danish town. Cross the Fosse Way where it left the city again through the northern gate, and before he knew it he would find the Gallowtree-gate, and the little white-limed church of St Margaret.

And from there it was no more than a step to the ale-house Gunnvor owned, the Wave-Serpent...

He could feel his will being jerked thither, like a nail answering the lure of the lodestone.

His palms were damp and his heart was dancing to an irregular drumbeat.

The way to the door was thick-packed with people. Could he reach it unnoticed?

He was vaguely aware that Kenelm was saying something to him. 'Sorry.' He blinked. 'What did you say?'

'What is all this?' Kenelm hissed. 'Tell me what's going on. Who is that horrible man?' He indicated towards Ketil, a furtive little movement that betrayed his fear even more than his voice did.

Wulfgar realised with a sudden pang that Kenelm could hardly have understood a word of the confrontation between Thorbjorn and Ketil's man back in Charnwood, or indeed any of the conversations since.

'That's Ketil Scar, Jarl of Leicester. We're his hearth-guests tonight.'

'Not his prisoners? He's not going to kill us? Or – or anything?'

Wulfgar shook his head, and Kenelm exhaled with relief, closing his eyes and making the sign of the cross, but he interrupted himself halfway through, his eyes jerking open.

'Are they pagans?'

'Ketil's been baptised.' Wulfgar choked back the uncertainty he felt as to any difference that that sacrament might have made. 'And he's inherited his brother's treaty with the Danes of York, to whose King we are sworn.' He glanced back at Ketil Scar, squatting over his fire. 'Kenelm, I have friends in Leicester. People I want to see.'

'That renegade priest?' Kenelm's face darkened as much as his pale features would allow. 'The Irishman?'

'Yes, of course, I forgot. You met him back in the spring.' Wulfgar bit back a sharper response, remembering what he himself had thought of Leicester's only priest, the first time they had met. 'But Ronan's Leicester born and bred, and no renegade. The people of Leicester are lucky to have him.' He looked at Kenelm, willing the other man to meet his gaze. 'I must go and see him, now we're here. Will you—'

Let Thorbjorn know, on the quiet, he had been going to say.

'Come with you?' Kenelm's face lit up. 'Of course.' Then he took in Wulfgar's expression. 'That's not what you were going to say, was it?'

Wulfgar groped after the least hurtful words he could think of.

'It might be dangerous, in the dark—'

'Don't leave me here on my own!' Kenelm's eyes were stretched wide with fear.

Wulfgar looked towards the door again, a hollow pit of yearning under his ribs. He clenched his fists, baffled and angered by the urgency of his feelings. This had to stop. What ludicrous, half-baked scheme did he have in mind? Even if he found her, and she were, unbelievably, glad to see him, what then? Was he really going to abandon his mission, return to Gloucester and announce his betrothal to an unbaptised Dane? Renounce his ambitions – or even, unthinkably, his ordination – and go back to the little Meon valley estate of Corhampton that his mother had left him? Was he expecting Gunnvor Cat's-Eyes Bolladottir to dwindle into a housewife?

He'd never thought that far.

He'd been daydreaming. Empty fantasies. Toying with her image as though she were no more than a pretty trinket. He put his hand to his breast, feeling the lump of the little pouch and the hard shape of the enamel brooch within. He had to choose, and he knew where his duty lay.

'Don't worry,' he said to Kenelm. 'I won't abandon you.'

Kenelm exhaled loudly with relief.

Wulfgar sighed in turn, and resigned himself to the inevitable.

'Everything's fine, you know. We represent the Lady. Ketil Scar's not an easy man to deal with, but we're his guests,' he said, trying to convince himself as much as Kenelm. 'Everything's going to be all right.' He swallowed hard. 'I'm not going anywhere.'

There was a tap on his shoulder.

Wulfgar turned to find the dark-haired man who had led the Charnwood ambush standing next to him.

'Englishman?' Gripping Wulfgar's elbow, he steered him round. 'Jarl Ketil wants you again.'

Indeed, Ketil Scar was beckoning him back, stabbing a finger at that little stool. As Wulfgar approached, the Jarl glowered at him.

'I want to talk,' he barked. He gestured abruptly, and his housecarls crowded away to the other end of the long fire, four or five yards away.

Wulfgar steeled himself to look up at the Jarl of Leicester, wondering why he had been summoned back. But Ketil seemed in no hurry to tell him. He was sitting forward on his chair, resting his forearms on his thighs, his hands dangling between his knees, and staring at the glowing hearth.

Wulfgar found it much easier to contemplate that wreck of a face when its owner wasn't returning his gaze.

'Three months now, I have been Leicester's Jarl,' Ketil said at last. 'Three months since my brother Hakon died.'

It felt safest to nod and say nothing.

'Do you know what I most fear, little Englishman?'

Wisest perhaps just to shake his head this time.

Ketil fell silent again. He reached forward to pull out a charred branch, and used it to stir the glowing charcoal.

'How many years do you have?'

Wulfgar jumped. He had been watching the sparks fly upward, and the newly awoken flames licking the logs. 'Twenty-four, my Jarl.'

'So many?' Ketil raised an eyebrow. 'I would have thought fewer. I had eighteen winters under my belt when I met the Mercian swords that did this to me.' He sketched a gesture towards his scarred visage. 'I would have died if my brother hadn't taken care of me.' He jabbed at the fire again. 'Thirty-two years, and in all that time no woman has come willing to my bed.' He shifted round to look at Wulfgar. 'I was a pretty boy once, Englishman.' His voice was edged with contempt. 'As pretty as you, maybe.'

Wulfgar sat very still, forcing himself to look up into Ketil's face.

'Maybe Hakon should have let me die, at Nottingham.' Ketil shifted away again and scowled into the fire. 'Look at them.'

Wulfgar blinked. 'Look at what, my Jarl?'

Ketil jerked his head, gesturing down the length of the hall. 'Women. Have you ever thought how strange it is that they all wear much the same, but one looks like a sack of turnips, while another looks like *that*?'

The woman he was indicating had her back to them. She was dressed in green, with a kind of train pinned to and falling back from her shoulders, her unveiled head held high, the silver ornaments in her coils of dark hair flashing reflected fire. She was talking to someone beyond her, her hands stabbing the air, punctuating her words with vivid movement.

Wulfgar would have known that arrogant back anywhere.

Gunnvor Bolladottir, known as Cat's-Eyes.

Had she been there all along?

She turned her head a little then, and he saw her falcon's profile, the proud lift of her chin and the rare curve of her smile. The demon of illicit longing, which he had thought exorcised only moments before, came screaming back.

Had she seen him yet?

Was she ignoring him?

'Not bad, eh, little Englishman?'

Wulfgar had almost forgotten Ketil Scar was still there.

Ketil snorted. He lifted a massive hand to his face and rubbed at his scar.

'It still troubles me, you know. My face.'

Wulfgar somehow found the strength to drag his gaze away from that compelling green-clad back.

'It troubles me more than ever, and the hinges of my bones hurt, and I'm growing old.' Ketil was rummaging around in the ashes with his stick, scattering grey-black powder this way and that. '*Dust thou art*, eh, Englishman? How does it go?'

Wulfgar nodded. His throat was still tight and arid, but he managed to say, '*And into dust thou shalt return.*'

'What I most fear, little Englishman, is dying like my brother.' Ketil paused, hawked, and spat accurately into the middle of the hearth. The coals hissed. 'Dying in the straw by the fire in a puddle of piss. Like an old woman, with womanish men like you fussing about me.'

Ketil Scar, coming to him for spiritual advice? Wulfgar felt both honoured and terrified. He took a couple of steadying breaths. The urge to squint down the hall again was almost overpowering. He could feel himself trembling, and it needed all the strength he had to keep the quiver out of his voice. 'But you have been baptised, my Jarl. You have accepted the—'

'Oh, *já*, I've worn the white robe. More than once. My brother told me to, and I was in no place to refuse him. But it's no faith for men.'

Wulfgar was silent.

The moment stretched itself painfully.

Ketil said, 'So? What do you say to that?'

'The Faith teaches us other ways to be men,' Wulfgar said at last. 'Better ways.'

Ketil gave a triumphant crow of laughter that set heads turning the length of his longhouse.

'And Knut of York is another one, a fool who's had his head wetted.'

Suddenly he was looming over Wulfgar, prodding him in the chest so hard that Wulfgar had to struggle to keep his balance on the little stool.

'You go to him. You tell him, Ketil of Leicester is not going to die in the straw. I don't know what he and the Lady of Mercia are brewing together, but' – prod, prod with that iron forefinger – 'you tell them, Ketil of Leicester is ready for the fight.'

Wulfgar nodded.

He had no idea how he got up from the stool or stumbled away from the still raucously merry Ketil.

When he got to the far side of the hearth, she was gone.

He looked long enough to be sure that no broad-shouldered house-carl of Ketil's was blocking his view, and he sagged with disappointment, his hand stealing again to the pouch round his neck.

Kenelm's gangly presence was hovering at his shoulder.

'What?'

'There's no need to snap at me.'

'Sorry.'

'I just had the strangest conversation,' Kenelm said. 'Someone came up to me. A woman' – he glanced back towards the hearth – 'I can't see her now. Very flashy-looking.' He pursed his lips disapprovingly. 'She came right up to me and said, "Are you the other Englishman?"'

'What?' Wulfgar's focused his whole attention on Kenelm.

'Well, I told her I was. And she said, "Tell your friend there's a message for him, from Cat's-Eyes." I suppose she meant you by "my friend". She can't have been talking about' – Kenelm's mouth tugged downwards as though encountering a bitter taste – 'Thorbjorn.'

'A message,' Wulfgar said. Suddenly hope was scrabbling its way up out of the pit. 'What message? Who was this woman? What did she look like?'

Kenelm's eyes had narrowed.

'So, you are a friend of this Cat's-Eyes, whoever he is?'

'What's the message?'

Wulfgar found he was clenching his fists as well as gritting his teeth. Kenelm's long throat with its protuberant Adam's apple had never looked so tempting.

'Oh, it was in Danish for some reason. I didn't understand it.'

'Try, Kenelm. Please, try.' Wulfgar tried to keep the desperation out his voice, but Kenelm was looking at him curiously.

'Who is this Cat's-Eyes, anyway?'

'Just – just an acquaintance of mine. A useful person to know.' Wulfgar swallowed. 'Kenelm, *please*.' He realised the other man was enjoying having the upper hand for once.

'Well' – Kenelm was relenting. 'It sounded something like *syow umpsti yor vik*, if that means anything to you. She made me repeat it back to her.'

'*Syow...*' Wulfgar tried to find meaning in Kenelm's garbled vowel sounds. 'Oh!' Revelation flooded through him like an undammed mill race. '*Sjáumst í Jórvík?* Was that it?' He found he was gripping Kenelm's elbows, looking furiously up into his face. 'Is that what she said?'

Kenelm was frowning. 'Let go of me. Yes, that sounds about right. What does it mean?'

'*Sjáumst í Jórvík*,' Wulfgar repeated under his breath. He wasn't going to tell Kenelm, but he knew exactly what it meant.

See you in York.

CHAPTER SIXTEEN

York

Two nights later, they had arrived in Knut's city.

They had yet to meet the King.

Kenelm was rolled in his cloak already and snoring relentlessly, but Wulfgar was far too tired to sleep. He lay on his side by the banked fire, trying to sort his thoughts into some sort of order. Thorbjorn had ridden them hard that last day, he and the other York men all eager to get home. The murk of July midnight was around them by the time they had trotted under the city's southern gate and guided their weary, stumbling mounts down the steep, muddy street to the river.

'We'll see the King tomorrow,' Thorbjorn had said, stifling his yawns, and he'd brought them back under his own roof, hard by the Ouse-bridge. Despite the lateness of the hour, hot meaty broth was waiting for them, with black bread and sweet ale and this stack of sheepskins. Wulfgar might find fault with many things in Thorbjorn, but never his hospitality. But, for all their fleecy softness, the skins were providing no rest for him. He sighed, and turned over yet again. Thorbjorn himself was snoring even more impressively than Kenelm, over on the other side of the house, on the sleeping platform he shared with his wife and two daughters and the baby.

Leicester still rankled. They had left Ketil Scar's longhouse before sun-up, and he had caught no further glimpse of Gunnvor. But now he had those cryptic words to cling to.

Sjáumst í Jórvík...

What could she possibly be planning to do in York? One of her many business deals? Could he even trust Kenelm to have heard the words accurately? He turned restlessly and pulled his cloak over his shoulders, but found little comfort in the rough wool.

Tomorrow – no, *today* – they would meet Thorbjorn's King, who held their lives as a boy might hold a beetle in the palm of his hand. Wulfgar shifted his aching hips, and sighed again. And he had to take the Lady's letter to Archbishop Lothward. Smile and bow, and spy on the man if he could. He understood why the Lady had asked him to do it, but that did nothing to warm the cold dread and colder shame that gripped his guts at the prospect.

And then there was Wystan...

Grey light was seeping round the edges of the shutters, and somewhere close by a blackbird was starting up its Matins hymn.

'Oh, Lord, open Thou my lips,' Wulfgar murmured wearily, 'that my mouth may show forth Thy praise...'

The next thing he knew, it was broad daylight.

The elder of Thorbjorn's two daughters, no more than a briefly glimpsed shadow the night before, was stretching past him to rekindle a flame at the hearth. Seeing him awake, she squatted back on her haunches to grin at him, a mouse-haired, narrow-faced girl, gawky in a dress of faded-blue herringbone twill, one long fat plait over her shoulder. 'Would you like a wash?' she said. '*Kambi*?' She held up a fine-toothed comb.

He was about to refuse when something in her eyes made him change his mind. She was so eager to please, and so touching in her youth and her readiness to take on the role of mistress of the house while her mother slept.

At his nod, she put the comb down and used wooden tongs to drop a couple of stones from the heart of the fire into a leather bucket of water that was standing ready.

'Face first?'

'I can do that myself—' he began, but again was stopped short by the pride in her expression. So he let her wipe his face with a square of linen, and rinse his hands, and dip first one then the other grubby bare foot into the deliciously warm water. Her breath was sweet and her thin hands gentle, and he could feel himself blushing even before she held up the comb again and gestured for him to lean back against her bent knees. He could feel her body quivering, and realised when he turned to look inquiringly at her that she was laughing, hard and silently.

'What?'

'Your hair.'

He lifted a hand. 'Oh, my tonsure.'

'It's good hair, she said firmly. 'Short. I can't see any louses.'

'Lice,' he corrected, absurdly pleased by her commendation.

'Lice,' she repeated, and gave him that transforming grin again. 'Very good hair.'

'Very good English.'

Thorbjorn had rolled over and was watching them, propped up on one elbow.

'Very good girl, my Gerd is.' He reached out and pinched her

110

cheek hard but with deep affection, and she smiled happily back at him. 'Not mardy like her little sister, eh, lass? Want a wife, Englishman? Tha could go further and find worse.'

Wulfgar shook his head, but joined in the smile.

'Not just now.'

He pulled his saddlebag over and distracted himself by rummaging for his long tunic.

'Art sure?' Thorbjorn winked at him with exaggerated lechery. 'She's ready for a man, that one. Needs a house of her own to run. She and her stepmam, they make it crowded in here.'

Wulfgar could feel the blood surging all the way up to his ears. 'You honour me.'

'No? She's young enough to break to thy will, and I'll see her well dowered.' Thorbjorn sat up and shrugged, still chuckling. 'What about thy pale-eyed friend, then?'

'Better ask him yourself.'

He realised then that the girl was blushing, too. She was leaning against her father, saying something in Danish in such a soft voice that Wulfgar couldn't make it out.

'She says, does tha want barley pottage? Honey?'

'That would be lovely.'

Kenelm was opening his eyes now, and it made Wulfgar feel pleasantly worldly, seeing how he bridled and batted away the girl's offer of a wash.

'Eat up your pottage,' Thorbjorn said, 'like the brace of good lads you are.' He stood up, rubbing his hands together. 'Gerd, fetch their saddlebags.'

Gerd jumped up at her father's words. Wulfgar watched her brisk movements for a little before shifting his gaze to the younger daughter – prettier, darker, warier – and their brisk stepmother, coming in from collecting the eggs with the plump baby on her hip and her distaff thrust through her belt. Yes. Thorbjorn was truly blessed.

Gerd had opened the door. He blinked in the bright sunlight. Thorbjorn was walking purposefully away, and Wulfgar hoisted his saddlebag over his shoulder and hurried to follow. They crossed the massive timber bridge and went up the slope the other side.

'That's our ainkirk,' Thorbjorn was saying. 'All Hallows.'

'Ainkirk?' Wulfgar followed the man's gaze to find a solid construction of timber and thatch at the side of the road.

'*Já* – nowt to do with thon Archbishop!' Thorbjorn seemed to think this was a huge joke.

Wulfgar intercepted an anxious glance from Kenelm. He fell back a pace, and muttered, 'I think he means it's their own church. Who *they* are, I couldn't tell you.'

'Thanks,' Kenelm said, and added, 'It does help, you know, when you tell me what people are saying.'

Thorbjorn had overheard their exchange. 'King's hearth-men,' he said. 'We paid for the building, and we pay for the priest. I buried my father there not six months gone. Happen you two'd like to kindle a candle at his grave, later?'

'Now?'

But Thorbjorn shook his head and hurried them on through the narrow, dusty maze of streets until they reached one that ended in a guarded gateway. On sighting Thorbjorn, however, the guards stepped back to let them through. Beyond them was a wide sunlit courtyard.

'King's Garth,' Thorbjorn said.

The yard was crowded and noisy with many armed men, their

voices raised in English and Danish. Thorbjorn slowed and frowned.

Wulfgar looked around him. To the left a tremendous hall reared up, a stack of startling wooden roofs zigzagging up into the sky, adorned at every gable with a snarling dragon-head finial. He wanted to stop and marvel, fascinated by its exotic lines, but Thorbjorn was hurrying them on again, still frowning, to a very different building that had been hidden behind the first.

Much plainer, this, much older, and far more familiar. It was constructed of massive stones, creamy gold under their flaking limewash, that rose in a façade easily thirty feet high with horizontal bands of fox-red tile threaded through the masonry. The wall was pierced by twin arches, each once wide enough to let a cart through but now boarded up, though one had a wicket gate let into it. Across the boarded arches, an exterior staircase built in raw-looking timber led to an upper storey with a pair of graceful, arched windows, like quizzical eyes. On a bench under the staircase, a couple of guards were playing dice, but their eyes, too, were watchful.

Kenelm was blinking, head tipped back. 'Surely no Dane built that,' he said, far too loudly for tact.

'It's a Roman gate,' Wulfgar said, his own voice low. 'You must have seen this sort of thing elsewhere, surely? At Canterbury, and at Leicester—'

But Kenelm was rolling his eyes. 'You think you know everything, don't you?'

'Wait here.' Thorbjorn still had that frown tugging his bushy eyebrows together. He spoke to one of the pair of guards who had left their dice-game to stand at the foot of the stair, and the man turned and clattered his way up.

'Knut is royally housed,' Wulfgar said to Thorbjorn.

Thorbjorn's red, flaky face cracked into a smile. 'He is a King.'

'And what's that building?' Wulfgar indicated the exuberantly carved stack of roofs.

'That's his hall. Up there,' Thorbjorn gestured, 'is his private bower.'

'Such different buildings!'

Thorbjorn looked at him levelly. 'He is a King according to the customs of his own people, as well as according to yours.'

The guard was calling something from the top of the stairs. He clattered down again and spoke in a low, rapid voice to Thorbjorn, who turned to his guests. 'King's in council.' He listened again. 'It'll take a fair time, from what yon man says.'

Wulfgar was certain there was more going on than Thorbjorn was telling them. He looked across the courtyard to where two young men were bringing buckets of hot mash for their horses and calling to each other in cheerful voices. English voices, he realised, and not Northumbrian English, either.

'Who could be more important than us?' He tried to sound as though he were joking, but Thorbjorn was finding nothing to smile at.

'What shall I do with you lads, meanwhile?'

Wulfgar remembered the Lady's words.

'We would very much like to be presented to the Archbishop,' Wulfgar said hesitantly, 'but it might be improper to meet him before the King has received us.'

'Go behind the wall? Aye, we can fettle that.'

'Behind?'

'The wall.' Thorbjorn stabbed the air with a stubby finger, and

114

Wulfgar realised that Knut's gatehouse-palace was itself set into a substantial stone wall that ran away north-east and south-west, almost hidden behind the packed thatch roofs of the stables and barracks that lined the courtyard. 'Now?'

'Why not?' Kenelm's face lit up.

Thorbjorn took them back the way they had come – 'Gate-guards'll know your ugly faces next time' – and along a broad, claggy track that bordered the river.

'This is the King's Street.' He gestured along the line of warehouses, and pointed out wharves, piers and slips visible in the gaps between them. 'The King takes all the tolls from here, not the Archbishop.'

Again, that gibing note when the Archbishop entered the conversation.

Now that Wulfgar knew the wall was there, he was aware of its massive, looming presence running continuously behind the houses on their right. After two hundred yards or so they reached a second and even more impressive stone gatehouse. Here the arches were still in use, and the guards in their shade were notably well turned out, swaggering in matching helmets with gilded nasals and crests, and hip-length cloaks of bleached wool trimmed with red and purple braid. Wulfgar had seen that livery before, he realised, in the Archbishop's entourage at his consecration in London five years back. Then, he had thought their finery assumed for a special occasion.

'Ambassadors, you say? Hostages? We've heard nothing of this.' The captain looked at them quizzically. 'From Mercia, and just the two of you?' He snapped his fingers for a subordinate. 'You, tell his Grace that he's got some southern visitors.' He turned back to Wulfgar. 'We'll see what he has to say about this.'

Wulfgar could see that Kenelm was feeling as snubbed as he was himself.

'He'll keep you lads kicking your heels,' Thorbjorn predicted. 'They like their petty games, behind the wall. I'm warning thee, Wulfgar – thee too, White-Eyes' – he swung round to Kenelm – 'don't you get too caught up with their tricks. You're the King's hostages, the pair of you. It's to him you're oath-sworn, mind on.'

Kenelm gave him a baleful look.

'We're clerics. The Bishop of Worcester's my uncle. You can't expect us to spend all our time in a barracks.'

Thorbjorn considered him, head on side, sucking his teeth loudly. Then he said, 'I'll show you lads somewhat.' He dug in the purse at his belt. 'Look.'

They had to crowd round to see what he had on the flat of his palm.

A coin. Rare in that it was gold and not silver, but fashioned in a familiar enough style: a little cross in the centre with the King's name laid out around it.

'Yes,' Kenelm said, a querulous tinge to his voice. 'So?'

Thorbjorn huffed with exasperation. '*Look*. Clerics, tha says? Clever lad, eh? Then track the letters sunwise and see what you make of it.'

'K at the top, and then T on the right?' Wulfgar frowned. 'That doesn't make sense... Oh, I see!'

'What?'

'Which of your kings in Mercia ever blazoned his faith like that?' Thorbjorn said. '*Whose is this image and this inscription?*'

Wulfgar gave Thorbjorn a startled look.

'*Render therefore to Caesar the things that are Caesar's, and to God*

116

the things that are God's,' he said softly. 'But this is a thing of Caesar's *and* a thing of God's.'

'What is it?' Kenelm demanded. 'What are you talking about?' He looked from face to face. 'I don't understand.'

'You tell him,' Thorbjorn said.

Wulfgar reached out for the coin, and paused. 'May I?'

Thorbjorn nodded.

Wulfgar picked up the coin carefully by its edges and turned to Kenelm.

'Look. You aren't meant to read it sunwise. You start at the top and go down to the bottom, then left, then right. You have to make the sign of the Cross with your eyes, to read the King's name.'

With the forefinger of his free hand he traced lightly over the letters. It was a lovely conceit, half puzzle, half prayer. He looked up at Thorbjorn.

'Was it King Knut's own idea?'

'*Já,*' Thorbjorn grunted. He seemed gratified by Wulfgar's response. 'This was minted in silver, to mark his crowning. But he had a few struck in gold as tokens for us hearth-men.'

'It's not what I would have expected from a Dane,' Kenelm said, sounding sulky.

But Thorbjorn just laughed. 'Happen that's the idea, White-Eyes. Tha'll find him full of surprises.' He tucked the coin carefully back in his purse. 'What, back already?'

The captain was turning towards them, gesturing his errand-bearer back to his post. 'His Grace says he will see you straight away.' He couldn't quite conceal his surprise.

'And I'll see you lads later.' Thorbjorn raised his hand and had half-turned away before visibly thinking again. His weather-beaten face had taken on a strained expression. 'Wulfgar, tha knows I'm standing surety for you two? You're my King's hostages. If one or other of you runs off, it's my neck. And my wife's, mind on. And my bairns'.'

'You have my oath.'

Thorbjorn nodded, still hesitating. 'What about White-Eyes?'

'I'm hardly going to *run off* anywhere on my own,' Kenelm said stiffly.

Thorbjorn still looked unhappy.

'I'm trusting you both,' he said at last.

CHAPTER SEVENTEEN

Their escort stopped at the broad door. The red leather in which it was clad muffled his knock.

'He's waiting for you.'

They went in.

A man in a plain white robe was standing at a writing desk, caught in a shaft of sunlight. It took a moment for Wulfgar to recognise Archbishop Lothward: his hair, which had been thick and black six years earlier, was still thick but now pure silver. But the face below was the same: round, broad, shrewd, with heavy-lidded eyes and strongly marked lines from the corners of his mouth up to his nose. He had been taking a step towards the door as it swung open, his arms extended and a bright look of welcome on his face.

When he saw them, however, he stopped. His gesture and his smile both froze. A shadow of perplexity passed across his broad, clean-shaven face, and he looked briefly beyond them, at the closing door.

He had indeed been expecting visitors, Wulfgar realised. But not them.

The Archbishop quickly regained his poise. 'Greetings!'

He was coming towards them, wreathed in smiles and words of welcome.

'From the south, my man said? And clerics!' He was clasping Wulfgar by the shoulders and looking him up and down. 'Welcome to York.'

'We have met, your Grace,' Wulfgar said. 'I was an acolyte at your consecration.'

'Of course!' The Archbishop bluffed well but Wulfgar was quite sure that he had no memory of him. And why should he? A nervous eighteen-year-old, hiding behind a silver ewer... 'Remind me of your name, young man? You're surely not still an acolyte?'

'Wulfgar of Winchester, your Grace. Subdeacon, and secretary to the Lord and Lady of the Mercians.' He bent to kiss the gold and sapphire ring. 'And this is Kenelm, a deacon of Worcester cathedral, and the nephew of Bishop Werferth.'

'Indeed!' More bows, broad smiles and embraces. 'How is my brother prelate of Worcester?'

'We have a letter for your Grace,' Wulfgar said.

The Archbishop was clapping his hands. 'Wine. Stools.'

He beckoned them forward. 'You can't have travelled all this way just to bring me a letter? Have you come north with these English visitors of the King's I've been hearing rumours of? Who are they? What can you tell me about them?'

'No, your Grace—'

Kenelm drowned him out. 'We're hostages,' he said, his outrage audible. 'The Lady sent us off here with hardly a moment's notice, and we had to stay with that dreadful man and carry our own bags—'

'Sit down, sit down. You've clearly had a very trying time.' The Archbishop's voice was soothing but Wulfgar had caught the sudden narrowing of his eyes. 'Perhaps I should see that letter?'

Wulfgar handed his silver cup of wine and water back to the attendant slave, and dug the wallet out of his saddlebag. He might censure Kenelm's tactlessness, but he too was feeling the humiliation of coming into the Archbishop's presence lugging his own grubby gear.

'I beg your pardon, your Grace,' he said, gesturing at their bags. 'We haven't seen Knut yet, and we don't know where we'll be quartered.'

'*King* Knut, while you're in York,' the Archbishop said reprovingly, but when Wulfgar looked up apologetically those knowing brown eyes were laughing at him. 'Drink your wine.' The Archbishop was unfolding the sheet of vellum and holding it at arm's length.

Wulfgar took his cup back and sipped from it, taking the opportunity to look around the room. They had been marched so briskly from the gate that he had taken in little more than scattered impressions of the Archbishop's little empire 'behind the wall'. The young guard had tossed out a litany of names – 'St Helen's, St Wilfrid's, our chapel of St Benedict, that's St Michael's mortuary chapel, the lay cemetery' – but there had been no time to do more than turn his head from side to side, taking in glimpses of the cathedral's solid towers, flanked by lesser churches and chapels, and a maze of other buildings from bell-towers to stables to forges. Then they had been escorted through a set of double doors into a stone-built hall with two rows of massive pillars, and out again into a small, private courtyard, and finally, thoroughly disoriented, to the door through which they had just entered.

He looked at it now. Heavy, on curlicued wrought-iron hinges, and covered in that dark red leather on both sides, it exuded opulence. A quality it shared with the rest of the room, he realised. It was a bright, pleasant place, the walls white-plastered, and the round-headed windows that flanked the door letting the morning sun flood the interior. Painted and gilded beams supporting a flat ceiling. The wine jug stood on a round tripod table with feet carved like lions' paws, complete with gilded claws. Wulfgar had seen pieces of furniture made in that mode – Frankish or Lombardic – in Winchester, but not many. The Archbishop's bed was an outlandish thing to him, however: the headboard flanked by rearing dragon-like beasts with savage open jaws, painted in red and white and black. At the bed-foot stood a carved wooden chest, coloured the same red and hasped with broad iron bands, its lid fastened with an elaborate padlock.

His gaze came round at last again to Archbishop Lothward, who was still leaning back in his chair, feet elegantly disposed on his footstool, squinting at the second page. Wulfgar took another sip of wine. Kenelm was holding out his chased silver cup for a refill.

Archbishop Lothward was drumming his fingers on the arm of his chair now. 'And any private message for me?'

Wulfgar shook his head. 'No, your Grace. Unless—'

He looked at Kenelm, but his face too was blank.

'Is this all?' The Archbishop flicked the vellum edge with a fingertip. 'Empty diplomatic mouthings?'

The contempt in his voice made Wulfgar start and nearly drop his cup.

'Where is the support I need?' He tossed the letter onto his writing desk. 'And this treaty with King Knut it mentions?' He sat up. 'Tell me about it.'

'It's to last till next year, your Grace. English Mercia and Danish York are to come to each other's support if either is attacked.'

'Really? So you two have been sent here for a whole year?' The Archbishop's heavy-lidded eyes had opened wide. 'Does someone want you out of the way?' His tone was teasing but there was an underlying seriousness to his words.

Wulfgar didn't reply. The cup of wine was suddenly unbearably heavy in his hands.

'Forgive me, your Grace,' Kenelm said, his tone indignant, 'but it's not like that. Not at all. We're not here for a whole year, thanks be to God, only for a season. And we haven't annoyed anybody. The Lady can't trust many people, you see. But she trusts us, that's why she's sent us here.'

Lothward leaned back, steepling his fingers and eyeing Kenelm thoughtfully.

'Is that so?' He waved a hovering slave away. 'Well. You're welcome to sleep and mess with my men while you're here. You'll probably find it more to your liking than' – he jerked his head towards the window – 'Knut's quarters.'

Kenelm exhaled with relief.

'We'd be most appreciative, your Grace.'

'Although we'd have to get the King's approval, your Grace,' Wulfgar added. 'We are sworn to him, after all.'

The Archbishop was still eyeing Kenelm.

'Servants of the Lady, eh? Then you might be interested in another letter I've lately received.' He reached over to the desk and pulled out a different sheet of vellum. 'From her brother, Edward of Wessex.' He squinted at it. 'He tells me I must be *groaning under the Danish yoke, longing for deliverance*. He offers his services as liberator.'

'To bring Northumbria back under English rule?' Kenelm's voice sounded bright at the prospect.

'Bring it back?' Archbishop Lothward was shaking his head. 'Bring it *back*? Do you see this yoke of which King Edward writes?' He gestured eloquently around his luxurious room. 'It doesn't chafe my shoulders. The heathen conquerors are dead or dying. Their sons were born here, to English mothers. Who baptised them in the rain-butt if there were no priest handy.'

Wulfgar said, 'Forgive me, your Grace...'

'Yes?'

He thought back three months to his one encounter with a Danish jarl born to an English mother.

'Toli Silkbeard of Lincoln, your Grace. I don't know if he was ever baptised, but he swears by Spear and Hammer. I've heard him myself.'

'So you know young Toli, do you?' The Archbishop gave him an appraising look. 'Well, you might get the chance to ask him in person whether he's been baptised, if you stay around.' He chuckled. 'No, I'm not afraid of little Toli, or any of the rest of them. Let them play their games. And I don't care whom the men of York call their king, as long as he realises he can't rule without my support. More wine?'

Wulfgar shook his head, too taken up with what the Archbishop had said about Toli, as well as Edward.

Kenelm held out his cup.

'I'm glad you like it.' The Archbishop beckoned an attendant. 'It's meant for the altar but this was such a good vintage that I've reserved most of it for my own use. Now' – and the smile fell away – 'tell me whom you rode north with. I've heard nothing, except that a large party of West Saxons has arrived. Are they Edward's men?' He picked up Edward's letter again and brandished it at them. 'If so, why are they paying their regards to Knut?'

'I don't know, your Grace,' Wulfgar said. He glanced at Kenelm. 'We rode up with King Knut's hearth-man, Thorbjorn.'

The Archbishop nodded.

Kenelm broke in, 'But when he took us to the King's court this morning we did see a lot of men and horses, and the King couldn't welcome us because he was in council with his other guests.'

The Archbishop had drawn in his brows. 'So?'

He was interrupted by a knock on the door.

'Your Grace?' The guard appeared, looking diffident. 'My apologies for disturbing you but' – he glanced behind him, at something hidden by the door – 'you have more visitors.'

'Tell them to wait,' the Archbishop said shortly.

The young man's expression grew agonised.

'In all good faith, your Grace, I don't see how I can.'

Behind his back, the door opened wide.

CHAPTER EIGHTEEN

A tall, slim, dark-haired man entered first. He was somewhere in his thirties, with a neat, modish beard and dressed in a slate-grey tunic with broad bands of woven silver at neck and wrist and hem. He was accompanied by a young woman, clad from veil to slipper in bleached lawn, linen and lambswool, embroidered white-on-white with glossy silk threads. An older, dowdier woman hovered in the doorway.

Wulfgar didn't recognise either of the women.

But he knew that dark-bearded man who was ushering the younger one in, his left arm guarding her back, hand cupping her elbow.

He had known that man for nearly twenty years.

Athelwald Seiriol, the Atheling of Wessex.

The Archbishop rose to his feet. 'Seiriol!' Relief and welcome were almost palpable in his voice. 'You've come!'

'My dear lord of York.' The Atheling was bowing low to kiss the Archbishop's ring, but as he straightened up the Archbishop seized him by the elbows and pulled him into a warm, back-slapping embrace. 'Where else would I come, exile and wanderer that I am?'

'But you arrived last night? And you went to Knut first?' Archbishop Lothward's tone sharpened with suspicion.

'Elfled and I thought it the politic thing to do.' The Atheling was laughing, making light of the Archbishop's evident displeasure, pulling the girl forward. 'We have to keep him sweet, for the time being at least.'

Hearing this, the Archbishop seemed to relax. He turned to the girl. 'My lady.' He gave her a warm smile.

'My Lord of York.' She bent in turn and kissed the offered sapphire, poised and stately, her crisp, carrying voice somehow familiar to Wulfgar.

'And you're here freely, my daughter?'

'With all my will, your Grace.'

The Atheling had not yet looked beyond the Archbishop. The sight of a brace of tonsured clerics hovering either side of the great man's chair would hardly warrant his special attention. While the Archbishop and the newcomers continued to exchange pleasantries, Wulfgar, glad of the temporary anonymity, struggled to make sense of the sensations that were rocking him.

What was the Atheling doing in York, of all places?

Wimborne, in Dorset, now that had been an obvious bolt-hole. A fortified manor, a royal nunnery, and the site of his father's grave. Going there had reminded all Wessex that Athelwald Seiriol was just as much a King's son as his cousin Edward was.

But *York*?

What business could he conceivably have here?

How did he come to be on such easy, familiar terms with York's Archbishop?

Who was that girl?

But, above all, he was aware of a brimming, indeed an over-flowing, sense of accomplishment, so powerful that he had to fight to keep the triumphant grin from his face.

It had been worth it, after all.

He had bowed his head and let the Lady slip the halter round his neck and break him to her will. He had put aside the demands of family and listened to the claims of his oath, and he had gone willingly into danger. He had endured Thorbjorn's coarse humour and Ketil Scar's menacing intimacy.

And here was his reward.

That for which he had longed so desperately had now, *mirabile dictu*, come to him.

The Atheling was all smiles and easy laughter, still keeping one hand on his companion's elbow, talking animatedly to the Archbishop, but turning to the young woman frequently, keeping her in the conversation.

'We'll need your blessing, though, my Lord. As I said in my letter, we thought we could rely on you to do the honours.'

Wulfgar realised he must have missed a great chunk of their conversation. Nonetheless, he had a suspicion he knew what the Atheling was referring to. He forced himself to concentrate.

'You still want it at once?' the Archbishop was saying.

The Atheling clasped the young woman's hand in both his.

'We need it done as soon as maybe. But by the book, your Grace. Nothing hugger-mugger.'

The Archbishop was nodding his agreement.

'Witnesses,' the Atheling said. 'We need witnesses. Independent ones. Men of good standing.' And then, at long last, he looked at the two clerics poised diffidently in the background.

He didn't even blink.

'Wuffa, by all that's holy!' He dropped the girl's hand and bounded forwards, the skin around his eyes creasing with evident delight. 'God sends you here in a good hour. And your friend – yes, I remember you. The Bishop's nephew, of Worcester.'

Kenelm was nodding and stuttering, his thin skin flushing pink with pleasure.

Wulfgar found himself bowing, still clumsy with shock. The Atheling's hand was resting on his shoulder now.

'You'd be doing me – us – a superlative kindness. We're here with no retinue but a handful of men-at-arms, and it's wonderful to see a familiar face.'

'My Lord Seiriol—'

The Atheling lowered his voice. 'I was appalled to hear about recent events in Winchester. *Appalled.* A man of your brother's standing and family, dragged before the court in shackles. Those summary executions, of well-regarded thanes.' He shook his head. 'The new Wessex, I'm afraid. Edward's Wessex. Despotism, wearing the mask of justice.' The hand tightened, giving Wulfgar's shoulder a little shake.

'Thank you, my Lord.'

In his mind's eye Wulfgar could see accusing faces: Judith's, Wystan's. They demanded answers and they deserved them. But what else could he possibly have said?

Not now, he told them silently. But soon. They were all in this together, united against the threat from Edward and Garmund. Just because he was hundreds of miles away didn't mean he wasn't fighting in the shield-wall at their side.

With his hand still resting, easy and companionable on Wulfgar's shoulder, the Atheling said, 'Come and witness our wedding, and then perhaps you can tell me what you're doing here. Are you part of the grand plan?'

Wedding? Grand plan? Out of the corner of his eye, Wulfgar thought he saw the Archbishop purse his lips and give his head a little shake, but when he turned Lothward was as bland and affable as ever.

The Atheling had turned back to his companion. 'My dear, let me present Wulfgar, secretary to my cousin of Mercia; and Kenelm – that's right, isn't it? Kenelm of Worcester cathedral, the Bishop's nephew.'

Kenelm preened and nodded.

'My bride, Elfled of Wilton.'

Wulfgar knew he had never before been introduced to this girl, but there was a familiarity somewhere, nonetheless, nagging as toothache, sharper when he heard her name.

To his surprise, she addressed him directly. 'I think your sister Cwenhild is a nun at Shaftesbury?'

He looked her full in the face for the first time. Her poise and self-possession made her striking, although her eyes were too small, her nose too sharp, for beauty. She was very pale, but there was a flush along her cheekbones and a glitter in her eyes that made him wonder whether she might not be slightly intoxicated.

'Not now. But she was, your ladyship.' He wondered how she knew.

'I spent my novitiate at Shaftesbury before I was sent to join the sisters at Wimborne.'

'My sister is at the Nunnaminster now, in Winchester.'

'I remember her mentioning you to me, more than once,' the girl said. She paused. 'I liked Cwenhild. She always treated me with proper esteem.'

'She is the very soul of kindness.'

His mouth opened and closed on the meaningless syllables while his thoughts scrabbled ever more furiously for purchase.

She was a nun. The Atheling was marrying a nun.

Not even a novice: a professed nun.

How could the Archbishop possibly give this union his blessing?

But that same Archbishop seemed to be taking everything in his stride and, watching him ring his little bell and issue orders about candles, incense and vestments, about guest accommodation and the feast to follow, Wulfgar began to have a suspicion that the Atheling's arrival in York, with this girl in tow, wasn't quite the shock to the Archbishop that he had assumed at first.

'And am I right, Seiriol, in thinking that you would prefer to have the blessing in Holy Wisdom?'

'Rather than the cathedral?' The Atheling was nodding. 'Oh, yes, I think so. Holy Wisdom has certain associations that we would like to invoke.' He smiled down at the girl on his arm.

The Archbishop rang his little bell again.

'Well, my children, I must vest myself with suitable splendour.' When the guard came in he said, 'Take these two' – he gestured at Wulfgar and Kenelm – 'to Holy Wisdom.' He smiled. 'We won't be far behind.'

CHAPTER NINETEEN

'Is that a *church*?'

Astonishment had forced Kenelm's voice up an octave.

They had been bustled back out into the sunny courtyard, through the gloom of the great stone-pillared hall, out again and past the cathedral. In the northern corner of the Archbishop's estate there was a broad open courtyard and standing within it was the most extraordinary building that Wulfgar had ever seen. Anxiety, confusion and exhilaration all took a step backwards at the sight of it, leaving him gaping-mouthed and silent.

'It's a very odd shape,' Kenelm said accusingly.

'Polygonal, it's called,' their guard said. He looked gratified by their response. 'Thirty altars: fifteen at ground level and fifteen in the gallery. You've not seen its like south of Humber, then?'

'Never,' Wulfgar said thoughtfully. Now that the guard had described its layout, he could see how that peculiar shape would work, with its upper and lower arcades of windows set into a creamy, mellow limestone that angled away from them to right and left.

'I'd show you inside,' the guard said, 'but this is where they'll be coming.' He gestured at the southern porch. 'They won't be long.'

They weren't.

Wulfgar knew he should be listening to every word, so that if it ever came up in court he could lay his hand upon his heart and swear that the marriage this man and woman had privately contracted had been publically blessed and acknowledged, but his thoughts were so tangled that he missed nine words out of every ten.

How soon after the nuptial blessing could a lowly subdeacon intercept a royal bridegroom, accuse him of the highest treason and demand an explanation?

Elfled's voice, cool and gracious in answer to the Archbishop's ritual questioning, cut through his anxieties. For a shocked moment, he had thought it was the Lady's voice. Was that why she had seemed so familiar?

And then, as though the old documents with the lineage of the West Saxon dynasty were under his hand, as though those lists of kings and kings' sons were inscribed in iron and oak-gall on the blank fall of the bride's veil, Wulfgar remembered who she was.

Elfled of Wilton, whose hand the Archbishop was now taking and placing in the Atheling's, now conjoining to her lord's with the long white ribbon of silk he had received from the attendant subdeacon – Elfled of Wilton was the daughter of the Atheling's older brother.

The Lady's cousin, and King Edward's, too.

Let the West Saxon bishops howl about incest, the Atheling

must have been thinking, a dispensation could always be got from somewhere.

Bribe Alnoth and Edric to kill King Edward, then ride into Winchester with apparently clean hands and a bride of the royal lineage perched on his saddle-bow, the union endorsed by the Archbishop of York, and wait for the Witan to offer him the crown.

But the plan had failed in its key aspect: Edric of Amport had panicked and confessed the plot, and Edward was still alive.

It was a long moment before Wulfgar realised that their little party was processing into the heart of Holy Wisdom.

He hurried after them.

The church was dark after the sun-dazzle of the courtyard, filled with incense and candle smoke. He slowly became aware of a great hoop of candle flames apparently floating in mid-air, and more candles on an altar, which, he realised, stood hub-like in the centre of the great church. He glanced from side to side to see that they were encircled by a ring of arches, every one leading to an altar where crosses and images glimmered like fire-lit eyes from dark caves.

A surreptitious glance upwards, and he saw that there was another storey encircling them, the gallery the guard had mentioned. That ring of fire resolved itself into a suspended wheel of delicate, lacy metal, a tiered circle a good yard across, supporting numerous socketed candles, and adorned with fragile-looking hanging crosses, large and small, and little oil lamps of glass, below which the Archbishop was now intoning the *Gloria*. It was a thing of extraordinary, ethereal beauty, bringing the blaze of the sun into the church's dark corners, and it took Wulfgar's breath away.

He realised with some small part of his mind that the Archbishop was speaking in English now, smiling affectionately at the couple in front of him.

'My children. We stand in a church built by my kinsman, Archbishop Albert, a long hundred winters ago, as a gift to the kings of Northumbria. But the dedication of this church, to the Alma Sophia, the Holy Wisdom of God, is eternal. *Give me wisdom,* King Solomon prayed, *that setteth by Thy throne: and reject me not from among Thy children.* Let us share in that prayer. No one needs wisdom more than those whom God has appointed as rulers of men.'

He smiled then, raising his hand in benediction. 'May God's wisdom inform your lives, as rulers, and as husband and wife.'

Wulfgar felt a frown tugging his brow. Rulers? *Exile and wanderer,* the Atheling had called himself and it was no more than the truth. All his lands lay in Wessex, and they were now surely as forfeit to King Edward as ever Wystan of Meon's estates could be.

Was the Archbishop endorsing not only this indefensible marriage but also the Atheling's claim to the West Saxon throne?

Or – and his throat constricted suddenly – could the Atheling still be eyeing up the lordship of Mercia? He had confessed as much after all, back in the spring, when the Lord of the Mercians had first been struck down by his illness. While he might love his cousin Fleda, did he love her enough to let her rule her little kingdom in peace?

Wulfgar found himself making the responses instinctively, with little or no awareness of what he was saying, his eyes entranced by the gleam and glitter around the altar while his mind ran through all the possible variations of political intrigue.

His head hurt.

'*Ite*,' Archbishop Lothward said at last, '*Missa est.*' The Mass is ended.

Wulfgar turned to watch the Archbishop leave, the candle-bearing acolytes in his wake.

The Atheling, his bride on his arm, had paused on his way out. Wulfgar almost walked into them.

'Look up,' the Atheling said.

Obedient, Wulfgar followed his gaze up, to the gallery.

In the bay above the main door, just visible over a balustrade of turned stone columns, there glimmered a white shape. Something rectangular, carved from a lambent white stone.

A great chair, he realised, positioned so that anyone seated there would have a commanding view of the central altar, and most of the church around it.

'Do you know what that is?'

'The Archbishop's throne?' Kenelm suggested.

Wulfgar shook his head. 'This isn't the cathedral. It can't be.'

'It's the ancient high-seat of the kings of Northumbria.' The Atheling turned and lifted his bride's fingers briefly to his lips, before turning back to Wulfgar, his eyes dancing with mischief. 'But no king has sat there for some thirty years. Not since York fell to the Danes.'

Kenelm was nodding approvingly.

Wulfgar was about to open his mouth again, to ask the Atheling if they could have a private word, and soon, when Kenelm interjected, 'Not King Knut? Despite his baptism?'

'A Danish upstart? On the throne of the Northern Kings?' The Atheling's smile dropped away, his eyes grown cold and fathomless as flint. 'He wouldn't dare.'

CHAPTER TWENTY

In all the Archbishop's great hall, there were only two women. Elfled and her middle-aged attendant were seated up on the dais. The rest of the benches were crammed with the Atheling's retinue – those *few retainers* he mentioned turned out to be a full five dozen men-at-arms – and the Archbishop's own dependants, clerical and lay. The arrangement of the hall was unfamiliar to Wulfgar: the dais was in the middle of one of the long sides, rather than at one end, with the long tables set out flanking it to left and right.

Wulfgar had been seated a long way from the dais, at a table largely populated by West Saxon soldiery. He could see Kenelm several benches away, half-obscured by those great stone columns, tucking into the sucking pig, the white bread and creamy green cheeses, the veal seethed in milk, the apple-beer and the sweet, sticky wine. All of the best, and enough of every dish for each to have his fill.

Wulfgar was being largely ignored by the jovial, hard-drinking men seated either side of him, and he wasn't sorry.

They were all traitors to King Edward. He hadn't recognised any faces, but he was willing to bet there were names he would know. If he could learn them, he could draw up a precise pedigree of West Saxon treachery to send back to his Lady, which she could then pass on to her brother.

But did he want to?

If it came down to it, on whose side would he find himself?

No, given the darkness of his thoughts he wasn't sorry to be left alone.

Nor, despite the excellence of the fare, was he hungry.

He stared at his piled trencher and wondered what, in God's good name, he was doing there. He felt like a straw tossed this way and that by a stream in winter flood, at the mercy of water and weather from far away, caught and whirled by unseen eddies and in perpetual danger of being sucked under and lost for ever.

Sulking in silence wasn't going to help his brother though, or the Lady; gathering information was.

So he plucked up his courage and, taking advantage of a lull in the conversation, asked his neighbour how long they would be staying in York.

The man rubbed a hand over his greasy whiskers.

'That's what I asked my Lord only this morning!' He belched loudly. 'And do you know what he told me?' His broad West Saxon voice was indignant.

Wulfgar waited.

'Till the wind changes! Now, what do you suppose he meant by that?'

Wulfgar shrugged and tried to look sympathetic. 'What?'

'I've no idea. *Till the wind changes*, indeed. Anyone would think we'd come by sea.'

'What do you—?'

Horns were blowing outside the hall.

Up on the dais, the Archbishop leaned sideways to listen to something the Atheling was muttering. He nodded, raising his eyebrows.

The tramp of feet outside, a barked command, the great double doors opening. Wulfgar twisted round on his bench to see what was happening.

Guards were coming in, and falling back to flank the doors, framing a single man who strode in, pausing just within the threshold. He looked around him, nodded, and waved his men back outside with a bold, confident gesture.

'I need no guards in the house of my friends.'

The hall's stone walls resounded with the sound of some hundred and fifty men scraping back their benches and clambering to their feet.

The Atheling too was standing, and raising his cup. 'My Lord and King!'

So this, at last, was Knut.

'Better late than never, eh, friend Seiriol?' His voice was guttural, but his English was clear and fluent. He took a few more paces into the room, and looked up and down the hall to left and right. 'I was in two minds about coming.' He gave the occupants of the dais a hard stare. 'But in the end I couldn't resist the prospect of drinking a toast to the bride. King Edward be damned, eh?'

An approving roar went up from the tables.

'Art going to make space for me beside the bonny bride, Archbishop?'

Wulfgar had heard men refer to Knut as *that old war-wolf*, and

139

he had expected a greybeard with a feral glint in his eye. But this man, for all his crumpled, well-worn features, was in his prime. Not tall, but powerful, bulky and splendid in an exotic, calf-length tunic of vermilion silk that tied across the front, woven with gold bands striping down from collar to hem. Close-cropped hair, growing to a point low on his forehead, and thick, dark eyebrows. Big-boned and jowly, with a neat moustache and beard, and the rolling shamble of a bear rather than the slinking lope of a wolf.

A sad face.

Wulfgar wondered why that thought had struck him. Looking again, he stood by his thought. There was indeed something melancholy about Knut, despite the festive occasion and the cheerful face the King was putting on.

'Archbishop?'

Wulfgar looked beyond the high table to where the Archbishop had returned to his high-backed wooden chair. His hands on the armrests were gripping the carved lions. His expression could have curdled milk.

Then the Atheling bent down and whispered something in his ear. Lothward looked up at him and laughed, over-loud and unconvincing. But he rose. Knut had timed his walk perfectly, so that he arrived at the vacated seat of honour just as the guests further down had rearranged themselves, freeing the place on the groom's right for the Archbishop.

There was a flurry of attendant hands, helping the King to settle on the silk cushions, bringing him meat and bread and wine.

'My Lord King!' The Atheling was still on his feet. 'You honour us beyond measure. With your leave, I'll order ale for your men outside?'

Knut indicated approval with a nod and a wave.

The Atheling waited for a moment, everyone's attention still on him.

Then, 'My dear Lords,' he said, bowing to King and Archbishop alike. 'My hosts.' He turned to the hall, holding out his hands, looking up and down the tables. 'My friends – old and new.' Finally, and tenderly, 'My wife.'

He waited for the applause and stamping to die down.

'I come to you a landless man, denied my inheritance. My wife has done me the honour of taking me as I am, dispossessed and exiled. York's great lords have given us shelter and consecrated our nuptials by their presence.'

Knut was leaning forward, resting an elbow on the table, his head cocked slightly, nodding every time the Atheling paused.

The Atheling was speaking to his hearth-companions now. 'You share my exile of your own free will. You have faith in me. I will not forget you when I come into my own.'

Wulfgar shifted his gaze to look at the rows of the Atheling's men. Most of them were close to the Atheling in age, and he suspected they had forged their bonds fighting shoulder to shoulder with him over the last twenty years. One face that caught his eye, however, was much younger than most: a pale lad with huge grey eyes and a shock of dark hair, who was watching his lord with an avid expression. Wulfgar wondered why the boy should be there among the forge-hardened warriors.

Never mind that wan boy: why should he and Kenelm be here at this bride-ale? He longed for a private conference. Somehow, they would have to get all this budget of news to the Lady of Mercia.

He tilted his beaker and watched the sticky apple-beer swill this way and that. He knew that she would take the word of this wedding very badly.

The encounter with Ketil Scar. She needed to know about that, too.

And the letter Edward had written to Archbishop Lothward. Was he planning an alliance with York's Archbishop in a counter-move to her treaty with its King?

Had she spoken to Edward yet, about Wystan? Asked for a reprieve, as she had promised?

He pushed the food around his trencher, still without appetite.

Perhaps he could find a friendly Danish merchant, one who traded south of Watling Street, willing to carry a letter.

And thinking about friendly Danish merchants led, inevitably, to other, connected, thoughts.

Sjáumst í Jórvík...

Gunnvor's throaty ring-dove voice spoke in his mind, although he had only ever heard Kenelm's stumbling parody of her words.

See you in York.

Or perhaps a better translation would be, *We'll see each other in York.* Danish could do some elegant things with verbs that English couldn't...

'Are you the Mercian hostage?' A young page, bright-faced at his shoulder.

'One of them.' Wulfgar indicated Kenelm, hoping the boy might nod and move on.

He shook his head. 'It's you the King wants words with.'

Wulfgar felt a prickle of guilt, though as far as he knew he had done nothing wrong. Looking up to the high table, he realised that, somehow, he had missed the end of the Atheling's speech. He clambered gracelessly backwards over the bench and made his

142

way up to stand across from the King, his head bowed and his hand on his heart.

Knut was leaning back against the Archbishop's cushions.

'Look me in the eye,' he said in English. Bright black eyes, at odds with the creased and folded skin around them. 'Thorbjorn tells me thy Lady will keep to the terms of her treaty.'

Wulfgar was taken aback by this direct approach.

'Indeed she will, my Lord King.'

'I am very fond of my nephews. My own boy died, see? And their mother trusts me.' He nodded to himself. 'Do I need to keep thee and the other one under lock and key? Lothward tells me he will find you both bed and board here.' He cocked a thick, black eyebrow. 'You two might prefer it, men of the cloth as you are?'

Against all his expectations, Wulfgar found himself warming to the man. 'You honour us, my Lord,' he said, 'and we have sworn our oaths not to abscond.'

'To Thorbjorn.'

Wulfgar nodded. 'But we will swear them again to you, if it please you.'

'*Nej, nej,*' Knut grunted. 'Thorbjorn is my right hand. An oath to him is true coin.' He looked Wulfgar up and down. 'I would be truly sorry to have to kill thee, and thy friend.' The King closed his eyes and shook his head: a tiny gesture. 'Enough politics!' He wiped the grease from his beard and dropped the crumpled napkin on the tablecloth. 'A toast, and a kiss for the bride!'

While the hall voiced its approval, and Knut embraced the acquiescent if unresponsive form of Elfled, Wulfgar contemplated the smiling bridegroom only a few feet from him. His lips half-framed the question that had pounded through his mind for a fortnight now.

143

It was unsayable.

The Atheling looked up, and caught Wulfgar's gaze on him. He raised a single, amused eyebrow.

Wulfgar felt the perfidious blood colour his cheeks. He said softly, 'My Lord Atheling. Please. A word at your leisure?'

'At my leisure. But not at my bride-ale.' He smiled. 'Tomorrow morning. After Prime. Here, in the hall.'

CHAPTER TWENTY-ONE

When they had gone into the cathedral for Prime, at first light, the alleys and courtyards of the Archbishop's citadel were thick with damp, white mist. But they emerged only a little while later into another day of blazing sunshine.

The day matched Wulfgar's mood. He was grateful to have found that Knut was no ogre.

What was more, the Archbishop's clerics had welcomed him and Kenelm. Avid for news of affairs in distant, glamorous Winchester, Worcester and Gloucester, they had kept their visitors up late into the summer night, chasing after every crumb of gossip. *The strangers are become my friends*: never had the words of the psalm he had chanted at so many thousands of Primes over his lifetime seemed more apposite.

The strangers are become my friends, he chanted again under his breath. *Who will lead me into the strong city?* He was still humming cheerfully as he made his way towards the Archbishop's hall, braced and ready to face the Atheling.

Someone bellowed his name.

The Archbishop's chaplain, with Kenelm standing at his side, was only a few yards from him. The chaplain, a plump, officious man, was flushed and evidently annoyed. 'Didn't you hear me? That was the third time I had to shout.' He gave Wulfgar no time to answer. 'The Archbishop's presence. Now.'

'But—'

'His Grace wants to see you both. He said so. He's waiting for you in his own chamber.' The chaplain was escorting them through the hall, and Wulfgar looked around wildly. There was no sign of the Atheling. Scan it as he might, the hall was empty of anyone other than a few of the Archbishop's guard, still sleeping off their excesses, and the slaves sweeping up the remains of the feast. As they left the hall for the calm of the private courtyard, Wulfgar had to hope that the Archbishop's business with him and Kenelm, whatever it proved to be, would be rapidly concluded.

Archbishop Lothward was alone. He dismissed his chaplain with a wave of his hand, and beckoned Wulfgar and Kenelm closer.

'I've looked again at that letter you brought me,' he said, without preliminaries, 'and I have to confess I hadn't realised what a treasure the Lady was sending me.' His eyes lingered on Wulfgar in particular. 'I gather from this you are a considerable scholar, despite your youth?'

'Your Grace.' What was this about? Wulfgar had to struggle to keep his eyes from looking longingly at the door.

'I have an important meeting with the King later this morning. The King and some others. We will be discussing York's future relationship with the Jarls of Lincoln and Leicester. I thought, in the light of this new treaty, and your roles in it, you would be interested to attend?'

Kenelm bowed. 'You honour us, your Grace.'

'Before that meeting...' the Archbishop took a step back and gestured at his desk, heaped with scrolls and sheets of vellum. 'I've been digging in my archives recently.'

Despite his anxiety to be gone, Wulfgar felt a tingle of curiosity.

'I found this charter. It concerns the midland minsters.' The Archbishop held out a single, folded sheet. 'I hadn't known about it; it's never been copied into the cathedral cartulary. I'd be grateful for an independent opinion.'

Wulfgar met Kenelm's eyes briefly. The two of them went over to the nearest window to get the benefit of the daylight. Wulfgar read through the text, which was written in a mercifully clear script, and felt the hairs slowly prickle on his nape. *Lothward wants Leicester*, the Lady had said. Had she known about this?

'Well?' Impatience broke through the smooth surface of the Archbishop's voice. 'Does it mean what I think it does?'

Wulfgar waited, hoping Kenelm would say something, but the deacon was still frowning over the lines of text.

After a long moment's silence, he said, 'Forgive me, your Grace.'

The Archbishop nodded his permission.

Wulfgar plunged in.

'It's not a charter.' Surely Lothward had known that? He tried to soften his words. 'Not technically, that is. It's a list of the monastic houses that owed allegiance to your hallowed predecessor, Bishop Wilfred, some two hundred years ago.' His throat felt scratchy. 'It's of great historical interest. I knew about Peterborough and Oundle, but not Wing, or Brixworth, or—'

'Leicester,' the Archbishop interrupted, his eyes gleaming.

Wulfgar had to shake his head. 'Not Leicester, your Grace.' He stopped, taken aback by his own temerity.

147

'It says Leicester.'

Wulfgar wasn't sure how to interpret that light in the Archbishop's eye. Was this a test of some kind?

'But not part of the list,' he tried to explain. 'The first part is the register of monasteries. Then it moves on to other houses, which acknowledge a connection, but not overlordship. That's where Leicester comes in.' He reached for the document. 'Look, your Grace. There.' He indicated with his finger. '*Etiam Ratae*, that's where the new sentence begins.'

'No,' Kenelm said.

The Archbishop turned to him. 'Go on.'

Kenelm darted a sideways look at Wulfgar. 'I think Leicester's the final item on the list. The monasteries – that's clear enough – and then the last house to belong to York is *also Leicester – etiam Ratae.*'

'But Leicester is a cathedral and subject to Canterbury,' Wulfgar said stubbornly. He thought over what Kenelm had said and felt a gust of outrage. 'And none of these houses *belongs* to York! They recognise the overlordship of a particular individual, namely Bishop Wilfred. York wasn't even an archbishopric two hundred years ago.' He looked through the troublesome text again, and felt even surer of his ground. 'This has no contemporary relevance.'

'I disagree!' Kenelm's eyes were fixed on the Archbishop, his face bright and eager. 'I think this certainly gives York a current claim to overlordship.' He took the document back and started reading it again.

'No.' Wulfgar felt he had to try to stand his ground. 'Not unless this can be supported by a later document, dating from after St Wilfred's death. In fact, from after York's promotion to an arch-diocese, demonstrating these houses' transfer of allegiance from

Canterbury...' He felt a sudden wash of impatience eddy through him. He needed to be in the hall, talking to the Atheling about his brother, not wasting time picking over the bones of long-dead, purely academic, ecclesiastical disputes. 'Your Grace?'

Bu the Archbishop was ignoring him.

'This *later document* you mentioned' – he put his hand on Kenelm's elbow – 'what might it look like? How would I know it, if I were to come across it in some dusty corner?'

Kenelm had gone bright pink with pleasure.

'Well, your Grace, there are various forms it might take. There could be a supporting charter from a Mercian king, granting rights to York.'

The Archbishop glanced at Wulfgar, who nodded reluctantly.

Kenelm was still talking.

'Or a letter from an Archbishop of Canterbury, or even something ratified by a Bishop of Leicester—'

'But,' Wulfgar said loudly, 'we gather there is no such document surviving in your archive, your Grace.'

Lothward smiled at him.

'I haven't seen one. But our archive is extensive, and largely uncatalogued. And then there are other archives – who knows what we might find at Oundle, or Brixworth or Leicester?'

A vision of Leicester's charred, scarred ruin of a cathedral came forcefully into Wulfgar's mind. A lump in his throat, he said, 'I can't vouch for the others, your Grace, but I can't imagine anything survives at Leicester.'

'Is he always such a pessimist?' The Archbishop didn't give Kenelm the chance to answer. 'This letter, or charter – how might it read?'

Kenelm was glowing.

'Well, it would be in Latin—'

Lothward snatched up a stylus and a pair of tablets from his writing desk.

'Jot it down for me.'

Wulfgar could feel a tic twitching away by his right eye, as though the skin were caught and tugged by some angler's hook. Couldn't Kenelm see the trap? But his colleague was scratching away, muttering *dono et concedo* under his breath, with Lothward watching him inscrutably from under those heavy lids.

Lothward wants Leicester...

But Leicester's true ruler was the Lady, even if Ketil Scar held it for the moment.

Wulfgar's lips tightened as he remembered all the jibes he had endured from Kenelm and the other Worcester cathedral clerics over the last year. Where was the much-vaunted *true-born Mercian* loyalty of the Bishop's nephew now?

Lothward was saying, almost casually, 'And can you do me a fair copy?'

Kenelm nodded. 'There must have been such documents once, your Grace.'

'Lost in the troubles we have suffered for so many years,' the Archbishop agreed. 'You'll find pens and ink on the desk.'

Wulfgar watched them in growing disbelief. Could Kenelm possibly be ignorant of what he was complicit in? Creating a forged document that would support York's claim to these contested churches against that of his uncle and the Lady of the Mercians.

He was finding it hard to breathe.

The Archbishop was ringing his little bell, telling a breathless slave to fetch a sheet of vellum from the scriptorium. Turning back to them, he said, 'I would appreciate it if you would both be present at the council meeting later this morning. A Mercian perspective would be invaluable.'

'Of course, your Grace,' said Kenelm, smooth as cream.

Wulfgar struggled to find his voice. He opened his mouth, wanting to protest. His mind was full of words like *forgery* and *treachery* and *wrong*. And then a cold little voice, an unfamiliar little voice, spoke to him. *Conceal*, it said. *Prevaricate. Dissemble.*

He was so certain that he had heard someone speak those words that he turned sharply. But the room was empty apart from the three of them. The curtain hung motionless on its bronze rings.

Neither of his companions seemed to have registered his sudden twitch.

Dissemble...

The little voice was right.

'Your Grace,' he said, trying to emulate Kenelm's unctuousness. 'If I might... ?' He indicated Kenelm's tablet.

The Archbishop moved back.

'Of course.'

His eyes rattled over Kenelm's scratchings.

'Good,' he said, his voice sticking in his throat. 'Good.' His mind felt barren; his diaphragm and larynx had constricted almost to stifling-point. He managed to say, 'But in whose name?'

Kenelm muttered, 'I didn't know... I can't remember much history...'

'You're a learned man, Wulfgar,' the Archbishop said. He smiled. 'Help us out here.'

Dissemble...

'Let me think.' Mentally, he leafed through the archived charters with which he had been working at Gloucester and

Worcester, wondering which Mercian monarch was least likely as a benefactor of York. With a strained smile, he said, 'What about King Offa?'

Was it too obvious a false trail? Surely one of these two men would know how unlikely it was that that particular King of Mercia should have enriched York?

It seemed not.

Kenelm's eager stylus was gouging the wax once more.

'Yes?' He looked at Wulfgar expectantly.

'You can draft a simple deed of gift, can't you?'

Kenelm got back to work. Wulfgar drifted towards the door.

'That looks ready for its fair copy,' the Archbishop said.

Wulfgar dug his nails into his palms, determined to say nothing more. He desperately needed air. Would the Atheling have waited for him?

'If you would excuse me, your Grace?'

Neither Kenelm nor the Archbishop so much as acknowledged his departure.

CHAPTER TWENTY-TWO

Wulfgar paced restlessly up and down the flagstone floor of the Archbishop's great hall as he had been doing for the greater part of an hour.

No sign of the Atheling, no message from him. He had tried several times to sit himself down on one of the benches and breathe deeply, but the tumult of his thoughts and feelings always had him up and pacing again.

It was only partly the prospect of this meeting with the Atheling that had him so agitated.

Kenelm. Stupid, stupid, stupid...

Wulfgar stopped in his pacing.

Stupid?

Or clever?

At that thought, Wulfgar sat down again.

If he was right, this was all his own fault. He had suggested that Kenelm should accompany him to York. He had even said to the Lady that Kenelm had never had a chance to set his own pace; that the Bishop of Worcester kept his nephew on too short a rein. Now Kenelm had been given his head, and just look at the result.

He groaned aloud. The Bishop of Worcester was a better judge of men's hearts than he would ever be.

And where had the Atheling got to? He had asked several different people, and no one had seen him in the hall that morning. The reactions to his question had ranged from polite unhelpfulness to a lewd snigger and a reminder that the man he was waiting for had passed the night in his bridal bed, and that even with such a scrawny, whey-faced bedmate he might be excused for forgetting an early appointment.

Not that early.

The sunlight was creeping round the wall and, even as he wondered how late it was, the bell for Terce began to ring.

The Golden Hour. The hour when the Holy Ghost had descended at Pentecost in the form of flame. The hour when the Saviour had received his sentence of execution.

It had never occurred to Wulfgar for a moment that the Atheling might default on his promise.

He stood up again.

He had no idea what to do, but he had had enough of waiting, and he walked out into the bright courtyard.

The day was already hot.

The summoning bell was being rung at the cathedral, but he found his feet taking him round its west front and beyond, to the church of Holy Wisdom.

Its door stood ajar. There was a middle-aged woman seated on the bench by the door, but from what he could see the church itself appeared to be deserted.

Why not?

The Lord and His Holy Mother knew, wisdom was what he so desperately lacked.

The church was indeed empty. Only a lingering scent of incense and beeswax evoked the ghost of the previous day's nuptial mass. The air inside was cool.

Wulfgar inhaled deeply, and found the sacred geometry of the place beginning to work its little miracle on his soul. The first altar was dedicated to the Blessed Virgin, and he felt a familiar uprush of devotion. *Oh, Queen of Heaven...Mistress of the Angels, Mediatrix of Sinners, Mother of Wisdom, we entrust ourselves to your intercession and also to your advocacy...*

He began to walk sunwise around the outer ring of chapels, pausing before each altar. The church wasn't as dark as he had thought at first. The candles might be unlit, but the little arched windows, one for every altar, let in an eerie underwater light through their thick, grey-green glass.

He had thought to kneel in one of those little ancillary chapels, but instead he found the beauty of the place drawing him round with the inevitability of water striking the blades of a mill wheel. He moved from altar to altar. *St Peter, pray for me; St Paul, help me; St Andrew, hear my prayer...*

Thirty altars, hadn't the guard said? That was only fifteen.

How did one get up to the gallery?

He walked the circuit again, paying less attention this time to the saints and their altars and more to the construction of the building. He found what he was looking for at last: a door set back into a tall, shadowed archway, so narrow that a stout man would have had difficulty getting through. He touched the handle, and the door swung open.

The stairway went up through the thickness of the wall, narrow and steep as a ladder, airless and absolute in its darkness. He climbed with one hand fumbling at the wall, the other extended before him. It was with relief that he felt his knuckles graze the studded wood of another door. He groped for its ring, and pushed his way out, blinking, into the greyish light of the upper gallery.

Another ring of altars. He was feeling calmer and happier as he made his way around this time. Up here, the window openings were filled with wafer-thin sheets of alabaster, and the chapels were dedicated to the Saints of York. Here was St Wilfred, and here the Roman Paulinus, interspersed with some local holy men and women of whom Wulfgar had never heard. But here was St Edwin, King and Martyr; and here – and Wulfgar gulped and sank to his knees – here was St Oswald of most blessed memory, whose bones Wulfgar had carried next to his heart for a few, brief, unforgettable days and nights.

Wulfgar, still kneeling, put his face in his hands and poured out his soul in inarticulate prayer. St Oswald had lived in the thick of this dirty world. He had known exile and enmity and the basest treachery. If anyone could help, surely it was St Oswald...

And all the company of Heaven.

Spokes and felloes of a great wheel, whose hub was Holy Wisdom.

He stood at last and looked into the well-like space surrounding the great altar. He was now above, and well placed to observe, that magnificent lamp-ring. It hung from a chain that was fixed by an iron hook built into the painted ceiling. Fifteen little vessels of blown glass and fifteen sockets, now empty of oil and candles, a light for every lesser altar, and all united to shine on the high altar itself. That glorious confection of glass and metal was never

English work. Lombardic, he wondered, or Roman? Or from still further east?

Polycandelon – the word swam up from some text once read and long forgotten by his waking mind. He tried it aloud and it sang on his tongue.

'Thy Word is a lamp unto my feet,' he chanted softly, 'and a light unto my path.'

However did they kindle the lamps and candles? There was nowhere to lean a ladder.

Looking back to his right he could see that he had walked straight past the answer. There was a simple arrangement of counterweight and pulley, terminating in a rope that was looped snugly around a hook in the wall. Following the rope and chains with his eyes, he saw how they would allow the polycandelon to be lowered in a controlled way, the oil lamps and the candles to be lit, and the whole glittering contraption hauled back into place. He wondered how much the whole thing weighed. The previous day, with the lamps and the candles lit, it had been a thing of glory. Even extinguished and in the dull, underwater gloom of the empty church, it was impressive.

Still caught up with his image of the saints endlessly circling in praise around God's throne like the constellations around the Pole Star, he turned away from the balustrade and looked for the last embrasure.

It held the high-seat of the kings of Northumbria, about which the Atheling had been so cryptic the previous day.

Curious, he approached.

And thought his heart had stopped.

There was someone sitting in it.

A pale figure, swathed in white.

Wulfgar was reminded forcibly of images of Lazarus three days dead and brought back from the grave in his linen cerements. He stood frozen to the spot, breathless, for a long moment.

'I thought it was you,' she said. 'Wulfgar of Winchester.'

He breathed again. But what was the Atheling's bride doing here, alone, the morning after the sanctification of her wedding?

'I've been watching you at your devotions.'

He nodded, self-conscious, glad of the semi-darkness.

'This throne is so cunningly placed, don't you think?' She ran her hands over the smooth armrests almost lasciviously. 'Six steps up to its plinth, just like the throne of Solomon. You can see nearly the whole church from here.'

He found his voice at last.

'I assumed it was limestone. The throne, I mean. But it's marble, isn't it?' He moved closer. 'With your permission, your Ladyship?'

At her nod, he reached out to caress the slick, polished surface, and found that his fingers, like hers, were drawn to caress its glassy planes. The white veins within the nacreous marble echoed the white-on-white embroidery of Elfled's skirts. He reached down the side, where it was too dark and cramped to see, and his tentative fingers encountered carvings that announced themselves as crosses, flowers, and something harder to interpret. Peacocks, perhaps. He was reminded of the alabaster of the windows. Like them, this seat had come from somewhere long ago and far away.

'This is older than the church,' he said. 'Older than Northumbria. Much older.'

'Very old, and very cold,' she said, rising to her feet. 'Your sister Cwenhild would tell me to shift my rump before I got piles. We will have to find a suitably splendid cushion for it.'

'A cushion?' He could feel he was gaping at her, and closed his mouth.

'Before my husband sits here with any regularity.'

It was as though a bolt of lightning had gone through him.

'Your husband?' And, with a sudden urgency, the question he should have asked at first. 'Where is your husband?'

She stepped down from the plinth.

'He will be King in York, you know. He was born to be King of Wessex. That was stolen from him.' Her voice had taken on the sharpness and clarity of thrice-forged steel. 'And I will be his crowned and anointed Queen, which is more than any king's woman in Wessex can title herself. And our sons will be doubly royal, and they will rule after us.' She stroked the cloth covering her stomach affectionately, as though she were already carrying the boys of whom she spoke with such confidence.

It made Wulfgar's skin crawl.

Hesitating, he said, 'There is a King in York already, you know.'

'Oh, I know that.' She was turning away from him. 'God grant your prayers be answered, Wulfgar of Winchester.'

CHAPTER TWENTY-THREE

'Why weren't you in Terce?'

Wulfgar ignored Kenelm's accusatory hiss.

'You should have stayed with his Grace and me,' Kenelm went on. 'He was very kind. He even said I ought to be ordained soon, that there was no point in keeping a talented man like me kicking my heels in the diaconate for a moment longer than necessary.'

'You're too young,' Wulfgar said. 'Years too young.'

He and Kenelm were walking along King's Street, heading towards Knut's palace, retracing the route that Thorbjorn had brought them.

'Under normal conditions, yes.' Kenelm preened. 'But if an Archbishop can't break the rules...' He looked sideways at Wulfgar. 'You really should have stayed with us, you know. You did yourself no favours, scuttling off like that. His Grace told me all about his plans for Leicester, and all about this meeting. But for once you don't know anything about what's going on, do you?' The waspishness in his voice was unmistakable.

'No,' Wulfgar said, trying to keep his voice steady. 'You're quite right. I don't.'

'That horrible man's going to get what he deserves.'

'Horrible?'

'Ketil Scar,' Kenelm said with vindictive satisfaction. 'He's going to be sorry he ever laughed at me.'

Wulfgar lengthened his stride. He didn't want Kenelm to see his face.

For all his extra height, Kenelm was struggling to keep up.

'Do we have to walk so fast? It's too hot.'

Wulfgar, looking at Kenelm's puce complexion, relented and slowed down a little. If Kenelm was that colour, then he probably was too.

'Why did you leave, anyhow?' Kenelm sounded peevish.

Wulfgar sighed. What harm could the truth do?

'I thought I had a meeting with the Atheling. But perhaps I mistook the day or the time.' He cast his mind back to their brief exchange of the previous day. He was quite sure he had not been mistaken.

'You must have,' Kenelm was saying, his voice rich with satisfaction. 'He went out hunting before the sun was up. Didn't you know?'

'Hunting?' Wulfgar stopped dead outside a warehouse whose open doors revealed stacks of baled furs. 'He did? How do you know that?'

'The Archbishop mentioned it, I can't remember why.'

Wulfgar started walking again. Hunting. He had broken his promise, or forgotten his promise – and Wulfgar wasn't sure which hurt more – to go *hunting*.

They were rounding the great tower at the southern corner of the Archbishop's enclave.

'Oh, that was it,' Kenelm said. 'The feast tonight. His Grace was hoping the Atheling would have good speed in his hunting.'

'I must have misheard the Atheling.' Wulfgar said. 'Misunderstood him.'

But he was certain that he hadn't.

The guard on the gate at King's Garth nodded them through.

'Oh, *já*, I mind you lads all right. You're expected.'

'I wish we had more time to look at that extraordinary building,' Wulfgar said, turning as he had done the previous day to marvel at the stacked and carved roofs of the timber hall. Anything to distract himself from thinking about the Atheling.

'Barbaric,' Kenelm said.

That wasn't quite what Wulfgar had been thinking, but he was glad to let the remark go by.

He wondered whether the Archbishop had arrived yet, or whether they would have to encounter Knut on their own. Leading the way up the stairs, he could hear the murmur of voices growing clearer as they went up. One voice in particular, and it certainly wasn't Knut's.

'What's that to me? I don't call Leicester home, not these days.'

Wulfgar had lifted his right hand, ready to pull the door curtain aside, but he froze then, the hair lifting on the back of his neck. He stared at his hand, the familiar shape of his fingers suddenly strange, the lozenge-patterned twill of the curtain shifting and re-forming.

Sjáumst í Jórvík...

Kenelm, hard on his heels, almost ran him over.

'What's the matter?'

Wulfgar let the curtain drop back into place.

A man's deep voice rumbled though from the other side.

'But for all that, lass, you surely don't want to see Leicester sacked and burned?'

And Wulfgar knew that voice, too.

'Can you be sure of that?' The first speaker again.

Wulfgar swallowed, painfully. There was only one voice like that in the whole of God's blessed Creation.

He was filled with a sudden, almost overwhelming, desire to run away.

Kenelm was looking at him oddly.

He took a deep breath and pulled the curtain to one side so gently that its gilt-bronze rings barely jingled.

Knut's inner sanctum was set out for an intimate meeting. It was a big, oblong room open to the rafters, with its two arched windows looking back down into the courtyard. A single chair stood next to a small table piled with sheets of vellum. There were three people in the room: the solitary man-at-arms standing to attention with his spear, and two others.

One was a man in late middle age: his hair, the grizzled black-and-white of a badger's pelt, was untonsured, he was bearded, and the chestnut gleam of a well-dubbined leather sword-belt lay over his left shoulder. But Wulfgar knew him for a priest, for all his layman's trappings.

The other was a woman, her thick dark hair unveiled and piled high on her head, braided and twisted with knots of shiny wire, the black cloak draped around her shoulders trimmed with wide bands of purple and silver, and skewered in place over her left collarbone with an elaborate silver brooch whose pin was long and sharp enough to make a very serviceable dagger.

The man had his back to the door. The woman was looking straight towards them. She raised her eyebrows and inclined her head.

Wulfgar tried to frame a greeting, but it stuttered and died in his throat.

The man turned.

'Is it yourself? Wulfgar of Winchester, by the Holy Name!' The priest's voice was a roar. 'God's Death, lad, but it's grand to see you.' Wulfgar found himself enveloped in a swamping hug, one he reciprocated from his heart. 'And what brings you here?'

'Ronan,' he said, his throat tight. 'It's good to see you, too.'

'Well, well,' the priest said, holding him by the shoulders and looking him up and down before embracing him again. 'I never thought to see you in York.'

'I'm a – we're hostages,' he said. 'Kenelm and I. A treaty with Mercia...'

Father Ronan was nodding to Kenelm now.

'The Bishop of Worcester's nephew. I remember you well; yes, indeed I do.' A little of the warmth had ebbed from his voice.

'And what are you doing here, Ronan?' Wulfgar shook his head, dizzy with delight and relief.

'Faith, I'm not sure exactly. We'll have to see.' The priest had dropped his voice. 'I had a summons from the Archbishop, which I thought I'd do best to obey.'

'And I thought I'd been invited to discuss affairs of state with important people!' Wulfgar turned as she spoke. 'Kings. Archbishops. Not grubby little subdeacons.' Amusement bubbled under the surface of her voice.

Wulfgar found himself looking indignantly down the length of his spotless tunic, glancing quickly at his hands with their gleaming nails, before he met her gaze again and saw the quirk of her eyebrows, the glint in her eye, and realised he'd fallen for her teasing.

He'd have sensed her presence even with his eyes closed. Not just that silky, ring-dove voice but the scent of her, that cinnamon-peppery-spiciness, the boiled-down essence of all the exotic goods she traded in.

He offered her his most formal bow, the one reserved for the Lady. 'Gunnvor Bolladottir.'

She returned the bow with a long inclination of her neck. 'Wulfgar Soft-Hands.'

'As ever, I am but your humble servant.'

'My thrall, even.'

Wulfgar nodded, a lump in his throat. Yes, he was, until he paid her back the money he owed her. But to repay her would be to sever that link between them...

'You're that woman from Leicester,' Kenelm said accusingly.

She nodded in her turn, holding up her hands.

'I confess, churchman. What of it? Did you pass on my message?'

Kenelm began to stutter something, but Gunnvor lifted her head then to look Wulfgar straight in the eye, obliterating his awareness of anyone else's presence in the room. How, in a few short months (though, God and His Mother knew, they hadn't seemed short), could he have forgotten the way her face was composed of curves? That the falcon-swoop of her eyebrow was an exact complement to the high arc of her cheekbone and the lofty bridge of her nose; that the full bow of her lower lip followed the line of her chin to perfection? Given a compass and dividers, he could have plotted the geometry, those perfect ratios, of her face...

'How's little Electus?' Ronan was asking.

'What?' Wulfgar dragged his attention back to the priest. 'Oh! Thriving, I'm told.'

Gunnvor said, 'Who's Electus?'

'Come on, lass! You've not forgotten the baby Wulfgar's fostering? You went to his christening for God's sake, woman! In my Margaret-kirk, remember? He'll be, what, six months now, Wuffa? Any teeth yet?'

'Oh, *that* baby.' Gunnvor shrugged, resettling the cloak around her shoulders. 'I'd forgotten its name.'

'I don't know about teeth,' Wulfgar said. 'I expect his wet nurse will tell me all the latest news when I'm back in Gloucester.'

'A rare happy outcome,' Ronan said.

Their mood had sobered. Wulfgar was thinking about that bleak day last April when Ronan had disentangled the wailing baby from the arms of his murdered mother, and from the priest's quiet face he guessed that Ronan was remembering it too. Ronan was looking tired. Shabbier, or perhaps just thinner, so that his tunic sagged over his shoulders and was held in redundant folds at his belted waist. His hair and beard were greyer, too.

'No doubt he is doing everything appropriate to a baby.' There was an acerbic edge to Gunnvor's voice.

Wulfgar turned back to her.

'I've been worrying about you.' The words came out against his better judgement, but now that he was face-to-face with her he found himself incapable of saying anything but the simplest of truths.

'Have you indeed?'

Damn his blushes.

'We heard things are bad in Leicester.'

'Things are bad in Leicester,' she echoed, mocking. Then she said, 'Our gracious Jarl, Ketil Scar, doesn't like me, but you know that.' She rubbed her right cheekbone meditatively. 'He's not dared hit me again, though.'

He wanted to ask her what she was doing in York; how she had known he would be there; and whether – just possibly – she had come to York because of his presence, but perhaps fortunately he was forestalled. A bustle had been going on below in the courtyard, and while Gunnvor was speaking the man-at-arms suddenly snapped to attention.

They all looked at the door.

The thunder of many feet resounded on the stairs, and a servant was pulling back the curtain.

King Knut came in first, in a swirl of red and gold, Thorbjorn in close attendance. The Archbishop, in a sombre grey-furred gown, with his red-cheeked chaplain at his shoulder, both clerics nodding a greeting to Ronan. More men coming in behind. The room was crowded suddenly and noisy. Knut was settling into his massive chair; a servant was setting out a purple-embroidered stool for the Archbishop. Thorbjorn caught Wulfgar's eye and winked.

Knut was looking round the circle, nodding at each face.

'Bolladottir. *Prestr.*'

Ronan bowed in answer.

'Toli *jarl.*'

Wulfgar's head jerked round in appalled disbelief, his jaw dropping, before he could even think of cloaking his instinctive reaction in the meaningless smiles of diplomacy. Toli Silkbeard Hrafnsson, the young Jarl of Lincoln, was standing just by his left shoulder, a brace of bodyguards behind him.

Wulfgar fought the instinct that was telling him to run. Toli Silkbeard had filled out. Grown into his father's shoes, perhaps. Looking less like a spoiled boy, more like a jarl. A shiver ran up and down between Wulfgar's shoulder blades. A maturer Toli was not necessarily a less dangerous Toli.

'Knut *konungr*.' Toli bowed to the King. 'Archbishop.' Another bow. 'Bolladottir.' He lifted a hand in salutation.

'Toli *jarl*.' Gunnvor responded with a deep curtsey, smiling as she rose and shrugging back her cloak to expose the red silk and diaphanous linen beneath.

Wulfgar registered that smile, and felt a tug of misery. When her smiles were so rare, why was she was wasting one on Toli?

If Toli had recognised Wulfgar he gave no sign of it.

The King was nodding and smiling too, but he never stopped scanning the room with those sharp black eyes in their pouchy settings.

'And the West Saxon Atheling? Our happy bridegroom? Where is he? Archbishop, you told me you had asked him to be here.'

Silence. Not so much as a muttered ribaldry.

Wulfgar waited for the Archbishop to speak up about the Atheling's hunting trip, but he was looking as baffled as everyone else. If he were feigning, it was well done.

Kenelm, too, was silent.

Knut jerked his head at Thorbjorn.

'Find out.'

The waiting was long and painful. Still no one spoke. Wulfgar, looking at the thunderclouds building in the King's face, was not surprised.

'My Lord King.'

Knut beckoned Thorbjorn forward.

'He has gone hunting with his men, my Lord. He left before dawn. He took the Archbishop's hounds with him, and his boar-spears.'

'Ah, so that's what's happened.' The Archbishop's frown was lifting. 'Then *mea culpa*, my Lord.' He smote himself lightly on the breast. 'It's my fault. I did offer him the use of my hounds. I didn't think he would go this morning, though.' He smiled drily. 'Perhaps the bridal bed proved less entertaining than he had hoped.'

Knut ignored the invitation to share a joke at the newlyweds' expense, though this time Wulfgar heard more than one stifled, sycophantic snigger coming from elsewhere in the room.

'Forgetting his invitation to this meeting,' the King said coldly. 'Hunting my hinterland, without my leave. Why does he ride around with so many men, landless exile that he calls himself?' Knut's voice was still cold but Wulfgar could sense the heat simmering beneath that lid. 'I will be less willing to welcome him, next time.' He pressed his lips together, nodding to himself. 'Thorbjorn, wait down in the courtyard for him. When he comes back, send him up to me.'

Thorbjorn nodded, and turned to go.

'Archbishop, if you would open our meeting?'

The Archbishop nodded, steepling his chunky brown fingers with their flash of gold and sapphire and bowing his silver head.

'Blessed Peter, chief of the Apostles, keeper of the keys of Heaven and Hell, and patron of York, deliver us from the hands of our enemies...'

'To our matter, then.' Knut crooked a finger. 'Archbishop, you suggested this meeting, and you invited our guests.' The Archbishop nodded. 'Your reasons?'

Lothward of York cleared his throat and spread those broad, powerful hands out before him on the table. Blunt workmanlike nails, albeit meticulously pared and cleaned.

'Disturbing rumours have been reaching us.' He stretched out one hand to lift a sheet of vellum from the squared stack in front of him. 'And now something a little more solid. Listen to this, and tell me what you make of it. *Edward, King of Wessex, greets Lothward, Archbishop of York, with love and friendship...*'

It was the letter that Wulfgar and Kenelm had already heard the Archbishop summarise.

By the time the Archbishop finished reading, Knut was growling low in his throat.

The Archbishop nodded. 'Edward's threat is implicit, but unmistakable. York is to acknowledge him as overlord. Or else, invasion.'

'*Call him lord*, he says. *Pay him tribute*, he says,' the King muttered. 'And he writes to you, Archbishop. Not to me. Why not?' His hands, resting in his lap, had curled into fists. 'We must counter this letter,' he said, louder now. 'He will learn that Knut of York is a king among kings.'

'We fight Wessex, then?' The Archbishop leaned back on his stool, apparently relaxed and comfortable, but Wulfgar noticed the way his eyes flickered across to Toli of Lincoln.

Wulfgar tensed, waiting for what seemed the inevitable affirmation.

But Knut's response was as unexpected as it was uncompromising.

'*Nej.*'

'No?'

King and Archbishop held each other's gaze for an endless moment.

'I am not in the fighting business any more,' Knut said at last. 'Not unless I am attacked first. I have too much to lose.' He pondered for a moment. 'We will write to him. As a brother. In Latin.' His head lifted and his lips curved in a sudden expression of pride. 'I am a King as much as he. Charles of the Franks is my friend. Make that clear to him in the letter.'

Wulfgar heard Toli of Lincoln, behind him, muttering something indecipherable in Danish.

'Not in the fighting business,' the Archbishop said pensively. 'There are some here, my Lord King, who are hoping to nudge your thinking along a different course.' He got slowly to his feet.

'Don't mistake me,' Knut said.

But he wasn't looking at the Archbishop. Instead, his gaze was directed up, over Wulfgar's shoulder, at Toli.

'I have won many fights before now,' the King went on. 'Believe me, I would love to show Edward who's the man and who the boy. But York cannot take war to Wessex.'

'Not yet,' the Archbishop said.

'And perhaps never.' Knut put his head on one side, pursing his lips, listening to his own words. 'Ach, we old men must learn our limitations, Archbishop.' He shook his head.

There was more discontented muttering among the Lincoln delegation behind Wulfgar's back. He could feel his hackles rising.

'Our present limitations, perhaps,' Archbishop Lothward said. His eyes were alight, his face tense with a peculiar concentration. 'But what say we annex Leicester? If York's rulers become the masters of Watling Street, what then?' He nodded towards each of their visitors. 'Perhaps we should now hear—'

'Did you hear me, Archbishop?' Knut was scowling now. 'I've told you this before: I don't like your scheme for Leicester. It's a distraction. We have our old treaty with Leicester. We have our new treaty with the Lady of Mercia.' He waved a hand at Wulfgar and Kenelm. 'Our honoured guests and pledges: *they* are our insurance against Leicester, and Wessex too. Furthermore, Ketil Scar has acknowledged me as King of York. I know him of old.' Knut chuckled nastily. 'He may frighten you, Archbishop; he doesn't frighten me.'

Wulfgar realised he hadn't breathed for some long moments.

But the Archbishop seemed barely to register the King's provocative words. He merely nodded, the heavy lids coming down over his eyes.

Toli Silkbeard said, 'My Lord King?'

Knut nodded, a wary look crossing his jowly face.

'I have no treaty with Leicester.' Wulfgar half-pivoted to look at the young jarl of Lincoln. His white-lashed eyes were bright, his red lips curved with delight. Such a deceptively sweet, girlish face. 'I have forty horsemen, good men, who keep their weapons honed.' He brushed a stray lock of spidersilk hair out of his eyes, and smiled radiantly. 'If you need us, we can be at Leicester's gates with two days' warning.'

Knut waved a brutally dismissive hand.

'Enough of this. We have no quarrel with Leicester. We will deal with Wessex diplomatically. I have spoken.'

When the Archbishop responded at last, it was through gritted teeth.

'My Lord King, these prominent citizens of Leicester have travelled at some personal inconvenience to assist with our plan.' A marked emphasis there on *our*. 'Not to mention Lincoln's Jarl.'

Somehow he and Toli had converged to stand side by side.

Knut stood up.

'Your plan, Archbishop. Not mine. Never mine. And Bolladottir and this priest are not accredited ambassadors from Leicester. They are private citizens with a grievance. As for you, Toli Hrafnsson' – he raised an admonitory finger to the Jarl of Lincoln – 'I welcome you here because you are your father's son, but do not presume on my old love for him.' He bowed to each of the three in turn then. 'Glad though I am to see you all, it was not I who summoned you. My apologies to you, if you have been troubled.'

He turned to the tight-lipped prelate.

'Archbishop, if you could see that they are well housed for the remainder of their stay? Reimbursed for their trouble?'

Phrased as a request, it was clearly a command. As far as the King was concerned, this meeting was over.

'*Thetta er allt?*' Toli Silkbeard's jaw was clenched so tightly that the tendons in his neck stood out like harp-strings.

'*Já,*' Knut said. 'That is all.'

Toli's voice was guttural with anger. 'I am summoned here like your thrall for you to tell me *this*?' He took a step towards Knut.

Knut's eyes flickered towards the door. Wulfgar thought he was looking for Thorbjorn, who was still down in the garth. Suddenly there was a twisting up of the tension in the room, so sharp one could almost smell it.

'Jarl Toli,' Knut said, 'you have my leave to go home.' He jerked his chin at the attendant man-at-arms. 'See the Jarl of Lincoln safely to his horse.'

Toli Silkbeard was quivering, like a leashed hound straining after a hare. 'I need no man's leave.'

His soft mouth was pinched in a straight line, his nostrils flaring in and out as he breathed. He and Knut stared at each other for an endless moment.

Silence.

Then Toli moved.

Wulfgar flinched.

But it was only Toli turning, lifting an empty hand, half-smiling round the room, though the smile never reached his eyes.

'My Lords. Another time, perhaps.' Aside, to one of his men, 'Saddle our horses.'

The man nodded, and darted from the room.

No one spoke as the Lincoln men jostled their way out of Knut's sanctum.

With Toli Silkbeard gone, the sense of imminent catastrophe ebbed palpably. The room felt more spacious, and Wulfgar could see their relief in the way its remaining occupants were moving, stretching, even smiling. Knut clapped his hands and ordered wine, and most of the remaining awkwardness was dissipated in the familiar ceremonies of pouring and bowing and drinking one another's health.

The wine was excellent, thick and syrupy even mixed with water, and Wulfgar felt its effects immediately, with a warm, buzzing sensation stealing through his veins. To his delight he found Father Ronan at his side, and they clinked cups and drank deep.

'What are you two doing here?' Wulfgar said softly.

Ronan leaned in and spoke so close that the bristles of his beard buzzed in Wulfgar's ear.

'Don't be too hard on our little Gunnvor. I've come along to watch over her as much as anything else. But mind you don't tell her that!'

Wulfgar pulled away and turned to look at the priest with a frown. 'What do you mean?'

'She—' but the priest stopped mid-word, holding up a warning hand.

'So, we conclude our meeting,' Knut was saying. 'A letter to Edward of Wessex. See to it, Archbishop. To the rest of you, my thanks. I am sorry if your time has been ill-spent.' He was all affability now, moving towards the door.

'My Lord and King.'

The men had all stepped respectfully to right or left, out of the King's way, but Gunnvor was standing firm.

'Gunnvor Bolladottir.' Low in the King's throat, but it was a rumble rather than a growl.

She inclined her head gracefully.

'You've grown up since I saw you last.' His expression softened into a smile, and those sad eyes warmed. 'I would be honoured if you would eat with me later. You, and any among your men who remember your father. We will drink to Bolli's memory.'

Gunnvor bowed low.

'The honour will all be mine, and my father's. We will drink with you with a glad heart, my Lord King.' She paused. 'But, my Lord, you really should hear the proposal we have brought you.' Her face was alight, its lines gentle for once, entrancing, the fingers of one hand resting on the gauzy linen swathing her breastbone, her other hand extended towards him.

How, Wulfgar wondered, could he fail to melt?

But Knut just grunted.

'You have already had my answer.'

She bowed again, her eyes lowered, and stepped sideways with a rustle of skirts.

'Later, my King.'

'Later, Bolladottir.'

Knut made as though to push past Gunnvor, but the sudden clatter of shod hooves on the cobbles outside made him pause.

Was it Toli of Lincoln, tardy in his leaving? They could all hear a sudden hubbub of loud, cheerful voices in the courtyard, the yipping of hounds and the jingle of harness.

No, not Toli.

It was the Atheling, returned from the hunt.

There was the patter of quick, confident steps on the outside stair. The curtain was drawn aside with a dramatic rattle of its gilt-bronze rings. The Atheling stood there, his dove-grey tunic spattered with mud and dried bloodstains.

Wulfgar wondered how he effected his entrances so perfectly. That one smudge of dirt on his cheek, which only served to show off the beauty of his bones, the brightness of his eyes...

The Atheling said, 'We'll feast tonight, my Lord.'

CHAPTER TWENTY-FOUR

The Atheling looked from face to face.

'By God, I'd forgotten it was this morning.'

He stepped into the room, and now his bride, Elfled, was visible behind him, immaculate in her white.

'You are discourteous.' Knut's voice was stiff.

The Atheling put his hand on his heart and bowed his head. When he looked up again he took in Knut's still-furious expression. One more lightning glance around the room, and he stepped swiftly forward. There was a new alertness in his face.

'My Lord.'

He went down on his knees. Gazing at the floorboards, he said again, 'My Lord. My King. Forgive me.' He clasped his hands and offered them up to Knut, his head still bowed, in an unmistakable act of homage.

'What is your excuse?' His voice remained gruff but Knut was already looking a little mollified.

'None, my Lord King. Only that the sun was shining, and I had word of a boar out Heslington way...' He looked up then, and smiled, and said, 'I thought to please you, my Lord. What can I say to make amends?'

And, miraculously, Knut's grim, set expression relaxed. He stepped forwards and took the Atheling's hands in his, pulling him to his feet. The two men embraced warmly, slapping each other's backs.

'It's a fine boar, my Lord King.' The Atheling's smile broadened. 'A quick kill, and gutted cleanly.' That bright, expectant look was still hovering about him.

Knut pulled away a little, still holding the Atheling by the elbow, reaching for Edward's letter with the other hand.

'You'll have seen this communication from your cousin of Wessex?'

The Atheling shook his head. 'His usual insolence?'

Knut passed the letter to him, and he scanned it quickly, his smile fading and his frown deepening as he read.

'So, what would your answer be to this?'

Knut folded his arms across his chest, looming impressively in his red and gold.

The Atheling pivoted to pass the letter to Elfled. When he turned back, he said, 'Destroy him. Take war into the heart of Wessex.' His glance flickered sideways to the Archbishop. 'We can mop up Leicester, and the rest of Mercia, afterwards.'

And Knut said, 'No.'

'We'll take Leicester first then? Use it as a base to—'

Knut cut him short. 'Neither Wessex nor Leicester. No. Not unless they attack us first.'

'Not this year, perhaps.'

'Never.'

'Never, my Lord? Are you sure?' The Atheling shrugged. 'That's unfortunate...'

Wulfgar never forgot the tiniest detail of what happened next.

The two men were still standing close, close as lovers. And, much as a lover would, Knut gave a little sigh and slumped in the Atheling's arms.

The Atheling staggered slightly with the sudden weight. He guided Knut back, and lowered him into his sumptuously carved chair with studied gentleness. Then, still holding the older man in that tender embrace, he looked up at Elfled, who had been watching every move like a cat at a mousehole. She nodded, and turned, and walked to the landing to call something to the men waiting below.

Knut gave another sigh, harsh and creaky, and his head lolled to one side as though it had suddenly grown intolerably heavy. The black eyes were wide open, but they were growing dull.

Evidently satisfied that Knut was safely propped in the chair, the Atheling stood up and stepped back, dusting his hands.

'My sword.'

One of his retainers was suddenly at his side, deft fingers already working the buckles.

Wulfgar bent to look at the silver-wire patterns inlaid in the hilt of the Atheling's belt-knife. A dance of tiny creatures. Lion, and ox. Eagle, and – yes – he could see if he leant closer – a little human face, staring back at him. The signs of the four gospel-writers. St Mark and St Luke. St John and St Matthew. *Orate pro nobis...*

Pray for us...

It was beautiful black-silver work, typical of Winchester. If he were to examine it closely enough, he could probably deduce whose workshop it had been made in.

But it shouldn't be sticking out of a man's belly at that jaunty angle.

He laid his hand on the hilt, ready to pull it out.

A narrow, pale hand with prominent blue veins rested on his, forestalling him.

'Please.'

He looked up blankly, only realising when her colourless face came into view that it was Elfled.

'Please,' she said again. 'Don't. If you do that, there'll be blood everywhere.' She gestured at herself briefly, a flash of sunlit gold from her ring. 'And I'm all in white.'

'Seiriol,' the Archbishop said.

The Atheling looked up from adjusting a final buckle.

'This isn't what we planned.'

'It's not quite how we planned it, certainly. How seldom things unfold precisely as one would wish, eh?' The Atheling's smile was tinged with irony. 'But one has to seize the moment.'

Wulfgar looked from face to face, not quite trusting his hearing. He felt very cold. Surely Knut would sit up in a moment, and he and the Atheling would be laughing together again.

He felt a hand on his shoulder.

Ronan.

He stood up, the blood ringing like clamorous alarm bells in his ears. He caught a glimpse of Kenelm's face, wild-eyed and greenish.

'We've got to get out,' Kenelm said. He sounded as though he were choking back the urge to spew. 'We're trapped in here. I want to get out.'

'Brought your sword, have you, deacon?' The priest sounded bitterly amused. 'Even so, you might have difficulty.'

There was shouting now, Wulfgar realised, and had been for some moments. Shouting and the clash of steel coming up from the courtyard, very close to the foot of the stairs.

Kenelm was right. They were trapped.

'You should be all right in here.'

The Atheling had gone to the window, Elfled at his shoulder. His voice was calm, almost happy.

'There are more of us,' he said, 'and we have the hounds.' He turned back to his sword-bearer. 'Get down there and see that they bar the outer gates, and stand a couple of men at the foot of these stairs. Then send someone behind the wall' – he looked at the Archbishop – 'with your permission, my Lord?'

'Of course.'

'Get the Archbishop's retinue. Tell them we need help tidying up.'

The Archbishop nodded his approval, but the man was already halfway down the steps.

Wulfgar's legs felt unreliable. He knelt at Knut's side again. The Atheling's words were still echoing meaninglessly in what felt like vast hollow spaces inside his skull. There seemed to be nothing real in all Creation but this man, still sprawled across the luxurious cushion of his chair.

Was there even the faintest hope that the King was still alive?

Wulfgar rested his fingertips on the warm, slightly chapped lips, but could feel no breath. He touched the dark-stubbled throat here and there, very gently, with questioning fingertips, trying to find the answering beat of a pulse.

Nothing.

When the Atheling had lowered Knut into the chair, one of his hands had come to rest on his chest. It slipped now, and the arm flopped to hang at his side. There was something about the movement, an awe-inspiring finality, that made it horribly certain to Wulfgar that Knut was dead.

He became aware that blood had begun to seep through the thick layers of splendid cloth, almost black on the fiery-red silk of the King's long tunic.

Wulfgar found his hands were clammy now, and shaking. He still couldn't fully believe what he had seen.

He blinked, trying to drive away the images, insistent as summer midges, of Knut's broad smile at the bride-ale, the smacking kiss he had given Elfled, the readiness with which only moments earlier he had held his hands out to the Atheling...

He looked at Knut's jowly face, still with that faint air of puzzlement about its features.

Men had called him the old war-wolf. But he had become the lamb to the slaughter.

'Let us destroy the tree with its fruit,' Wulfgar whispered. 'Let us cut him off from the land of the living, that his name be no more remembered.'

Was this what it meant, becoming one of the holy fraternity of Christian kings? To hold to the oaths of baptism and coronation: to uphold the peace and protect the people; to fight no unjust war ...

Thorbjorn loved this man.

Did Thorbjorn yet know his King was dead?

Hot liquid was searing the rims of Wulfgar's eyes. He reached out to draw the King's lids over that dulling gaze. He was vaguely aware of Ronan at his side.

Dona ei requiem... Give him eternal rest, O Lord, and may perpetual light shine upon him...

Kenelm had backed himself into the corner furthest from the door, his face still that underwater green, his lips moving in ceaseless entreaty.

Elfled had moved to the window. She watched for a moment, then, 'We have the advantage of surprise,' she said, approval in her voice.

'Indeed.' Gunnvor, dry and faintly mocking.

Wulfgar didn't look up from his muttered requiem. Ronan was making the sign of the cross on Knut's forehead, and his paling lips, and over his heart.

Elfled turned back to the room, a halo of sunlight behind her. 'Wulfgar?'

He looked up at last.

'Don't you want to know how the fight is going?'

He shook his head. This was no fight of his.

'After all,' she said, 'we're the only other West Saxons here. You and me. If my Lord loses – which God and His Mother forbid – we're the ones Knut's men will take particular pleasure in hacking to pieces.' She sounded exhilarated. 'We'll get the blame.'

'Your equanimity is commendable, your Ladyship.' Even he could hear how brittle his voice had become.

'What do I have to lose?' She smiled radiantly. 'I've been buried alive all my life. Of course I would prefer not to die now. I have something to live for at last. But I'm ready to go down fighting.'

'I'm not,' Gunnvor muttered from somewhere behind Wulfgar's shoulder and through the icy miasma of his shock he found himself wishing, desperately, that she were anywhere but here.

Crossing himself one last time and hauling himself to his unsteady feet, he went over to join Elfled at the small arched window. He had to force himself to look out.

Some twenty feet below, there was a furore of running and slashing and shouting men. As he watched, different patterns began to come clear to him. He had no experience of reading a battle, but even he could see which side was winning.

As he watched, Knut's surviving men were offering up their swords one by one, allowing themselves to be searched for hidden weapons, removing their helmets and handing them over. A member of the Archbishop's bodyguard was standing over a growing pile of battle-booty.

The Atheling's voice came up to them, bouncing off the wall, addressed to a small group of a dozen or so men who had been backed into the north-eastern corner of the yard. Wulfgar leaned out a little way to see more clearly. All the cornered men were facing outwards, swords bristling. His heart in his throat, he realised Thorbjorn was in the vanguard.

'Throw down your weapons,' the Atheling was shouting.

There was a ragged growl of reply.

Wulfgar couldn't decipher the precise words, but their meaning was unmistakable.

'Throw down your swords, and you will find us merciful.'

Another growl, and a blinding flash of noonday sun on brandished metal.

'Your King is dead. Are you the heroes of old songs, to die to the last man?' His voice lower, more intimate, the Atheling said, 'Thorbjorn, don't be a fool. Don't throw yourself away. You could be a great man under my rule. I could make you Jarl of Leicester yet.'

Thorbjorn spat for answer.

'He makes big, easy promises, doesn't he?' Wulfgar realised that Gunnvor was somewhere very close behind him.

'Give up!' one of the West Saxons at the Atheling's shoulder shouted. 'Time to serve your true King!'

As he did so, another man came pelting across the courtyard, pointing behind him to the gate, shouting something incomprehensible.

The Atheling turned. 'Unbar,' he shouted. 'Our reinforcements are here.' His attention briefly elsewhere, he failed to notice Thorbjorn and a brace of other men shattering the cordon around them, swords wielded like threshers' flails.

Elfled gasped: the first crack in that marmoreal façade.

But, at the last possible moment, the Atheling turned back, his sword at the ready. Even from twenty feet above his head, Wulfgar could see his smile.

Then they all piled in, the Atheling, and the West Saxons with him, and those of the Archbishop's men-at-arms who had been in the yard already. Knut's men were hopelessly outnumbered. They disappeared beneath a pile of screaming, hacking men. Wulfgar failed to see how, for the life of him, one might distinguish friend from foe in that pitiless scrum.

He heard Elfled's fierce whisper. 'Kill them, my Lord. Kill them.'

When the rest of the Archbishop's men came clattering into the courtyard only moments later, the fight was already as good as over.

'Don't fail me now.' Wulfgar turned to find Ronan beckoning him towards the staircase. 'We're needed, lad.'

'What? Go down there?'

Ronan nodded.

'Aye. There'll be men hurt down there. We didn't raise a finger to stop this, Wuffa, and that's on our souls. We have to tend whom we can, now.'

His bluff face looked grey and weary, gaunt even, behind its badger-striped beard, but his jaw and his shoulders were resolute. Just seeing him standing there, foursquare and infinitely trustworthy, did Wulfgar some good. His feet were leaden as he walked across the room, skirting the chair with its tragic burden, out under the curtain rail into the steamy sunshine, and down the hollow, wooden stairs, but they did his will.

Tend whom we can, but the Atheling's men had done their job almost too well. Welcomed as friends, lacking their swords but carrying their freshly honed hunting knives and wicked boar-spears, their assault on Knut's followers had come entirely unawares. Ronan and Wulfgar moved among the ranks of the butchered, closing dead eyes and mouths and straightening still-pliant limbs, noting with sickened hearts how many of the dead men's wounds were those of men attacked from behind, with the razor-sharp blades used for the disembowelling of game.

So many cut throats.

The cobbles of the yard were slick with their life-blood, and long before he and Ronan had completed their rounds Wulfgar's sleeves and knees were stiff and sticky, and his forehead bloodied where he had wiped the sweat from his eyes. The air was thick with the smell of slaughter, and ever greater numbers of fat, glossy-black flies. A periodic *cark cark* from overheard told him that the ravens and their kind had already detected the smell of death.

As he moved from corpse to corpse, Wulfgar had been looking

out for Thorbjorn's body, with fear and trembling and without success.

Could he have survived, after all?

But that tiny flame of hope was at once extinguished by the cold memory of the slicing and slamming of axe and blade and fist and boot.

But if not here, where could he be? Wulfgar looked in vain in the north-east corner of the yard for anything resembling Thorbjorn, or any of the other men who had been part of that hopeless, loyal, little band.

Something glinted gold under the red at his feet. He stooped to pick it up without thinking.

'Keep it,' a passing soldier said. 'Lucky man! We're all entitled to what we find.'

Wulfgar stared after the man without comprehension before opening his palm to look at what it contained.

A coin.

A gold coin stamped with a cross and the King's name patterned around it, inviting one's eyes to go from north to south, from west to east, to make the sign of salvation and invoke a blessing on the name of the man commemorated there.

One of the special issue coins, minted for Knut's hearth-men.

Had Thorbjorn dropped it?

Careless of him to let it fall: he would be wanting it back.

Then, with an emetic jolt like a blow to the gut, Wulfgar realised what he was looking at.

At his feet, there was an unspeakable pile of mud and filth, reaching into the corner. The corner into which Thorbjorn and his friends had been backed. He had thought it no more than a blood-drenched midden.

Now, having drawn closer, he realised that it was less midden than butchers' offal.

Corpses.

Human corpses, but so hewn and minced that they were barely recognisable as such.

He pressed his fist against his mouth.

There would be no body to bury next to Thorbjorn's father in their little *ainkirk* of All Hallows.

How in the name of Heaven could this news be brought to Thorbjorn's house?

The clop of hooves behind him.

Voices raised in cheerful greeting.

Wulfgar knelt down on the bloodstained cobbles and hid his face in his hands.

CHAPTER TWENTY-FIVE

It was only slowly that Wulfgar became aware of a figure standing next to him. Even as he realised someone was there, the man reached out and rested a warm, consoling hand on his shoulder.

Ronan again. He put up his own hand to grasp his friend's, longing for the comfort it could provide. *I'm so glad you're here.*

It was the Atheling.

'Don't grieve.'

Wulfgar snatched his hand away; he couldn't help himself. Scrambling hastily to his feet, leather soles skidding on the slick cobbles, he bowed and muttered a hasty greeting to mask his revulsion.

The Atheling shook his head at him.

'You're not pleased with me, Wuffa, are you? I remember that look from when you found me broaching a pipkin of wine reserved for my uncle's table from behind the old steward's back.' He smiled and shook his head. 'What was his name? That tall man, bald, with the—'

'*Don't*,' Wulfgar said. 'My Lord.' He didn't want this man to call him Wuffa. He didn't want to remember how he had trotted adoringly after him when he was seven and eight and nine. He wanted him never to call him Wuffa again.

The Atheling smiled then, but his eyes stayed sober.

'Dear Wuffa. As I've always said, you're far too good for this dirty world of ours.'

Wulfgar's chest and lungs had been feeling tight, too tight for breath or speech. And then suddenly, as though an iron hoop had been sprung from a barrel, his voice was unleashed.

'I killed a man once, my Lord. You know I did.' He lifted up his stained and sticky hands. 'And you know why. It was self-defence, even though I did stab him in the back. And I did my best to kill another man, to avenge the innocents he had killed. I did my best and he got away from me.'

He looked at his hands as though they belonged to a stranger, caked with the drying blood of so many different men.

'But this, my Lord? This?'

He gestured around him. The astonishing torrent of words was drying up. He looked around him at the scene of bustling industry. The dead bodies were being dragged by their heels over the cobbles and stacked in a corner by that strange, towering wooden hall.

There was one last question he felt compelled to ask.

'Will you see they have proper burial, my Lord?'

'What do you think, Wuffa? Shall I send to their families? Let them know that they are welcome here, to find and claim their men?'

Wulfgar closed his eyes. *Their families.* Empty words to the Atheling, but not to him.

He had a sudden prophetic vision of that sweet, bony, competent, mouse-haired girl in her old blue dress, tugging at the corpses, turning them over, looking for her father and finding, finding...

Bile and acid rose gagging and burning in his throat. Swallowing hard, he said, 'Knut thought he was your friend. He and his men were taken unawares.'

'And where's the honour in that?' The Atheling nodded. 'There's no shame in crying for them, Wuffa.'

He blinked back the treacherous tears and tightened his lips. Then he said, 'It's just – I've seen fights. But I've never been in a battle before.'

Another voice, mellow and urbane, came from behind them.

'I don't think the chroniclers will dignify this little skirmish with the title of *battle*, do you, Seiriol? More a little mopping-up operation, I'd say.'

'My Lord Archbishop.'

The Atheling straightened. Wulfgar, still dizzy and nauseated but imprinted from infancy with respect for the episcopal office, tried to do the same. He became aware of other people, coming and going. The clean-up of the bodies continuing. Soldiers alert in the gateway. Ronan moving, grim-faced, among the dead and the dying. Gunnvor in her black and purple cloak and Elfled in her white dress and veils, standing on the staircase, safely above all the blood and guts.

'The captain of my guard,' the Archbishop was saying. 'He would like to report to you in person.'

The Atheling nodded, and the young man snapped to attention, gilded helmet under one arm.

'My Lord! We have the King's Garth secure within and

without. All Knut's bodyguard are dead. We've lost seven men so far. Six of yours and one of ours. Two horses. Half a dozen nasty injuries, and a lot of lesser ones.'

'Good man!'

The captain glowed.

The Atheling said, 'Have you York men in your party?' The young captain nodded. 'Go through the streets. Explain what has happened and that nobody will be hurt. Tell them that the killing is over. Get your local men to talk to the heads of their families, and the same for the priests of the city churches. Spread the word, as reassuringly as possible. Do it now.'

'My Lord.' The man turned on his heel.

The Atheling frowned. 'Wasn't Toli of Lincoln expected at this meeting? Didn't you summon him?'

'I did, and he was.' Archbishop Lothward's tone was drily amused. 'Knut clipped him over the ear and sent him about his business.'

'Order a man after him, on a fast horse.' The Atheling didn't sound in the least entertained. 'I need all my hounds.'

'Indeed.' The Archbishop looked thoughtfully around the courtyard, at the shambles those few brief moments had generated. 'Not what we planned,' he said, 'but a very neat operation for all that.' He exuded satisfaction like a cream-fed cat.

A passionate desire to escape from these smug men gripped Wulfgar. His voice a rasp, he said, 'My Lord Archbishop, your man mentioned the wounded. Might I tend them? I'm no leech, but—'

'Good man,' the Atheling said again. 'Do what you can.' He patted Wulfgar on the shoulder, as one might a little boy when

192

telling him to run along, and said to the Archbishop, 'I was just telling Wuffa here that he's too good for this life.'

Wulfgar didn't wait to listen to their laughter.

He was directed towards the great wooden hall with its zigzagging, dragon-decked stack of roofs. He had said to himself that he would have time and leisure to explore that mysterious structure while they were in York.

Now here he was, inside it.

And he had no eyes for its uncanny craftsmanship at all.

It was being ransacked. Men were ripping embroidered hangings down from their hooks; iron-bound chests were being carried carefully out through the wide doors even as bodies were lugged gracelessly in; lesser furniture – benches, tables, stools – was being hauled into a pile close to the still-glowing hearth. In the dim, dust-mote-laden shafts of light filtering down from the little louvred windows, Wulfgar could see that there were half a dozen living, bleeding bodies variously prone and supine on the floor where they had been dragged and dumped, and at least as many more for whom earthly help had come too late.

Where to start?

He looked down at his filthy hands and realised he was still clutching Thorbjorn's coin. The first thing was to put that safely away in his pouch.

Then, water.

Bandages.

He turned back into the courtyard, found a terrified-looking stable boy, and sent him to fetch a bucket of water and a length of clean linen.

He started doing what he could. The first two men beside whom he knelt had lost too much blood to live, and the third looked as bad, with delicate pink froth bubbling at his lips: a lung wound. Wulfgar tried to wipe it away but even as he did more came gurgling up. The man was panting, trying to say something.

'Ssh,' Wulfgar said helplessly. 'Don't worry. Don't try to talk.'

But the man was clawing at his arm, a look of peculiar intensity on his face. 'She – I can see – I can see her coming...'

His wife, or his mother?

Wulfgar scrabbled for what he could remember of the last rites. 'The Lord pardon you whatever sins—'

But the man's eyes were tipping back into his head, and darker blood came gushing from his mouth even as his head lolled sideways.

Wulfgar hated to leave him, but there were others claiming his attention; others with a better chance of living. The fourth man had no more than a nasty gash in his arm, and Wulfgar set to work with relief.

'You're the Mercian hostage, aren't you?'

He nodded, intent on wiping the wound without provoking the blood to flow again.

'But not the Mercian one. I mean, you've come from Mercia, but you're the West Saxon one.'

'That's right.'

'Wystan of Meon's brother.'

Wulfgar nodded again. Familiar, stifling guilt hovered at the fringes of his awareness, but he pushed it away. Now was not the time for self-indulgence.

'Alnoth of Brading was my father.'

And, at that, he did look up.

Under the blood and the grime, a beardless boy, with tousled dark hair and grey eyes and a fine-drawn face, gazed back at him.

Now that he was paying attention, Wulfgar could see the marked resemblance.

He didn't know what to say.

'My name is Alwin,' the boy said. His mouth twisted. 'Alwin of Nowhere.'

Wulfgar sat slowly back on his heels and wrung out the bloody rag into the bucket of pink water, taking his time to twist it first one way and then the other, watching the drops as they fell.

He remembered now: it had emerged at the trial that the lad had been offered a place as one of the Atheling's hearth-companions.

It shouldn't, therefore, come as such a great shock to find him here, in the midst of the slaughter. Where else did the boy have to go, after all?

It shouldn't be such a great shock, but it was.

He dabbed meaninglessly at the boy's wound.

'You saw them hanged,' Alwin said.

'I was there.' He couldn't honourably say a simple *yes*. He hadn't had the courage to watch as Edric and Alnoth had kicked and struggled and choked their way out of this mortal life.

'How did my father die? I mean, I know they hanged him, but did he do it well?'

Wulfgar twisted the bloody rag into the pail again, to give himself something to do. He wanted to find comforting words, but his thoughts were disjointed and clumsy.

This boy deserved honesty.

'Hanging is never a kind death,' he said. He couldn't meet Alwin's hungry eyes. 'Your father was brave. I prayed with him. But it's still horrible.'

'Yes,' the boy said. 'And it's worse that they lie in the pit.' His voice took on a new intensity and he frowned, his thick black brows making one horizontal line. 'Have you seen the pit, up at Harestock?'

Wulfgar nodded his head, not trusting his voice.

'I haven't. But it's got a lot of names,' Alwin said. 'The thieves' pit. The heathen pit. The traitors' pit.' His voice wobbled. 'The pit of Hell. They say that, if you're buried there, even if you led a good life, you're damned for ever.'

Wulfgar shook his head again in fervent denial.

'I heard, they just threw him in,' Alwin went on. 'In the filthy, stinking clothes he'd been hanged in. That you could still see the corpses of the last men who'd been cast there, rotting away for the rats and the foxes. They don't bury them properly or at all, really, that's what they told me. There's no holy words, or anything. They just scatter a little bit of earth on top—'

'*Stop it*,' Wulfgar said ferociously. He felt remorseful at once. More gently, 'Where are your family? Where's your mother?'

'My grandfather's taken her back, and my sisters. But it's hard on them. I'm all right. My Lord Seiriol is looking after me. But they've got nothing left.'

'Yes, I see.' Wulfgar tore off a strip of clean linen and began winding it around the boy's upper arm.

'I hate Edward,' the boy said with a sudden passion. 'He's the traitor. Not my Lord Seiriol. I'm going to kill him.'

Wulfgar wondered who else might be listening to this conversation.

'Don't use that arm more than you can help.'

'I hate Edward,' the boy said again. 'He promised my father his life and then he hanged him.'

Wulfgar tied the ends of the bandage as neatly as he could. If

Wystan had been hanged with the others, would he himself have had such a simple hunger for revenge? He looked up at the carved boards decorating the tops of the walls. Impossible animals biting one another incessantly: legs and tails and ears all caught up in long jaws, all tangled hopelessly in a maelstrom of strange, sprouting tendrils. There was no telling where one creature started and another left off, the first beast's tail in the last one's teeth.

'Pray for your father, Alwin. And for Edric of Amport.' *And for my brother*, he was going to add, but he bit back the words. This boy didn't need reminding that one life had, however provisionally, been spared. 'They need our prayers as never before.'

'It's too late for that. They're in the pit. They're damned.'

The child's bitterness stabbed at him like a spear-thrust. Wulfgar shook his head fervently.

'It's never too late, this side of Judgement Day.' He put all the conviction he could into his words, but they rang hollow in his own ears.

Alwin turned his face away.

Troubled and tired, Wulfgar picked up the bucket of bloody water and his dirty rags, looking for his next patient.

'Everybody out!'

There was a bumping and a darkness in the doorway, heavy footsteps booming on the floorboards and echoing round the cavities of the gable-spaces far above them.

'What?'

He turned to see some of the Archbishop's soldiers, dragging in more corpses by their heels.

'There are wounded men in here,' Wulfgar said to the weary-looking young man who seemed to be in charge.

'Better get them out, then.' He shouted over his shoulder, 'Can someone give me a hand here? Is there a cart we can use to get the rest of the carrion in here?'

'Cart?' A voice from outside. 'A shovel'd be more use for some of these.'

'You can't move these men.' Wulfgar tried to sound authoritative. 'They're your own men. They're hurt.'

The young man grinned at him, teeth white in a filthy, blood-smeared face.

'They'll be worse hurt if they stay.' He dumped the corpse he had been lugging and turned back to the door.

Another man, grey-haired, more patient, said, 'We're going to fire this place. Bring all the York dead in here and burn the hall.' He bent to wrench a gilt pin from the matted cloak of the body he'd just bumped across the floorboards.

'No.' Wulfgar shook his head. 'The Atheling said he would let the families have the bodies.'

But the Atheling hadn't said anything of the sort. He had answered one question by asking another, but he hadn't promised anything.

'On your feet now, lads! Those who can walk, can bloody well walk.' The grey-haired man turned back to Wulfgar, his face rendered a devilish mask of bloodstains. 'Who's too far gone?'

'To walk? That man there, and those three.' He indicated. 'They'll need stretchers...'

But the man had pulled his belt-knife.

Looking at Wulfgar's stricken face, he said, 'It's better this way, you know. Really, it is.' And he knelt by the side of the man with the lung-wound. 'Ach, I think this poor lad's gone already. Best make sure, though.' He lifted his blade to strike at the base of the throat.

'No!' Wulfgar grabbed the kneeling man by the shoulders and tried to haul him off. 'He was speaking to me a moment ago – you can't kill him. Help me get him out of here!'

But the grey-haired executioner was already sliding his knife back out. 'You've a fair bit to learn, lad,' he said, wiping the sticky blade on the dead man's sleeve. 'Sometimes the kindest thing a friend can do is finish you off.'

Appalled, Wulfgar stared at him for a long moment.

'You've a lot to learn,' the man repeated.

Wulfgar shook his head. 'I don't think so.' He turned to offer his arm to young Alwin. They went out together into the kindly, late-afternoon sun.

CHAPTER TWENTY-SIX

The pyre blazed all through the brief summer night and into the following day. Knut's stripped and battered body had been added eventually to the pile of corpses.

Wulfgar was sitting on the stone seat outside Holy Wisdom, watching those endless black roils of smoke rising over the cathedral, when the Atheling's messenger caught up with him.

'In the King's chamber. Now.'

'But the King is dead.'

The smart young man ignored his words, looking him up and down. 'He said to come straight away. But you can't go like that.'

'Like what?'

Had this spruce young warrior been part of that screaming, hacking mob the previous day? He looked little older than Alwin, barely old enough to shave. Wulfgar looked at the extended hand and felt revulsion at the thought of touching it. But, weary beyond belief and incapable of argument, he let himself be led away to a quiet corner, a pail of hot water and some of the Archbishop's own soap. The young man's kindness had him on the brink of tears again.

The blood and smuts scrubbed away at last, stinging with cleanliness and in a fresh tunic, he was conducted back past the cathedral and hall and through the interconnecting wicket gate under the great gatehouse to the King's Garth. There were armed men everywhere. In the courtyard ahead the great smouldering timbers still glowed and crackled. As they climbed the stairs, he recoiled both from the tangible heat that was welling up almost visibly, and from the thought of all the men's bodies rendered down to fuel that heat.

'Wuffa!'

The Atheling sprang up from the chair and came forward, arms wide. Wulfgar stood like a wooden post in his embrace, but if the Atheling noticed his lack of response, he ignored it. When he stood back, Wulfgar noticed that Kenelm was already there, standing at the Archbishop's shoulder.

The Atheling had seated himself again.

'How good to have you with us.' He raised his eyebrows. 'You are with me, Wuffa, aren't you?'

His voice was warm and calm, but Wulfgar could see from the play of his fingers of the carved ends of the armrests that he was twanging with nerves like an over-tuned harp.

It was hot, he told himself, really hot. It wasn't just him, shivering and sweating in this airless room.

He realised he had missed some of the Atheling's words.

'Honoured guests, of course,' he was saying now. 'The freedom of the cathedral close, isn't that right, Archbishop? And my house and hall.'

'We're not hostages any more?' The roof of his mouth was

painfully dry and his voice was a hoarse whisper. The thought hadn't occurred to him before, but of course, it was true. The treaty between Knut and the Lady had been rendered void the moment the Atheling's belt-knife had gone home under the King's ribs. He and Kenelm were free to leave. He could go home to Winchester...

But what was the point of going to Winchester, when the man he wanted to question was seated in front of him, clapping his hands and ordering wine as though this household had always been his to command?

'We want you to serve in the Coronation ceremonies, Kenelm,' the Archbishop was saying now. 'I'd like you to be part of the Coronation Mass itself, in the cathedral.'

'I'd be delighted.' Kenelm was looking sleek and pink. It was hard to connect this smiling visage with that green-and-livid corpse-mask he'd been wearing yesterday. Could he really be fatter? Surely not. They'd not been in York long enough. But that air of strain, of unresting resentment, that had always spoiled Kenelm's features had retreated.

Outside, a rumble of thunder had them all jump.

The Archbishop smiled. 'Knut's men would have yelped, *Hammer protect us!* for all their baptism.'

'But the Hammer didn't, did he? Protect them, I mean.' The Atheling gave a little bark of laughter. 'And what would you say that sound signified, Archbishop?'

Archbishop Lothward was still smiling. 'I would say it's the sound of St Peter slamming the door on their accursed souls, and throwing away the key.'

Wulfgar felt a violent shiver up and down the ridge of his backbone. 'What will happen to the little boys?'

He hadn't meant to speak: he hadn't even known he had been worrying about them until the words were out of his mouth.

'Little boys?' The Atheling was frowning.

Wulfgar was wishing now he had never spoken.

'I think Wulfgar must mean Knut's nephews,' Kenelm interjected smoothly. 'In Gloucester. His sister's sons. The hostages the Lady has been holding.'

'Ah. Yes.' The Atheling looked thoughtful. 'How old are they?'

'Nine?' Kenelm said. 'Ten, perhaps?'

'Not nearly so old,' Wulfgar said hurriedly. 'No more than five and seven.'

'You mean I needn't worry about them for a year or two?' The Atheling relaxed but Wulfgar, looking at his face, could see exactly what he was thinking. He wished, more than ever, that he had never mentioned them. His throat was still lined with soot and dust, despite the sips he had been taking from the chased silver cup.

'Whom will you send to Mercia with the news, my Lord?'

There was another, louder, boom of thunder.

When it died away at last, the Atheling said, 'Oh, I'll let the news filter through on its own.' He was really smiling now. 'To Gloucester, and to Winchester too, for that matter. Every day that my little cousin Eddi remains blissfully ignorant that I've won myself a crown to match his is another day for us to make ready. Word will get south soon enough: there are plenty of officious souls who'll make it their business to spread the news.' He stood up then and walked to the window.

They had changed the cushion. It had been white with gold embroidery yesterday, now it was green.

Of course. The old one must have been thick with Knut's blood.

The dead man had been left lying in that chair for a long time before they finally tumbled his stripped body down the stairs. Trying to forget his last memories of York's late King, Wulfgar found himself staring at the floorboards. They were freshly scrubbed, almost to whiteness, with still a few damp patches lingering here and there.

Knut had been wiped out.

Obliterated, with only those ingenious coins to stand as his memorial.

His right hand strayed to the hidden pouch where Thorbjorn's gold coin nestled next to the little enamel brooch. Knut's legacy. And, for perhaps the thousandth time, *God have mercy on his soul.* His index finger sketched a tiny cross: north–south, west–east.

The Atheling was still at the window. 'Here they come. Just ahead of the cloudburst, by the look of that sky.'

He turned back and settled himself down again. He, too, had been transformed by the events of the last few hours. That rangy, winter-wolf look that had characterised him as long as Wulfgar could remember had gone. He was pack-leader now, and it showed.

Slow footsteps trudging their way up the staircase.

What now? Wulfgar was dreading another shock.

To his immense relief, Ronan stood framed in the doorway, a look of weary resignation on his face. 'My Lords.'

If the Atheling had been expecting congratulations his desire went unsatisfied.

The Atheling frowned. 'Are you alone?'

'No, *herra*, he is not.'

Ronan walked into the room, to reveal Gunnvor standing behind him.

'Welcome.' The Atheling nodded at each of them in turn. 'My friends. You come as spokesmen for the interests of poor, ill-governed Leicester. Please, accept my apologies for any upset yesterday. And believe me when I say I will listen with more consideration than I gather my predecessor showed.'

And that, it seemed, was all the acknowledgement that yesterday's bloody mayhem was going to get. *The dead know nothing more*, Wulfgar recited under his breath, *neither have they a reward any more: for the memory of them is forgotten*. He lifted his eyes and found Ronan watching him. *Their love also, and their hatred, and their envy are all perished; neither have they any part in this world, and in the work that is done under the sun* . . .

'And you're a priest, you say?' The Atheling's brows were raised.

'That I am, my Lord. Ordained in Armagh in Ireland, but I serve the people of Leicester, at St Margaret's Kirk in the Gallowtree-gate.'

The Atheling leaned back and looked at Ronan levelly.

'And you speak for Leicester Cathedral as well as this church you speak of, this St Margaret's? In effect, for the whole Christian community of Leicester?'

Ronan nodded again. 'Such as it is, aye. It all falls to me. I'm the only priest left in Leicester, nowadays.'

'And we have your backing, and that of your congregation?'

'Backing, my Lord?' Ronan sighed. 'That's tricky to say, when I'm not privy to your plans. But Ketil's hard on his folk. He lets his bullies have their way with them.'

He gave the Atheling a long, hard stare before going on.

'We had law under Ketil's brother, our old jarl, Hakon. If you bring law back to Leicester, then, aye. I can't offer you help, my Lord, but I won't stand in your way.'

He closed his eyes briefly, and Wulfgar felt an upsurge of sympathy. The two of them had spent the night in prayer, a lonely vigil lit by the flames of the burning hall, constantly interrupted by the drunken antics of West Saxon and Northumbrian soldiery alike.

But Ronan, unlike Wulfgar, had evidently found no opportunity for a wash or a change of clothes. And Ronan was more than twice Wulfgar's age, and again Wulfgar found himself noticing the new hollows at his friend's temples, the extra grey in his hair.

Gunnvor, however, was looking as fresh as she had the day before. She wore her red silk overdress pinned at the shoulders with filigree tangles of silver, swags of crystal beads looped between them, all over a tunic of creamy, pleated lawn. There were silver polyhedrons bobbing at her earlobes and more silver winking out from the unruly dark coils of her unveiled hair. Taking his wistful inventory, Wulfgar had to fight a swell of bitterness. What, after all, would be the point of blaming her? She had been an innocent witness to the slaughter, just as he had been himself.

But he should have known she would miss no sleep over the dead-and-done-with.

The Atheling had lost all interest in Ronan.

'Gunnvor Bolladottir?'

'*Herra?*'

'You represent the merchants of Leicester?'

'I do, *herra*,' with a graceful bob and dip that set her trinkets jingling. 'Only the disaffected, mind you. But we are surprisingly – or perhaps unsurprisingly – numerous under Ketil Scar's new tax regime.'

The Atheling was appraising her, eyes narrowed, a faint smile on his lips.

'Why would they send a woman?'

Gunnvor arched her eyebrows, returning his gaze unblinking.

'Because I am the richest, maybe? Because it is widely known that Ketil Scar is my enemy? But' – and now she was laughing – 'nobody sent me, *herra*. I am here of my own free will.'

Wulfgar wondered again why he had ever thought that little enamel brooch would appeal to her.

'And no one else came with you? None of Ketil Scar's men?' The Atheling had a calculating look on his face.

'We didn't suggest it to them, *herra*. We don't want the chickens smelling fox in the wind.'

'Are they still loyal?'

'Are you asking me to give you names?' She showed her teeth. 'That can be done, but it might be expensive.'

'An old priest, and a young woman.' His tone was provocative. 'It's hardly the support I was hoping for.'

'But at least you know that, should we turn against you, you can fight us off without too much trouble.'

'Are you saying I can't trust you?'

'You can rely on him!' She indicated Ronan with a flashing glance and a lift of the chin. 'He's that house built on rock he talks about. But' – and her eyes met Wulfgar's for a fragment of a second – 'no one should ever trust me.'

'Let me set out my counters.' The Atheling sat up, still talking to Gunnvor as though there were no one else in the room. 'I have York.' He clapped his hands together, as though trapping a fly. 'Give me a couple of weeks, and I'll have York's hinterland secured. A month, and all the lands between Humber and Tees will answer to me.' He rubbed his hands together like the two halves of a quern. 'But that's not enough.'

'Enough for what, *herra*?'

'Knut was right about one thing: Wessex can't be fought with York's resources. I need to start moving south, setting up bridge-heads.' The corners of his mouth twitched as though at some private joke. 'The Lady of Mercia may not help me fight her brother, but somehow I don't think she'll stop me. So, I need a base in the midlands, defensible, with good lines of communication by land and by river.'

Gunnvor nodded. 'I see, *herra*. You need Leicester.'

'I need Leicester.'

They were both smiling, but the Atheling's smile faded then. He turned to Wulfgar, who braced himself anxiously. 'You brought me a message from Ketil Scar a few months back.'

Wulfgar nodded, wary. 'My Lord.'

'Remind me what it was.'

Wulfgar swallowed. 'He said to tell you, *when I need him, I will send for him.*'

The Atheling had received the original message with a smile, a word of thanks, and a clap on the shoulder. Only now, watching the tightening edges of the Atheling's mouth, did Wulfgar realise quite how that thorn in his flesh had been festering.

He felt a sudden, unforeseen spurt of anxiety on Ketil Scar's behalf. Much as he feared the Jarl of Leicester, he wouldn't have wished the Atheling's enmity on anybody.

Archbishop Lothward had been tapping his fingers with increasing impatience all through the Atheling's sparring with Gunnvor. Now he stepped forward, clearing his throat.

'Good! So, we're all agreed. We need Leicester.'

He clapped his hands and Kenelm was at his elbow at once, an obsequious smile on his face.

'Thanks to the diligence of my staff' – the Archbishop beckoned

Kenelm forward – 'I find I am in a position to assert York's lordship over Leicester's cathedral.'

Kenelm held out two pages of vellum, one smooth with rubbed, brown edges, the other fresh and creamy.

So, thought Wulfgar. This was what Kenelm had been doing while he and Ronan had been dealing with the bodies and souls of the slaughtered. Scratching out a fair copy of his forgery, or as fair as he could in his abominably poor excuse for handwriting.

The room was getting darker by the moment. The sky outside had turned a purplish grey.

The Archbishop was nodding benevolently at Kenelm. 'Go on.'

'I'll do what I can in this light, your Grace.' He unfolded the first of the sheets and began to read it aloud.

'In English, please,' the Archbishop said.

Kenelm stopped halfway through a word and started again, fumbling his way through an inelegant but reasonably accurate translation.

Wulfgar couldn't help but listen and nod. He felt as though he knew that old list of the midland monasteries by heart by now. And – to be fair – he could understand why it might have excited the Archbishop so much on first encounter. Read superficially, it did sound as though the taxes and renders from those houses, including Leicester, were due in perpetuity. And when one took into account the comparative impoverishment of the northern archbishopric after the Danish wars, and the magnificent achievements of earlier archbishops of York, many of them Lothward's own kin, it was hardly surprising that the current incumbent of York's *cathedra* should want to claw back as much as possible.

But...

But that list was two hundred years out of date.

But those houses had been looted and burned, their lands confiscated and redistributed, their clerics driven out.

Those few that still clung on could surely boast little more than a couple of old priests subsisting on a few hides of land and local charity: they were no more able to provide the Archbishop with the listed abundance of bullocks and timber and sesters of honey than they were to fly to Heaven's threshold on home-made wings.

He glanced at Ronan. The priest was quietly alert, pursing his lips from time to time, his eyes glued to the Archbishop's face rather than Kenelm's.

Kenelm came to the end, and looked around for praise.

The Archbishop nodded at him. 'The next one.'

Wulfgar tensed.

'*Ego Offa Rex*—' Kenelm stopped. 'I'm sorry, your Grace. Do you want this in English, too?'

'If you could.'

Kenelm had done a much better job than Wulfgar had expected.

He had to admit to himself that, had he stumbled across the worn, creased original of that text in a dusty corner of the archive, even knowing the complex history of King Offa's relationship with York, it might have convinced him of the validity of the Archbishop's claim.

As Kenelm finished, the loudest clap of thunder yet broke right over their heads with a rumble as deafening as barrels being rolled down a wooden ramp. They all waited for its final reverberations to die away.

'So, you see, Seiriol,' the Archbishop was all smiles now, rubbing his hands together, 'you claim Leicester for the world, and I claim it for God.'

'Let me see those.'

At the Archbishop's nod, Kenelm handed the pages over. The Atheling scanned them rapidly, nodding as he did so.

'Yes, I see. And how does this most convenient discovery change matters?'

The Archbishop was still rubbing his hands together, making a rustling sound. His broad, brown face bore an expression of intense pleasure. 'We send news of these documents to Ketil Scar. We make our claim over Leicester's cathedral. We ask for two hundred years' worth of unpaid renders. He has the cathedral and its lands. He is liable.'

The Atheling nodded.

'Forgive me, *herrar*.' Gunnvor dipped another curtsey as she addressed both men. 'Ketil Scar will cut off your messenger's head and send it back with these' – she indicated the documents contemptuously – 'stuffed in his teeth.'

'Precisely,' the Archbishop said. 'He gives us our excuse. And then we go to war.'

CHAPTER TWENTY-SEVEN

At least the storm was quenching Knut's funeral pyre.

Wulfgar and Ronan had been dismissed from the war council as supernumerary, but the torrential rain had prevented them from going far. They were sitting on the bench under the sheltering staircase, looking at the filthy mess left in King's Garth, watching the downpour hammering the ash and charcoal and blackened timber into a sea of dark mud. Steam was still billowing out as though a great worm slumbered somewhere below. The stench of wet, burnt wood permeated everything.

'So Edward broke his word,' Wulfgar finished, 'and he hanged them out of hand.'

'But your brother's still alive?'

'To the best of my knowledge.'

'And you want him to stay that way?'

'Doesn't that go without saying?'

Ronan grinned. 'Don't look at me like that, lad! I'm teasing you.'

'Sorry.'

'Let's try to work out what we know. Four men are accused of plotting to kill the King.' Ronan looked at Wulfgar. 'Edric of Amport, King's thane. Dead. Alnoth of Brading, King's thane. Also dead.' He looked up. 'Both ambitious men, is that fair?'

'I suppose so. I only ever knew them by reputation before Wystan's trial.'

'Athelwald Seiriol, Atheling of Wessex' – Ronan glanced up at the underside of the wooden treads of the staircase – 'and now presumably about to style himself King of York. Also an ambitious man. Would you say that's fair, now?'

'Yes, I think that's fair,' Wulfgar said, trying to match the priest's dry tone. He was already beginning to feel calmer. Out in the yard, men with sacks over their heads and shovels in their hands had come to prod at the margins of the drowned pyre.

'And Wystan of Meon.'

'The least ambitious man anyone could imagine,' Wulfgar said.

'Is that so? Really?'

Wulfgar thought about it, staring out into the yard. It was raining harder than he had thought possible, splattering droplets of ash-water and mud over his shoes and clean leggings. He pulled his feet back under the bench. The workmen were shouting at each other but the drumming of the rain rendered their words incomprehensible.

'In that way, yes. Really.'

'So, the way you read it, then, is that the plot existed? Edric and Alnoth were guilty. But King Edward and your brother Garmund Polecat, whom I remember well—'

'Don't call him my brother.'

Ronan looked at him for a moment.

'All right. Edward and Garmund see the opportunity to bring Wystan down by implicating him falsely, so Edward can reward Garmund with his family lands.'

'We're not his family.'

Ronan looked at him in evident frustration. 'Lad, if you carry on like this I'll begin to have some sympathy for Garmund, and I never thought I'd hear myself say that.'

There was a long pause.

Wulfgar stared at the spreading puddles, each one now running into the next and threatening to turn King's Garth into a single lake.

'I know Garmund is my father's son,' he said at last. His shoulders were hunched and even he could hear the furious resentment in his voice. 'But his mother was a slave. Not even a house-slave. Just a field-woman.'

'And that was her doing, you think?'

Wulfgar said nothing. He could feel Ronan's eyes on him.

'Do you recall what I told you once about my own blessed mother?'

'She was an Irish slave-woman,' Wulfgar said slowly, 'and your father a canon of Leicester Cathedral.' Flushing with shame, he said, 'I'm sorry, Ronan, what must you think of me? And – oh, Queen of Heaven – I don't hold Garmund's birth against him: it's not his fault, and the Lord knows I can't – and I don't – blame his poor mother.'

'So who is the culpable one here, exactly?'

Ronan gave him a hard stare.

'My father. Forcing himself on his slave-women...' He shuddered violently, feeling the gorge rise in his throat. 'Every time I see Garmund, I think—'

'Steady, lad,' Ronan said. 'I just wanted you to slow down a little and listen to yourself.'

Wulfgar nodded, still hot with embarrassment and revulsion.

'Go on,' he said, at last.

'So. After Alnoth and Edric are arrested, they're tutored in a story that's close to the truth but smears Wystan. Is that what you think?'

'In a horribly convincing way.' Wulfgar drew in his breath, remembering. 'They'd woven their truth and lies into a cloth so tight you couldn't pick a hole in it.'

'The King made a deal with them, but the Witan overturned it, and Edric and Alnoth were condemned?'

'Edward must have made a deal of some kind with them,' Wulfgar said. 'Why else would he let them go into exile?'

Ronan raised an eyebrow. 'Trying to be a merciful king?'

Wulfgar felt the shutters come down across his face.

'Just playing devil's advocate.' Ronan shrugged, shaking his head. 'I agree with you.'

'But why wouldn't Wystan swear to his innocence?' Wulfgar thought back to that exasperating conversation in the stable-yard in Winchester.

'If everything you say is true, lad, the likelihood is he thought he hadn't a hope.' Ronan sighed gustily. 'Despair's a powerful thing. Poor, poor man.'

'And Edward does plan to give Garmund our lands. Doesn't that prove the truth of Wystan's accusations?'

'It bears them out, certainly.' Ronan patted Wulfgar's shoulder again. 'And I suspect Edward was glad to see the other two hanged and silenced. Perhaps he knew all along that the Witan would never let them live. He could afford to appear generous in the knowledge he'd never in all likelihood have to follow through on those promises.'

'That sounds like Edward. And he agreed straightaway to hanging them the same day, too.' Wulfgar looked at his friend in renewed anguish. 'But if Edward's prepared to twist the truth and bend the law like this, then how can I do anything to save Wystan? Edward will just change the rules again, and hang him anyway.'

'Aye, lad, and I think you have to prepare for that chance.' Ronan nodded heavily. 'But you also have to talk to yon slippery Atheling.' He jerked his head upwards. 'For your own peace of mind, if nowt else.'

Wulfgar bit his lip. 'I know.' But something else was nagging at him. 'Ronan, the day before yesterday—'

It was almost impossible to cast his thoughts back, past the shield-wall of horror.

'Mm?'

'You said something about Gunnvor. Not to be too hard on her. What did you mean?'

'Ach, don't read too much into anything I say.' The priest stared out into the rain. 'Leave it, Wuffa.'

But Wulfgar couldn't let it go so easily. 'Tell me.'

Ronan spread out his grimy hands and contemplated them. 'Faith, she'd never confess it, would Cat's-Eyes, but she's had a very sheltered life, you know.'

'*Sheltered?*' Wulfgar swivelled to gape at the priest, thinking of some of the things he'd heard Gunnvor say, and seen her do.

'Aye, in some ways she has. It depends how you define it. Ach, yes, she always comes out fighting. But look at where she's come from. Adored pet of a shocking-rich father. No mother, no siblings to share the sunlight. And then the last few years as the Jarl's woman.'

'But I thought Hakon never married her.'

Ronan shrugged. 'The Danes, they don't see marriage quite the way we do. She had all the trappings of marriage – carried the mead round in his hall, shared his bed – though the state Hakon was in, I don't suppose there was much going on there.' He stared out across the courtyard. Its far side was hardly visible through the pouring curtain of water. 'Will this rain never end?'

Wulfgar was suddenly aware of his heart, beating so hard that he felt nauseated.

'That side of things worrying you, lad?' Ronan laughed, but without any real amusement. 'Hakon was neither a young man, nor a well one. And he liked his wine unwatered. There was never a sign of childer, any road. To no one's great surprise. As I just told you, Cat's-Eyes has had a much more sheltered life than she knows of. There's plenty of lasses her age married to hard-fisted men, lasses who've had ten bairns by now.' He shifted his weight on the bench and yawned. 'A more sheltered life than she knew, I should say. The last few months, since Hakon died, have opened her eyes a little.'

'Richest woman in the Five Boroughs?' The words left a bitter taste in Wulfgar's mouth.

'It's what they call her, sure enough. And there are a lot of men out there who fancy a bit of that. But they go about it the wrong way. Grab, grab, grab. She doesn't like it.'

Wulfgar thought of Gunnvor's fastidious, cynical nature. 'I can understand that.'

Ronan sighed even more deeply.

'I've known that lass since she was knee-high to a handworm, and I fret about her. I'd like to see her settled, and soon. I'm afraid of what she might find herself doing.'

Wulfgar nodded. He had no idea what to say. When he did open his mouth, it was to find himself asking another question that had been preying on him for the last day. 'Ronan, are you ill?'

'Ill? Nay, lad. Just getting too old for this game, and dog-tired. But not half as tired as you, by the look of you. Lean on my shoulder, if you like, and close your eyes.'

Pounding footsteps on the wooden stairs above his head woke him. It felt as though only a moment had passed, though the painful ache in his neck suggested he hadn't moved for some time. He blinked in confusion. He had sagged sideways, his head lolling at an awkward angle.

The clattering of feet had given way to shouting: there were men running across the courtyard and horses were being led from the stables. There was the Atheling, vaulting into his saddle: Wulfgar knew him at once, even with the hood of his cloak up around his head. He was in the company of a couple of dozen of his men, and they were riding through the veil of rain and out of the gates.

'What's happening?' He had been startled out of deep sleep and was still hopelessly thick-headed. 'Is he attacking Leicester?'

'I should have brought my clogs.' Gunnvor was looking at the filthy yard with an expression of extreme disdain.

He levered himself off Ronan's shoulder, uncomfortably aware of the priest's amusement. 'What's going on?'

'Make room for me to sit down, Wulfgar Soft-Hands, and I'll tell you.' She settled herself on the edge of the bench, spreading out her cloak. 'Let's hope Knut kept his gutters well maintained.

This rain should clear out some of the worst muck, at least.'

'Go on, lass.' Ronan yawned hugely. 'What have you and your fellow plotters been conniving at, since Wulfgar here and I were told to clear out?'

Gunnvor ignored him.

'I like your Atheling,' she said to Wulfgar. She looked at him, her head tipped to one side, her eyes gleaming. 'Move up a bit. I like him very much indeed. I like the way he does business. No nonsense.'

'You mean he *has* gone to attack Ketil Scar? Already?'

'Not quite yet. He's gone off to meet some of his new subjects.' She laughed softly. 'By midday yesterday he had already sent out harbingers to the Wolds and north into Ryedale and west, to tell the Yorkshire drengs what had happened. Knut wasn't even cold.'

'He's gone away?' Wulfgar was shocked into wakefulness. 'But I need to talk to him!'

'He'll be back for his coronation,' Gunnvor said. 'A week, he told us. As I said, I like him. He doesn't waste time.' She shook her head in admiration, setting the silver bobbing in her ears.

'You and Knut were planning to drink to your father's memory,' Wulfgar said.

She shrugged and nodded. 'So?'

'Knut was your father's friend. And now you're talking like this about his killer.' Wulfgar turned away, lifting a shoulder as if to protect himself against her.

'*Let the dead bury the dead,*' she said. And then, in a mockery of an apology, 'Oh, how foolish of me. That's your creed, I believe, not mine.'

There was an uncomfortable pause.

'Would you be happier if I'd fought for Knut? And been hacked down along with Thorbjorn? Truly?' She folded her arms. 'Men die. These things happen.'

Ronan snorted. 'And now you're ettling for Ketil Scar to go the way of his old friends from the Great Army days, like Knut.'

'And you're not, *prestr*?' She drew herself up very tall on the bench. 'You'd be perfectly happy for word of where you are right now to get back to the Jarl of Leicester, eh?'

'If it suited your needs, lass, I've no doubt you'd be telling him.' The priest was shaking his head. 'It's a bad deed we've done this day, I'm thinking.'

Gunnvor's face grew scornful. 'You want Ketil in his grave as much as I do.'

'In his grave, aye. That's as maybe. But I don't fancy seeing him with his head on a spear-end and the dogs at his corpse.'

CHAPTER TWENTY-EIGHT

'You stand here.' The Archbishop's chaplain glanced from the altar to the door and back again. 'Yes, that leaves plenty of room. There'll only be his Grace and the King. And a couple of guards, but they'll be over there by the door.' He frowned, calculating. 'I'll see if we can't assign one of the altar boys to help you: the thurible and the cross and the benedictional will be a lot for you to manage, otherwise.'

'Thank you,' Wulfgar said drily.

'You don't mind, being in here and missing the coronation itself?' The chaplain's plump, owlish face bore an even more anxious expression than usual. 'It's a compliment, really. The King is very eager to do this properly.'

'I know.'

'We just have to hope he's back in time. He chose the day, after all. Word came last night he was in Sherburn, so he could be back this evening.' He ran his hands through his hair. 'Just go through it again for me.'

Wulfgar stifled a sigh. 'I come in early and prepare the thurible, kindling the charcoal and getting the incense ready. As the Archbishop enters I fall in behind him, holding the cross. I place it in its stand' – he pointed – 'pick up the thurible, give it to his Grace. He censes the altar and the Atheling—'

'King.'

'Yes, and he gives it back to me. I replace it, pick up the benedictional, and give it to the Archbishop. I pick up the cross again. He reads the blessing while the – the King kneels before the altar. His Grace places the book on the altar, and we all process out again, with me in the lead.'

The chaplain smiled. 'Well, you're one thing I don't have to worry about, clearly.'

The rain had stopped at last. Three days of torrential downpours had given way to a more sweltering heat, of a nature that suggested further storms were brewing. Through the open door of Holy Wisdom, Wulfgar could see the towering clouds moving slowly across the deep hazy blue of the sky, behind the roofs of the cathedral. It was a relief to go out of the stuffy church, into the steamy air.

Tonight.

The Atheling would be back tonight. And Wulfgar would be waiting for him.

'Soft-Hands.'

He jumped. 'Cat's-Eyes.'

'Come on,' she said. 'Come for a walk with me. I want to talk to you.'

'Come where?'

She jerked her head and he followed her, nervous, drag-heeled and reluctant, wondering who might be watching. She led him under an archway and down an old metalled road towards the north-west gate of the Archbishop's enclosure.

'Where are we going?'

She slowed a little and let him catch her up as she reached the shade of the gatehouse.

'I'm tired of sly, sneaking, clerical eavesdroppers,' she said. 'Let's walk down to the river.'

The grass was wet and waist-high. She stopped just before the ground dipped down to the water's edge. It had been in flood, and whole branches and great matted tangles of grass were still being whirled along on the thick brown water.

'That's far enough.' She turned to look past him. 'No followers.'

'Why are you so nervous of being spied on? You're in the inner circle. You're part of their plans.'

'And you're not? I waited for you for ages, outside that church.'

'Holy Wisdom.'

'If you say so.' She reached forward and he flinched away. 'There's a clegg on your neck,' she said.

'What?'

'Stand still.'

He felt the feathery brush of her fingertips under his left ear as she batted away the noxious insect.

'Thank you.'

'Ronan's angry with me,' she said bluntly. 'He wishes we'd never come to York. He thinks even Ketil Scar's a better bet than your Atheling, now he's seen him at close quarters.' Her chin jutted defiantly, but he could guess how much she minded the priest's displeasure. 'Are you angry?'

'At your support for the sack of Leicester?' he said slowly. 'Yes, I suppose I am.'

'And you want Leicester saved?'

He recoiled at the jeering note in her voice. 'I don't want people to get hurt,' he said, painfully aware of how his mind was still running on the shimmering possibility the Lady had offered him. Did he really care about the people of Leicester? Or was it just his worldly vanity, hankering after that tantalising possibility of a bishopric? He pressed his fingertips to his temples. What did he really want?

'People get hurt,' she said briefly. 'Get used to it.' And then, 'I don't want Leicester sacked. Of course I don't. That sort of thing is very bad for business. But I do want Ketil gone. Dead or dispossessed or gone on pilgrimage to Jerusalem, for all I care. But he's ruining my markets.'

'And that's really all that matters to you?'

She looked at him levelly, her eyebrows slightly raised and her lips parted. There was green in her eyes, and brown, and flashes of gold, like sunlight angling between beech leaves to coruscate on the surface of a slow-moving, trout-rich stream. What had Thorbjorn called her? *Hatchet-faced bitch.* But poor, butchered Thorbjorn could never have seen her like this. It was as though he had called a wild peregrine falcon out of the sky and she had perched on his unbelieving wrist.

'You should know the answer to that question,' she said at last.

He shrugged, afraid of what folly he might utter if he opened his mouth. He couldn't hold her gaze any longer, and he looked away, along the overgrown riverbanks. They were standing against a dense thicket of elder, some sprays still with their thick, creamy, scrambled clots of flowers giving off an intense, unnerving tom-cat scent; others where the tiny blossoms had given way to the first green dots of berries.

Summer was beginning to give ground to autumn.

In the dark green shadow of the elder, the brambles were still in bloom though, their petals pink and palest white, their spiky shoots, yards long and as thick as a man's thumb, arching up and over the path, their tips ready to strike earth and root again. Up through the brambles and elder grew the nettles, some of them standing taller than him, their menacing leaves interspersed with swags of pale-green flowers. And over everything the goosegrass and the bindweed, strangling and choking.

The air was so hot and damp he was finding it hard to breathe.

He was trying to frame some way of saying, *I brought you a present*, when Gunnvor broke their silence. 'Ronan said you had troubles at home. In Winchester.'

He nodded.

'Your brother. Not the Polecat. Your real brother.'

He nodded again.

'Tell me.'

'Can we walk?'

She nodded and they set off upstream, along a path that was much used by cattle, judging by the frequent steaming cow-pats, each with its population of swarming orange flies. Large brown butterflies and small white moths fluttered away from their steps.

He rattled through what was becoming a well-trodden tale to him: the accusation; the farce of a trial; Edward's unexpected reversal of his judgements; Edric and Alnoth hanged; Wystan in prison. He glanced at her from time to time, but she was watching where she put her feet and didn't return his gaze. He was perversely glad to see that she too was looking less fresh now, the hem of her green dress soaked and draggled and dotted with the burrs of goosegrass, tendrils of her hair come loose and sticking to her damp forehead and cheeks.

He fought the urge to brush the strands of hair away from her face.

It felt little short of sacrilegious to be taking pleasure in her company while Wystan was shackled to a post in a shed in Winchester, while Edric and Alnoth rotted in the pit at Harestock, while Knut and Thorbjorn's charred and crumbling bones lay God knew where. But, since he could change none of that, since he could help none of it, since none of it had been his fault, then perhaps the angels and saints would allow him to be glad that he was walking here, along the line of these linden trees big and shadowed as cathedrals, with this woman of all the women in the world.

There was so much goodness in her, if only she knew it. If only she would let him show her.

Finishing his story, he felt a little, illicit thrill of pride in the way he had told it.

She nodded, thoughtful, and said nothing.

They walked a few more paces, and then, unable to restrain himself, he said, 'So? What do you think?'

'Your Atheling.'

He stared at her. It was so far from anything he had thought she might say. 'What about him?'

The corners of her mouth twitched. 'Do you remember what he's called among the Danes?'

'*Athalvald inn hungrathr*,' he said. 'Athelwald the Hungry.'

'And he'll always be hungry, that one. Now he's King north of Humber, with his delicate, high-born bride. And it's not enough. It'll never be enough.' She tugged idly at the long swaying heads of the grasses, flicking the seeds from her fingers. 'And Athelwald *Seiriol*,' she said, lingering over the syllables. 'I've heard men call him that, too. Where does he get that eke-name from?'

'Seiriol's not an eke-name, it's a second baptismal name,' Wulfgar corrected her. 'From his mother. She was Welsh, though she took an English name when she married.'

'What does it mean, *Seiriol*?' Again, that caressing of the word.

'I don't care about the Atheling,' he said angrily. 'Haven't you been listening to a word I've been saying? What about Wystan?'

'Your brother the traitor.'

'Not a traitor.'

'No,' she said. 'A traitor.'

He stopped, mid-pace. 'What?'

'Wuffa, face it. He's obviously guilty.'

'Who?'

'Wystan. It stands to reason.'

Don't do this. He said, 'Are you teasing me again? Because if you are, please don't.'

She shook her head.

'No,' he said again. Then, 'How do you know?'

She sighed. 'Look at the facts, as you've given them to me.' She pushed the damp locks back from her face with both hands. 'And forget what you think you know about your brother. Think instead about the sort of man your Atheling is.'

He gave a jerky nod.

'The plot existed, would you agree?' Index finger of her right hand to the thumb of her left.

'I suppose so.'

'The other two thanes—'

'Alnoth of Brading and Edric of Amport.'

227

'*Já*. They were guilty, by their own admission.' She tapped her left index finger and the spiral of silver on her knuckle flashed in the sunlight.

Another nod.

Middle finger. 'Their testimony implicates your brother.'

He swallowed. 'Deeply.' He was mesmerised by the articulate flicker of her hands.

She extended her ring finger. 'There are no other witnesses, but with such a small and secret plot you wouldn't expect there to be. If this was really a confection of lies, you would surely expect more people to be brought forward to speak against your brother. A small number of witnesses suggests the plot was real.' She frowned. 'And, finally, Wystan refuses to plead his innocence. Five counts against him.' She held up her left hand, palm towards him and fingers splayed.

Wulfgar couldn't look at her any longer. He stared down towards the river, where a herd of almost motionless cattle was swishing restless tails against the unrelenting flies, and the children who should have been watching the cattle were splashing naked on the muddy beaches the Ouse had made in its flooded meandering, the water levels retreating after the lashing storms. The odd grumble of thunder still lingered high in the upper air.

'He refused to plead at all,' he said. 'Weren't you listening?'

Out of the corner of his eye, he could see her looking at him levelly, eyebrows raised in mild reproof. 'I'm trying to help you here.'

'Sorry.' But he felt no repentance.

'So why won't a man plead his innocence, if he's innocent?'

Wulfgar cast his mind back to that conversation with his brother in the enclosed stable-yard in Winchester: such a short time ago, he realised, when tallied in mere days.

'He told me that there's a plot against him to steal his estates, that he's in a trap.' He frowned. 'That it's been fixed.'

'By whom?'

'King Edward. And Garmund Polecat.'

'And Garmund has definitely been granted the land?'

'Garmund tried to give us that impression. But I don't know. I was summoned back to Gloucester, and then sent here. I just don't *know*.' He was finding it hard to think clearly about Winchester, such a yawning gulf seemed to have opened up between his life then and now.

'I think I'd call that cause enough for treachery,' she said drily.

'What? What cause? But – how could anyone conceivably have suborned Wystan?' He was feeling frantic in his need to convince her. 'You should have heard the witnesses at his trial! Everyone said the same: there has never been a less likely traitor.'

He found he was thumping his fist into the other palm, and shouting. He took a deep breath and tried to find a place of balance.

'Gunnvor.' He heard the crack in his voice as he spoke her name and realised he was on the edge of breaking down. 'All he has ever cared about is his land. And now his son.'

'Wuffa, there are ways of getting to people.' Gunnvor's voice was so gentle that he hardly recognised it. 'Some are easy to bribe. Wystan clearly isn't one of them. But perhaps someone threatened to take his land away from him if he didn't join the plot.' She shrugged. 'Or made him think that the King was planning to take it away – whether or not that was in fact the case.'

'You mean...' He tailed off, failing to follow her unstated implications, shaking his head and feeling obtuse.

'I mean, that if those other men, those ones who've been hanged already—'

'Alnoth and Edric.' It seemed to him very important that their names not be forgotten.

'Yes, them – if they were telling the truth, this could help us to understand how the Atheling got to Wystan. Not by bribing him or threatening him in any usual sense, but by playing on his fears. By feeding him a story: that Garmund and Edward were scheming to take his land.'

'And thereby turning him against the King,' Wulfgar said slowly. He could feel the sweat running down his back, his linen sticking uncomfortably to his skin, the wool tunic stifling him, his leggings chafing his thighs.

'Wystan seems to have been all too ready to believe this was the case.'

'Oh, yes.' Wulfgar remembered his brother's wild, weary eyes. 'He certainly believes it.'

He stood silent and still for a very long time.

'Let me see if I understand you,' he said at last. 'What you mean is that Edward may, *now*, decide to grant the confiscated estates to Garmund. They will have to be granted to someone, after all.' He searched carefully for each word before giving it the weight of speech. He remembered Garmund in the hall at Godbegot, his deep, lazy voice saying, *Someone needs to administer the estates till we do manage to hang him*. 'They can call it a temporary arrangement while he's in prison, then hang him, and make it permanent. But you're saying that that was never Edward's original intention? And that Wystan only believes it was because the Atheling fed him lies to that effect?'

Gunnvor's cynical edge had returned, curling her lip and putting a glint in her eye. 'By trying to forestall his worst fear, Wystan has brought it down upon his head.' She smacked her hands together, making Wulfgar jump. 'Oh, he's a clever man, your Atheling. I do like the way his mind works.'

Wulfgar said, 'But that – that would be ... I don't understand. It can't be true. It can't.' There was a fuzzy dark patch at the centre of his vision. 'What you're suggesting the Atheling did – it would be wicked.'

'Worse than stabbing your host as he's holding out his hands to you?' Her tone was light but her eyes were blazing.

'*My Atheling*, you call him,' he said. '*My Atheling.*' He sat down on the wet grass in an ungainly huddle, his head in his hands.

The water meadows around them were as peaceful as ever, but to Wulfgar they suddenly seemed full of menace, of fast black shadows. There was a screaming inside his head. He put his hands over his face, pressed the pads of his palms against his eyes until he saw fiery devils in the darkness.

It all hung together. He could hear Alnoth of Brading saying, *lies, like a serpent dripping its slow venom.* Believable lies. Hardly lies at all, just the truth given a little nudge off course. Poisoning Wystan's mind, driving him mad with anxiety, harrying him relentlessly, until there seemed to be only one possible solution ...

Killing King Edward.

It felt like a long time until he could breathe again.

At long last, he looked up at her. 'Gunnvor, the Atheling has always been my friend.'

She squatted down next to him and took his left hand in both of hers. He looked down at her strong, shapely hands, the swirls and tendrils of filigree silver twining round her fingers, the neat ovals of her nails. He could see her hands, but he could hardly feel them.

'You're cold,' he heard her saying in surprise.

He pulled his hand away from hers to rub his right wrist, feeling for the reassuring pulse.

'You're getting very damp,' she said. 'Come on. Let's go.' She stood up in one easy movement, and turned away, back towards the gate.

He struggled to his feet, his ears still ringing. He felt a sudden surge of anger against her.

'I can't believe it,' he said. 'I refuse to.'

CHAPTER TWENTY-NINE

'The hostage? From Winchester?'

Wulfgar spun round, startled. The man had spoken right in his ear. It was twilight of the same day. He had just come from Vespers, trying to forget what Gunnvor had said to him, and to work up the nerve to confront the Atheling.

'That's right.' He looked curiously at the stout, well-dressed figure. He had the look of a merchant: solid and prosperous, respectable enough, but not many merchants came into the Archbishop's enclave.

'Then I've word for thee.'

'A message?'

'Better nor that.' The man had a richly embossed leather satchel over his shoulder, jingling with little gilt buckles and strap-ends, and he bent to dig through it.

Wulfgar felt his guilty conscience go to work, but he could think of no reason why anyone in York should need to use some unknown go-between. And this man struck him as a most unlikely errand-boy. If the new King, or the Archbishop, wanted to send him a message, they had a dozen more suitable agents.

'Ah.' The man straightened up, a sheet of creased vellum between finger and thumb. 'Nearly got into a faddle there, thinking I'd lost it.'

Wulfgar felt a visceral reluctance to take the folded sheet from the man's hand. 'Who sent it?'

'Happen *thank you kindly* would be a more gracious answer.'

Wulfgar reddened. 'Sorry. You're quite right. Thank you.' He took the sheet, still folded, and looked at it, still curiously repelled.

The man sighed, and relented. 'I trade south to London. A man met me after mass at St Mary by Billing's gate, said he needed a letter taken to York. To Wulfgar, the hostage. Guards at gate said that was thee.'

'Who was he? I don't know anyone in London.'

'He was no Londoner, not by his voice. Open it, lad. Put thysen out of thy misery.' The man grinned at him. 'If that's all, I've work to be doing.'

'I must pay you,' Wulfgar said, embarrassed. 'Let me—'

'Let be, lad.' The man raised a hand.

Wulfgar watched him walk back past the chapel of St Benedict, still turning the sheet of vellum over in his hands. It was poor quality, he noticed without really thinking, dotted with little holes where warble-flies had bitten the living calf.

He supposed he had to open it.

It was a round, workaday, slightly old-fashioned hand.

Wulfgar, it began without preamble. *Please, come back to Winchester. Garmund is at Meon, living like its lord, and trying to have Wystan's boy Helmstan named as his foster son. I am very much afraid. Everyone talks as though Wystan were already dead. We have heard the frightening news from York and don't understand why you are still there. Your most loving sister, Cwenhild.*

The simple, direct sentences went like knives into his heart.

She was right: he was no longer a hostage.

He would ask Seiriol for proof of his brother's innocence, and then he would go home.

Why was he finding this so hard?

Crushing the letter in his hand, he turned down St Peter's way, towards the garth he still thought of as Knut's.

'My Lord.' Wulfgar stepped between the two guards and bowed deeply, to hide his confusion as much as to show reverence.

'Wulfgar.' The uncrowned King of York put down his stylus. 'I was just writing to your Lady.' He smiled that irresistible, dancing smile. 'What do you think she will make of all this?'

'She loves you, my Lord.' Saying those words felt as though he were taking carding combs to his own heart.

'I haven't had a chance for a proper talk with you.' He looked around the room. 'Fetch me a stool, Alwin.'

Wulfgar watched the boy's slight figure dart through the door and clatter down the steps. Alwin still looked as though he were dressing up in his father's too-big cloak and sword-belt. He returned within moments with a three-legged stool that would have been more at home in a byre, but the King nodded and thanked him graciously. Wulfgar saw the boy stand taller at the words of commendation.

'Now, Wuffa, what can I do for you?' He glanced at the window, checking the angle of the sun. 'I've not got long. I'm being crowned tomorrow, after all.' A quick, complicit smile.

'My Lord' – Wulfgar gestured at Alwin and the other guard –

'a word in private?' Bad enough anyone hearing what he had to ask, but he couldn't have borne young Alwin being in the room.

The King jerked his head. 'Search him.'

Wulfgar stood up reluctantly and allowed them to take his belt-knife, and to run their hands briskly up and down his body. At last, with a nod, he was allowed to reseat himself, and Alwin and the older man left the room. He was very sure, however, that they were just on the other side of the curtain, and when he did speak, his voice was hardly louder than a whisper.

'My Lord, I have to ask you about my brother. Wystan of Meon.'

The King nodded.

'Yes. I thought you would, sooner or later.' He sat quiet for a long moment, his eyes pensive, as though fixed on something far away and long ago. 'What an unworldly pair you are, you and he,' he said at last.

'My Lord?'

'No one would ever think you were brothers, at first glance. Perhaps not even after long acquaintance. But you've unworldliness in common. Where does it come from? Not from your father, God rest him.' The King shook his head, his expression somewhere between sorrow and amusement.

Wulfgar swallowed. 'My Lord, the plot to kill King Edward—'

'Are you as sorry as I am that that never bore fruit?' The King smiled. 'Sorrier, I should think. How you must hate my little cousin Eddi. And with every justification, God knows, Wuffa. Remember how he and that slave-born son of your father's used to lie in wait for you when you were coming back across the water meadows from your Latin lessons, before Grimbald moved into that little house in the cathedral close in Winchester?' He sat up

236

a little, his voice livelier. 'Do you remember, there was that one time I had to rescue you?'

'My Lord!'

It was a shout, torn from his throat by desperation. Wulfgar put his hand across his eyes. He couldn't look at that familiar, adored face any longer, not while he was saying what he had to say.

'Was Wystan part of the plot to kill Edward? Did you – did you talk him into it?'

There. He had said it. Let the heavens crash down around his ears, but let justice be done.

There was an agonising silence.

Wulfgar felt a craven urge to speak, to fill the empty space with any kind of inane gabbling but, with his fists clenched, his teeth gritted and his eyes fixed to those well-scrubbed floorboards, he managed to remain still and mute.

At long last, he heard a rustle, a scrape of wood on wood and the creak of a floorboard.

'Wuffa?' The King was crouching at his side. 'Look at me.'

Slowly, reluctantly, he turned his eyes to the other man's.

'What do you need to hear from me?' That humorous, mobile face, those warm brown eyes: they revealed nothing but concern. 'This is tearing you apart, isn't it?'

He nodded stiffly.

'You want me to tell you that he is innocent? That he has never had any part in my wicked machinations? That he loves King Edward?' Seiriol shook his head. 'How could anyone love both you and Eddi? And be very certain, Wuffa, your brother loves you dearly.'

'The Lady.' He stopped and started again. 'My Lady – she loves me, and she loves King Edward.'

237

'Oh, Fleda!' The King crowed with laughter. 'Darling Fleda! And she loves me, and she loves the Bishop of Worcester and half the world besides!' The King dropped his voice. 'That's if a tenth of the rumours that come to my ears are true.' He shook his head.

'My Lord!'

'Wuffa, how I wish I could tell you that your brother Wystan was as innocent of ill-wishing King Edward as any newborn lamb. But of course he's not, any more than I am, or you are yourself.' He stood up. 'But I can promise you this, Wuffa: Wystan never wanted to kill Edward.'

He stretched out a hand to Wulfgar. 'Come on, old friend. Have a cup of wine with me, and smile. Stay for my coronation tomorrow, then go home and do your damnedest to save your brother's life.'

Wulfgar looked at the offered hand, strong and tanned, with an ancient scar white across the knuckles.

He longed to take it.

'Can you say that again, my Lord King?' He half-hated himself for his graceless, grudging disbelief.

'I can do better than that.' The King smiled. 'Come with me to Holy Wisdom and I'll kneel before the altar and swear it on my hopes of salvation. By any saint you care to name.' He seemed elated suddenly. Now he was holding out both hands. 'Come on, Wuffa! Let's go there now.'

Clean hands. Strong hands. Hands that could dispense both justice and mercy. Hands that would be sure on the reins, steady on the tiller, guiding a kingdom.

'There's no need, my Lord. I believe you.' Wulfgar looked up at the older man's face with an overpowering sense of relief and gratitude. *Deo gratias.* 'Of course I believe you.'

CHAPTER THIRTY

Holy Wisdom, York

Wulfgar checked the thurible for the fifth or sixth time. The charcoal had bedded down and was smouldering obediently. The little lidded dish containing the incense was to hand, with its spoon. Before his arrival, the candles and lamps had already been lit in the great circular polycandelon, which hung like a glimmering diadem of metal hammered and soldered fine as spiderweb above the high altar. The air in Holy Wisdom was stuffy and he found himself longing for another mighty thunderstorm to cleanse the atmosphere. At least the still air meant that the candles were burning down slowly and evenly.

He had wanted to go straight to Winchester and proclaim Wystan's innocence from the rooftops and the borough walls, but he had been persuaded to stay one more day in York. Kenelm was in the cathedral, one of many clerics participating in the coronation liturgy, but Wulfgar had been singled out for this more personal ritual. The look of bitter envy on Kenelm's face had confirmed his decision.

Somewhere out there, momentous events were happening. The Archbishop would be solemnly intoning prayers fitting for a coronation over the figure of Athelwald Seiriol – Wulfgar was finding it increasingly easy to think of him as *the King* – who would be lying prostrate before the high altar in the cathedral. The freemen of York – merchants and soldiers and landowners alike – would be acclaiming him as their ruler. With Elfled serene at his side, he would be processing through the streets, sumptuously clad and triumphant. A mighty prince, come into his own at last.

And then the last element in the ceremony before the great feast: a private, and unprecedented, concluding blessing in Holy Wisdom, the church of the Northumbrian Kings.

Knut had been dead for a week.

There had been no protest, no rallying of support, from the Danish kindreds of the city's hinterland.

'Faith, they've got too much to lose,' Ronan had said. 'They're farmers these days, not fighters. Happen it's heads down, and get the crops in.' His face was freighted with sadness. 'If only more men thought like that, eh, lad?'

Wulfgar found himself nervously checking the thurible again, for lack of anything better to do. Of course they were running late; it was only to be expected, with all the elaborate to-ing and fro-ing. He would have to be careful when they did get to Holy Wisdom, with the tricky juggling expected of him with incense burner and cross and benedictional, especially as he was in a borrowed alb which was too long for him, and a tunicle which was too wide, embroidered though it might be with silver and gold thread. There had been no sign of the altar boy whom the chaplain had half-promised him.

No doubt the man had forgotten, with all the other claims on his attention.

His stomach was tight and acidic. There was nothing to occupy him other than prowling, picking up and replacing a candlestick, straightening the little volume of benedictions where it lay on the pristine white linen of the high altar, wandering to one or another of the lesser altars and peering at their icons and votives. He checked again that the grand processional cross was stored just inside the door, just where it had been when he had last checked it a few moments earlier, and he hefted it once more, tested the weight, brought it down to peer closely at the engraved silver plaques. It was a good eight feet in length, but he'd handled longer, less wieldy ones in his time. Peering outside, he could see the crowds still waiting: the cathedral doors weren't visible from here but he would have plenty of warning when the new King and the Archbishop did emerge into the sunlight.

He was just putting the cross back on its stand when he caught a flicker of movement out of the corner of his eye.

Something had shimmered past an archway, up in the gallery.

Had a sparrow fluttered in and got trapped?

He would have to try and get it out, before it panicked and soiled the altar cloth.

He watched again for a long moment.

There was no sign of anything there now, and he had just decided that his overactive imagination had dreamed it, when he heard a faint sound. Had he not already been alert he would have heard nothing.

'Hello?' he called, tentative.

Silence.

He cleared his throat. 'Is someone there?'

There was no response, but he decided to go up to the gallery anyway and check. It would take no more than a moment and it would give him something to do.

He groped his way up the narrow stair, wary of the cobwebbed walls and his borrowed splendour. The gallery curved away from him to right and left. He set off to the left, whence he thought the sound had come, and peered through the arches at altar after altar.

No one.

There seemed nowhere to hide.

He was just about to turn and go down again when his ear caught the quick, furtive scuff of leather on stone, somewhere behind him.

Picking up his skirts, he turned and pelted back towards the door to the stairs.

Someone was there, wrestling with the heavy iron ring.

A slight figure, a thick plait of mouse-brown hair falling down her back, a blue dress almost grey in the dim light.

He recognised her at once, although he couldn't call her name to mind.

'Don't be afraid! It's me.'

He was at her side now. She was still scrabbling at the ring.

'What's the matter? Can I help?'

Gerd, that was the child's name.

'*Gerd.*'

She turned and saw him. Her eyes went painfully wide, and she turned for the door again.

'Gerd,' he said again. 'I'm Wulfgar. You combed my hair.' It sounded fatuous, but it was the best he could manage. 'Last week. Don't you remember?'

And the sheer incongruity of it seemed to get through to her.

She threw her head back and breathed in, blinking furiously. Then she nodded. '*Já*. I remember.'

'Why were you running away?'

'I – I wasn't sure I should be here.' Her eyes flickered sideways.

'Were you praying? Did I disturb you?'

She nodded again, but she still wouldn't meet his eyes.

'Were you praying for your father?'

She looked up then.

'I saw him die,' Wulfgar said. Suddenly young Alwin's face came vividly to mind, with his passionate devotion to the Atheling and his violent words blaming King Edward for his father's death. How many more furious, bereft children were out there, after these horrible events?

They must be much of an age, he realised, Gerd and Alwin.

Sixteen? Surely not more.

Gerd was watching him intently now.

'Thorbjorn died a hero, Gerd.' He spoke slowly, hoping to be given the right words. 'And a priest and I prayed for his soul. All night we prayed, for him, and King Knut, and the men who died with them.'

She was dry-eyed, though the freckles were standing out on her wan face. She looked so much younger and smaller than when she had been playing the confident hostess in her father's home.

She muttered something, he wasn't sure what. Then, very clearly, she said, 'They're all coming here. Is that right?'

'Yes. After the coronation. For the new King's blessing.'

Her mouth worked, and he was worried for a moment that she might cry. Instead she turned her head and spat, hard, on the floor.

It took him aback.

'You shouldn't have done that. Not in here.'

She stared at him for a long moment before reaching out with her shod foot and smearing the spittle this way and that on the stone of the floor.

'Better?'

Wulfgar bit back on his indignation, counting and breathing.

'You really need to be out of here before the blessing,' he said, when he had mastered himself, 'but I shouldn't think they'll be here for a little while yet. Do you want me to leave you in peace, to pray?'

She put out a grubby little hand and grasped his white sleeve.

'Stay with me.'

She looked very small, so very young.

His heart wrenched with sudden sorrow for her predicament.

'I can't.' He suppressed an impulse to put his arms around her, to offer what inadequate comfort and shelter he could.

'Why not?'

'I'm going to be helping at the altar when the Archbishop and the Atheling – I mean the King – come. I've got to be down there when they arrive.'

'*You?*'

He felt a little affronted. 'Yes, me.' Why not him?

Her eyes flickered down and up again.

'Tell me what you will do, when they come.'

He stood up a little straighter.

'I'll meet them at the door. I'll walk before them, conduct them to the altar. I'll hand the Archbishop his book, and then wait to one side until he's finished reading...'

He had lost her, he could see that. Her eyes were focused on something very far away.

Gently, he said, 'I interrupted your prayers. I'll let you get back to them.'

She nodded, and turned away.

'Wait,' he said suddenly, groping in the pocket round his neck for the gold coin he had found by Thorbjorn's body. God knew, he certainly had no claim on it. He fumbled the heavy little disc out with clumsy, nervous fingers, and held it out to her.

'This is for you.'

He hurried down the stairwell without looking at her again, hoping she would have left before the Archbishop and the King arrived. Her hand had left a faint dusty mark on his white sleeve, he noticed, when he got back into the better-lit lower church. He brushed at it, but it wouldn't shift.

CHAPTER THIRTY-ONE

Wulfgar handed the processional cross to the acolyte to hold for him, returned to the altar, genuflected, picked up the beautifully bound benedictional in both hands and passed it, two-handed, to Archbishop Lothward.

Holy Wisdom had become a place of eye-watering glitter and dazzle. The Archbishop and the Atheling – the King, the anointed and now the enthroned King – were wearing white and silver and gold. Outside waited Elfled, the clergy, the nobility of Northumbria, the wealthy merchants of York, their bodyguards, and crowds of lesser well-wishers besides, but here inside the church there were only the two great lords of church and state, Wulfgar and a single acolyte to help him, and a brace of the Atheling's hearth-companions just inside the door.

And God, and His angels, their wings almost tangible in the thick air.

The King and the Archbishop had just been up to the gallery, and the King had sat at last in the seat of Constantine and repeated his coronation oath. The uncanny acoustics had picked up his voice and boomed it round the church until it was hard to tell whence the sound actually came. He and the Archbishop had been round all the altars, upstairs and down, asking each of the saints in turn for their aid and approval. Now they were returning, for the final benediction, to the main altar.

The heat and scent were stifling, intoxicating, the air swimming and shimmering above the candle flames.

The Archbishop bowed and Wulfgar retreated, taking careful steps backwards until he felt the security of the pillar against his shoulder blades and the small of his back. He received the cross again from the acolyte. The new King was kneeling before the altar now, his head bent under the golden diadem that signified his sovereignty, the Archbishop standing in front of him, head bowed over the still-closed book.

Wulfgar blinked.

It really was very hot.

He had the sudden, shaming notion that he was going to faint. Shadows were swimming, growing longer and shorter as he watched: the room looked as though it was moving.

Then something made him look up.

The great metal polycandelon was swaying, just a little.

There was no time to think of a plan.

No time to shout a warning, even.

He hurtled forward, head lowered, still holding the cross. Barrelling into the Archbishop, shoving him out of the way, turning to grab the King's arm, hauling him to his feet, throwing both of them sideways, tripping over the shaft of the cross that, somehow, he was still holding.

He was still too close to the altar. If the polycandelon came down now he would be underneath it. The cross was still tangled up between his shins, in the folds of his vestments. Frantic, he struggled to stand.

And found the point of a spear at his throat.

The two guards stationed within the doorway had come rushing forwards. One was holding him at bay. The other was helping the King to his feet.

The Archbishop was glaring at him, furious, uncomprehending.

Wulfgar gently laid down the cross and lifted his hands, a gesture of helplessness, of prayer. The guard held the spear-tip level with his throat.

'It was going to fall,' he stammered. 'I thought it was going to fall.'

The King seemed to be recovering most quickly.

'You thought it was going to come down on top of us? That great lamp?' He gestured impatiently at the guard. 'Let him up.'

Wulfgar nodded, clambering slowly to his feet and backing away from that honed spear-tip.

'My Lord, I'm sorry if I made a foolish error of judgement. I acted in good faith.'

He was beginning to shake, now that the danger seemed past.

Past, or imaginary?

They were all looking up at the polycandelon now. It was motionless. Fifteen candles and fifteen oil lamps burned with a steady flame in the airless church.

'It was moving, my Lords,' Wulfgar said. He had little hope that they would believe him. 'I would swear by all my hopes of Heaven that it was moving.'

'The last thing I need today is a hysterical little subdeacon.' The Archbishop had muttered the words through gritted teeth, but

Wulfgar knew he had been meant to overhear. 'Shall we—'

And the polycandelon crashed to the floor.

The sound was overpowering, a great smash and shatter of glass, and a clang of metal on stone like a great bell, echoing, and reverberating and humming in the stonework of the church for an eternity.

The central well of the church had gone dark.

No one moved.

It had missed Wulfgar, but only by inches: he felt the rush of wind as it came down, and now his feet were spattered with hot oil and broken glass. The great ring had bounced off the altar on its way down, gouging the stone slab, and was itself buckled and broken. The altar candles had been knocked sideways, but their wicks were still smouldering, and oil was spilling across the altar cloth. Even as Wulfgar watched, frozen and horrified and heart-broken at the destruction of so much beautiful craftsmanship, wicked little flames began to spring up from the surface of the linen.

'Put that out!'

It was the new King. He gestured brusquely at Wulfgar and the equally shocked acolyte. 'You two' – he wheeled on the men-at-arms, one of whom still had his spear levelled at Wulfgar – 'come with me. If someone did this on purpose, we'll find them.'

Wulfgar stepped carefully towards the altar, the broken glass crunching like ice under his thin-soled shoes. The stains from the oil that were splattered across his beautiful tunicle would never come clean. He and the acolyte tried to pull the burning altar cloth out by its edges from under the twisted metal, but it wouldn't come.

'Leave it.'

It was the Archbishop, sounding irritable.

'It'll burn itself out.' He looked around at the shattered glass and metal on the floor. The candles and lamps from the polycandelon had extinguished themselves in the fall. 'Just make sure nothing hot gets on to the floor, with all that oil.' He glanced at the candles still flickering in the side-chapels. 'You' – he gestured at the young acolyte – 'snuff those.'

There was a shout from the gallery.

Wulfgar's heart was thundering.

The King and his men came jostling back through the narrow doorway down from the stairs, shoving the slight, blue-clad figure of Gerd in front of them.

'What were you doing up there?' The Atheling was breathing hard. 'Did you untie that lamp? Where were you hiding when we were up there a few moments ago?' He lifted his hand, and she flinched away in a half-crouch. He didn't hit her, but he gave her a shove that made her stagger. 'Give me an answer, damn you.'

'Are you alone?' The Archbishop was closing in. 'Was this your idea?'

She whimpered with terror.

'Your Grace,' Wulfgar tried to say. 'My Lord King—' He stepped forward, pushing between Gerd and the King.

'You were in here before us.' The King rounded on him. 'Did you see anything? Did you see her?'

Wulfgar caught a glimpse of Gerd's face, and wished he hadn't.

'My Lords, I know this girl.'

That got their attention.

'She's' – he groped for the right words – 'simple. Harmless. Look at her.' God and His Mother knew that just then, with her slack mouth and fearful eyes, she looked simple enough. 'And feeble-bodied. I don't believe she could manage that lamp, even if she were bright enough to understand how the counterweights worked.'

She was cowering, looking even smaller, even younger, than when he had encountered her up in the gallery. She put out a thin hand as she had done earlier, and clutched at the sleeve of his alb.

And, to his bafflement, the King burst into laughter. 'Oh, Wuffa, can't you do better than this?'

'My Lord? Look at her—'

'That's what I am doing.' The King laughed again, so loudly that Wulfgar wondered whether he were on the verge of hysterics. He struck Wulfgar gently on the shoulder with his fist. 'Couldn't you find a prettier girl than that?'

The Archbishop had been listening carefully, his shrewd brown eyes narrowed.

'Is that what this is about? Wulfgar smuggling in his shabby little quean? His mistress, on this day of all days?' He looked at Gerd with distaste. 'Is this how Winchester clerics conduct themselves?'

Wulfgar's first, furious instinct was to deny their smutty allegations, to shield both Gerd and himself from the contamination of their salacious looks, from the nervous, knowing sniggering of the guards.

But, instead, he found himself saying to Gerd, in a tender accent he hadn't known he had in his repertoire, 'Were you playing with the lamp, you silly thing? Surely you're not strong enough?'

And Gerd did the wisest thing she could possibly have done.

She burst into tears and flung herself into his arms.

'We've been in here far too long.' The Archbishop shot a vicious glance at Wulfgar. 'I'll deal with the pair of you later.'

'Turn round, your Grace,' the King said. The corners of his

mouth were still twitching. 'You're fine. Just a little oil on the hem there: there's nothing anyone will notice. You' – he jabbed a finger at the nervous acolyte – 'get that cross, and lead us out of here.'

As the door opened, Wulfgar felt the shouts of the crowd like a tide of sound bearing down on him. He looked down at the damp, snuffling bundle of young woman clinging to the front of his tunic, and he wondered what in Heaven's Name he was supposed to do now.

After a long minute he pushed her gently away from him.

'Come on,' he heard himself saying. 'No matter what the Archbishop says, we can't leave the place looking like this.'

She nodded, and stepped away from him, wiping her eyes with her cuffs.

Had she released the polycandelon? Or had it fallen on its own? The breath of God, he thought, shivering. He wanted to ask her, but he didn't want to hear the answer.

He took one side of the battered metal frame of the polycandelon, and together they lifted it down onto the floor, and then rolled up the heavy, scorched, stained altar cloth. The flames had gone out, but Wulfgar didn't trust it.

'What about the broken glass?' she said in a very small voice.

'You go home. I'll find someone with a broom and we'll get all this cleared up.'

CHAPTER THIRTY-TWO

The night was overcast. Truly dark still, although it was long past midnight. Summer was hurrying on. Wulfgar knew all too well that he had stayed overlong in York. He could have slipped away the previous evening, after the coronation feast, but there was one last job still to do.

He opened the door and stepped cautiously into the hall of the Archbishop's palace. It was pitch-black in here and he waited for a long moment, hoping his eyes would adjust. The hall was full of the Archbishop's sleeping retainers, or those who had not gone with him and the new King at least, and Wulfgar was wary of tripping over one of the recumbent, snoring figures and rousing the whole room. He would have to say he had been walking in his sleep across from the clerics' dorter by the cathedral, where he and Kenelm were housed. He was revolted by what he was about to do, but the prospect of being caught and having to lie and stammer his way out of it was almost equally repellent.

Inch by inch, he shuffled forwards, aided by guesswork rather than vision, towards the door on the far side to the right of the dais. He stumbled against a sleeping foot, but steadied himself, and to his relief the foot's owner slumbered on undisturbed. Although the new King and the Archbishop had ridden out of York that morning, those who were left had continued their celebrating of the coronation for a second evening, and Wulfgar had been counting on them largely having drunk themselves insensible.

Ronan was getting the horses. But Wulfgar knew he owed the Lady something and he had refused to leave without trying, at least. And this was his last chance, though he hadn't planned it that way.

Nor had he planned a visit to Leicester, on the way home. But Ronan had just looked at him.

'Do I have to?'

'Ketil will listen to you,' the priest said.

'You could tell him.'

'He despises me.' Ronan shook his head. 'He won't pay heed to me.'

So, unwillingly, Wulfgar had agreed. Before he could report back to the Lady, before he could attest to Wystan's innocence, he would do as his friend asked: go back to Ketil Scar and tell him of the army being raised against him. He also – and here, even alone and in the dark, he could feel his cheeks grow warm – he also wanted to leave York before anyone else asked him whether it were true that he'd been caught huddling with some town-quean on the very high altar of Holy Wisdom.

That story had spread like the Ouse in flood and lost nothing in the retelling.

And he wanted to leave before the Archbishop and the King returned. They had said nothing more about the disastrous incident with Gerd and the polycandelon, but he hadn't forgotten that look of vicious dislike on the Archbishop's face.

That his life had been saved, and the King's, seemed to impress the Archbishop not at all.

Here, at last, was the far door.

He trailed his fingers over its nailed surface until they encountered the latch and eased it up, allowing the door, on its blessedly well-oiled hinges, to swing noiselessly towards him.

Or almost noiselessly.

There had been a slight scraping noise and he stopped dead, but it had come from the hall behind him, rather than the door in front. He paused, holding his breath for a long moment, but there was no repetition of the sound. He slipped through the door like a shadow, and out into the little courtyard.

After the darkness of the great hall, the way through the yard was plain. He fully expected that the courtyard would be guarded. That the Archbishop's room would be locked and barred. That the Archbishop would have taken the objects of his quest with him, with all his other valuables. But he had to try. He had searched the muniments room in vain. There were only so many places they could be.

And the courtyard was empty.

He walked carefully across to the door of the Archbishop's private bower, found the ring and pulled, and again the door swung open silently.

It was like a dream.

He stood in the doorway, trying to remember how the furniture was arranged. The massive chair stood at the end on the right, he remembered, the dragon-prowed bed over against the far wall. He could see it now, neatly made, flat and empty...

'Wuffa?'

He thought his heart was about to leap out through his mouth. It was all he could do not to yelp in terror.

The hood of her cloak was pulled down low, making her a darker shape in the darkness. But he knew her at once. Gunnvor.

'What are you doing here?'

'I was wondering the same thing of you too.' Even when she was whispering, he could hear that light, amused note in her voice. 'I've been hearing all sorts of things about you.'

'They're not true,' he said, too quickly.

'But you don't know what I'm talking about.'

'Were you following me?'

He felt her hand push him gently between the shoulder-blades. 'We'd do better to have this conversation inside, with the door closed. There's no guard now, but there'll be one doing the rounds before long.'

He let her shepherd him across the threshold, and the grey rectangle darkened behind her as she closed the door.

'Yes, I was following you.' Laughter bubbled under the surface of her voice. 'I saw you outside the cathedral and wondered where you were sneaking off to, so cat-footed and sly.'

'You recognised me in the dark?'

'Does that surprise you?'

'What were you doing wandering around so late?'

'I'd been talking to the agent for the York dyers in Hundgate. I suspect I can undercut their current clubmoss supplier. The evening ran away with us.' He could hear her smile. 'And you? What's your excuse for this spot of house-breaking?'

He sighed, and gave in to the inevitable.

'Those documents. The old list of minster renders and Kenelm's forgery.'

'Kenelm? That straw-headed gowk who's so full of himself?'

He had to smile himself at the aptness of Gunnvor's brusque characterisation. His eyes had once more adjusted to the gloom, and he could see the outline of the chest at the foot of the bed now, although there was no way of telling its colour in this light, where everything was grey. He could hear the Lady's voice quite plainly. *Listen at doors. Go through document chests. Bribe. Steal. Lie. For the love of God, Wulfgar, how clear do I have to be?*

He squatted and ran his hands over it, trying to heft the lid.

'But it's locked,' he said, his disappointment battling with relief. He gave the ornate iron padlock a tug and a twist but it was a solid thing, for all its elaborate wrought-iron squiggles. 'I can't open it.'

'Why do you want them?'

'I've got to take them to the Lady,' he said. 'I promised her I would.' He had been trying all night to convince himself that his motives were pure: that this was only about keeping his oath of loyalty to his Lady. That he didn't have a delightful image, at the corner of his vision, of the Bishop of Worcester's face when the irrefutable proof of Kenelm's treachery was put before him.

She stayed silent for a long moment.

Then, 'So, you're on Ketil Scar's side, not mine.'

'How can you say that?'

He put his attention back to the padlock, gripping it with both hands, and twisting till the metal bit into his palms. It was a solid thing and it fought him all the way.

Wincing, and massaging his hand, he said, 'I serve the Lady. You know that. I have to do what's in her interests. And she's not on Ketil's side. Of course she's not! She wants Leicester back under Mercian control.' He could hear the equivocation in his own voice; he doubted he could fool her for a moment.

'Anyone who stands in the way of this attack on Leicester supports Ketil.'

Her tone was light, but it didn't fool him.

'All right then.' He bent over the chest again. 'Go on. Believe I'm on Ketil's side, if it makes you happier.' He paused. 'You're the one who said these documents' – he tried to put all her scorn into the words – 'would be no use to the Archbishop. That' – what had her exact words been? – 'that Ketil would send them back stuffed in the messenger's teeth.'

'Is this really Wulfgar Soft-Hands I'm talking to? You're learning fast, aren't you?' She was silent for a moment, then, 'What will you really do with those bits of writing, if you find them in the kist?'

'Take them to the Lady.' He tried to keep his voice steady. 'I told you. Not to anyone else. She needs them. She has plans for Leicester. The cathedral—'

'Don't tell me. You'll be the first bishop of the new dispensation.' When he didn't answer, he heard her chuckle, deep in her throat. 'Oh, Wuffa. I'm right, aren't I? Aren't I?'

He was silent.

'When are you going to stop hiding behind your tonsure?'

'My tonsure?' He lifted his hand to the crown of his head. 'What's that got to do with anything?' He was glad she couldn't see his hot face.

'And will you call on Ketil on your way south? Show them to him? Tell him an army is on the march? Tell him Gunnvor Cat's-Eyes is out for his blood?'

The dark hid the sudden reddening of his cheeks. Again, that

258

sudden impulse of pity for Ketil Scar. How could anyone hold out with Gunnvor and the Atheling in league together against him?

He took a deep breath. He could not tell her the truth but he refused to lie to her. Would she read through the gaps in his words?

'The plan is to get back to Gloucester with them. And I don't have any time to waste. I have to go to Winchester as quickly as possible.'

'Oh, *já*. Of course. To save your brother the traitor.'

'He's not a traitor! The Atheling told me so himself. He swore an oath.'

'And you believed him.' Her tone was rueful, almost amused.

He opened his mouth to protest, but she spoke first. 'Out of my way.'

Even in that dim room enough light came from somewhere to glint on her blade.

He took a stumbling pace backwards.

'What are you doing?' He sounded panicky, and he despised himself for it. 'Gunnvor?'

'Helping,' she said. And then, as she realised, 'You thought I was going to use this on you?'

'I—'

'What a very low opinion you do have of me.'

She pushed him out of the way, gently but firmly, and bent forward. Wulfgar realised she was delicately inserting the tip of her knife into the lock's aperture, testing and pressing with those cunning, experienced fingers.

'You're right,' she said. 'It's a good lock.'

He was still on fire with confusion. 'Let's leave it then.'

'Not so fast.' Her voice was tense, controlled, but he could hear the quiver of excitement. 'If you can't get in through the front door, it is just...sometimes...worth trying the back.'

There was a grinding scrape of wood over wood as she dragged the chest forwards a few inches.

'Fancy iron hinges, *já*, but they're only as strong as their nails.' Even as she spoke she was working fast, prising them out with her knife. 'That's all four nails from the first one.' She pressed the cold, sharp little objects into his hand. 'And, here, from the second one.' She was breathing quickly. 'Put them somewhere safe. I'll hold the lid up while you rootle around inside the kist. There's not a lot of play with that fancy padlock holding the hasp so tight at the front, but you should be able to get your hand in.'

Obediently, he counted the nails out of his hand, onto the flat surface of the bed. She had moved round to stand in front of the chest and was leaning forwards, lifting the lid up. He squatted down again and slid his hand inside. She was right: there wasn't a lot of room and the chest was a good three-quarters full. His questing fingers slid over what felt like leather bags stuffed with coin, embossed metal cups and folded silks, probing and searching and rejecting.

'Come on,' she said from somewhere close above his head.

'I don't think they're here,' he said doubtfully

'Make up your mind.' Impatience put an edge on her voice. 'This is heavy, and it will be getting light soon.'

He had pushed his hand in as far as it would go. The hard edges of the wood were pressing painfully into the flesh of his forearm, and he was just about to give up when his fingertips stroked something smooth and cool, a texture he knew intimately.

'Yes!'

He found the edges and pinched and pulled them triumphantly out. The lid thudded back down.

'Both of them?'

'Yes, I think so.' Two folded sheets of vellum, certainly. He peered down at them. 'It's still too dark to read but I'm sure this is what I'm after.'

'Then give me the nails back.'

Tucking the documents under his arm, he scrabbled on the counterpane for the little spikes of metal and dropped them into her hand. One stuck to his sweaty palm and, when he gave his hand a shake to free it, it rattled on to the floorboards.

'Oh, Queen of Heaven...'

'Leave it.' She was pressing the rest of the nails back into their holes. 'It won't be very strong, but they may not notice for a while.' She hefted the chest back into place.

'I have to find that other nail.' He was on his hands and knees, groping under the bed. 'I think it's rolled right to the other side.'

He got up and went round to the far side of the bed, next to the wall.

'There it is—'

Suddenly she was next to him, pulling him down against her on the cold, hard floor, in that cramped little space between bed and wall.

'What?' He fought her for a moment, startled and excited by the soft weight of her body, the pressure of her arm, the sweet warmth of her breath.

Then he heard it, too.

Quiet voices, the light tread of shoes.

Squinting under the bed, he could see the texture of the floorboards shift as the door opened, letting in that early morning greyness. It was much lighter outside than he had realised: it must be nearly time for the cathedral clerics to haul themselves from their beds and blunder their way to matins.

As though echoing his thoughts, a cock crew somewhere nearby.

CHAPTER THIRTY-THREE

Though it seemed a small eternity, the guards only stayed for a moment before closing the door again and continuing on their rounds.

Gunnvor murmured, 'Why do I ever agree to help you with your lunatic undertakings?' Her mouth was only an inch or so from his ear and her arm was still around his waist. Surely she could feel his heart, hammering inches from her own?

He rolled on to his side away from her and started to get to his feet, hampered by the bed.

'Don't forget these.'

He almost snatched the documents from her, then slowed, conscience-stricken. 'Thank you,' he said briefly. And then, touched by her concern to help but still confused, 'Why are you doing this?'

She pushed past him and went to stand by the window.

'Courtyard's empty again.' She nodded at the door. 'You go first. Where shall I come and find you?'

'Find me?'

'I want to see if you've got what you came for.'

'I'm sure I have.'

His mind was whirling. Ronan had said he would be waiting with the horses in the King's Garth. She would never forgive them if she knew they were riding to warn her old enemy of the Atheling's plans. He had to point her in the wrong direction.

'The cathedral,' he said. 'The crypt.'

'Where the old kings are buried?'

He nodded, hating himself for lying to her. He couldn't believe that she hadn't noticed. He felt as though his very skin was transparent, and the lies within him plain to see. Not just the lies, but everything else he was thinking and feeling.

'Go on, then.' She made a shooing gesture.

'Wait.'

He tucked the folded vellum sheets under his arm again and loosened the knot on the leather thong around his neck.

'I've got something for you,' he said thickly.

It was now or never. He got the little hide pouch free, his nervous fingers fumbling with the tightly drawn neck. He could feel her amused gaze on him. He tipped it sideways and a little disc, hardly bigger than his thumbnail, fell out into his cupped hand.

A gold coin, carrying the name of a murdered king.

He shook the bag again, but it was unequivocally empty.

She was looking at him, her head on one side, eyebrows raised.

He closed his fingers over the coin, his mind a perfect blank.

'It's not here,' he said.

'Another time, then.'

He looked at her hungrily, marvelling once more that the lines of her face could be so soft and yet so fierce at the same time. He felt quite sure he would never see her again.

'Go *on*.'

He went.

He could never remember in any detail how he made his way back through the hall or along St Peter's way to the gatehouse that divided the Archbishop's estate from the King's Garth. In the last week, the arches under the gateway had been unboarded, and he came through to find Ronan standing in the dawn, the garth full of blackbird song and the horses saddled and laden.

'Any luck, lad?'

He nodded.

'Well done! Anyone see you?'

He smiled. 'Gunnvor. She helped me.' He unstrapped his bag and tucked the sheets of vellum inside.

Ronan had one foot in the stirrup and was about to swing himself up into the saddle, but he paused, and stared. 'What, Cat's-Eyes? She helped you? Did you tell her our plans? She's not with you?' Ronan looked back through the gate. 'It's not that I don't trust her, exactly, but...'

Wulfgar shook his head. 'I only said that I was going to take them to Gloucester.' He wanted to admit to Ronan that he had lied to her, but he couldn't do it.

He tightened the buckles on the bag with a savage yank, hoping Ronan would leave well enough alone.

But the priest was frowning. 'And did she say what her reasons might be for helping you?'

Wulfgar thought back. 'She didn't. I thought she was trying to prevent me at first, but then she seemed to change her mind.'

He remembered, still further ashamed, that heart-stopping

moment when he had thought she was going to use her knife on him.

'Ronan, are we going over the Ouse-bridge on our way out of York?'

'Have to, lad. Unless you want to go a very long way round?'

'No, no. But there's a call I have to make. A house just over the bridge, near the bottom of the Mickle-gate.'

'We've time, and plenty,' Ronan said with exaggerated cheer. 'York to Leicester in three days, the way I ride.'

The thought of the guard on the outer gate of the King's Garth had worried Wulfgar a little, but the yawning lad on duty let them through on the nod. He knew their faces, and he wasn't there to keep people in, after all. They walked the horses past the little church of All Hallows of which Thorbjorn had been so proud. Wulfgar crossed himself and sent up yet another heartfelt prayer for the man's soul, and all those who had died with him.

They clattered over the bridge. The Ouse was back within its normal banks.

'Wait here, just a moment,' he said to Ronan, slithering down from his saddle.

He hoped they would be stirring. From the rows of houses around them he could hear yawning morning voices, and smell the smoke that was curling up through the thatch even if he couldn't see it in the early mist and murk. He rapped with his knuckles on the smoothly planed boards of the wall.

It was Gerd herself who opened the door. She must have been having her hair combed; it was unplaited and floated light and loose over her shoulders. Her eyes were red-rimmed, wide and wary, but when she recognised him her face lit up.

'I—' he looked over his shoulder at Ronan. 'We – we're leaving York. I wanted to say goodbye.'

She nodded, and he watched her smile fade. He could hear someone from inside the house, her stepmother or her sister, asking who it was. Gerd stepped out into the street and pulled the door to behind her. In the dawn light she still looked thinner and smaller than he remembered from his previous visit to that house.

'I made a mistake,' he said. 'I meant to give you this instead. The day before yesterday, in Holy Wisdom.' He had the gold coin ready in his hand, and he had been planning to ask for the return of the little enamel brooch, but the breeze lifted a skein of that gossamer hair and he saw it pinned to the neck of her tunic. The words died in his throat.

She took the coin wordlessly, and stared at it.

'It was your father's.'

She nodded again. She still hadn't spoken.

He said, 'Are you— you and your family – are you all right?'

She shrugged. 'My stepmother has a cousin.' It was hardly more than a whisper. 'He said he'll take us in, if we work.'

Her face was still closed and cautious. Wulfgar had a sudden overpowering desire to see her smile properly, to hear again that ready giggle that had so pleased him – pleased him and embarrassed Kenelm – on their first morning in York.

Only ten days ago. How could that possibly be true?

He said, 'If there's anything I can do...'

Her eyes flickered past him, to Ronan. 'Who's that?'

'My friend, Ronan. The priest from St Margaret's Church, in Leicester.'

'Is that where you're going?'

Was it wise to tell her? He surely owed her that much.

'Yes, Leicester, first. And then I'll be going back to Mercia.'

She nodded, looking down at her clasped hands. 'I see. A long way.'

Suddenly, to his horror, he found her clinging to him as she had two days before in Holy Wisdom, her head on his chest, her hair fanning out in a wavy, woodsmoke-scented cloud. 'Take me with you,' she said, her voice muffled against his tunic. 'I don't want to be a poor relation.'

She looked up at him, her hands still clutching the stuff of his tunic, her face fierce. For a brief, insane moment, she reminded him of Gunnvor.

'I am Gerd Thorbjornsdottir,' she said proudly. 'The elder daughter of my father's house.'

The door behind her opened and he found himself gazing over Gerd's shoulder into the eyes of Thorbjorn's sharp-faced widow. Her eyes were narrowing.

There would be other interested eyes, Wulfgar knew, peering from behind neighbouring doors and window-shutters.

And he could sense Ronan's amusement from where he was standing.

He looked down, helplessly, at the girl.

'Gerd...' Her grip tightened. 'Gerd, I can't take you with me. We need to ride hard. And anyway, what would I do with you?'

He felt her stiffen.

Her stepmother snapped something and stepped forward, her hand upraised.

Wulfgar put his hands over hers and gently unfastened her fingers. He had expected resistance, but he met none. All the fight had gone out of her.

'Gerd, I want to help. Let me know if I can help with anything.'

He stepped back, feeling increasingly useless and in over his head. 'Word sent to me in Gloucester will always reach me. To the Lady's hall at Kingsholm.'

Her stepmother was reaching for the girl's wrist, swinging her back towards her, hustling her indoors. '*Óhapp*,' she hissed, with one last glance at Wulfgar.

Unlucky... He couldn't argue.

The door had closed behind them.

Ronan's smile faded when he saw Wulfgar's face. He shook his head.

'You and your waifs and strays.'

They turned their horses' heads up the Mickle-gate hill, and out of the city.

CHAPTER THIRTY-FOUR

Leicester

They would reach Leicester before sundown. Wulfgar was still regretting that he had ever agreed to carry word to Ketil Scar. All the more so, because the ride from York had taken so long.

Three days, Ronan had bragged.

But it had been nearly twice that, and to Wulfgar's unspoken surprise it wasn't he who had been slowing them down. Ronan tired very quickly in the saddle and he had to stop and rest two or three times in the course of each day. His appetite was poor and by evening there was an unfamiliar sallow tinge to his skin.

Five long days to do the hundred-odd miles in a damp, westerly breeze and the occasional spell of heavy rain.

The wind had changed at last.

Leicester, he thought, and then headlong to Gloucester, to Kingsholm palace, to find the Lady. And then, at last, return in triumph to Winchester, with the Atheling's sworn word that Wystan was innocent. It was still only late July. He had weeks and weeks in hand.

Nonetheless, Wulfgar was thankful from the bottom of his heart when they had skirted the marshes of the Humber's hinterland and negotiated the endless branching tributaries of the Trent to pick up the steady, straight miles of the Fosse Way. It led them due south-east into what had now become a familiar landscape to him, the rich farmland around Leicester, where the branching streams flowed down from rocky Charnwood.

'Surely Ketil will be glad to see you back? Even if you're not friends, you're the only priest in Leicester. How will he have managed while you've been away?'

Ronan barked with laughter.

'No,' he said. Then, 'Have you learned nowt, lad? You still don't understand, do you? Old Hakon was a true son of Mother Kirk. A bad one, like most of us. But he chose his path and he stuck to it.' He shrugged. 'But Ketil Scar – Ketil endured the font and the white robe because his big brother told him to. Now he's rebelling. He wants to change everything his brother did, good along with bad. That's why he'd like to ruin Gunnvor, if he can't have her.'

Wulfgar chose to leave the last remark alone. 'So what does it mean for your St Margaret's?'

'It might be easier if Ketil hadn't taken against me. Or if I had a successor.'

'Your altar boy...'

'My little Kevin's twenty years off priesthood.'

'That's what I was going to say.' Wulfgar's horse, sensing his rider's mind was elsewhere, had slowed to a walk and was now stretching his neck after a succulent clump of grass. He yanked on his reins. 'You're in a cleft stick then, aren't you? Getting rid of Ketil Scar is the only way of making things better in Leicester.

But the only way of getting rid of Ketil Scar is to support this invasion.'

'And since when did sacking and burning a city make anything better?' Ronan completed the thought. 'I reckon my flock has had enough to thole, without that.' He sighed gustily. 'You've never seen a city sacked, have you?'

Wulfgar shook his head.

'A sack's not like a battle,' the priest said. 'There's nothing clean about it. And nothing prepares you...I was barely twenty last time. The young heal quickly. Supposing I survived another sack myself, I think dealing with the dead would kill me too, this time. Folk I'd married. Bairns I'd baptised.' He stopped for a moment. 'So, any road, we've got to warn Ketil.'

'We do.' Wulfgar couldn't see any way round it. 'We warn Ketil, and then I go home.'

They were riding through rich, open farmland now, the fields like gold damask shot through with just a little green as the barley grew close to ripeness, the flowers of the harvest scattered among it like so many sapphires and garnets. The trees were sending long shadows over ditch and hedgerow, stretching out eastwards as the sun sank slowly over Charnwood. They would be in sight of Leicester's great walls soon. It was a scene of great tranquillity. War was unimaginable.

Ronan said, 'Wuffa, I need to warn you—' He stopped abruptly.

Wulfgar waited.

The priest started again. 'Happen you don't remember the name of the gate St Margaret's stands on?'

'Gallowtree-gate.'

'Aye, that's right.'

Wulfgar waited for the priest to make his point. Eventually he said, 'Well, a gallows so close to the city would be rather unusual in Wessex.' Wulfgar closed his eyes against a sudden image of dark shadows against the sun, struggling their lives away up at Harestock. 'But maybe the Danes do things differently.'

Ronan sighed. 'Not that sort of gallows. I'm not referring to due process of law, Wuffa. *Gallowtree*.'

'You mean?'

'He's not dared sacrifice men. Ketil Scar, I mean. Dogs. Horses, yes. But not men. Not yet. It's too soon. But now, when he guesses war's coming...'

Wulfgar looked at the road ahead, between his horse's ears. It was widening out, becoming better trodden. Leicester couldn't be far now.

'He told me he didn't do that sort of thing, when I saw him in April.'

He reminded Ronan of the Jarl's exact words.

Ronan snorted.

'*Not for his own pleasure*! He would say that. I can hear him now.'

He was silent a moment, then he said, 'For his own pleasure, maybe, no. But with war in the offing...'

When the Northgate came into sight at last Ronan took them away from it on a loop to the east, outside the old walls and through the densely packed streets of the Danish town that had grown up outside the Mercian city, to his little church of St Margaret. Kevin came out to greet them with whoops of delight, his little dog running at his heels. They rubbed down the weary horses and left them with oats and water in Kevin's willing care, and then, slow-footed, they walked back through the streets and yards to where Ketil Scar had his longhouse, near the river.

Ronan was kept busy greeting his parishioners, who were clearly very glad to see him again, shouting his name and slapping his back and chaffing him for having been away from home for St Margaret's own feast-day. Wulfgar had nothing to do but smile, and nod, and forget names as soon as he heard them. At least it slowed down their progress.

Nonetheless, the long low curve of Ketil's roof, bracketed by its pairs of carved finials, came into sight all too soon, silhouetted against the sunset in the north-western sky.

'He may not be at home,' Wulfgar said, half-hoping.

But he was, and his sentries ushered them through.

At the last moment, Ronan fell back. 'You go in.'

Wulfgar stumbled, turning round, 'But—?'

Ronan was shaking his head. 'He's got no time for me. He knows you. You parted on good terms last time, from what you told me.' He gave Wulfgar a gentle push. '*Go.*'

And then suddenly the guard at the door was searching him for weapons, and he was ducking his head under the low, carved beam, and the steward was coming forward and asking the guard for his name, and he was being ushered forward to where Ketil Scar sat at the board, flanked by hostile, bearded faces. At least, he thought they were hostile. He was so dazzled, and the room was so smoky.

He fell to one knee in the straw, bowed his head, put his hand on his heart.

He heard the steward saying his name.

And he waited.

At last he heard that thick, guttural voice speaking low, saying something in rapid Danish, something he didn't (and, he suspected, wasn't meant) to understand.

Then, louder, '*Litill Englis-mathr.* Little Englishman. Little Wolf. What brings you back to me?'

He hadn't been invited to stand, so he stayed kneeling, but he lifted his eyes as far as the table edge and focused on the white linen, the red and blue and green embroidery. His eyes were stinging.

'I come from York, my Jarl.'

And at those words the mood in the longhouse shifted – he could smell it.

'What news from York?'

The patterns on the linen blurred and reformed.

'King Knut is dead, *herra*.'

'I knew that.'

'Athelwald Seiriol, Atheling of Wessex, is anointed King in his place.'

Ketil hissed, long and slow between his teeth. It was perhaps the most menacing sound Wulfgar had ever heard. Then, 'I know that, too. *Athalvald inn hungrathr*. Do you bring me word from him again?'

'No, my Jarl. But he has designs on Leicester, my Jarl.'

Dogs sewn in silk the colour of old blood and blue-grey horses and a green swirly linking pattern that twisted and tangled and branched and seemed to be nothing but pattern...

Ketil was growling now.

'Yes, *herra*. The Archbishop has found some documents.' He paused. The smooth, folded sheets of vellum burned against his skin, under his linen. He fought the urge to pull them out and pass them over before Ketil could order him stripped, and find them, and hang him for his duplicity. 'The Archbishop believes they give him authority over Leicester. That he can make you pay him geld. Acknowledge his authority over the cathedral.'

Ketil barked with laughter.

'Do you think that frightens me? Me? Your little Atheling and his tame Archbishop! If they come here I will burn their documents and make them eat the ashes. Go back to them, *hej*? Tell them what I say.'

Wulfgar nodded.

'Look at me, Englishman.'

He felt his gaze dragged remorselessly upwards. He managed to halt at Ketil's broad chest, the fine twill of his tunic, the great circle of silver on his shoulder.

He heard Ketil say, 'Tell them I will burn the cathedral to the ground with every Christian I can find in this city locked inside it before I see that happen. Leicester is mine.'

Wulfgar never doubted for a moment that he meant it.

'My Jarl,' he said loudly. 'You need to know, King Athelwald Seiriol of York is raising an army against you now.' He hated himself for saying it, for giving Ketil fair warning.

But it wasn't about Ketil Scar, or even about Ronan, much as he loved the old priest.

It was about Ronan's son, Kevin. Kevin's mother. All the people of Leicester, who loved their houses and workshops, and their pigs and hens, and the honour of their daughters, and their sons' lives.

Ketil was silent for a long moment.

When he spoke, it was in Danish. Wulfgar understood enough to know that he was reporting the news to his house-carls. There was a grumble, and a mutter, which Ketil silenced with a brusque gesture. He stood up then, swinging a stiff leg over the bench behind him, and walked down behind the line of his men until he reached the far end of the table. Wulfgar, his eyes still on the embroidered table linen, heard the lurching steps approach him.

'And have they marched?' Ketil jabbed a finger into Wulfgar's shoulder, nearly overbalancing him. 'Are they at your heels, little Hare-Foot? Eh?'

'No, *herra*.' Wulfgar shuffled round towards Ketil Scar, still on his knees. 'At least, I don't think so. You should have time. We came as fast as we could.'

'And I am ready for the fight.' Ketil growled again, deep in his throat. 'I must reward you, then. Let no man say Ketil Grimsson Scar is not grateful.' He was tugging at one of his swollen joints; a series of rapid jerks that hurt to watch, but the evident pain didn't stop him chuckling under his breath. 'Put out your hands.'

Wulfgar offered his cupped hands, his head still bowed. Despite the heat of the longhouse, the exposed back of his neck felt terribly cold. Something warm, small and heavy dropped into his palms.

'Thank you, *herra*.'

He brought his hands down and opened his eyes.

A massive gold hoop nestled in the shelter of his palm. He turned it, knowing without having to look that it was set with a carnelian the precise hue of fresh blood. The Bishop of Worcester's relic-ring. His own gift to Ketil.

He was aware of his hackles rising, of Ketil's gaze burning the crown of his head.

'Well? Do you like it?'

When Wulfgar spoke he was astonished to hear how calm his voice sounded.

'If you return my gift, *herra*, does this mean you withdraw your protection from me?'

Ketil Scar guffawed. 'Wetting yourself, little Englishman? Do you think I'm going to hang you, for bringing me useful news?'

'I only know your reputation, *herra*.' Again, astounding calm.

Ketil sputtered with laughter, like water thrown into a pan full of hot fat.

'I don't give gold away every day.' He gestured impatiently at Wulfgar's hands. 'Take it. Put it on. When I want to make a sacrifice to the Spear I hope I can find a fitter victim than you.'

More laughter, loud and mocking, from the men standing around the long table.

Somehow Wulfgar fumbled the ring onto his thumb. Even there, it was too big.

There was a sudden clatter and a shouting from outside the longhouse. A startled horse whinnied.

Everyone turned to stare at the door at the far end as it was hurled open and a dark-haired man came bursting in. 'My Jarl,' he shouted.

It was the man who had ambushed Thorbjorn's party back in Charnwood. The man who had served Gunnvor and then shifted his allegiance to Ketil Scar. He was taking great lungsfull of breath, and trying to speak through his wheezes.

'My Jarl, York is sending its army!'

'I know that,' Ketil growled in Danish. He indicated Wulfgar. 'I have better servants than you to bring me news. We have good warning. We can ready ourselves.'

'*Nej*, my Jarl!' The man was beginning to master himself. 'They have crossed the Trent. They are south of Newark.' He rasped another breath. 'They will be here tomorrow.'

278

CHAPTER THIRTY-FIVE

Gallowtree-gate and the ginnels leading off it were being transformed from a sleepy, midnight haven into a scene of frenzied activity. Three of Ketil Scar's house-carls were going down the street, hammering on every door and shouting the news of the impending attack. People tumbled into the muddy roadway in every state of dress and undress. Every cart was being commandeered, baskets of cackling hens and protesting geese were being loaded alongside folded bolts of cloth, and tools, pots and pans of every size. White-faced men were arguing with Ketil's bodyguards, while equally ashen women were shoving children over the tailgates. The air was raucous with the bleating of distressed animals and the cackling of fowl, and the names of relatives and outlying villages were being shouted back and forth as Leicester's frantic citizens made their plans for escape before the men of York arrived.

'The old and the ill will be abandoned to shift for themselves,' Ronan said grimly. 'All but the very lucky ones.'

He turned back under the low thatch of his doorway.

'We'll have to ride the horses again, even if they aren't rested.' Wulfgar hovered on the threshold. 'When are we going to leave?'

Ronan looked at him, his face floating fire-lit against the darkness of the room. '*Leave*? You leave if you want to. I'm staying. I'm needed here.'

Wulfgar swallowed. It hadn't even occurred to him that Ronan – after everything he had had to say about the horrors of a sacked city – would be staying.

Ronan was still looking at him, his dark eyes hollow and expressionless under his greying brows.

'You don't have to stick by me.'

Wulfgar thought of everything he and this priest had endured together. He gazed at him beseechingly, registering how weary he was looking, the creased skin around his eyes visibly yellowed with strain and exhaustion even in this poor light. He tried to say something but the words wouldn't come.

'I know you're no coward, Wuffa. I'll think no worse of you if you decide to leave. You're a valuable man to your masters, after all.' Ronan turned away to reach for something against the wall.

'Ronan, that's not why!' Wulfgar followed him, ducking under the low lintel. 'I've got to get back to Winchester, to Wystan.'

'Of course you do.' Ronan's voice was a little gentler. 'I've got no choice, Wuffa, that's all. And much, much less to lose than you do.' He was kneeling in front of the rough-planked box near the hearth that held all his possessions, and he turned back to his rummaging.

Wulfgar watched him, his thoughts roiling like milk in a butter-churn. Ronan was quite right. He had so much to lose. All those years at school in Winchester. Hundreds and hundreds of hours of old Grimbald drilling him in Latin. The liturgies. The psalter. The law-books and the histories...His masters had invested hugely in him. Undoubtedly, he was a prized commodity.

But was that all he was?

He lifted his chin. 'If you're staying, then so am I.'

'Now there's the pity.' The priest smiled wryly, clambering to his feet, his arms full of a shapeless bundle. 'Because I was going to ask you take charge of my harp.'

'You mean Uhtsang? St Cuthwin's harp?'

Ronan nodded.

'Aye. Take her to a place of safety. She's not a gift, mind.' The priest held out the beaver-skin bag. 'You're just her next caretaker.'

'Until I see you again, you mean.'

Ronan laughed.

'She's not mine either, lad. I meant, one of these days we'll see Leicester Cathedral thriving again, and then you can give Uhtsang' – he patted the bag – 'back to the saint I borrowed her from.'

Wulfgar couldn't resist unfastening the bone toggle and peering inside. The great-beaked silver-gilt birds of prey that adorned the arch of the harp winked back at him with their fire-lit garnet eyes.

'Do you mind if I play her sometimes?'

It felt the grossest of presumptions.

'Mind? Nay, lad. I insist.'

Wulfgar fastened the thongs again and went to wrap her carefully up in the spare linen stored in his saddlebags. This gesture of trust, more than anything else, was bringing home to him the depth of Ronan's fears.

'What will you do, now?' he asked, his back to the room.

'Pray.'

Wulfgar turned. 'But will prayer be enough?' He thought again of the ruthlessness of the Atheling's hearth-men, how Thorbjorn and his mates had fought valiantly and still gone down under that terrible storm of swords.

'Oh, Wuffa, haven't you learned yet?' Ronan raised his eyebrows. 'All prayers are answered.'

Wulfgar nodded, dutiful as ever.

'It's just that sometimes the answer is *No*.' Ronan grinned and clapped Wulfgar on the shoulder. 'Cheer up, lad. I shall go into St Margaret's and give sanctuary to anyone who claims it. And who knows, God and St Margaret willing, an army sponsored by an Archbishop may even respect my little kirk.' His eyes held Wulfgar's and he smiled. 'Dear heart alive! They can't be worse than the Danish Great Army, thirty years gone, any road.'

'Ronan, I—'

'Stop your gibble-gabble, lad, and get on your horse.'

CHAPTER THIRTY-SIX

Excellent advice.

He couldn't act on it, though.

When Wulfgar and Ronan had watered their tired horses earlier that night, they had left them tied behind the house to recover from the ride from York, their nosebags full of oats. Now Wulfgar, a saddlebag in each hand, one heavier by the considerable weight of a harp, was staring in disbelief at the empty hitching post.

'Nabbed,' Ronan said succinctly, coming up behind him. 'Ah, well. All's fair, as they say. If you're going on shank's mare, you'd better shift yourself.'

'Walk? To Gloucester?' But that would take him weeks. 'You don't think perhaps I could buy a horse?'

Ronan shook his head. 'You'll not find one, lad. Not if ours have gone. Even those with no time for the Kirk wouldn't have dared touch the priest's horse, without it was the only beast left in Leicester.'

Wulfgar, looking at the hard, straight lines of Ronan's mouth and eyebrows, didn't doubt his word for a moment.

'Then I'm staying a little longer,' he said slowly, trying to make sense of it. 'I must be meant to stay. After the battle, I'll find a horse from somewhere.'

Wystan and Judith would understand. They'd have to.

Ronan looked at him levelly. 'You might still find a corner in someone's ox-cart.'

Wulfgar let a little smile tug the corners of his mouth upwards, though he knew it wasn't reaching his eyes.

'Ox-cart? The way they're laden, I'd be faster on foot.'

Ronan nodded. 'Then the sooner we set up boundary markers and declare sanctuary, the better. And, Wuffa?'

'Mm?'

'I'm glad of the company.'

'Father?' A toothless woman, arched and humped with age, appeared at his side. 'They've all gone, Father.' She shook her head. 'Can the kirk take me?'

Ronan sighed. 'She won't be the last,' he said to Wulfgar, and, 'Gladly, old mother.'

They went back to the presbytery to catch what sleep they could.

At first light, Ronan shook Wulfgar out of slumber, and they went down to the river where he joined the priest in cutting hundreds of long wands of willow and staking them a few inches apart all round the perimeter of the church and churchyard and the presbytery with its little yard. Before twenty wands had gone into the ground they were joined by more of Ronan's refuge-seeking parishioners. As the priest had predicted, it was the old and infirm, for the most part, who had been left behind. But there were few so incapacitated that they couldn't whittle a willow wand into a sharp point. The long, slim green leaves fluttered like so many dozens of tiny flags.

'I don't see those keeping an army out for long.'

Ronan gave him a long look. 'We're not building a stockade, lad. We're making a point.'

Wulfgar bit his lip.

'Crosses, now,' Ronan said briskly.

Linden, this time. A dozen uprights, the height of a man, and crosspieces to lash to them with more long withies of willow. Again, they staked them around the perimeter, among the willow staves.

More people were coming all the time, bringing their little treasures to entrust to the altar, along with their lives. And every newcomer brought another titbit of gossip. If half of them were true, the Archbishop of York and his new King had had more luck in recruiting soldiers than any war-leader in the history of the English kingdoms, and more skill in arming and marshalling their troops than any general since Joshua outside the walls of Jericho.

And wings – they seemed to have grown wings.

Nearly all the rumourmongers were in agreement that the army was less than a day from Leicester.

Ketil Scar and his men had set up their camp along the Fosse Way to the north of the city, the route along which they expected the York army to come.

'With any luck,' Ronan said, 'they'll do all their fighting in the fields and never come near us until it's all over, one way or the other.'

They waited all day for news, but nothing more solid came to their ears. Ronan celebrated Mass as if it were any other Sunday.

By evening the churchyard was thick with the smoke of cooking fires and cluttered with temporary shelters rigged out of cloaks and hurdles and yet more woven willow.

'Wuffa, can I ask a favour?' Ronan asked.

'Anything,' Wulfgar said. He was weary and red-eyed from the effects of anxiety as much as the endless toil of the day.

'Don't laugh.'

'Laugh?' He had never felt less like laughing.

The corners of Ronan's mouth quirked. 'I know what you think of me, lad, in your secret heart of hearts. A priest with a sword. Singing lewd songs in ale-houses. A son, and never a wife. And no tonsure. Well, there's not much I can do about the rest, but would you shave me? Before it gets too dark and you take half my scalp off with it?'

Wulfgar put a hand to his mouth to hide a smile he couldn't repress.

'Is that all? Why now?'

'Oh,' Ronan said lightly, 'I suspect it might be politic to try and look as much like a man of God as possible. You're overdue a trim yourself, come to that.'

'Have you got a whetstone?' Wulfgar asked, looking doubtfully at the blunted blade of his belt-knife.

They submitted to each other's tonsorial attentions in turn. Wulfgar, pulling lock after lock of Ronan's grizzled, wiry hair tight and carefully trimming it close to the roots, was surprised by the difference it made. Ronan looked naked, vulnerable somehow, even a little foolish. Like a baby bird, before it had fledged.

Innocent.

Harmless.

Gormless, as Ronan might say. *Nesh*.

'Have you finished?' The priest ran a tentative hand over the crown of his head. 'Ach, that feels strange. Is that the best you can do?' Ronan brushed the shorn ends of grizzled hair from the shoulders of his tunic. 'Now, vestments. You borrowed the cathedral dalmatic once before, if you remember?'

'I—' Wulfgar looked at his feet, remembering that Easter Sunday dazzle of decaying red silk tricked out with gold. 'I'd prefer something less eye-catching.'

'Aye, lad! No point in looking like loot to any soldiery, even an Archbishop's. I've a plain alb you can borrow, though we'll need to pin it up or you'll be tripping over the hem. But I think I'll put my stole and chasuble back on, now the dirty work's done. They're not grand things, but I feel at home in them.' He grinned cheerfully at Wulfgar. 'And if it goes awry with us, I'd like to think I might be buried in them.'

CHAPTER THIRTY-SEVEN

Wulfgar, conditioned by his long years of stumbling sleepily to matins in the small hours, woke long before sunrise.

He felt a powerful urge to be out of the stuffy little room and under the sky. He unrolled himself from his cloak, pulled the long white alb that Ronan had lent him over his underlinen and leggings, and went to the presbytery door.

All looked peaceful and still. The birds were awake and singing. The church, with its luminous whitewashed walls and the cross on the end gable, stood proud against the cool, greying light in the sky. The rowan tree in front, a bell hanging in its branches, was laden with green berries. He paused by the little arched niche outside the church door with its flaking painting of St Margaret of Antioch, one elegantly shod foot pinning the dragon casually to the floor. It was hard to tell in this light, but he thought the saint had a look of Gunnvor about her. Not the sweet, painted face, but that proud neck, the arrogant head, the way she disdained to notice the scaly monster at her feet.

'Help me,' he whispered, and found he wasn't sure whether he was addressing the Martyr of Antioch or her flesh-and-blood counterpart.

What had woken him up? He shook his head, trying to clear the fug of sleep from his mind. There had been a noise ... Had he been dreaming about battles? Had it been the sound of battle?

Silence, other than the birdsong, and the crowing cocks.

He walked past the church door and into the little churchyard, the enclosure of the dead. He had spent time enough here the previous day but he had hardly had a moment to look about him. Most graves were unmarked other than by the long, green bump in the turf. A few had carved wooden planks laid down along their length, a few had simple crosses. Ronan had pointed out the grave of Hakon, Leicester's late Jarl, close by the church's south door and marked by a painted board.

Wulfgar found his feet drawn that way now. Although plenty of shelters had been put up in the graveyard, the Leicester folk had left a wide berth around this particular grave.

Three months, nearly four months dead. The sprightly summer grass and weeds were growing back over the lumpy, disturbed soil, but it was easy enough to see the outline of the rectangular grave, cut wider in all directions than the carved and painted board.

Wulfgar knew from Ronan that Hakon Toad had died and been buried with all decency, with all the rites that poor little Margaret-kirk could furnish.

He had left a good name behind him, too. *We had law under Hakon*, Ronan had said to the Atheling. That was a good last word: any man could rest proud of that.

From somewhere, a fragment from a Danish song came into his mind.

> *At kveldi skal dag leyfa . . .*
> *Praise no day before sunset;*
> *No ale till it's drunk;*
> *No ice till you've crossed it;*
> *No wife till she's buried . . .*

Queen of Heaven, but theirs was a harsh ethos.

He hunkered down on his haunches, wondering what sort of death he himself would make when the time came, what sort of grave would house him. Could it really be right that Edric of Amport and Alnoth of Brading were damned because they were buried in that dreadful pit at Harestock? What of valiant Thorbjorn, and poor, trusting Knut, whose ashes and cinders and calcined bones had been shovelled like so much midden into York's town ditch?

'Hakon,' he said, under his breath. 'Hakon Toad, can you hear me?'

He looked left and right. None of the sanctuary-seekers had yet emerged from their makeshift tents. He reached out a clammy hand and picked up a clod of earth from the grave. A pinkish-grey worm wriggled away from him, pouring itself back into the soil.

'She was your woman, Hakon Toad. For years.'

He crumbled the clod, watching black earth shower down between his fingers.

'How did you keep hold of her? What was your secret?'

He waited.

Was he really expecting an answer?

His guts were taut with a painful cramp that he realised after a few moments was jealousy.

Wulfgar was shocked at his own stupidity, but it didn't make the sensation any less raw.

Hakon was dead and rotting, he told himself. He could counter that Danish song with an English one: *Three bedmates shall hold you, Grit, and mould, and worms...*

And what gave him the right to be jealous of any lover of Gunnvor's, living or dead?

He tried to push thoughts of her away, but they nagged at him like fleabites. Would she be riding with the approaching army? He couldn't quite see her as one of the camp followers, content to jolt along in the baggage train.

Wulfgar curled his hands into fists, grubby nails digging into the soft fleshy pads of his palms.

'What do your hands look like now, Hakon?' he muttered. 'Bones?'

No, surely it was too soon for bones. Leicester's old Jarl hadn't been that long in the earth.

'Were your hands like your brother's, Hakon Toad?'

He could see Ketil Scar's hands in minute detail, puffy and discoloured and freighted with rings around the swollen finger-joints. He closed his eyes against the sudden and frighteningly vivid image of those hands in contact with the smooth, creamy planes and curves of Gunnvor's body, below all her distracting gauds and frippery.

He shuddered.

Whatever Hakon's hands had looked like in life, they wouldn't be very pretty, not now.

Wulfgar tipped forward on to his knees and bowed his head. *Absolve, we beseech Thee, O Lord, the soul of Thy servant Hakon from every bond of sin . . .*

He trusted that Hakon could hear him. And God.

Getting awkwardly to his feet, he wiped the soil of the grave from the knees of his leggings and was brushing what was left from his hands when he paused. Again glancing right and left, he leaned down and took another little clod of earth between his right finger and thumb. A handy dock leaf served to wrap it into a compact parcel. Delving down the collar of his tunic, he pulled out his pocket and tugged its thongs apart to tuck the little parcel carefully inside.

He had to hope no one had seen that peculiar little action. He would have been hard pushed to explain his motives.

There was grave soil still under his fingernails and he picked at it as he walked away. The circuit of willow wands and crosses was complete, apart from a narrow gap allowing entrance to the churchyard and the church, and Wulfgar stepped with self-conscious boldness through the gap, feeling a strange, shocking thrill as he left the demarcated ground of the sanctuary.

The Danish settlement seemed to be a ghost town, other than the encampment at St Margaret's. An unmilked cow lowed in protest from a fenced yard. A blackbird sang, loud and sudden from an elder tree heavy with hard berries, their green flushed with the first purple.

His feet were still pulling him on, willy-nilly, up to the old stone gatehouse, the *porta sinistra*, reminding him forcibly and unwillingly of Knut's former stronghold in York, and the scene of his murder.

Through the arch, and into the ancient walled city, home of St Cuthwin, the first bishop.

Bishop of Leicester.

It could be him, one not-too-distant day.

His Lady had said as much, and she had never broken her word to him yet.

He straightened his back and lifted his chin as he walked into the cathedral close. It was all too easy to imagine the awed crowds falling back as he walked under the archway towards the cathedral for his consecration, barefoot and humble, deep in prayer, oblivious to their admiring cheers. Through the gate, and there the clerics would be standing – *what clerics*?

Never mind. This was his vision. Clerics would be drafted in from somewhere – the clerics of the whole diocese waiting to greet him. Ronan of course: he would appoint Ronan his archdeacon – and at the thought he felt a thrill of pleasure. The cathedral doors would be wide open, allowing him to process into the church and be vested in a sumptuous godweb cope of purple shot with gold, a gold-embroidered mitre... The Archbishop – *which Archbishop*?

Canterbury or York?

Again, never mind. He would work out the details later – the Archbishop would already be at the high altar, with the Lady in a seat of honour—

But – this was a new thought, and an unfriendly one – would the appointment be in the Lady's hands?

If York's army were to take Leicester, York's rulers would choose Leicester's new prelate. And he knew as certainly as he knew anything that he had utterly undermined his chances of favour from the hands of York's Archbishop. He looked at the cathedral with new eyes, fierce, proprietary eyes. It looked smaller, now that he had come to know York's churches, but its stone walls still had the beauty of proportion that had moved him so profoundly on his one previous visit.

He had to wonder why Ronan hadn't chosen the cathedral for their place of sanctuary. So much more robust and in its own yard: it would have been a much easier building to defend, with that massive oak door on its strong hinges...

We're not building a stockade, lad. We're making a point.

He forced himself to breathe deeply, to push his fears away with every exhalation. Ronan was right. They weren't warriors. They were servants of God. Lambs among wolves.

Ronan was always right.

Ronan always won, and the trouble was the old priest didn't even know there was a competition.

A mutilated stone cross stood in the forecourt of the cathedral and Wulfgar sat down on the chilly stone of its plinth to regain his equilibrium in contemplation of the west front. A lot of work was needed – there was a nasty crack wandering this way and that through the stonework to the left of the door and a bulging wall above it – but not impossible, surely, given men and money.

Or pull it down and start again.

But there were angels, carved of golden stone, warm even in the cool grey light of this dull dawn, flanking the west door. Angels with solemn, transcendent faces, despite the weathering and flaking of paint and plaster. Angels too beautiful to throw away.

And that wistful thought reminded him tangentially of Edward's ambitious building works for his new abbey in Winchester. He remembered his indignation at the demolition of so many of Winchester Cathedral's beloved ancillary buildings, including his own dormitory, when he had passed through the close on his way to see Wystan.

What a fool he had been, to agonise over stone and mortar when a man's life and soul were at stake.

And the realisation struck him like a blow from a thresher's flail.

He was doing it again.

How could he possibly dally in Leicester, twiddling his thumbs and pondering plaster till the army arrived and the city's fate was settled one way or another?

Leicester didn't need him, and neither, to be brutally honest, did Ronan.

But Wystan did.

He could walk, of course he could. He could walk all the way to Winchester, if he had to.

He got to his feet.

CHAPTER THIRTY-EIGHT

'*Herra! Herra!*'

Wulfgar fell back against his perch, startled. A boy was running into the cathedral yard, a small yellow dog at his heels. Ronan's altar boy and son, the irrepressible Kevin.

'*Takk vera Guthi*, I've found thee!' The boy was panting hard. 'I've been up ginnel and down gail, all through Dench town, brevitting about for thee, *herra*.'

Although Wulfgar missed half the sense of the lad's gabble, his general meaning came through loud and clear.

'Why? What's going on?'

'Fight's started!' Kevin had grabbed his arm now and was tugging hard, trying to get him to his feet. 'Shift thysen, *herra*! Happen they're coming this gate!'

Wulfgar looked wildly around the yard. Every alleyway was a potential conduit for the Atheling's hearth-men, wielding their swords as mercilessly as butchers do their axes.

Even as he hunted for a way of escape, he became aware of a

distant roar. It might have been breakers on a rocky shore or a rising wind in autumn trees, but he guessed the sound had no natural cause. There was no telling which direction it was coming from.

Sanctuary. Somewhere to hide the boy. But where?

The cathedral.

The great west door stood ajar.

'In there.'

'Nay, *herra*! They'll nab us like rattens in a pudden bag.'

'They wouldn't dare.' He gathered up the skirt of his too-long alb and walked, with as much dignity as he could muster, towards the west door.

'Come on.'

But Kevin lingered.

'What about Conan?' He indicated the little dog at his feet. 'I can't take him in kirk,' he said miserably.

The noise was certainly getting louder. Wulfgar's reluctant ears could distinguish details now: thump and clang and clash and bellow.

'Yes, you can,' he said. 'Of course you can. These are special circumstances.'

Kevin still looked doubtful, but even as he stood dithering a man came hurtling into the courtyard and threw himself around the corner of one of the buildings. He leaned back against the wall and then bent forward, his hands clutching his knees, gasping loudly and painfully. His hair was matted with bright blood.

Wulfgar grabbed Kevin's shoulder and hustled him through the door.

'Where shall we stow oursens, *herra*?' Kevin had scooped the wriggling little dog up into his arms.

Wulfgar looked around the dim nave.

If he had the faith that Ronan practised so effortlessly, he would refuse to hide. He would prostrate himself before the high altar, and chant the psalms appropriate to Prime, whose hour it was. Even as the men of violence raised their swords, he would look them in the eyes, and say, *Forgive them, Lord, for they know not what they do...*

He looked doubtfully at the struggling dog. 'Will he keep quiet?'

'*Já, herra.*'

Behind the high altar there were curving stone benches built against the wall for the lesser clergy and, in the middle, the bishop's high-backed *cathedra.* They squatted down behind the altar. Kevin had let his dog wriggle onto the floor, and it was skittering around, its toenails making a nerve-racking commotion. The boy caught Wulfgar's eye and made a ghastly face, half-deprecatory, half-apologetic. He hauled the dog back into his arms where it struggled and whimpered, but Kevin was murmuring now, and scratching it behind its ears, and it seemed to be settling. The cathedral was eerily silent.

Wulfgar could feel his ears straining for sounds.

Nothing.

Had the battle gone another way? He caught Kevin's eye and looked away again, but not before he caught the boy's grin.

'Never fret thysen, *herra,*' he whispered.

Wulfgar tried to smile.

Ronan would be worrying about the boy now, as well as his folk and his kirk. There was no sound from outside the thick stone walls, and Wulfgar wondered if the battle had gone in another direction. Not to St Margaret's, he prayed with a sudden passion.

As his sight adjusted to the gloom, he became aware of an

unnerving number of eyes gazing at him. He twisted round to see that the back wall of the apse was lined with painted saints, some tonsured, others mitred, one carrying a staff, another a tiny model of the church.

'That must be Bishop Cuthwin,' he whispered.

Kevin followed his pointing finger. '*Já, herra*,' he murmured. 'Who owned the harp, tha ken? And see that one gainhand, with the pot? He looks like thee.'

Wulfgar squinted harder at the nearest image, with its soulful dark eyes and gentle mouth. 'I think that's a woman,' he said.

Kevin was chuckling at his discomfiture. 'Got you there, *herra*!'

Wulfgar couldn't meet his eyes. He leaned back, to look at the image in the ceiling of the apse, far above their heads. Returning his gaze was a vast, bearded face, smoke-blackened but still recognisable.

The Saviour, Ruler of All.

Wulfgar felt a tingle run up and down his spine, meeting that gaze of infinite sadness. *A man of sorrows, acquainted with grief* . . .

Somewhere down the nave, a door banged.

They both froze.

After a moment, Kevin reached out and grabbed Conan, immobilising his jaws.

They heard the door again, but more quietly this time, as though someone had remembered how heavy it was, and what careful treatment it needed.

Footsteps. Leather-soled shoes that sounded as though they were sticking slightly to the floor with every step their owner took.

That owner was taking his time, criss-crossing the nave as though paying his devotions at every side-chapel, but growing steadily nearer.

Wulfgar felt irrationally convinced that whoever it was knew that he and Kevin were hiding there, that he was drawing out their agony on purpose. It took all his will-power to restrain himself from jerking to his feet and shouting *Here we are*! Only the knowledge that he was responsible for the child's safety prevented him.

They crouched down behind the altar, making themselves as small as they could, both ducking their heads and hunching forwards as though thereby to render themselves invisible.

The footsteps were very close now.

They slowed, and stopped.

There was a sharp intake of breath.

'*Gratias tibi ago, Domine.*'

A familiar voice.

Breathless with relief, Wulfgar raised his head.

Ronan was rolling his eyes, crossing himself with his left hand and supporting himself against the altar with his right. He looked shattered.

'Both of you, here,' he said. He looked at them, huddled and grubby. 'You can come out now. It's over.'

'What is?' Wulfgar forced himself to speak through the shock of relief.

'The great battle of Leicester, of course.'

Kevin shot to his feet, shouting some incoherent, ululating war-cry, and he sped for the west door, Conan scrabbling after him.

Ronan closed his eyes briefly. 'The lad knows better than to laik about like that in a kirk.'

Wulfgar smiled. 'He did ask my permission before bringing the dog in here.'

'Aye, and had you said no he'd have stayed without and got himself gralloched, like as not.'

'What happened, Ronan? Was it' – he struggled for a word – 'bad?'

'Not as men reckon these things. A handful of dead. Come and see.'

Must I? But, looking at Ronan's face, the words died on his lips. Instead, he said, 'How did you know we were here?'

Ronan smiled at last. 'Call it an inspired guess.' He buffeted Wulfgar gently on the shoulder. 'Sometimes I think I know you better than you know yourself.' He glanced obliquely at the bishop's *cathedra*. 'Why I wasted time looking in the side-chapels, I don't know.'

They walked down the nave together.

Wulfgar asked again, 'What happened?'

They had reached the west door. Ronan paused, his hand on the twisted iron ring. 'Anyone else would have asked who won, you know that?'

Wulfgar looked away, unsure whether the priest was laughing at him.

'It didn't last very long,' Ronan went on. 'They met in the fields by the Northgate. Ketil was in his wagon, his joints being too sore to let him mount a horse.' Ronan shook his head. 'Two lines of men flyting insults at each other. And then they stopped shouting and started fighting, around the gate and into the streets.' He looked at Wulfgar. 'You don't need to know much more than that, do you? It didn't last very long, because Ketil was killed' – he paused for a moment, looking at Wulfgar as though wondering how much to tell him – 'and his men threw down their weapons.'

'Ketil...killed?'

301

'Aye.' Ronan pushed the door open.

'But, how?'

Ronan shook his head. 'Come on, let's get ourselves up to the Northgate and greet the victors before they get carried away.'

But they were forestalled.

The victors were coming to meet them.

The army of York was advancing down the straight street that ran from the Northgate past the apse at the cathedral's eastern end.

First came the earth-shaking pounding made by the hooves of the horses and the tramp of men.

Then the banners.

Then the sun glinting on spear-tips.

Voices, singing.

The horsemen were in the vanguard, a dark mass of riders, the rising sun on their flanks, helmeted faces in shadow. But the Archbishop and the Atheling – the *King*, Wulfgar had to remind himself once again – were easy enough to pick out, riding in the place of honour as they were. He wondered whether they knew yet that he had stolen those documents. He could feel them again in their place of concealment under his linen, like pages of flame against his skin. Would they spot him in the crowd, haul him out, condemn him on the spot?

They were flanking a third man, one Wulfgar didn't know, and then a couple more riding close behind them, obscured by the standard-bearers.

The third man was holding a shaft aloft, and at its top, instead of a blade or a banner, there was a strange, battered lump.

And then the sun slid out from behind a wisp of pink cloud, and Wulfgar realised he was looking at the head of Ketil Grimsson

Scar. He put his hand to his mouth. *Lord, have mercy...*

Ketil had got his wish. No straw-death for him.

Wulfgar was not the only one to have recognised it. There were half-muffled cries from the other people who were now emerging like worms from the woodwork, a flurry of fingers as some crossed themselves, while others made the horns to avert evil.

He wondered, with a sudden pang, whether Ketil had given him back the Bishop's ring because he had known what was coming to him.

Lord have mercy...

But even the appalling sight of Ketil's severed head failed to hold Wulfgar's attention for long. A few paces behind the Atheling, another horse and rider – riders, he realised – had come out from behind one of the fluttering standards. A fine bay horse, with a plethora of glinting gilt discs adorning the bridle, was carrying a bleached-fair young man who was sitting far enough forward on the white and silver saddle-cloth to allow the other rider, tucked up behind him with her green skirts kilted, to clasp him tight round the waist and rest her cheek against his broad back.

He knew them both at once.

The young man on the bay, his white-blond hair lifting in the breeze, was Toli Silkbeard Hrafnsson, Jarl of Lincoln.

And the woman clinging so intimately behind him was Gunnvor Cat's-Eyes Bolladottir.

Ronan had fallen to his knees.

Wulfgar looked past him, to Seiriol of York saying something affable and meaningless; to Archbishop Lothward smiling and bowing, mounted on a huge white mule, whose long ears were the only clue to its parentage; to the triumphant young man whose spear was crowned with its hideous burden; to a bevy of mounted clerics with Kenelm in their midst; to Elfled sitting stiff-backed and regal on a grey mare; to Toli of Lincoln, and Gunnvor.

She must have seen him; she was only feet away from him. But she gave no sign as they came past. He could have reached out his arm and stroked the twisted silk-and-silver braids that hemmed her black cloak. He dug his nails into his palms and concentrated on his breathing, staring ahead unseeing until they had ridden past, followed by the thundering hooves of the hearth-troops of York and Lincoln, the tramp of the Northumbrian levies, the rumble of the hooves of the oxen and the great solid wheels of the supply carts, laden with spears and barrels and sacks, and cheering camp-followers, with more women and girls running barefoot in the drifting dust.

Only when the noise and stink of an army on the move had begun to fade did he begin to breathe again.

'That's a well-disciplined mob, any road,' Ronan said. 'I doubt me there'll be much burning and looting, other than Ketil's longhouse and his treasury.' His voice took a wry turn. 'We might even get our horses back.'

Wulfgar nodded.

'I need to return to the Lady,' he said carefully. 'She claims jurisdiction over Leicester, of course. I trust any council they hold will include her.' Neither of them, he thought, could admit what was really in their hearts.

They stood in shared silence, watching the tail end of the baggage train vanish.

CHAPTER THIRTY-NINE

Much Wenlock

'My Lady.'

'Wulfgar. What do you have for me?'

Was he imagining it, or was her manner colder and more remote than he felt he had a right to expect? She looked exhausted, dark shadows under her eyes, and was swathed in a light woollen wrap despite the warmth of the summer evening.

Get the worst over with.

So he told her in detail about the Atheling's wedding to Elfled; about Knut's death at her cousin's own hand; about the fall of Leicester. Her neat little face was expressionless throughout his long recital, though he told it as fluently as he knew how. He suspected that little of what he was saying was news to her, in outline at least, though she might not have been aware of the minutiae. He also had the distinct and contradictory impressions that she was both impatient for him to finish and yet dreading him reaching the end.

'Yes,' she said, at last. 'You confirm everything I've already heard. My cousin Seiriol has won himself a kingdom at last, and he inaugurates his reign with an act of aggression against Leicester. Mercian territory. *My* territory.' Her mouth twitched. 'So much for my dream of an alliance with York.'

He couldn't read her face clearly but there was something about it that chilled him.

'He and Archbishop Lothward are very close, my Lady. The Archbishop – he's used to working with kings.' And getting rid of them, he thought, but he didn't say it. 'He may have met his match in your cousin Seiriol, though.'

'Is that all your news?'

'Not quite.'

He took out his stolen documents and explained what they were and what he'd done to get them.

She listened carefully, and let him read them to her, nodding and occasionally asking him to read something again.

'I thought that by stealing them, I would damage York's claim to Leicester, my Lady,' he said. 'Perhaps fatally. But it doesn't seem to have made any difference.'

'Oh, it does,' she said, and for the first time a strained smile flickered across her face. 'This one' – she held up the old list of minsters and their renders – 'might have been very useful to the Archbishop, had you left it with him. And this one' – the forgery – 'shows just how very close to home treachery has come. I look forward to presenting it to Kenelm's uncle.' She nodded at him. 'Well done, Wulfgar. After you'd gone, I thought I might have made a terrible mistake in sending you to York, but you've proved me wrong. What a lot you've managed to achieve in one little month.' Her voice had a ragged edge.

'And then I came to you.' He managed a tremulous smile in

return. 'I went to Worcester first, and they told me to come here to Much Wenlock because you were on pilgrimage—'

'Wulfgar.'

He stopped mid-word.

She got up and went to the carved chest at the back of the room. When she rose and turned round again, she was holding out a sheet of vellum. Not one of those he had brought her. Wider and shorter and covered with writing. He could see a block of text, and then what looked like a long list of subscribing names.

He reached for it, but at the last minute she pulled back.

'Perhaps I should explain first. I only got this four days ago – oh, dear God, Wulfgar. I've been dreading your return ever since.'

He stood very straight, squaring his shoulders in unconscious anticipation of a blow.

'Wulfgar, I – it's bad news about Wystan.'

He was very still.

She had an imploring look on her face.

'I wrote to Edward. I did. I asked him to exile your brother, if the verdict went against him in September. But soon after that we got the news of Seiriol's accession to York. And that you were in the very room when Knut was killed. I suspect that's what tipped the scales against you.' She paused and swallowed. 'Wulfgar, Edward's so angry. He thinks you were in league with Seiriol, as well as Wystan.'

His face felt as though it was made out of wood. He forced his stiff lips to say, 'He promised me the summer.'

She nodded forcefully. 'Until the equinox. I know. But the killing of Knut changed everything.'

'What's happened?'

She offered him the sheet of vellum again and he took it with numb, trembling fingers.

'He is innocent,' he said. 'I have the Atheling's sworn word.' The words blurred and shifted in front of his eyes. 'I can't read this.'

She said, 'Edward was scrupulous in observing the law. He sent round to every last man eligible to attend the Witan, asking each one whether he thought Wystan was culpable.'

'Culpable...?'

'And they said yes. From what I've heard, there were no dissenters.' She stood up in her agitation. 'He felt waiting for September was too dangerous. When he heard you were with Seiriol in York, he took it as confirmation that both you and Wystan had been part of the plot to kill him.' She let out a long breath. 'And this damnable marriage doesn't help. Elfled of Wilton was supposed to be safely locked away in her nunnery.' Her voice wavered a little. 'Seiriol wanted to marry me, once. Did you know that? Before I was promised to my Lord. But my father and the bishop said no. You're too close in blood, they said. And now look whom he's married in the end! All my cousins, uniting against me.' Her tone had become too bright now, too brittle, her smile ever tighter at the corners. 'If my Lord had died at Easter, Seiriol might have married me, after all.'

Her words flowed over him, tugging at his understanding but little of their meaning coming through.

'Wystan is innocent.' He frowned hard. 'So am I.' He was still having difficulty understanding exactly what she was saying to him. 'You mean that there won't be another trial?'

'As you can see.' She gestured at the sheet of vellum he was still holding in his shaking hands.

'I can't see,' he said. His head and his heart were pounding, and there were black dots intruding on his vision.

'You need to read what it says, Wulfgar.'

He nodded, pinching the sheet tight in his numb hands, forcing his rebellious eyes to focus, his quailing mind to take in the sense of what he was looking at.

By agreement of the King and the Witan of the West Saxons, Wystan of Meon is to be struck down for his treachery, without shrift, and his body cast into the traitors' pit, there to lie until the Day of the Lord's Judgement, when body and soul he shall be damned to suffer hell-torments in eternity.

✠ *Ego, Edwardus Rex Occidentalium Saxonum, confirmavit.*
✠ *Ego, Denewulfus Episcopus Wintoniae, subscripsit.*
✠ *Ego...*

The witness list ran into dozens of names. Many of them were men whom Wulfgar – and Wystan – had known all their lives.

Edward had been taking no chances with the legality of the judgement this time.

Carefully, he said, 'And when will sentence be carried out?'

'Oh, Wulfgar.' Tense, now, and snappish to the point of breaking. 'Don't you understand? This isn't an order, it's a record of an order.' She sat down again, exhaling heavily.

'What do you mean?'

She looked at her lap, silent and shrouded for a long moment. Then, very softly, 'He's dead.'

'What?'

'He's dead.' Louder this time. He couldn't pretend he hadn't heard, or understood.

'No.'

Unlike her, to have made such a foolish mistake.

She was shaking her head at him.

'No,' Wulfgar said again. 'That can't be right. I'm going to go to Edward and explain, you see. It has all been all a terrible mistake. The Atheling told me so himself.' If he could only make things clear to her, he could put her silly misconception straight. 'He swore me his solemn oath that Wystan never wanted to kill Edward. So I need to tell Edward that, and then he'll let Wystan go home at last. To Meon. To his wife and son.'

She was staring at him with a look of terrible pity on her face.

CHAPTER FORTY

Winchester

Wulfgar was shocked by the change in Cwenhild. She had aged
visibly in the seven weeks since he'd last seen his sister and the
bright sunlight was doing her no favours. She had never been
beautiful as the world measured such things, but her plump cheeks
and gappy grin, her direct gaze, her warmth and energy, had
always more than compensated. They were sitting in a corner of
the kitchen garden at the Nunnaminster among the rows of beans.
The air was thick with their scent and the hum of bees. She was
talking, but he found it hard to concentrate on what she saying,
too distracted by the mottled, discoloured skin around her eyes –
eyes that wouldn't meet his for long – her dry, flaking lips, the
continuous nervous pleating of her coarse brown skirt.

Cwenhild's words were out of character, too. She was rambling
on, coming out with vague platitudes about the fine weather,
about the novices, nothing of importance.

'Cwenhild, this isn't what I'm here for. I'm tired, I'm dirty, and
I've only just stabled my horse—'

'Of course!' She looked mortified. 'You must need all sorts of things before you beg your audience with Edward. Food, a bath—' Her fingers reached out and tore off a spray of rosemary. 'Here, smell this. It'll restore you. Or shall I find you some balm? Your uncle swears by balm, steeped in—'

'How is my uncle?' He felt the now-familiar churn of bitterness in his gut, remembering how his uncle's words had smoothed his brother's road to the gallows.

'Not well.' She blinked. 'You should go and see him. He finds it hard to leave his bed, most days. And he misses you.' A tremulous smile. 'We all do.'

He chewed his lip, absorbing this. 'And Judith? And the little one, Helmstan?'

'I – I haven't seen them for a while. You've really not heard any Winchester news, then? Fleda's not said anything?'

'The Lady? No. She's had a lot to contend with lately.' The collapse of the treaty with York, for one thing.

'She's not unwell, too, is she?' Cwenhild frowned. 'I did hear a rumour...'

'Everyone seems to have heard rumours.' He rubbed his forehead, thinking back to that difficult reunion with his Lady four days earlier. Had she been ill? Weary, and short-tempered, certainly, and swathed in that heavy shawl despite the warm day...

'I hope not,' he said at last. 'That would mean the end of Mercia, I think.' But she certainly hadn't been herself.

'Poor Fleda.' Cwenhild shook her head. 'It's one blow after another, these days. We were staggered at the Nunnaminster when we heard about dear little Elfled marrying—' She stopped so abruptly that Wulfgar wondered whether she'd bitten her tongue. She stared for a long moment at the spray of rosemary she

312

was holding. 'If King Edward, if...' she lifted her eyes to his. 'Wuffa, what are you going to do?'

He stared at her.

'Please, don't fight...' Her voice was barely audible.

'*Fight?*' But Cwenhild was too close to the truth for Wulfgar to feel entirely comfortable. His first desire, once the Lady's dire news had finally sunk in, had indeed been to ride at once, headlong to Winchester. Burst into the King's presence; call him murderer; strike him down.

He finally understood young Alwin's simple, blind hatred, his longing for revenge for the death of his father Alnoth.

He felt them himself.

'I won't confront him,' he said slowly. 'Not in any way that might bring more trouble down on our heads. I wanted to. But the Lady talked me out of it.'

And more than that. After she had broken the news to him of Wystan's execution, the Lady had waited patiently, letting him rave himself to a standstill.

Then, 'Listen to me. Attacking Edward won't solve a thing.' He had turned away from her earnest face at those words. She grabbed his arm and tugged him round to face her. 'You cannot win that fight. How will your death help your brother? *Listen to me.*'

'Nothing can help Wystan now. He's damned.'

Be good, he remembered his wet nurse saying to him, *or I'll put you where the bad men lie...*

'Then get him reburied. Damn it, Wulfgar' – and now she was shouting at him. 'You've convinced me he was innocent! You can convince Edward.'

'*How?*' He could feel his expression was that of a sulky schoolboy, and he tried to relax, breathe, and listen.

'Throw yourself on his mercy.' The Lady was gripping both his hands now, her nails gouging the skin of his knuckles. 'You know Edward. He loves feeling powerful. Appearing generous, especially when that generosity will cost him nothing. Tell him what you've told me.'

Those words were still ringing in his ears, here in the sheltered haven of the Nunnaminster vegetable garden. Cwenhild was hauling herself to her feet.

'Come on. I'll get one of the novices to heat some water for you in the guesthouse. Do you need a comb?'

He had a sudden, poignant memory of young Gerd in her blue dress, so bright-eyed and eager to help.

'No. Thank you, though.'

And still, neither of them had so much as mentioned Wystan's name. The dreadful fact of his death hung in the air between them like some tangible, dark phantasm, and their shared knowledge underpinned every word they spoke. Wulfgar had not been able to raise the subject in so many words, however, and he suspected Cwenhild was feeling the same.

But now, as she turned away from him, he said, 'Were you with him? At the end?'

She closed her eyes and gave a tiny nod.

'You saw him hanged? And buried?'

Another tiny nod.

He hated forcing her to remember, but he had to know.

'Buried in the pit up at Harestock?' He heard again the *thump thump* of bodies falling from the gallows.

'*Yes*,' she said violently, and swung round to hurry back up the path between the tall, laden bean-plants.

He hadn't told her any details of why he needed to see Edward.

Time enough after the interview.

If the King listened to him, and believed him.

As he headed westwards the short way down Cheap-Street from the Nunnaminster, Wulfgar told himself it was unlikely the King would even receive him. Cwenhild had told him that Edward was continuing his father's practice of hearing petitioners in his bower after Mass, but his hopes of being admitted to the royal presence weren't high.

However, when Wulfgar walked into the precinct and found a messenger to take word to Oswin that he craved a word with the King, he found the way made suspiciously smooth before him. Other petitioners, having been told to wait their turn, muttered and grumbled at the sight of him being ushered through ahead of them. He heard more than one startled whisper of *traitor*!

Could Edward have been expecting him?

He was still as sick and churning inside as he had been back at Much Wenlock, his guts as rancid as the residue from a tannery. But to the fascinated eyes of the outside world he was neatly and suitably clad, clean and trimmed and composed.

Edward was seated on the kind of light iron faldstool his father used to take on campaign. Two of the men in attendance Wulfgar knew well: one of the palace chaplains and a deacon from the cathedral. The third, a layman by his beard and a thane by the quality of his dress, he didn't recognise.

Oswin stood back to announce the new arrival. 'Wulfgar of' – he paused, visibly at a loss for a moment – 'of Meon, my Lord King.'

Wulfgar felt profoundly grateful to the reeve for that vote of confidence.

He and Edward looked at each other for a long moment.

315

Wulfgar bowed his head but his legs were braced. He would not kneel to this man.

'Wulfgar.' Edward stepped forward and rested his hands on Wulfgar's shoulders. 'My old school...friend.' He smiled, and shook his head sadly.

Wulfgar stared down at the killer's hands clasping him with such apparent affection, and shuddered: he couldn't help himself. It was as visceral a reaction as vomiting after drinking an infusion of groundsel.

Edward contemplated him, his head on one side, his expression one of concern. 'Leave us,' he said in an aside to his companions.

'Check him for weapons,' the chaplain said. He shot Wulfgar a venomous glance.

Edward narrowed his eyes. 'No,' he said. 'I have nothing to fear from this man.'

Wulfgar wondered whether he really looked as harmless as Edward's words implied. Was the King was insulting him or paying him a compliment? As the three men shouldered past him, he couldn't help overhearing the bearded thane saying, 'We'll leave the door open. I'll be standing just outside, with my sword.'

Edward dropped his hands and stood back. 'You see?' he said. 'I'm not afraid of you.'

'You shouldn't be.' Wulfgar raised his hands, palms outward. 'I have never tried to harm you and I had nothing to do with the killing of Knut of York, either.'

'Yes,' Edward said. 'So I have been told.' His blue eyes were opaque. 'Swear your oath to me and I'll believe you had no part in this.' He settled back down in his chair. 'A man with your skills will be welcome back in Winchester.'

Wulfgar gaped at him.

316

'That's why you've come crawling back, isn't it? To assure me of your loyalty?' Edward smiled. 'I knew you would. With Mercia' – he was shaking his head, the smile evaporating – 'on the brink of collapse, where else could you go?'

'Mercia *collapse*, my Lord?'

'Fleda's husband will never be well again.' Edward's face tightened. 'And Fleda can't hold out for long. She hasn't the faintest idea what she's doing.'

'She has held Mercia steady for nearly half a year,' Wulfgar said. He tried to keep the anger out of his voice. 'It's not her fault, my Lord, that the treaty with York failed. She didn't kill Knut.'

'She should have seen it coming, though.' Edward waved a dismissive hand. 'She and Seiriol spend enough time together. And, while we're on that subject, she should never allow these rumours about the parentage of her brat to circulate.'

Her brat...

'If I were in her shoes,' Edward was going on, 'I'd be putting men's eyes out for the things they're saying...' He shrugged. 'But she's soft. Always has been. Soft and foolish.'

Her brat. Wulfgar's numb lips were still shaping the words, but from somewhere he found the common sense not to utter them. Edward must not realise he hadn't known. Suddenly the tangle of innuendos and anxieties that had been plaguing him for so long resolved itself and revealed its hidden pattern. His Lady's fragility, her sense of being elsewhere. Thorbjorn's coarse teasing. The persistent, scandalous rumours. That oath. *If I divulge what my Lady tells me, may I burn eternally in the pit of Hell with Lucifer, Judas and Arius, and all the other traitors...*

But how could he have divulged something that he had been too obtuse to understand?

He wanted to groan aloud, to put his head in his hands. But Edward was still talking.

'You're missed, the minster-men tell me. They say I could use you. We'll stick you in a dusty corner of the archive, and after a few years most people will have forgotten whose brother you once were—'

'My Lord.' It was a foolish man who interrupted a king, but Wulfgar couldn't help himself.

Edward's face darkened, but in the end he nodded.

And then Wulfgar did fall to his knees. 'My Lord King, if you can believe me innocent then you can do the same for my brother.' He paused, and forced himself to slow down. 'I had hopes of tracking down your cousin Seiriol in Wessex. Of asking him to tell me the truth. And then I found him in York, of course.' He looked up, and met Edward's eyes, willing the King to credit him. 'I asked him, in so many words, whether Wystan was guilty. And, my Lord, he said *no*. He said Wystan had never wished you harm. Had never wanted to kill you.' Those words were seared into his brain.

There was a long silence.

Wulfgar stared down at his hands, knotted as though in prayer.

Edward's iron stool creaked as the King shifted his weight. 'You really believe that, don't you?'

'My Lord, it is the truth.' Wulfgar could feel a whole summer's worth of grievance building up and threatening to burst forth: it was with an effort at the limits of his endurance that he kept his voice calm. 'My Lord King. We both know that that trial, back in June, was not well conducted.' He paused, trying to measure out his words judiciously. 'My brother refused to plead. By law, therefore, your court should have handed him over to the Church, to undergo the ordeal. If you hadn't – if the proceedings hadn't been ended so abruptly, I was going to say as much. The ordeal would have established his innocence beyond all possible doubt. Instead, he has been hanged, still without having submitted a plea, against all the laws of Wessex. Hanged and – and buried in the pit.'

Darkness and pain for ever.

Furiously aware of the tears threatening, fight them as he might, he lifted his face to Edward's again. He wasn't sure what he wanted any more. His hope, that Edward might allow Wystan to be exhumed and reburied at Meon, at the little family minster, seemed risible now.

He was fully expecting Edward's scornful dismissal.

But instead the King's narrow face was thoughtful, his brow creased and lips pursed.

'Get up,' he said. He snapped his fingers. 'Wine.'

When it came it was in blue glass cups trailed round with a green spiral. The King gestured for Wulfgar to be served first.

'Not well conducted?' Edward's voice was low and level. 'That's your considered opinion?'

Wulfgar nodded.

'And if you think that, then every man in Wessex who knows the law will think the same?'

He nodded again.

'Tell me then, Wulfgar, how are we going to resolve this? You want to redeem your family name. I want to be seen as a just *and merciful* king.' He put his head on the other side and fixed Wulfgar with that sudden sharp blue gaze. 'We'll never be friends, you and I. But we sat in the same schoolroom for all those years. We both' – he paused then, and his voice hardened – 'we both loved my father.'

Wulfgar sighed, and suddenly he found the tension ebbing from his body. This was about the law now, and he knew the law.

'My Lord, it was always going to be a difficult case. On the one side, a man of excellent record, awash with character witnesses attesting to his honesty, his loyalty, *et cetera*. On the other side, two men who were self-confessed traitors and therefore by definition untrustworthy, but telling such a circumstantially detailed story that it was very hard to disbelieve.'

Edward was nodding, listening closely. Where was the familiar sneer? Wulfgar went on, not knowing what else he could do.

'The judgement of the Witan was the harshest the law permits, and that is in itself a testimony to how much the senior men of Wessex have invested in you, and how far they will go to support and protect you against treachery.' He sighed again. 'But was it the *right* judgement? Putting all my own feelings to one side, I would have to say that the court had reached an impasse in Wystan's case. The law of men can only go so far.' He looked down at his cup. 'A fairer judgement, in an impossible situation, might have been to hang him for the presumption of treason, but give him decent burial and the chance of redemption in the heavenly court. Judge his body, but not his soul.' He stopped, swamped by the returning wave of bitterness.

Edward nodded. 'And so we come to the law of God.'

'And that's why I was going to plead that Wystan's case merited the ordeal, my Lord.' He bit his lower lip. 'A man's sins, his crimes, are woven into the very fabric of his body. At the heavenly judgement our bodies will become like glass – *clear* glass,' he amended, looking down at the murky blue of the vessel he was still holding. 'All our evil deeds – and our good ones – on show. But the ordeal, by fire or by water, foreshadows that judgement. It lets the truth shine through the dirty clay of the living body.' He winced at his trail of mixed metaphors, but the King didn't seem to have noticed.

320

'You want the truth?' Edward asked. 'The truth is, those men wanted me dead. To kill me. To drag me out of my saddle and gouge out my guts with their belt-knives.' He hunched his shoulders, clutching his abdomen and shivering suddenly. 'I had faith in them, you know. I would have rewarded them for their loyalty, even, if they had revealed to the plot to me at the beginning. Rewarded them beyond anything Seiriol might promise.' He swallowed, as if choking down a bitter draught. 'I trusted all three of them. Now I don't know whom to trust. What's going on behind men's faces?'

He stood up then, and walked over to examine the embroidered hanging on the wall. The *Gesta Alfredi*: the old King's great deeds immortalised in linen and wool and silk. Some of Wulfgar's earliest Winchester memories were of the Lady and her mother working on it, for what felt in retrospect like half his childhood. Edward must have known every stitch, but he still appeared to be scrutinising the scene closely: his father, youngest of four brothers, the ultimate survivor, being acclaimed King.

'They served my father. Why wouldn't they serve me?'

Wulfgar wasn't sure he had been meant to hear those words.

Edward still had his back to him. 'You're a churchman, and they tell me you're a good one. Is the truth really absolute? Eternal? God's truth?'

'It must be, my Lord.'

'The truth wasn't strangled, up there at the Harestock hanging-place?' He turned round abruptly.

'No, my Lord. And—'

'Then *you* take the ordeal.'

'What?'

'Will that make you happy?'

'Is this a jest, my Lord?'

'Be your brother's proxy,' Edward said. 'Come through the ordeal unscathed and I'll have Wystan out of the pit and buried with every honour. In the cathedral itself, if you like. With the Bishop presiding.'

Wulfgar's eyes had gone wide, his face frozen.

'Come through the ordeal, and I will admit in public to an over-hasty judgement by the Witan,' Edward went on. 'And the world will see me as a monarch who cares for the truth. God's truth.'

Wulfgar nodded meaninglessly. He had a sudden and overpowering memory of Wystan's terror when the ordeal had been mentioned. And he – God forgive him – had been so glib in his reassurances. He could hear his own voice, *And, if you are innocent, the ordeal will proclaim it. Beyond all doubt.*

He still believed that.

And he believed in Wystan's innocence, even though the King so patently didn't.

But his brother had been no coward. Why, if Wystan had been innocent, would the prospect of the ordeal have frightened him so badly?

'Good,' Edward was saying. He came and sat down again. 'Do drink that wine,' he said, irritation tinting his voice.

Wulfgar put the glass to his mouth but he still couldn't swallow. He managed to say, 'But, my Lord, what if I don't come through?'

As soon as the words left his lips, he wished them back again.

Edward gave him a hard blue stare. 'Then men will know your brother for the treacherous, murderous, cold-hearted bastard he was.'

CHAPTER FORTY-ONE

'I need to talk to Judith,' Wulfgar said.

He had gone straight back to the Nunnaminster guesthouse, convinced he was coming down with some terrible ague, he was so hot and shivery. But Cwenhild, after checking his tongue and the insides of his eyelids, had concluded it was nothing more than shock.

'And what could be more natural than for you to be shocked?' She had finally convinced him to drink a cup of steeped mint leaves. 'Undergoing the ordeal for a man already hanged. No one's ever heard of such a thing.'

He twisted round on his stool to look up at her. 'You think it's a bad idea?'

'No one can demand that of you.' But she wouldn't meet his eyes.

He cradled the warm horn beaker between his palms and breathed in the fragrant steam. 'No one can demand,' he said slowly. 'But they could ask.'

She frowned at him. 'What?'

'What would it mean to you, to have Wystan buried at the cathedral?'

'Well, Judith might change—'

'Not Judith,' he said. 'You.'

Cwenhild closed her eyes and leant back against the shelf.

Wulfgar waited.

After a long moment, she said, 'He visits me, you know. In the night, when I can't sleep. He's calling to me for help. It's as though we're children again, and he needs me. He's lost something or broken something and he needs me to come up with some plausible story.' She chuckled softly. 'He always did need me to get him out of trouble.' She opened her eyes then. 'What am I saying? You don't know, Wuffa. Of course you don't. You're too young. You never knew us as children.' Her chin trembled.

'You're very tired, aren't you?'

She nodded.

'Do you think it's possible, that my undergoing the ordeal for him would work?'

'I don't see why not. The truth remains the truth.'

'Right, then.' Wulfgar stood up. 'I'll do it, and I'll send word to Judith. Has she gone back to Kent yet?'

'No. She's at Meon.'

Wulfgar had been about to drain the last cooling liquid from his beaker, but he stopped with it halfway to his lips.

'*Meon?* But isn't Garmund there?'

'Garmund, speaking as the head of the family, has offered her and her son shelter.'

'And she's taken it?' He felt as though he had been kicked in the face.

'Helmstan is Garmund's nephew, too,' Cwenhild said. And, in response to his look of outrage, 'Don't think I like it any more than you do. Judith was a poor wife to Wystan, but that little boy made everything worthwhile for him.'

Wulfgar had to sit down again.

'I've been trying not to judge her. But as God and his Mother know, she's in an impossible position.'

'If I come through the ordeal,' Wulfgar said, 'and Wystan is shown to be innocent, then Edward will have to take the estates back from Garmund. He'll *have* to. It's the only fair thing. He'll have to let someone administer them for Helmstan, until the boy's old enough. In all justice.'

Cwenhild reached forward and took the beaker from him. 'We can pray.'

Wulfgar nodded, thinking of Ronan saying, *All prayers are answered. But sometimes the answer is No.*

A knock on the door, sharp and sudden.

It was that same cathedral deacon whom Wulfgar had recognised at his audience with Edward. 'Wulfgar? You're wanted.'

He scrambled to his feet. 'The King?' Had Edward changed his mind?

But the man shook his head. 'Your uncle. And the Bishop. Now.'

They were in an upper room, part of the cathedral's huddle of ancillary buildings. The had been debating vigorously when he came in, and they hardly broke off to acknowledge his appearance.

'Wulfgar is *not* a priest.' Denewulf of Winchester was shaking his head. 'Trial by Communion Host is only available to priests. Wulfgar is merely a subdeacon.' He glanced at Wulfgar. His soft pink face was looking deeply unhappy.

325

Wulfgar's uncle was propped up in a chair with several cushions. 'Do something about it, then.'

'And what do you suggest?'

Through the open shutters Wulfgar could hear hammering, the metallic chip-chip of the masons' chisels and the shouts of the King's workmen. Over the summer they had finished digging the foundations of Edward's great new minster and now they were laying the first courses of stone and erecting great forests of scaffolding.

His uncle was looking at him with concern.

'You're looking swimey-headed, Wuffa. Can someone get the boy a stool?'

'I'm all right,' he said, and, 'I'm sorry, I missed the first part of what you were saying.'

His uncle said to the Bishop, 'Ordain him now. Make him eligible. Why not? Right now. I'm still the archdeacon of your diocese. I'll vouch for him.'

Bishop Denewulf tapped his fingers on the table, visibly ruminating.

'That's not impossible. We'd have to promote him to deacon first, of course.'

Wulfgar looked from one to the other.

'What do you mean, my Lords?' He had a terrifying feeling that he knew, though.

'Ordain you priest, of course.' His uncle was smiling to himself, looking very pleased. 'With immediate effect. Then you're eligible to take the ordeal by consecrated bread.'

Wulfgar stood very still, waiting until he was absolutely sure he had understood everything his uncle had said. Then, carefully, 'I'm too young. I should be made deacon next year. Canon law says so.

But I can't be a priest until I'm thirty. Not without a dispensation.'

The Bishop of Winchester chuckled, his jowls quivering.

'And who do you think grants dispensations, boy? The King may be robbing my cathedral of all sorts of privileges, but he can't take that one from me.'

They were offering him everything on a plate. An easy ordeal and the absolute certainty of redeeming Wystan. With ordination to the priesthood thrown in. No more of Kenelm's little jibes. No more fears that he might be stranded as subdeacon and secretary for ever.

He could feel the skin of his face growing tight and warm.

'Would you really do that for me?' Give him what he so badly wanted without making him work for it? He put his hand to his scalp in his habitual gesture, and as he did so, he heard Gunnvor's voice, as bell-clear as though she were at his elbow. *When are you going to stop hiding behind your tonsure?*

He shook his head. 'I don't deserve this, my Lords. I'm not ready for it.' He bit his tongue. Surely the Bishop couldn't be suggesting the holy sacrament of ordination be treated as a legal loophole, an administrative convenience.

What sort of priest would such a ceremony create?

One who could take communion and swear Wystan's innocence, his hand on the high altar and the consecrated morsel still unswallowed.

But he knew he would choke on sacred words and host alike, and fail.

And his failure would have nothing to do with Wystan's innocence, and everything to do with his own guilty conscience

Wulfgar opened his mouth to try and explain something of this, but he never got the chance.

A loud bang resounded through the room. The door of the Bishop's upper chamber went swinging right back on itself, hard enough to slam into the wall. One of the King's hearth-companions glanced in, then stood back.

King Edward was darkening the doorway.

'Your decision, Bishop?'

'We were just considering the possibility of ordaining Wulfgar priest, my Lord King.' Bishop Denewulf produced a nervous smile. 'To enable him to undergo the ordeal by communion host—'

'I thought as much,' Edward said. 'As soon as I heard the three of you were closeted in here, I thought you'd have some ruse like this in mind.' He spoke directly to the Bishop. 'I won't have anyone doubting the validity of this ordeal. Hot water. Up to the elbow. And Grimbald will administer it. No one ever called *him* soft.'

Wulfgar could hardly miss the little smile the King had thrown him as he was leaving the room. No doubt Edward intended it as a threat, but Wulfgar for a stunned moment took it at face value. For the first time in his long acquaintance with Edward, Wulfgar was feeling something verging on gratitude.

'Wulfgar, you're being used.' His uncle sounded apoplectic.

'We all are,' the Bishop said.

The Archdeacon was wheezing painfully. 'That may be true, Denewulf, but no one's asking you to put your hand in boiling water.' He stopped, fighting for the next breath. When he had recovered, he said, 'The King wants Wystan's guilt established, and his verdict justified.'

Wulfgar nodded stiffly, still trying to grapple with that sudden grateful impulse he had felt towards the King. He was unsurprised by his uncle's conclusions. Exhuming Wystan would mean Edward admitting he was wrong. And even as a schoolboy, he had never been any good at that.

'My Lords,' he said, with all the deference he could muster, 'if Abbot Grimbald is still the man I remember, the King won't be able to bully him into any perversion of right practice. Surely the ordeal is as safe in his hands as it would be in your own.'

'Once I would have agreed with you,' the Bishop said. 'But why did Grimbald accept this appointment to the new abbacy?' He shook his head in disapproval.

Wulfgar's uncle was doing the same. 'Up to the elbow. The triple ordeal! It's not necessary. The wrist would do perfectly well.'

Wulfgar found himself stroking his wrist again. His dear hand. His good and faithful servant.

Together they would demonstrate Wystan's innocence with the whole world looking on.

'I'll see if I can't have a word with Grimbald,' the Bishop was saying. 'I'm still Bishop of Winchester, after all. I'm still his superior, no matter what the King thinks.' He glanced sidelong at Wulfgar. 'They say the Lord measures the wind to a close-shorn sheep, but sometimes He needs a little earthly help.'

'My Lords. Please, don't. Please, just stop trying to help me. I've got to go through with this.'

The two old men were looking at him in surprise.

'Don't be silly, boy,' his uncle said. 'You're like the man sinking in a bog, who prayed for God to help him. And what happened?'

'What?'

'A man came along with a rope and threw it to him, and he refused, saying he had faith in God. And then what?'

Wulfgar could feel himself shivering.

'He drowned.' His uncle sounded exasperated. 'God works through men as well as through miracles, you know. We don't want you to drown, Wuffa. I can't believe it to be God's will that King Edward's abuse of our cathedral should go unchallenged.' His voice had hardened. 'Or that that slave-born nobody Garmund should keep your family lands. It's not just Meon, remember. Corhampton belonged to my sister before it was yours.'

'Corhampton?' Wulfgar was distracted by what seemed a total irrelevance. 'What about Corhampton? That's mine. It's inalienable. Wystan was just administering it for me.'

But Wulfgar's uncle was shaking his head.

Wulfgar recoiled. 'It's not forfeit. It wasn't Wystan's.'

'Tell that to Garmund,' his uncle said drily.

And for the first time Wulfgar truly understood Wystan's visceral rage at the threat to his estates. *That little upstart...* his brother had said. Not words he would ever have hit upon himself to describe Garmund, half a foot taller and five years older than Wulfgar himself. But from Wystan's lofty heights... Wystan had already been ten at Garmund's birth. How had he felt, seeing their father take such pride in his strong, handsome, slave-born son? Wulfgar was ashamed to realise that that thought had never occurred to him before.

Like finding a cuckoo's egg in the nest.

Upstart.

Usurper.

Thief.

'There will have been an administrative mistake. Someone must have misread the records.' He felt an unreal sense of calm. Corhampton was his very own. It always had been, ever since his mother had died thirteen years earlier. The mill, the meadows, the little wooden church. 'I'll sort it out,' he said.

The Archdeacon was smiling through his wheezes. 'I thought you had more fight in you, Wuffa, and see? I was right.' He turned to the Bishop. 'We've got three days.'

But this wouldn't do.

It wouldn't do at all.

Wulfgar might have been shocked to discover how much he loved that little parcel of land on the west bank of the river Meon, but if he couldn't connive at a rigged ordeal for Wystan's sake, he certainly wasn't going to do it for a few acres of God's green earth. When he spoke, he was surprised by how firm he sounded.

'God will use the ordeal to demonstrate to the world that Wystan was innocent.' He let out a ragged sigh. 'And that's all that matters.'

CHAPTER FORTY-TWO

By midday on Thursday, the feast of St Lawrence, Winchester Cathedral was packed for the ordeal mass.

However, when Wulfgar and his onetime tutor Grimbald had entered some hours earlier, they had been alone. The only other person in the whole, echoing building was the sacristan, who had been detailed to stand at the door and keep out all intruders.

They had knelt before the high altar, uncomfortably close to where the charcoal lay heaped and ready beside the iron cauldron of water.

'Are we doing it here? The ordeal, I mean? Right in front of the altar?' Wulfgar's voice, even to his own ears, came out as painfully ragged.

'The King insists.'

Wulfgar was dressed only in the white linen shift of a penitent, and the stone of the floor was cold and painfully hard on his bare knees. Freshly shaved and tonsured, damp and chilly at scalp and ears and nape, he felt naked and inexplicably ashamed, as if some guilt of his own were being called into question.

332

He couldn't help sending sideways glances at Grimbald, new abbot of the King's still unbuilt new minster. Virgil, the old man had taught them. St Augustine. Rhetoric. How to measure the passing of time, and foretell the dates of Easter and Pentecost and the Lord's Ascension. He looked as spare and saturnine as ever, his thin hair still dark despite his age.

'Your confession next, I suppose, to go by the book.' The newly promoted abbot got to his feet and sat down a little gingerly on a fragile-looking stool next to the altar. 'It's an unusual case, this. But since your brother can't be with us to confess, I'd better hear yours. It's your right arm, after all.'

'My Lord.' Wulfgar shuffled forward, still on his knees. He groped for the familiar formula. 'Bless me, Father, for I have sinned. It has been' – this was a shaming admission – 'nearly three months since my last confession. These are my sins...'

How often had he said these very words, in this very church? This should be so easy. 'I have been disrespectful to my uncle,' he said. His mind had gone blank. Where had he been, for those ten weeks? What had he been doing? What were the eight capital sins? Sloth? Wrath? Covetousness?

'I stole some documents from the Archbishop of York.'

He bit his lip, remembering the warm pressure of Gunnvor lying next to him on the hard floor while the Archbishop's guards stood in the doorway in the thin grey dawn.

'I have desired a woman.' He closed his eyes. 'And I lied to her.'

A less welcome image next: sleek, smug, pink Kenelm.

'I have envied another his good fortune.'

He paused.

'Pride?' Grimbald inquired.

'Oh, I expect so,' Wulfgar said wearily. He felt his cheeks burn, remembering how he had thought himself too valuable to be killed in the sack of Leicester. 'Yes, pride.'

'Is there anything else you should tell me, my son?'

He shook his head.

Grimbald smiled. 'We'll exonerate you from gluttony, since you look to me to be verging on the emaciated.' His voice was dry, still tinged with that Frankish accent despite his decades in Wessex. 'Let me hear your act of contrition, then.'

'Have mercy on me, O God...'

But although he mouthed the words dutifully, his heart was full of images of Wystan. His eyes kept straying to the painted image to the left of the high altar, of the crowned Queen of Heaven. He hoped she would remind her Son that this ordeal wasn't about Wulfgar's own soul, his own sins. It was about his brother Wystan, and one particular accusation levelled at him. Of which Wystan was innocent.

'*Dominus noster Jesus Christus te absolvat...*'

Grimbald stood up and beckoned to the sacristan. 'Get this going, will you?'

Wulfgar stood to one side, watching the fat little man bustling around. He shifted the tripod and the heavy iron pot into position over the ready-laid fire, and started filling the pot, jugful by jugful, from the adjacent butt of water.

'Can we just check the depth?'

He beckoned Wulfgar forward.

'Put your arm in – you need to touch the bottom– no, watch your sleeve! Too deep. I'll take a little out.'

'It was only just up to my elbow,' Wulfgar said, drying his arm on the skirt of his penitent's shift, wanting to be helpful.

The sacristan gave him a scorching look. 'Are you telling me you *want* it deeper? Besides, if it's bubbling it'll splash up higher than that.'

'Bubbling,' Wulfgar repeated, nodding his head. Queen of Heaven, how inane he must sound.

Wystan was innocent; the Atheling had sworn it.

If Wystan were innocent, he had nothing to fear.

Edward and Garmund were the guilty ones. Not him. Not Wystan.

The sacristan had brought a little pot of glowing coals and a bundle of tinder with him and was working on the fire now. Grimbald was watching from just in front of the high altar, his face drawn and shuttered.

Wulfgar, in search of some distraction from the treadmill of his thoughts, said, 'My Lord Abbot. I haven't congratulated you yet.'

'For what, exactly?'

Wulfgar blinked. 'Why, your new post. Your preferment.' He gestured vaguely to the north, in the direction of the building site on the other side of the cathedral wall.

Grimbald's dark eyes flickered left and right. He said, in a voice too low for the sacristan to hear, 'You think I welcome this?' He leaned in closer to Wulfgar. 'When I first came to Wessex, the late King offered me the Archbishopric of Canterbury. Did you know that?'

'No, my Lord! I had no idea.' Wulfgar shook his head. 'But you?'

'But I turned him down. All I wanted was to be his tame scholar. And teach bright little boys like you.' His eyes gleamed suddenly. 'And now I'm an old man, I want only to live in my *monasteriolum* in the close, with a couple of clerics to help me.'

'So why—?'

'Edward has thrust this post on me precisely because he knows that all I wanted was a peaceful retirement.' Grimbald's face was fastidious with disgust. 'Wuffa, you of all people should understand his devious little ways.' He shrugged. 'I never treated him with the deference he thought the King's son merited.'

'And why did you agree?' Wulfgar's eyes were drawn ineluctably to the now-glowing coals beneath the pot. He wanted to keep talking although he could hardly concentrate on his own words, never mind what his old tutor was telling him. He could feel that radiant warmth reaching its fingers out to him.

'It was the least of several evils. He was threatening to send me into exile if I didn't accept. I'll do a good enough job in the few years God may have left for me, and I didn't know whom he might appoint in my stead if I continued to refuse. And I certainly don't fancy returning to Saint-Bertin, not at my age and after nearly twenty years. It may surprise you to learn that I don't mind if I never cross the Channel again.' Grimbald sighed. 'But I have made an enemy of my old friend Denewulf, which is a sorrow.'

A bell began to ring, sonorous and doom-laden.

'Enough of this self-indulgence. You are my first care.' Grimbald nodded at the sacristan. 'Is it heating up? Then put the lid on, and go and open the doors. But' – and he held up a warning hand – 'no one is to come nearer the altar than the end of the nave. There.' He gestured back towards the chancel arch, and the plump little sacristan hurried to do his bidding.

Wulfgar watched him go.

'Wulfgar?'

He jumped.

Grimbald was looking at him steadily, a sober look on his creased, sallow face. 'Wulfgar, you are doing a wonderful thing.'

After that everything was a blur.

Suddenly, or at least it seemed suddenly, the nave of the cathedral was thronged with ranks of pale, gaping faces. He knew King Edward would be there in the middle of the front row, and no doubt Garmund would be somewhere at his shoulder, and a dozen other familiar figures besides, but Wulfgar had no desire to pick them out of the crowd.

For once in his life the holy liturgy of the Mass was a gabble of meaningless syllables.

Now Grimbald was drawing him to one side. An acolyte had appeared out of nowhere with an aspergillum and a bowl of holy water, and he heard Grimbald intoning a rapid Latin blessing. Other clerics were appearing, one with a processional cross, another whose hands were reverently supporting a book, a third who was solemnly clanking a censer to left and right, producing acrid clouds of incense smoke. The water in the pot was reaching boiling point. Wulfgar's eyes stung in response to the incense and began to produce water of their own.

'Oh, holy water! Oh, blessed water! Water that washes the dust and the sins of the world, I adjure thee by the living God that thou make manifest and bring to light all truth.' Grimbald had pitched his voice low and true and it resonated off the curved wall of the apse and back through the arch into the nave.

The crowd, great as it was, had fallen still and silent.

Grimbald nodded at Wulfgar, and he found his legs somehow were propelling him forward.

'Wulfgar of Meon, I command you, in the presence of all, in the Names of the Father and the Son and the Holy Spirit, by the tremendous Day of Judgement, by your precious vows at baptism, by your veneration for the Saints, that if you are guilty' – Grimbald faltered for a moment, before picking himself up and moving

337

swiftly on – 'that if *your brother* is guilty in this matter of plotting the killing of King Edward, if he has done it, or consented to it, or if he knew who did it, that you, on his behalf, confess now and admit your – his – guilt.'

Wulfgar found the strength somehow to shake his head vehemently.

'You need to say it,' Grimbald muttered.

He took a deep breath. 'I assert Wystan's complete innocence. I will undertake the ordeal on his behalf, my Lords.'

Grimbald beckoned him still closer. He could see little puffs of steam escaping round the lid of the pot. The young acolyte offered him a cup of the holy water and he crossed himself before taking a sip. *Holy water, blessed water, help me to the truth.* Grimbald took Wulfgar's left hand in his and clasped it lightly and firmly. Wulfgar drew strength and reassurance from that cool, dry grip. His own hands were shamefully clammy.

Grimbald raised his right arm then, holding up a smooth grey stone for the crowd to see.

'Oh God, just Judge, sanctify this water being heated by fire. Bring the hand of your child, Wulfgar, safe and unharmed from this water.'

'If he's innocent!' A shout from the front row of the crowd.

Grimbald's gaze never shifted from Wulfgar.

'Lift the lid, please.'

The sacristan took the lid from the pot, which gushed steam.

Grimbald dropped in the stone. He mouthed something at the cleric with the incense-burner, and there was a sudden wild clanking. Further clouds billowed out, enshrouding them in the bittersweet smoke.

'Wulfgar' – it was a mutter in his ear – 'you should move your

338

ring on to your left hand. The metal might burn you worse than the water.'

His ring? The Bishop's ring. Ketil Scar's ring. He had put it on almost as an afterthought, praying fervently as he did so to the nameless saint whose relic it contained. He felt an almost painful surge of gratitude for Grimbald's foresight. Nodding, he pulled it off his right thumb and transferred it to his left. As soon as he had done so, Grimbald took his left hand again in that comforting grasp.

'Wulfgar?'

Grimbald was indicating the steaming cauldron.

'What, now?'

Grimbald nodded. 'Can you see the stone?' The grip on his left hand tightened comfortingly.

It couldn't hurt him.

Wystan was innocent.

It couldn't hurt him nearly as much as damnation would hurt Wystan.

Another young cleric was standing by with a roll of white linen, and Wulfgar realised it was the bandage with which Grimbald would wrap his arm as soon as he pulled it out again. With the stone in his grip. But he couldn't see the stone. He could hardly see the pot. So much steam was issuing from it, the water must be boiling away. Or was it incense-smoke? His eyes were watering.

He couldn't see.

That gentle voice again. 'Wulfgar, it's time.'

He hesitated. Put his arm in that bubbling vat voluntarily? It went against every instinct he possessed; every nerve in his body shrilling *No!*

'Wulfgar?'

He closed his eyes, and plunged his right hand into the water.

CHAPTER FORTY-THREE

'Is that the same stone?'

Edward picked it up and looked at it curiously, his head on one side.

No one responded.

Wulfgar watched, hunched over his right arm, which lay, still bandaged and concealed, in a loose sling across his chest. Tentative, wincing, he tried to straighten his fingers within their cerements of white linen, his flesh remembering the violent, shocking sensation of the water, how his fingers had curled immediately, reflexively around the smooth planes of the stone. The slick, egg-like contours had slipped free of his grasp, and he had had to scrabble after it before holding it securely at last. His arm had come erupting out of the water and Grimbald had plunged it at once into the cold water of the butt standing close by. He had only nebulous memories of pulling it out again and having it wrapped in wet cool linen.

How strange, he remembered thinking as his arm entered the

bubbling vat. Was this a miracle? It didn't hurt. It didn't hurt at all.

And then the agony had come, flooding in like a full-moon tide with a howling gale to herd it.

Through the cacophony of the pain, he had heard someone, somewhere, saying, 'There's nothing to see. Stand back, please. Forgive me, my Lord King.'

He had been dizzy with shock, vaguely conscious of the curious, gawping faces around him, slightly more clearly aware of the fact that his arm seared hot from fingertips to elbow, and that, when the shock wore off, the pain was going to be so much greater.

'He's in my care, my Lord King. Three days, and then we'll see if his arm be clean or foul.'

Edward's voice, angry and indistinct.

Then Grimbald again.

'God will write His message in Wulfgar's flesh, be sure of that, my Lord. And we will abide by it.'

Three pain-filled days and restless nights of care and rest had followed, in what Grimbald affectionately called his *monasteriolum*, that quiet little house in a far corner of the close, so familiar from Wulfgar's childhood. There had been few visitors. He had a blurry recollection of Cwenhild calling with a pot of some herbal salve and Grimbald sending her away with it unopened. No medicine allowed. Nothing but rest and awaiting the verdict of God.

Grimbald had found him a pile of thick springy rush mats in a quiet corner where he had nothing to do but lie still, wrapped in his cloak, and listen to the wind and the rain. He slept a lot, lying on his left side, and if he turned over on to his right, shocked awake as though he had rolled into the smouldering hearth.

God will write His message… As he had for Belshazzar the King, in the midst of his impious feasting. But the writing wasn't on the wall this time, he remembered thinking hazily.

God had written on his arm instead.

Weighed in the balance, he remembered with dread, *and found wanting.*

Wulfgar felt as though he had a whole lifetime's worth of sleep to catch up on. Even when he was awake he felt disoriented, heated and restless, very ready to drink a cup of warm ewe's milk and honey, and fall back into darkness.

His dreams, though, were vivid and exhausting. He saw a lot of Gunnvor in Toli's arms: heated images that he couldn't altogether blame on the fever.

And other, even darker, visions.

The battered lump carried on a triumphant spear-blade that had once been the head of Ketil Scar.

Thorbjorn and his men going down, the Atheling's men wielding their swords like threshers' flails and the scraps of flesh scattering like so much chaff.

Knut's look of infinite sadness and surprise as the Atheling's evangelist-adorned knife drove home.

Matthew, Mark, Luke and John, bless the bed that I lie on…

Edric and young Alwin's father going to the gallows.

Visions of Wystan, too, but not, mercifully, his death.

He did see Wystan at high table in the hall at Meon, talking enthusiastically about the need to spile the riverbank and marl the water meadows.

Wystan striding between the pens at eaning time, pointing out the likeliest of the new crop of lambs.

Wystan wielding his billhook with skill and enthusiasm along mile after mile of hedge, never ashamed to join his men in the meanest of labours.

Wystan red-faced, loud and blithe at his wedding, whirling his prim bride at the head of the procession of dancers.

That was a happy image. He hung on to that one, although he was vaguely aware that something felt wrong there too.

With whom was Judith dancing now?

The dance wheeled and turned, and the tall, broad-shouldered groom who was swinging the bride round had a black beard and red lips and sharp white teeth.

And then the darkness returned.

At last he had become aware of Grimbald squatting next to him, and a young acolyte with a cup of water – the same lad who had administered the holy water to him in the cathedral, he realised.

'Are you awake, Wuffa?' In an aside to the acolyte, Grimbald said, 'I've never seen anyone so much in need of rest.' He held out a hand. 'On your feet, if you can. It's time to see the Bishop, and you need to look as hale and well as you can. You might want this?'

And he held out the smooth, grey stone.

Now Edward was putting the same stone back down on the altar. They were in the cathedral, in the same place in front of the high altar where the cauldron had stood three days previously. He could see no sign, now, that a fire had ever been kindled on those smoothly mortared flagstones.

The cathedral was dim and chilly, the thick walls keeping out light and wind, the lingering smell of old incense adding to the aura of holiness. The Bishop of Winchester stood to one side of Wulfgar, and Grimbald flanked him on the other. The King was standing in front of the altar. The attendant thanes and clerics, a great cloud of witnesses, were waiting back in the nave, on the far side of the chancel arch. With a pang, Wulfgar recognised that thane with a beard like freshly carded fleece in the front row, the man who had argued so forcefully that Wystan and Alnoth and Edric should be hanged, and hanged forthwith.

Edward was in a high-collared tunic with gold thread to stiffen it, keeping his head erect. He gave Wulfgar a calculating look. Wulfgar did his best to keep his own head as high.

The boy was holding open the service-book, finding the page, angling it so that Grimbald could see the words.

'As Lazarus died, and was wrapped in the winding sheet and laid in the grave for three days, and yet came forth at the Lord's command, and was unwrapped and found to be whole and sound,' Grimbald read sonorously, 'so may this man, Wulfgar, submit his arm to be examined for the signs of life.'

He beckoned Wulfgar forward.

Wulfgar had been, surreptitiously, gingerly, feeling his arm through the clean, neatly folded bandages. The skin beneath was certainly still very sore and agonisingly tender; it felt taut, burning hot even now, and he flinched at the thought of so much as swivelling his wrist or extending his elbow. But, if there were blisters or weeping sores hiding under there, no matter was seeping through the linen. But then again, the bandages were thick enough to keep any foulness under wraps.

Clean or foul? It was such a familiar formula. But what did it mean? Clean burial, he thought carefully, is a proper funeral, the last rites having been administered, the dying man having made his full confession, professed his faith, been absolved. Closing your eyes on the things of this world, the faces of your weeping household, the roof of the house growing dim, fading into darkness. Opening them again to the sight of the gates of Heaven swinging open and the loving faces of the saints as they call you in. Home, at last.

And a foul death? Unforeseen, unconfessed. Lying in a ditch. In a pit. Food for the fox or the raven. Swinging from the branches of a gallows-tree. At the hand of a man you had called your friend. Darkness and pain for ever.

Obedient to his old teacher, Wulfgar held out his swaddled arm.

Grimbald sprinkled the linen with holy water and returned the aspergillum to the acolyte. He untucked the bandage's tidily wound end and began to unravel. Wulfgar held his arm as straight and as still as he could. He was finding it hard to breathe. He wanted to look away but he forced himself to keep his gaze on Grimbald's narrow, sallow-skinned hands, methodically coiling the end of the bandage as he went.

Now the first layer was off, and handed to the acolyte to place on the altar next to the stone.

Untuck, unroll.

Edward was standing uncomfortably close. Wulfgar could hear his breathing, the restless shifting of his leather soles on the tiles around the altar.

The second bandage was off now.

One more to go.

And this last one was hurting. The gauze of the linen was sticking to the skin, pulling at it, and he gasped with pain. He had closed his eyes, he found, and now he couldn't open them. He didn't want to see, didn't want to know what that familiar friend, his right arm, might now look like.

There was some muttering behind him: it sounded like King Edward and the Bishop of Winchester, but Wulfgar was unaware of any meaning in their words.

The last of the linen was off now. He could feel it. The sore, hot flesh felt cooler in the cathedral air.

'Wulfgar?' It was Grimbald.

He opened his eyes.

No wonder it hurt.

His head swam as he felt the shocked blood drain away.

Fingers, palm, wrist, arm: all were swollen and lumpish, a puckered spectrum of angry colours ranging from a background of dark pinks to archipelagos of violent purple-orange. In places the skin had erupted in blisters filled with amber liquid; in others it was peeling off in ragged grey trails.

Clean?

Foul?

It didn't even look human.

Grimbald took the arm carefully in his hands, turned it this way and that. Wulfgar winced and shivered, trying not to whimper. He was very aware of Edward's intent gaze. He swallowed, feeling a wave of icy nausea building, rising, threatening to overpower him.

Grimbald lowered his face to the scalded and inflamed skin, peering at it, inhaling deeply through his nose and closing his eyes as though savouring some rare vintage.

How could he bear to come so close to that horror?

Foul was the least of it.

It was hideous.

Wulfgar felt monstrous, deformed, exposed. He had been telling himself for a week that it Wystan's virtue that was being put to the proof, not his own. That seemed specious now. It was all the sins of his own past, the petty, the venial, the gross, the mortal, made manifest in the loathsome testimony of his own body. If this were a foretaste of the Last Judgement then he would never sin again. No earthly satisfaction could possibly be worth a repetition of the crushing humiliation of this horribly public moment.

And, worst of all, the final thought before his knees buckled.

Wystan was guilty, despite everything.

Wystan had been guilty after all.

CHAPTER FORTY-FOUR

When he came to his senses, queasy and disoriented, he found he was lying on the hard stone floor, his head in Grimbald's lap. The young acolyte was crouching nearby, watchful and concerned, still holding his bowl of holy water. The cathedral sanctuary appeared deserted otherwise.

'Where's Edward?' He tried to prop himself up on his left elbow and look around.

'Gone off to sulk, no doubt.' Grimbald raised his eyebrows. 'It always was among his least edifying characteristics. But he knows how many ordeals I've administered. He knows I'm impartial. He couldn't argue with God's verdict.'

'Argue?'

'He's none too pleased by the state of your arm.' Grimbald looked down at the limb in question. 'If you don't mind, Wulfgar, we'll leave it unwrapped for a little. Being in the air won't hurt it.'

Wulfgar's frown tightened.

'But I thought – have I done him an injustice, then? Is he

disappointed? Did he really want Wystan exonerated, after all?'

He looked at his arm. Every bit as hideous as he had thought on first revelation.

Shuddering, he closed his eyes.

'What do I do now?' he asked from that place of blessed darkness.

'Now?'

Wulfgar, disbelieving, heard the smile in Grimbald's voice. He opened his eyes again to find his old tutor beaming at him, his narrow, scholarly face utterly transformed.

'Now we arrange for Wystan's funeral, of course, with every honour the churches of Winchester can furnish.'

That made Wulfgar sit right up, and the pain be damned.

'What are you talking about?'

'Your arm's healing very acceptably.' Grimbald took in the extent of Wulfgar's shock, and smiled again, very gently this time. 'Didn't you realise? Oh, it looks a mess, I'll grant you that. But it's all superficial. There's no rot, no pus in the blisters. It smells fine.' He patted Wulfgar's shoulder. 'Light a candle to St Lawrence, why don't you? He knows a thing or two about burns.'

Wulfgar breathed deeply, staring at the flagstones, trying to assimilate this new perspective. His arm was fine. Grimbald said so, and so it must be true.

He would heal. He would be able to use a pen. Play the harp.

And then, like the sun breaking through clouds and a thousand trumpets sounding, *Wystan is innocent*. Grimbald's words about the funeral had finally sunk in.

And, hard on the heels of that thought, *if Wystan is innocent, then so is the Atheling*. Oh, Athelwald Seiriol was guilty of many crimes and sins, undoubtedly, but innocent of that peculiarly cruel method of corrupting Wystan, which Gunnvor had evoked so vividly.

Wulfgar started to get to his feet. The young acolyte hurried forward and offered him a hand. He turned to Grimbald. He was doing his best to look solemn, but the corners of his mouth were tugging irresistibly upwards. He felt like dancing.

'Exhume him today? Now?'

Footsteps, coming rapidly, heavily, up the nave.

They all three turned to see what was coming.

A dark shape, hooded and cloaked, approaching fast through the shadows, into the candlelit sanctuary. Raindrops gleaming on the hood, the shoulders.

Wulfgar took a step backwards towards the altar, lifted his left arm, hunched his right arm against his ribs, ducked to deflect the blow he knew was on its way.

But Garmund shoved him instead, a hard, contemptuous push that pinned his right side and his sore arm against the unyielding stone of the altar. He gasped with the pain.

Garmund's hood had fallen back. He was scowling, his black eyebrows drawn into a straight line, his white teeth clenched and bared. When he spoke he was barely articulate.

'You little—! Clean? Let's see it.'

He grabbed Wulfgar's shoulders, turned him round and threw him back against the altar, grabbing for his right arm. Wulfgar ducked again, but he was no match for his enraged half-brother. Garmund seized his right arm, one hand clamped just below the elbow, the other encircling the wrist with strong fingers.

Wulfgar screamed.

Garmund stared down at the arm in his grip, his upper lip

curling with distaste. He let it drop as though it were some long-dead, stinking thing. 'Call that clean?'

Wulfgar collapsed to his knees, hunched forward over his wounded arm. Tears were pouring down his face from shock as much as pain. He was aware of Grimbald and the young acolyte only feet away. He knew they wanted to help him. But this was something he had to do for himself. He forced himself to lift his head.

'But you've won, haven't you?' he said to Garmund.

'What?'

'You've won,' he said again. Somehow, leaning against the altar, he hauled himself up to standing, shaking his head at Grimbald and the young acolyte. 'No, I'm fine. Really.' He needed them to believe him.

He turned to face Garmund then, trying to stop himself shivering.

'You and Edward. You plotted to destroy Wystan. That good, true, faithful man. You blackened his reputation and broke his heart. Then you stole his lands, and offered him hope, and then you hanged him. And then you put me through this, in the hope I would fail.' The anger burst out, shattering the fragile crucible of his self-mastery. 'And what about Judith and Helmstan? What are they doing at Meon? How long will Helmstan live, under your care? Little children die all the time, don't they? No one will ever know—' His rage and misery were choking him. He put his hand to his mouth, pressing back the thoughts he couldn't bear to speak in case speaking them made them true.

Garmund's eyes had gone very black, impenetrable pools of polished jet, giving nothing away. 'Wystan was a traitor.'

Wulfgar pushed himself forward, lifting his puce and blistered arm. He noticed, as he brandished it in Garmund's face, that his half-brother's rough handling had burst many of the blisters. The wet smears of lymph gleamed in the candlelight from the altar.

'Look! Look!' He gestured wildly towards Grimbald. 'Ask *him* if you don't believe me. It's clean. It's healing.'

Garmund took a step backwards, his face pinched with distaste.

'What difference does that make?' He shrugged then, laughed. 'You're right. I've won. I don't know why I was so angry.' A flash of white teeth. 'Because it doesn't matter, does it, Litter-runt?'

'What doesn't matter?'

'Whether your arm heals or rots and drops off. Whether you dig up that grave. He's dead.' And Garmund threw back his head and shouted at the rafters. 'He's *dead*!' He grinned at Wulfgar, the tension visibly ebbing from his jaw and shoulders. 'And none of your oh-so-virtuous posturing can bring him back. Not after three weeks in the ground. He's dead and he's stinking.' He rolled his shoulders, stretched easily, yawned. 'And, as for Judith and Helmstan, I'm not exactly keeping them prisoner at Meon, you know. She can go back to Kent any time she likes. If Judith trusts me with her brat, then don't you think you ought to do the same?'

Wulfgar was speechless.

'I love that look on your face, Litter-runt.' Garmund's expression was pitying. 'The cornered leveret, not knowing which dog is going to leap first and tear its throat out. You do it so well.'

Wulfgar wished that when he was angry he looked a quarter as intimidating as Garmund. He tried to wipe the fury and terror from his face, to find a place of calm from which he could ask about something that had almost slipped his mind.

'What about Corhampton?'

'What about it, Litter-runt?'

'It's mine. It was my mother's morning-gift. It was never Wystan's. I want it back.'

Garmund nodded judiciously. 'And, knowing you, you'll have all the documents to back up this claim.'

'It's not a *claim*.' Wulfgar could feel his anger building again, in thunder-headed clouds. He took a deep breath, tried to hold it at bay. 'It's a fact. You know it as well as I do.'

Garmund spread out his hands.

'Produce the charter, then.' He was still smiling. 'I'll gladly see you in court. But with the King backing me, I don't think you'll have many supporters.'

Garmund turned as though to leave, then appeared to change his mind.

He glanced at Grimbald and the young acolyte, quiet witnesses in the shadows, and back to Wulfgar.

Their eyes met.

'Wuffa, he was a traitor, you know.'

Wulfgar returned his gaze, stony-faced.

'Liar,' he said calmly.

Garmund shook his head. 'You never saw that side of Wystan, did you? Big, solid, simple, cheery Wystan, eh? You think he was innocent.' He gestured contemptuously at Wulfgar's arm. 'You think that proves it. But I know how he treated me. What he called me.' His expression was stony now. 'He deserved everything he got. And so do I.'

CHAPTER FORTY-FIVE

They dug Wystan up again a week later, on the feast of St Helena. Beacons had been raised on the downs for the celebrations of the first sheaf to be brought in, and in the light of the late afternoon Wulfgar could see them still burning on the hilltops around Winchester and beyond. He could smell the smoke, too, and see it, hanging in heavy skeins in the motionless air.

Wulfgar was standing very much where he had stood when Edric and Alnoth had been hanged and, just as he had on on that day nearly two months ago, he was staring fixedly at the clump of grass at his feet. The sheep had been moved on, and the grasses were longer and heavy with their burdens of seed, the flowers harder to see. The yellow of vetch and bird's-foot trefoil had been joined by the various purples of knapweed and scabious. He was concentrating hard on that square yard of meadow near his feet, knowing that in a moment he would have to go over the rise, to the pit where no flowers grew.

The scrape and thud of the digging stopped.

Edward's reeve, Oswin, was coming towards him.

'Wulfgar, we've found the part of the pit we need. We'd like you to come and say which body is your brother's.' He grimaced. 'We need to make sure we get the right man, after all.'

Nodding heavily, Wulfgar followed Oswin's broad back. His hands had clenched so tightly he could feel his nails gouging holes in his palms. He concentrated on swallowing, on breathing, on moving one clumsy foot in front of another.

There was no need for the reeve's squad of stout young men to dig all three prone bodies out of their shared shallow grave, or even to turn them over. Wystan's fox-russet mop of hair was still recognisable emerging from the pale chalky earth, thick-speckled with little nodules of flint, distinguishing him easily enough from Alwin's dark-haired father or the fair Edric of Amport.

No surprises there.

Wulfgar nodded and pointed, and the lads stepped forward, spades at the ready.

This should have been a triumph. One of the great days of his life. But instead it was proving heartbreakingly anti-climactic. He turned to look to the south-east where, concealed by the inter-vening twenty miles of hills and fields and woodland, the lost estates of Meon lay. He had sent one of the King's own riders with a message to Judith, telling her in terse words what was happening and asking her to bring Helmstan to his father's funeral.

The man had come back stony-faced, saying only that there was no reply.

He could hear scraping, slithering sounds from the pit. He kept his back turned and tried to breathe through his mouth.

'Oh Lord, King of Glory,' he sang softly, 'deliver his soul from the pains of Hell.' He swallowed painfully. 'From the bottomless pit deliver him; from the jaws of the lion...'

Another voice chimed in on his right, loud and out of tune but very welcome for all that.

'Let your holy standard-bearer, St Michael the Archangel, lead him towards the light...'

It was Cwenhild. She reached out her large, red-knuckled hand and he twisted round to receive it with his left, gripping it with profound gratitude. His right hand and arm were still healing cleanly, but Grimbald had said it could be weeks before he was free of pain. Their voices grew stronger as they turned to watch four of the sturdy young men carrying their mercifully shrouded burden to the waiting cart.

'Lord, make him pass from death to life.'

There were curious crowds lining the streets in Winchester, and many more avid faces in the cathedral yard, where the grave had already been dug. Wulfgar had ordered it to be lined with purifying charcoal and the sacristan had taken him at his word. A good cartload of the stuff had been tipped in. Wulfgar picked up a stray lump from the graveside and turned it between his fingers, looking at the black grainy smears it left behind, taking care not to smear the purple and gold of his tunicle, the same one he had worn for his ordination as subdeacon the previous year.

Wystan had gone unconfessed to his grave.

Wulfgar thought of Ketil Scar, then, poking the dusty ashes and the glowing charcoal of the hearth in his longhouse...

Remember, man, that thou art dust, and into dust thou shalt return.

He thought of the black smears on men's brows on Ash Wednesday, that outward sign of inward penance. Was there anything more that he could do that would mark Wystan out as a penitent before the great throne of Judgement at the end of the world?

He looked at the approaching Bishop and the bevy of richly dressed clerics in his train, his old tutor Grimbald among them; at the boys clanking their thuribles and threatening to stifle the crowds with incense, the psalm they were singing soaring up to the canopy of dull grey cloud. *Open to me the doors of justice...* All the thoughts and needs of Wystan's immortal soul, his bitterness and his dread as well as his hopes of joy, expressed through the powerful, well-trained voices of Winchester's singing men.

Edward had kept his word scrupulously. Even the workmen digging the foundations of his new minster had downed their tools to join the throng. The very location of Wystan's second grave was a mark of honour: only a few yards from the little *habitaculum* that sheltered the grave of St Swithin. If there were anything that human activity could do to help the soul of Wystan over the threshold of Heaven, then it had surely been done.

Wulfgar felt his jaw tighten. No matter how much the King was spending on this funeral, it wouldn't begin to compensate him for the loss of his little Corhampton, never mind the Meon estates, which were as firmly in Garmund's hands as ever.

In the cathedral graveyard, the sacristan was shovelling in the last lumps of claggy soil.

The crowds were drifting away.

Cwenhild rubbed her hands together. 'Come back to the Nunnaminster?'

Wulfgar shrugged. 'I should return to Gloucester. The Lady needs me.'

'What, at once? Don't be ridiculous.'

He shrugged again, and gave way in the face of her anxious expression.

'You go ahead. Heat me a cup of wine. I'll follow in a little while.'

She gave him a searching look but eventually nodded.

He watched her threading her way through the rows of wooden grave-markers to the arched passageway under St Martin's Tower. Her sturdy, brown-clad figure vanished into the growing shadows. Only when he was quite sure he was alone did he turn back to his brother's grave.

The story was finally over. It was nearly two months since Wystan had been arrested, and he himself had come riding into Winchester with Alda, the reeve of Meon, certain that Wystan's life was his for the saving. He could hear the cathedral bells ringing the clerics into Vespers. Shadows were long in the last shaft of sunset light shining from the west past St Martin's Tower and over the freshly turned soil.

'I'm sorry,' he whispered.

Nothing but death. But it was over now. Wystan was at rest; and he himself could go home to Gloucester, to his beloved, dull, quotidian round of prayer and administration.

The next time that the Lady needed someone to racket around the country on a fool's errand, she could find someone more suited to the task.

There were jackdaws swooping and calling around the bell-tower, and, unwillingly, he remembered the ragged, black-winged rooks and ravens gathering in the sky over the King's Garth in York. Wystan had been spared that carrion ravaging, at least. Gerd's face floated into his mind. He would be thankful till the day of his own death that she hadn't had to confront what the

Atheling's men had left of her father's body. There were plenty of reasons to be grateful.

He squatted by the grave and was confronted at once by another recent memory: his one-sided conversation by the graveside of Hakon Toad. He must have been mad. It had all the lurid, half-remembered quality of a dream. His lips tightened at the memory of his last glimpse of Gunnvor, riding triumphantly into Leicester with Toli Silkbeard. Yes, a bad dream.

Everything that had happened in Leicester was safely behind him now, and the same was true for York. The political scene had shifted and tilted, and the Atheling's conquests meant that many things had changed. Edward would be raising his levies and looking nervously to his northern borders.

His own dreams of becoming the new Bishop of Leicester a few years from now had evaporated, as do the mists that lie low over the meadows when the sun rises.

And the Lady?

He would worry less about himself, and more about her. He was oath-sworn to her, after all, and in terms at least as binding as any marriage, as any bishop's consecration. His place was at her side and she needed men on whom she could rely without question.

Yes, this story was over.

CHAPTER FORTY-SIX

St Oswald's Minster, Gloucester

'If I were no longer here, would you still serve Mercia?'

She was kneeling at the shrine, her back to Wulfgar, who had been waiting for some time for her to finish her devotions.

He thought she was addressing her words to the saint whose bones were concealed beneath that embroidered pall.

'Would you, though?' She turned, enough so that he could make out her profile. 'Wulfgar?'

'Why do you ask, my Lady?'

She got stiffly to her feet, grimacing a little but saying nothing more.

'How do I know?' Distress was making him abrupt. 'If you weren't here, and your Lord were still ill, how could there be a Mercia for me to serve? Who would lead her?'

She snorted then, almost laughing. 'I can think of any number of candidates.'

She walked towards him, and together they turned and looked

360

at St Oswald's shrine, its silks and gilt gleaming softly in the gloom of the chapel.

'Wulfgar, do you remember, before you went to York, I asked you to swear a new oath to me?'

'Remember? Yes, I remember.' *If I divulge what my Lady tells me, without her permission, may I suffer for eternity in the pit of Hell, with Lucifer, Judas and Arius, and all the other traitors.* The words were branded into his memory.

'I made you swear, and I never told you why.' An ineffable sadness tinged her voice. 'I tried, but you thought I was talking about Athelstan, and then I lost my nerve.'

'My Lady—'

She held up a hand. 'Edward's promising boy. But I wasn't, you know – talking about Athelstan.'

He did know, of course. And so, it seemed, did all Mercia and most of Wessex. He had been angrily dismissing slanderous rumours for weeks. Of course the child was her husband's. It had to be. He suspected that her attendant women had leaked the word at first; and every mouth that had picked it up since had tarnished it a little in the telling.

She had clasped her hands now, and was looking down at them, the veils falling forward, hiding her face. 'Our Lady and St Oswald have interceded for me.' A sigh. And then, 'Come Candlemas, there will be a true heir to Mercia.'

Wulfgar was very aware of his breath moving in and out, fast and shallow. He must not show that this miraculous news was no news to him. 'A child of yours, my Lady?'

She nodded.

He had to say something. He forced air down into the depths of his lungs, fighting the constriction of his ribs, the lump in his throat, searching out the right, the tactful, phrase. 'My congratulations, to you and your husband. And my prayers.' A sudden thought came to him. 'Is he – is he well enough to understand?'

'He is not.' She shook her head, a sudden trembling of the veils. 'Please, yes, pray for me. For both – for all of us.'

She looked up then at the reliquary of St Oswald.

'I have you to thank for this.'

For one shocked, ridiculous moment Wulfgar thought she was speaking to him. But no, of course not. Understanding followed.

'St Oswald, of course.'

Candlemas. Five months away.

And five months since her Lord had had his stroke.

She turned her face to him then, and he realised that she must have been crying for some time. The tracks of her tears glistened but her little face was composed, even hard.

'I load too much on your back, Wulfgar, but there are so few people close to me, and even fewer on whose word I can rely.' She closed her eyes briefly. 'My cousin Seiriol – I still trust him, despite everything. I have to. I'm caught between him and Edward.' Her voice had dropped to a murmur, as though she were talking to herself. 'I know Edward wants Mercia; I only suspect it of Seiriol. If only I could talk to him, or even get private word to him...He needs to know about this child.'

Wulfgar had a nasty suspicion he knew what she was going to say next. He concentrated on the muted sunlight coming through the little splayed window in the wall to the south of the shrine and falling across his hands, the glint of gold on Ketil Scar's ring, still on his left thumb. His right hand and arm were healing, but still tender, puffy and itchy, the skin taut and puckered.

'My cousin is back in Leicester,' she said. 'I don't know for how long, though. Are you well enough to ride?'

'Now?'

He'd made his return journey to Mercia in an ox-cart, fearful that he might not be able to manage a horse. His bones could still feel every jolt and rattle. Never again. Better to find some amiable and aged nag, and bunch the reins in his left hand all the way.

'As soon as you can.' She was still staring up at the reliquary. 'Yes, I mean. Now.'

Wearily, he said, 'Yes, my Lady.'

Back to Leicester. A Leicester ruled by the English.

Toli and Gunnvor wouldn't still be there. They'd be in his hall, in Lincoln's Silver Street. Drinking sweet eastern wine out of Toli's chased-gilt cups, and making jokes about Wulfgar Soft-Hands. If they even remembered he existed.

She said, 'I've made you swear too many oaths already. Will you swear one more?'

He nodded. Did he have a choice? What was coming now?

'Swear to serve me and my child after me, come what may, until the day you die.'

Come what may...

'I swear, my Lady,' he said rapidly. 'By my soul, and the Holy Trinity, and the bones of St Oswald whose intercessions made this miracle possible.'

'You and the saint, both,' she said fiercely. 'You brought St Oswald here, and now I have conceived a son, and together we will build a new and powerful Mercia.'

She dismissed him then without another word, turning all her attention back to the saint before whom she was once more kneeling, her shrouded figure now lit by that one oblique shaft of sunlight. He backed silently out of the sanctuary, through the tall, narrow archway, trying to control his treacherous face.

Come what may, he had sworn to be true to the child growing in her womb.

For sixteen years, she had been longing for a child. And now this ambiguous, challenging, answer to her prayers...

He did his calculations yet again, feeling like the coarsest of village rumourmongers, and came to the same reluctant answer. If she were due when she thought, then her husband was most unlikely to be the baby's father, not by any of the usual laws of God and nature.

A miracle, she had said.

Miracles happened, certainly, and some people would be satisfied with that.

Others might be – no, they would be, and indeed he knew they were – putting a grosser interpretation on events.

He headed through the nave for the west door, his head still spinning. He had promised her he would go to Leicester, to get word to Athelwald Seiriol. That promise needed keeping.

'Wulfgar?'

A low, urgent voice, close behind him.

He didn't want to stop but his feet halted him against his will: obedience to his superiors was too deeply engrained. The priest caught up with him in the narthex.

'Wulfgar, the Bishop arrived in Gloucester this morning. He's let it be widely known he wants to see you, in his bower.' He paused. 'That was some time ago. And he didn't sound very happy.'

Wulfgar felt a familiar flush of irritation. He might be sworn – doubly, triply sworn – to the Lady, but the Bishop saw all

364

churchmen in his diocese as answering only to him, and these peremptory orders came all too often. But a bishop was a bishop, and Wulfgar did as he was told. The Bishop of Worcester had his own accommodation on the edge of the palace at Kingsholm, and this would only take a few moments. Then he could go and sort out a horse. A nice, gentle, soft-nosed, understanding horse.

'Wulfgar, what is this I hear about my nephew?'

Where to start?

'My Lord—'

'It's your fault. The boy's a fool, a vain, self-important fool. Did you know he's been ordained priest?'

'No, I didn't—'

'By York's Archbishop, whose pet it seems he has become.' The Bishop knuckled the puckered socket of his vanished eye. 'How did it happen?'

'My Lord—'

'Oh, never mind. I can imagine.'

'My Lord, if that's all...'

'Why are you in such a hurry? Sit down, boy.' The Bishop irritably indicated a stool.

Wulfgar stayed on his feet. 'My Lord, is there something important?'

'Please, sit down.' The Bishop's voice acquired a grudging courtesy and Wulfgar, astonished, sat. 'You've been with Fleda, haven't you?'

He nodded.

'And what is the wide world saying about her?'

Wulfgar knew the answer was written on his face. 'That the Lord of the Mercians had no part in the getting of this child,' he said in an almost inaudible mutter.

'And is there any consensus among the gossips about a name for the father?'

Wulfgar shook his head, unable to meet the Bishop's eye. 'I've heard a dozen different men suggested,' he forced himself to say. His tongue deserved to be torn out with iron pincers for giving those words voice.

'And each less likely than the last.' The old Bishop nodded. 'Let's hope for her sake that the child comes early.'

They shared a long moment of silence.

'Wulfgar, you've been with Seiriol. What kind of a king is he?'

The change of tack caught Wulfgar unawares, like a blow to the back of the head.

'My Lord, you know how he became King of Northumbria?'

A nod.

'He has tremendous energy,' Wulfgar went on cautiously. 'He knows very well how to make men love him. He makes decisions quickly. He shows men the advantages to be gained by serving him.'

'How does he measure against King Edward?'

Wulfgar felt his face tighten. The rock and the hard place...

The Bishop said, 'Nothing you tell me will go any further.'

Wulfgar believed him. He had to shake his head though. 'My Lord, I am not the man to judge. King Edward hanged my brother without giving me the time he promised me to prove Wystan's innocence. And, despite my best efforts, he has taken and kept all our family land – even the one estate that was in my private name.' He choked back the fury that threatened to rise and engulf him. 'I would like to believe that it was incompetence rather than malice in the first instance which made him accuse my brother, but...'

Words failed him.

To his disbelief the Bishop was smiling. 'And you say you're not qualified to judge?' He raised an enquiring eyebrow. 'To which man would you give the high-seat of Mercia?'

'My Lord!' Wulfgar found he was standing, looming over the old man, his fists balled and ready to strike. He looked down at his hands, appalled, and slowly his fingers uncurled and his hands fell back by his sides.

The Bishop chuckled, without any real mirth. 'That burn must be troubling you less, boy. Answer my question.'

'You accuse me of being a traitor,' he said stiffly.

But the Bishop was shaking his head. 'It's a necessary question. Fleda cannot rule Mercia much longer. The Lord is dying – inch by painful inch – but he's dying. Do we sit back and let the wolves tear us to pieces, which they will do? Or do we invite the strongest wolf in and give him our support?' He spread out his hands and looked from one to the other. 'Seiriol? Or Edward? And believe me, Wulfgar, it's not a choice I take any pleasure in making. But I see no third candidate.'

Wulfgar sat down again, slowly and carefully. 'You're her godfather,' he said. 'And now you're betraying her.'

The Bishop had drawn his eyebrows down until his good eye looked as dark and shadowed as his empty socket. The guttering flame sent little flickers of light over the crags and hollows of his face.

'Go back to your Lady, Wulfgar,' he said at last. 'It's not too late. Tell her to go home to Wessex. Become a nun, in decent retirement somewhere. She could go into exile. Pavia.' He shrugged. 'Rome, even. The door isn't closed. Not yet.'

CHAPTER FORTY-SEVEN

Leicester

Despite the Bishop's no-doubt-excellent advice, Wulfgar had not gone back to the Lady. He had requisitioned what the quartermaster swore was the most long-suffering horse in the Kingsholm stables, and headed out that same evening. It was only ninety miles to Leicester. How hard an errand could this be?

'God bless you, Wulfgar. How did you know to come?'

The plump, sloe-eyed woman whom Wulfgar had only ever known as Kevin's mother stood in the low doorway of the presbytery. The September wind chased the first ragged brown leaves around her skirt hems.

'Know?' He shook his head. 'The Lady sent me.'

'Whatever brings you, we're right glad you've come.' But she didn't look glad. Her face was weary and laden with sadness. 'You'll find another friend of yours here, too.'

He frowned, more confused than ever, then suddenly had a moment of revelation. 'Gunnvor?' His heart skidded.

But Kevin's mother was shaking her head, almost smiling for a moment. She turned and called something over her shoulder. To Wulfgar's utter disbelief, her summons was answered by a neatly dressed girl in a white apron-dress, her long plait of light brown hair neatly looped and tied back on itself.

'*Gerd*?' He must be hallucinating.

She ducked her head but he couldn't mistake her shy smile. He turned back to Kevin's mother. 'How did she get here?'

'Let her tell you. You should know this much, I've been blessing you for giving her our name. She's been a daughter to me.' Kevin's mother pushed past Gerd and went back into the dim presbytery.

'I came with the army,' the girl said softly, still looking down. 'You said, St Margaret's Kirk. But you were gone when I came.'

'You followed me?' He was appalled by the risks she had taken. 'A girl like you, with the camp-followers?'

'People were kind,' Gerd said defensively. 'None kinder than here.' She gestured behind her. 'I was going to go on to find you' – he watched her cheeks redden – 'but I was needed here.'

'You've been here for a whole month?' He shook his head at her. 'Whyever did they need you here?'

'You don't know?' She looked him full in the face for the first time, her grey-blue eyes startled and sorry. 'Oh, Wulfgar...'

He lifted his own head then, heart full of a sudden sickening premonition. She stepped away from the door and motioned for him to go inside. As he stooped under the lintel a stale gust of air came from the room behind her.

'You said you weren't ill! You were lying to me!'

Till Kevin's mother put her finger to her lips Wulfgar hadn't realised he'd been shouting.

He squatted down by the rush mat.

Ronan turned his head, and Wulfgar had to stifle a gasp. The stink – old piss, decaying flesh, illness – was overwhelming. His friend's robust flesh had melted away like candle wax, and what was left was like wax too, dark yellow and horribly smooth, taut over cheekbones and the curved dome of his skull. Even the whites of his eyes were stained yellow.

'Yes. I lied.' The mellow, humorous voice had gone too, replaced by a rasp. Ronan forced a grin. 'How did you know I wanted you, Wuffa?'

He couldn't say, *I didn't.*

'The Lady let me come.'

It wasn't much of an answer but Ronan seemed to accept it.

Wulfgar reached over and picked up the withered hand that lay on the bedclothes. It was clay-cold, with only its moistness and slight quiver betraying that its owner was still alive.

'What's wrong with you?'

Ronan closed his eyes. 'There's a crab attacking my guts. Eating me from the inside.' He shuddered. 'I can feel it, Wuffa. I can feel it moving. Growing. Like a woman quick with child.'

Wulfgar swallowed his disgust. 'How long... ?'

'Have I known?' The priest rolled his head from side to side. 'Oh, I suspected in the summer.' His face tensed and contracted, eyes squeezed shut. 'I've seen it before,' he said. 'In others.'

Wulfgar felt a spring tide of panic rising within him, driven forward by shock, revulsion, fury. He scrabbled for something to say.

'Can I get you anything?'

'He can't eat.' Kevin's mother was squatting at his shoulder, her face impassive. 'He can't even drink. When his mouth gets dry I wash it out with beer.'

Ronan shook his head. 'Too sore.' He lifted his other hand to gesture at his mouth.

'I can't believe this,' Wulfgar said. He stroked the clammy, shaking hand, feeling useless. 'I wish I'd got here earlier. I wish I'd never left you.'

'No matter. You're here now.' Ronan gestured feebly with his free hand. 'She's yours if you want her.'

For one giddy moment Wulfgar thought Ronan had to be referring to Gunnvor. He looked wildly into the shadows the priest had indicated, the angle where daub wall met corner post.

No one there.

Ronan was still pointing.

He looked harder. A pile of clothes, a bag, propped against a chest with its lid standing open.

A bag.

Realisation came slowly.

'Uhtsang,' he said. 'Your harp.'

Ronan nodded.

'Bring her.'

Wulfgar picked up the beaver-skin bag and, drawing out the harp, made to rest it on his friend's lap but stopped when he saw him tense.

'Sorry,' Ronan whispered. 'It hurts.'

Wulfgar nodded. 'Do you want to play her?'

Ronan shook his head, and swallowed, in obvious pain.

'You,' he grated.

Queen of Heaven, what to play, for this audience? His thoughts raced while his fingers moved slowly and gently, tightening the strings with the little bronze key. All his eyes could see was darkness.

'What shall I sing?'

Ronan's mouth twitched.

'Do you remember the Cuckoo Song?'

'The one you sang in the Wave-Serpent, the evening we first met?'

'The look on your face.'

Wulfgar tried to laugh with him. 'I was shocked,' he confessed.

'And, God forgive me, I was trying to shock you. Such a sweet, wide-eyed little subdeacon.'

Wulfgar looked down at the instrument lying in his lap.

'I wanted to ask you to teach me to play the way you do.'

'That's a compliment, coming from you.' Ronan winced and panted for breath, but he batted Kevin's mother away when she leaned over him.

'Hold her more upright,' he said when he could. 'Use your right elbow to keep her in place. Let her talk to you...'

Ronan tried to lever himself up the better to see but slumped heavily back on the mat, a sheen of sweat on his jaundiced forehead. After a moment he shook his head from side to side in frustration.

'We've left this lesson too late, Wuffa. Damn it.'

He closed his eyes.

'I should never have left you,' Wulfgar said in a sudden moment of blind passion. *Let the dead bury the dead.* 'God would have looked out for Wystan, and I could have stayed with you.'

The priest's eyes were still shut.

Kevin's mother pushed in next to him, felt the bony wrist for a pulse. 'He's with us yet,' she said. She picked up Ronan's hand, turning it over and pressing the palm to her lips. 'Gerd, bring some water. We can wash him while he's asleep.'

Wulfgar turned away, feeling the outrage of his intrusion into this woman's private anguish. But when he turned back she was smiling at him.

'Will you be staying tonight?'

'*Here?*'

'Please,' she said. Then, 'It won't be long, you know.' She paused. 'He's been asking for you a lot.'

So he stayed. She and Gerd offered him food but nobody had any appetite. They sat by the hearth. Ronan dozed and woke, and cried out, and muttered, and they looked after him and kept him clean as well as they could.

It was the longest night of Wulfgar's life.

In between tending to Ronan, Kevin's mother told him that, yes, the Atheling was in Leicester with his bride (only she called them the King and Queen, and Wulfgar couldn't for a moment think whom she meant); that he had spent the month since the battle going round the little warlords of the East Midlands, commandeering the loyalty of the lesser jarls of places like Derby and Nottingham.

'They're calling him Lord of the Five Boroughs,' she said, 'as well as King of York.'

'Lord of the Five Boroughs,' he said thoughtfully. The title had a fine ring to it. 'That's most of eastern Mercia, then. Old Mercia, I mean.'

'Aye,' she said. 'Before the Danes came.'

'What does Toli of Lincoln have to say to that?' Wormwood and gall, just having the name in his mouth.

She snorted, and reached out to poke the smouldering logs. Rain and wind rattled the thatch. 'Toli's regretting ever allying himself with Seiriol, or so men say.'

Ronan moaned, and muttered something. She rose in a single,

fluid movement and went to his side, bending down low and close. Then she stepped to the door.

'I'll be but a moment. Gerd, watch the fire.'

Gerd nodded. She had said little all night, but Wulfgar had seen how quick and deft she was, how ready to anticipate need, and he wanted to say something to her of how very grateful he was.

He was about to open his mouth, but Ronan spoke first.

'Wuffa.'

Wulfgar's head snapped round. 'I'm here.'

'Sing to me.'

Ronan's voice was surprisingly loud and clear.

'But is that the best thing, when you're so exhausted? You should confess, and be absolved.'

But how, without another priest?

'The last rites...' he said, increasingly anxious. 'I could do what I can to help, if you have the chrism oil.' He peered frantically around the dark little room.

'Let be, lad.' Ronan's sweating face cracked in a wry smile. 'God and I know each other too well for that.'

Wulfgar opened his mouth, only to close it again. His mouth was painfully dry.

'If you're sure.'

'Aye, Wuffa, lad. I'm sure.'

'Very well.' He drained the last of his beer and reached for the harp. He had no idea what he was going to sing. Start with the harp. *Let her talk to you...* The weight of her pressed against his right arm, which burned and smarted in response, but he embraced the pain with a savage joy.

'Uhtsang,' he chanted, his voice low and unsure, singing less to his friend than to the old instrument nestled so trustingly in his lap. 'Sweetest of harps, truest of singers.' He hesitated, his fingers sore and clumsy, his voice breaking like a boy's. It would be dawn soon, a stormy autumn morning. What would sunrise bring? He swallowed. Uhtsang, whose name meant dawn chorus, what was she telling him?

'Song before sunrise,' he started again tentatively, 'the babble of birds, oblates and elders, singing their matin-song, fresh at first light.'

He was finding pace and rhythm now, his voice still low but richer, firmer, truer as he groped after each word, his fingers barely brushing the strings. He hardly registered Kevin's mother coming back in, with the son whom Ronan had fathered huddling close against her skirts like a much smaller child, his face sombre and fearful.

'But I cannot sleep the summerlong night. Milky glimmer marks the midnight north. Each girn of gull, cry of curlew, brings back my friends, my lost loves, oh! To have them at my hearth again, with the cheering cup, the harp's sweet song. I falter and fall short, weave a waking song of the road still reaching before me, the pilgrim path, and, oh, I recall how so many loving lords and true thanes, they have trodden the track before me, their shadows already slipping out of sight—'

He looked up for the first time. Young Kevin was sitting close to him, holding hands with a sombre Gerd. Kevin's mother was looking at him as he played, her face streaked with tears. Ronan's head was in her lap, her hands stroking his hair, keeping gentle time with Wulfgar's low singing. As Wulfgar watched, she bent low over Ronan, her eyes wide and her expression intent. She held up one hand, and he trailed his fingers over the strings once more, and stopped.

There was a long shuddering gasp, and silence.

CHAPTER FORTY-EIGHT

'Where is he?'

Wrapped up in the shroud of his own misery, it took Wulfgar a moment to recognise her. Gunnvor pushed back the hood of her dark cloak and slithered down from the saddle, staggering slightly as her feet hit the ground. She glanced left and right, taking in at a single glance the meaning of the bustle of mourners going in and out of the presbytery where Kevin's mother and her gossips had been washing and preparing Ronan's body. Even as they watched Kevin staggered out with a pile of soiled mats and bedstraw, ready to add it to the growing stack in the yard.

Although the rain had stopped earlier that morning, she was sodden, he realised, and filthy, her hair darker than ever, with long strands worked loose from their silver pins and plastered in thick strips against her face, which was streaked and splattered with mud, mottled with cold and exhaustion.

'I'm too late.'

'He was so ill, Gunnvor. He wouldn't have wanted you to see him like that, not at the end.'

He expected her backlash of anger: he would have welcomed it, but instead she just nodded dumbly.

He took a step towards her. 'Let me take your horse.'

She stared at him.

He gestured at the reins, still clutched in her strong white hand. 'She needs a bran mash, at the very least.'

'We rode all night,' she said.

'We?' He looked around, hit by a sudden, gut-wrenching, conviction that Toli had come with her. But she was alone, and he realised she meant her grey mare. 'You've come from *Lincoln*?'

She nodded.

'You rode fifty miles in the dark? On your own? Have you gone raving mad? Ronan wouldn't want you with a broken neck...' He was beside himself with fury.

'Ronan,' she said, in a tiny voice, and let the reins go just before she crumpled gracelessly to the cobbles.

Wulfgar stared at her, his anger evaporating. What was he supposed to do now? He looked around helplessly, hoping for Kevin's mother or some other competent woman to take over, but no one was near. Reluctantly, he knelt beside her with some vague thought of checking whether she had hit her head.

'Come on. Sit up.' Daring greatly, he put his left hand on her arm and shook it slightly, but he met no response. 'Gunnvor?' He bent forward. He couldn't hear her breathing. In a sudden rush of anxiety he pressed his fingers to her lips and after a moment, to his fathomless relief, he felt the faint warmth of her breath come and go. 'Gunnvor,' he said again. 'This isn't like you.' He tried to get his good arm around her shoulders, to pull her up.

377

She looked so small, lying there.

'Leave me alone,' she muttered. 'I think I'm going to be sick.'

'Please, don't.' He looked around in renewed panic. 'Come on, we need to get you dry and warm.'

She was rolling over now, levering herself up to sitting. Her face was very pale, with a bluish tinge to her lips but, even as he watched, she began to look more like herself. 'I'm not wet. This cloak keeps everything out. Were you with him?'

He nodded.

'Who's going to bury him?'

The question astonished him. 'Why should you care?'

'You think that's your prerogative, don't you?' She pushed the wet strands of hair away from her face and swallowed, visibly fighting nausea. 'He deserves the best your Church can give him.'

'I could bury him.'

'You? You're not even a priest.'

But he could have been. Indeed, he would have been ordained priest by now, Wulfgar realised, had he only been prepared to let his uncle drive a horse and cart through canon law when they had offered him an easy version of the ordeal, back in Winchester. And now, it seemed, his high-minded refusal was putting Ronan's soul in peril. What a fool he had been.

She was getting to her feet now, angrily pushing away the hand he was offering. 'So find him a priest.' She hugged herself under her cloak, shivering. 'Go on. What are you waiting for?' She turned away from him and started walking towards the presbytery door, her head high. Kevin's mother was ducking out from under the low door with a pile of linen but, on seeing Gunnvor, she dropped it. The two women embraced and went inside.

But Ronan was the only priest in Leicester, Wulfgar found

himself thinking foolishly. And then he remembered: Leicester wasn't the jarldom of Ketil Scar any more. It was in the possession of a Christian, West Saxon king. How could he have forgotten, even for a moment?

He began walking towards the walled city. Somewhere, in the King's train, there would be a priest.

As he went through the Eastgate, an old woman walking by stopped and peered back at him. 'Priest's friend?'

He nodded, not trusting his voice.

'Thought I knew you, from staking sanctuary. How does he?'

Wulfgar crossed himself, and the woman's eyes widened. 'Gone? No!'

He nodded again. Licking his lips nervously he said, 'Where's the Atheling – I mean, the King – lodging? Is there a priest with him?'

'Aye,' she said. He tried not to flinch as she took his arm. 'Come along of me.'

He was hardly aware of being led through the maze of buildings and out beyond the wall again to where a sprawling tented encampment stood, of being passed from sentry to sentry, until he heard his name being called in a voice he didn't recognise.

'There you are!'

Wulfgar turned, startled, hardly aware of the old woman bowing and edging away.

'Someone told the King he'd seen you last night, but I was beginning to think he must have got it wrong.' Young Alwin was coming towards him. 'I looked for you myself, weeks ago, but they said you'd left York. I wanted to thank—'

He cut through the boy's words. 'I need a priest.'

Alwin stared at him.

'Does the King have one with him?'

'Yes, of course he does,' Alwin said. 'Didn't you know?'

'This priest – where might I find him?'

Alwin shrugged. 'In the cathedral, most likely.' He looked at Wulfgar's anxious face. 'But that will have to wait. My Lord King wants you. He said so last night. He said, if anyone else saw you—'

'No,' Wulfgar said, shaking his head. 'Not now.'

'I don't know what's more important than seeing the King.' Alwin looked uncomfortable. 'He won't be very pleased if I have to go back and say you've refused to come.'

'But—' Wulfgar looked at the boy's anxious face and bit his tongue. Alwin was right. What was he in Leicester for, anyway, if not to carry the Lady's message? He turned to follow him towards the largest and grandest of the tents.

'What happened to your hand?' Alwin asked, looking in fascinated horror at the still discoloured, swollen, peeling skin.

What could he say? Any proof of Wystan's innocence only served to brand this boy's father a liar as well as a traitor. 'Burned,' he said shortly, stumbling over a guy-rope.

The wind was picking up and the canvas and the banners were rattling and cracking with every gust. Alwin was speaking to the guard at the royal tent, who ducked under the lowered flap and reappeared almost immediately.

'He'll come out to you.'

Hardly had he finished speaking when the King followed him. Wulfgar sank to his knees but felt himself being pulled upwards, warm, friendly hands on his shoulders pulling him into a fraternal embrace.

'No ceremony among old friends.' The King stepped back and

smiled warmly. 'I was so sorry to hear you had left York so suddenly, but I know what it was that was calling you back to Winchester.' He shook his head, and glanced at Wulfgar's arm. 'And you're a brave man, from what I hear. There's not many would do that for a dead man, no matter how beloved.'

Did Athelwald Seiriol know that he and Ronan had carried news of the invasion to Ketil Scar? But what difference did it make, now? Ketil had known the army was coming, and he had readied himself, and he had still lost.

Treaties with Knut of York, treaties with Ketil of Leicester, blown away on the wind like so much chaff, like bonfire ash...

There was a stir at the tent-flap, and Wulfgar saw Elfled looking out. She nodded an unsmiling greeting.

Wulfgar took a step closer to her husband.

'My Lord King, a private word?'

Seiriol took his elbow and turned them away slightly from the curious eyes.

'I'm learning that a King has no privacy,' he said.

Wulfgar found himself stammering even before he got to the meat of his message. The King was looking at him with curiosity and amusement in his dark brown eyes. Wulfgar was sure Elfled could still hear them.

He breathed, 'The Lady your cousin...'

Seiriol nodded, still smiling.

'My Lord King, she is expecting a child come Candlemas.'

Was there even a flicker of surprise? The King's smile broadened to show his white, even teeth. 'Then my heartiest congratulations to my cousin and her Lord. Perhaps this news will be the beginning of his return to health.' His voice was pitched to carry, and his gaze flickered over Wulfgar's shoulder, back towards the royal tent. 'Tell her that my bride and I hope to have equally joyful news to share before long.'

Wulfgar opened his mouth again, wanting to ask about a priest. But he was too late.

The King was still patting him on the shoulder, but his attention had already moved on. 'I'm sorry we're in no position to receive you as you deserve. As you can see, we're still on a war footing when we're in Leicester. Next time, eh, Wuffa? In the meantime, go and ask my quartermaster to see you and your horse are fed.'

It was an unambiguous dismissal.

Wulfgar bowed deeply, and backed away, shuffling to avoid tripping over those treacherous guy-ropes that threaded over the grass like autumn gossamer.

The cathedral was quiet.

Wulfgar peered around, reacquainting himself with the battered, cave-like interior of shabby stone and smoke-damaged plaster. He walked from side-chapel to side-chapel, remembering how Ronan had done the same thing a brief month since, but the place felt empty. He peered through the chancel arch, into the sanctuary. A candle was glowing on the altar, and he bowed his head.

He was vaguely aware of another presence at his side.

Alwin. The boy must have seen him and followed him.

'It makes my skin crawl, this place,' he heard Alwin mutter. 'It's those eyes…'

Wulfgar looked up. From the curved ceiling of the apse the painted face of the Redeemer gazed down at him. Alwin was right: the eyes were terrifying, a mixture of anger and heartbreak, and as he moved they seemed to follow him. He crossed himself and murmured a last prayer before getting to his feet.

Even before the tall, fair-haired figure turned towards him in the gloom of the candle-lit nave, Wulfgar knew whose face he was going to see. The whole thing had an awful inevitability about it.

He forced his voice into obsequiousness.

'Kenelm, I need your help.'

Kenelm said nothing, only raising an eyebrow.

'Help only you can provide. Father Ronan has died and we need you to bury him.' Wulfgar's voice broke on the last words.

'Died?' Kenelm's pale eyes narrowed. 'And who attended his death-bed?'

'I did.'

'No final unction, then? No confession? No reconciliation?'

Wulfgar's heart began an agitated irregular thump. 'Ronan's soul was hallowed by a lifetime in God's service.'

'So you say.' Kenelm had drawn himself up to his full height, his arms folded across his chest. 'But I've heard from other people that he was a violent man, who went armed, with blood on his hands. A disgrace to his orders.'

'But—'

Kenelm uncrossed his arms and wagged a warning finger. 'He was a lecher, who kept more than one woman, and saw no shame in letting his by-blow serve at the altar.'

'He—'

'Hear me out, Wulfgar. He dressed as a layman, and he behaved like one. He was a slave's son with no right to the priesthood. No one even seems to know who was the bishop that ordained him or indeed if he ever was ordained at all.'

'He was one of the best men I've ever met.'

Kenelm shook his head reprovingly. 'So stubborn, Wuffa. I've had cause to reprove you for that before, you know.'

'Don't you call me Wuffa.' Wulfgar felt a most unholy rage beginning to build. 'You mean you won't bury him?'

'On reflection, yes.' Kenelm assumed a sorry expression. 'That's what I must conclude.'

'Wulfgar!' He turned at Alwin's cry but the boy was there, in front of him, holding his arms down.

'What are you doing?' He struggled. 'Let me go.'

'Put your knife away,' Alwin gasped. 'You mustn't draw your knife, not in a church, and you a man of God.'

Wulfgar looked down at his hand in shock. The boy was right: four inches of cold honed iron gleamed in his fist. His arm dropped back by his side.

Kenelm was cowering back against a pillar, but he recovered quickly. 'Fortunate for you,' he said, 'that you have your nursemaid with you. Now, if you don't mind, I have a meeting with the master stonemason.'

Wulfgar turned to see a leather-aproned workman standing patiently in the shadows.

'Yes,' Kenelm said, almost purring. 'We are going to rebuild the cathedral, Wuffa. My Lord King and my Lord Archbishop are even talking about reviving the bishopric. And, now you tell me that the living of St Margaret's has come free, I will have to see about appointing a priest to the benefice.'

Wulfgar gawked at him. Was this what he himself looked like? When he wrapped himself in his cosy thoughts of a nice warm cathedral, and a well-endowed bishopric, with clerics and craftsmen at his beck and call – did he too have that smooth, self-satisfied note in his voice? No wonder, if so, that Gunnvor despised him.

'It's only justice,' Kenelm said. 'I am acting entirely according to canon law. Your so-called priest is only getting his just deserts.'

Wulfgar pushed his belt-knife slowly back into its sheath. 'Kenelm,' he said, 'come into the sanctuary with me.'

Without waiting for an answer he walked through the narrow arch – *eye of the needle*, he thought – and into the sanctuary. He lifted his gaze to the face of the Saviour.

'Look what the artist has done,' he said softly. There was a rustle somewhere behind him, but he had no idea if Kenelm – if it were Kenelm – could hear him.

'Look how he has painted the left side of His face narrower than the right, and how the hollows and shadows are more exaggerated on that side. That's part of the reason He appears to watch you as you move around.' Wulfgar crossed himself. 'And do you see how the eye on the narrower side has a frowning aspect, with the eyebrow crooked and the eyelid slightly lowered? But the other' – and now he did look round, to find Alwin at his side, and Kenelm framed by the archway – 'the other eye, His right eye, is wide open. Its expression is soft and mild.' He peered up into the darkness. 'Even the pupil is larger.'

'So?' Kenelm sounded impatient. 'Are you saying the painter didn't know what he was doing?'

'No.' Wulfgar felt for a moment as though his heart would break. 'The painter was wonderfully skilful.' He turned back to Kenelm. 'You mentioned justice a moment ago. Well, here it is. This is the face of the Lord as He will look at the Last Judgement. But justice is only half of the story.' He felt the passion building in his voice again and took a moment to breathe. 'Look at His face. There's mercy there as well, Kenelm. There's love. There's forgiveness.'

But Kenelm's face was cold. 'I'm not giving in to your bullying.' He turned on his heel and walked away.

CHAPTER FORTY-NINE

It was raining when Wulfgar left the cathedral, it was raining as he walked back to St Margaret's and it was raining as a full half-dozen of Ronan's brawnier parishioners laboured to dig the priest's grave. Wulfgar was working alongside them doggedly, his teeth gritted, ignoring the pain in his arm. It was miserable work, the heavy, claggy soil threatening to snap the shafts of their spades, clinging to the blades when they tried to scrape them clean, the sides of the grave collapsing back into the trench, water puddling in the bottom. Wulfgar was the only one wearing shoes, and he soon had to discard them; their slick leather soles had left him scrabbling stupidly for purchase.

'Where's the priest then?' Gunnvor raised an eyebrow.

'He wouldn't come.'

Her eyes flared with anger, but she paused then and looked hard at his face, and in the end she nodded and pulled her hood more closely about her head. 'Go on.'

The rain continued throughout the brief burial liturgy. Wulfgar, his heart full of bitterness, read such prayers as his subdeacon's orders entitled him to from Ronan's tattered and greasy Service for the Dead. Somewhere up there behind that pall of cloud, veiled from their eyes, the gates of Heaven were swinging open, and the Divine Light was pouring forth as the angels ran singing with joy to bring Ronan home. But from down here all he could see was a sky of unrelieved grey.

'*In memoria æterna erit iustus,*' he sang, loud and true as he could, the tears and the rain trickling indistinguishably down his cheeks. '*Ab auditione mala non timebit.*' Never had the familiar words of the Gradual seemed more appropriate.

'So, what did all that gabble mean?' Gunnvor asked.

The grave had been back-filled over the swaddled corpse, which already seemed to have nothing to do with the man Wulfgar had been honoured to call his friend. The other mourners, one by one, had departed.

He glanced at her.

'Well, first I sang the Requiem, asking God to grant him eternal rest. Then the Gradual – *He shall be justified in everlasting memory, and shall not fear evil reports.*' He bit back the inappropriate words that threatened to burst forth, about Kenelm and his vile words. 'And then, at the end, the *In Paradisum* – how the angels will be leading him even now into God's very presence...'

Pain caught his diaphragm.

She was silent. He could hardly see her face; her hood was pulled so low. When she did speak, he had to strain to hear. 'First my father, Bolli. We burned him, by the river, and raised a mound to his memory. Then Hakon.' Wulfgar couldn't help glancing briefly over at that other grave, with its wooden marker. 'And, now, Ronan.' Her voice, usually so musical, was entirely without expression. 'It's as though I've woken up to find the sky gone.' She pushed her hood back then, glancing upwards as though to check the truth of her words. She had rebraided her hair, and the dark twists and plaits gleamed with silver pins. He thought again of giving her that little enamel brooch, before remembering with a jolt where he had last seen it, pinned to the neck of Gerd's tunic.

'You're getting wet again,' he said foolishly.

She laughed harshly. 'And have you looked at your own self, Wulfgar Soft-Hands?'

He knew without looking down that he was a mess of mud: he had seen what the other grave-diggers looked like.

'Have you got any clean linen?' she went on. 'Where are you sleeping tonight?'

'I thought—'

He looked across the graveyard to Ronan's presbytery, and as he did so a sudden blow of a thought slammed into him. He didn't even know whether he managed to stammer his excuses: he ran in a most unclerical fashion through the little graveyard and past the church, into the yard in front of the presbytery. Despite all the rain, the bonfire of Ronan's bedstraw and moth-eaten blankets was still smouldering sullenly.

'Kevin,' he bawled frantically, running towards the pile of wet, smoking ash. 'Kevin, where are you?'

He was about to plunge his hands into the detritus of the fire when he felt a hand on his shoulder.

Gunnvor said, 'It's the harp, isn't it?'

'They've burnt her.' He staggered to his feet, staring around in a frenzy. 'They've burnt Uhtsang.'

He would do anything, even undergo the ordeal again, to make it not have happened.

'Wuffa, no! No one would think of burning the harp!'

He had picked up a stick and was beginning a frantic stirring of the ashes. 'There might be something left – one of the silver birds…'

'Wuffa, *listen* to me. I've got the harp. I took her back to my house by the Wave-Serpent.' She was in front of him, holding his elbows. 'Look at me. Uhtsang is safe. I'm keeping her for you.'

He did look at her then, that treacherous tic tugging like a fish-hook at his eyelid. The sense of her words began to seep through, and his breathing steadied as he realised how irrational he was being. She was still gripping his elbows, staring hard into his eyes.

'Come back with me,' she said.

'I was going to sleep in the presbytery—'

She shivered and glanced upwards again. 'No.'

'At Kevin's mother's, then.' He tried to pull away.

'Wuffa, what are you afraid of?'

He felt the treacherous blood rush up through the veins of his neck, his chin, cheeks, brow; and he was profoundly grateful for the autumn dusk, and those splatters of mud, serving to veil him.

She dropped her hands.

'My Nonna is there,' she said. 'My old nurse. She'll chaperone you.' For the first time all that endless, weary day, a hint of the old mocking amusement had crept back into her voice and, perversely, it made him want to weep.

'Come on,' she said.

Although he had been to the Wave-Serpent before, he had never known which part of the labyrinth of little wooden buildings was her private quarters. Old Nonna was ecstatic, fussing round Gunnvor remorselessly, dropping stones into pails to heat water, bearing off Gunnvor's great black cloak to air.

Once she was satisfied that her chick was warm and dry, she turned her attentions to Wulfgar, brushing and wiping the mud from him, and clucking over his fresh linen – 'I don't know whose cack-handed thrall mended this' – and shamelessly seeing him into a change of clothes, having first banished Gunnvor, near-hysterical with laughter, into the bed-alcove.

She fed them too, with a rich apple-gruel and little bannocks and hot wine flavoured with cinnamon and pepper.

After they had eaten, Gunnvor ferreted through a pile of grizzled sheepskins and pulled out a familiar beaverskin bag. Wulfgar hadn't doubted her word, but when he saw the harp bag he felt a new and almost painful sensation of gratitude and relief.

'You can go,' she said to the old woman. She turned her head to look at Wulfgar briefly, then back to Nonna. 'Don't worry about us.'

He didn't think she had been talking to him, but he did worry, he couldn't help it. He was slightly drunk, more on her presence than the spiced wine or the sweet scents of pine and applewood that came from the fire. She was moving about the room, opening a small carved box and putting her great silver cloak brooch carefully away inside. She left the lid open, and, lifting her arms, she began to unpin her hair. He was unable to tear his gaze from her. She stood sideways to him, the fire casting highlights and shadows across her strong, proud face.

The fire crackled, and snapped occasionally as a pine cone burnt away, and again and again there came a tiny ringing sound as she took out another silver pin and dropped it into the box. Some were decorated with tassels or bells or further loops of wire that glinted in the firelight as they moved in her hand down from her head and into the box. There were so many of them. It was a steady rhythmic movement, rather like watching a woman at the loom. Her braids were uncoiling now, snaking down her back, and now she was unbraiding them and letting her hair ripple loose. He had never seen her before with her hair down around her face. Rather than softening her raptor's features the black waterfall sharpened them, giving her a feral, witchy quality that was new to him.

He shifted, a little uncomfortable now on the bench, and she looked at him for the first time. She raised her eyebrows, unsmiling, and reached both hands up to first her left and then her right collarbone to unpin the brooches that kept her green overdress in place. The silk-trimmed linen slithered to the floor, and she stepped out of it. He watched, entranced, as she bent to pick it up, shake out the folds and smooth out the creases and then roll it up like a scroll before putting it in the larger of the two chests that stood at the foot of the sleeping platform. She sat down on the edge of the bed and pulled up the skirts of her linen underdress to untie her shoes and unroll her stockings.

He tried to speak, failed. Swallowed, and tried again. 'Gunnvor—?'

She nodded without looking up, her hair falling past and concealing her face.

'Gunnvor, where am I going to sleep?'

She stood up then, the stockings balled in one hand, the shoes dangling by their thongs from the other.

'Let me put these away.'

He closed his eyes. He felt she might as well have been naked, dressed as she was by then in nothing but her white shift, with the distractions of her silks and silver and gilt all carefully bestowed elsewhere. And her feet were naked, slim and high-arched and somehow eloquent, catlike on the smooth floorboards.

He heard the pad of bare feet, a rustle of linen, and he knew she was standing in front of him.

'Wuffa,' she said.

He had lost the ability to move. He waited, eyes still shut, putting all his energy into keeping his hands loosely clasped in his lap.

He felt her fingertips trace the sides of his face, from his temples down over his cheekbones, encountering the close-shaved stubble of his jaw, meeting each other at his chin and then drawing away.

'You are beautiful, you know.' Then that achingly familiar, throaty laugh. 'No, you don't know, do you? You haven't the faintest idea.'

He was shaking, quite hard.

'Gunnvor, tomorrow—'

He found he still couldn't open his eyes, though he wanted to. He found her fingers now pressed against his lips.

'Ssh. Let tomorrow look after itself.'

And then her fingers splayed and she grasped his chin, and he did open his eyes, to find her mouth fastening on his, as sweet and soft as figs, as honey, as eager as any bee diving after nectar. He was holding her, warm in his arms, and trying to keep up with her kisses, and it was as his dreams had been – so many dreams – but better, indescribably better.

And now he was kissing her, and pulling her down beside him on the bench, and her hands were hard and probing and demanding under his tunic and his linen. He cried out with terrible desire, pleasure that was merging with pain, he wanted her so badly, and it was so wrong.

She pulled away from him then, her lips red and swollen, her creamy skin flushed with more than firelight, her eyes heavy, more beautiful than he could possibly have imagined. He looked away, unable to bear it.

'Wuffa, you've never been here before, have you?'

He tried to answer.

Couldn't.

He shook his head. It was a while before he dared look at her face, and the expression he saw then rocked him to his foundations. A softness there, a tenderness entirely new to him.

Oh, Gunnvor Bolladottir, he thought, *whenever I think I've learned you by heart you amaze me all over again.*

Their eyes met. He felt as though his heart was going to break.

She picked up his left hand in both of hers and held it gently, still gazing into his eyes. Her shift had slipped sideways, and he could see her collarbone and most of the white curve of her shoulder. She was stroking the back of his hand now, kneading and squeezing his fingers, rubbing the tip of her thumb against his palm. He could feel the thunderheads of desire beginning to build again and, sharper than he meant to, he pulled his hand away before he could be plunged back into that terrifying storm.

She began to reach after him, and then, quite suddenly, she stopped, looking at his face, and she drew herself back. Her expression had changed. The softness had vanished.

'Gunnvor,' he said, pleading now, 'I – I don't—'

She stared at him.

He tried to speak, but he had no idea what he might say to her.

She stood up. The rustle of her linen, which had sounded so warmly inviting only moments ago, hissed now like the north wind with snow at its back. He put his face in his hands, humiliated and speechless and still incapacitated with longing.

'Gunnvor—'

'Don't say anything.' Her voice was tight, each syllable weighed out scrupulously.

He tried to think of a response, but, before he could, she said, 'You know, men – powerful men, rich men – have asked me before now, and been refused. Men have *begged* for what you – you—'

He had never heard her at a loss for words before. It frightened him. He was terribly thirsty, suddenly. He pressed his palms against his eyes.

'Why not?' She exhaled then, a ragged expulsion of breath. 'Am I not good enough? Hakon's whore, is that what you're thinking? Toli's whore?'

He shook his head desperately. And it was the truth: none of that mattered to him, although he knew perhaps it should.

'Or are you afraid Toli will come after you?'

The contempt in her voice cut him through to the marrow. He lifted his head at last. He still couldn't look at her: the sight might sear his eyeballs. Staring at her feet, firmly planted less than a yard in front of him, he said, below his breath, 'It matters too much.'

'What?'

'*You* matter too much.' His mouth was still painfully dry. He prayed desperately for the strength to find the right words. 'I don't know – I don't understand exactly what you're offering me, only that it's a treasure above rubies.' He lifted his eyes to her face to find that she was gazing fixedly away from him, her chin lifted and her jaw set. He contemplated that proud, hawk-like profile for a moment, waiting for her reply, but she said nothing.

He hauled in his courage, and went on.

'Look at me, Gunnvor.' He got to his feet then, holding his arms away from his sides. 'I've got nothing to give you any more.

I can't marry you. Garmund's got my land, as well as my brother's. I used to be a son of the House of Meon, but now—'

'You make me sick.'

'What?'

'Listen to yourself! *Nothing to give you! I can't marry you!* Who's asking you?' She whirled on him. 'I know exactly what you've been thinking. You want to save me from myself, don't you? Just as you wanted to rescue Leicester Cathedral. I can read your mind, Wulfgar Soft-Hands. *What an honour I could pay her, turning down a bishopric for her sake!* That's it, isn't it? That's what you've been thinking. So noble, so high-minded.'

But it wasn't like that! He shied away from the reflection she was holding up. Waves of nausea were threatening to rise and swamp him. It wasn't like that at all. Was it? His hands crept back to his eyes, shielding himself from the furious vision.

Misery, heavy and cold as a pig of iron, was settling in the sediment of his gut.

'Here.'

He said nothing.

'*Here.*'

He forced his hands away from his face, but he still couldn't make himself look up.

'Take her,' she said.

He recoiled, not understanding.

'He wanted you to have her. The harp for you, and the sword for Kevin, just in case, for some inexplicable reason, the lad doesn't want to be a priest after all.'

The harp bag, with its thick, lustrous beaver fur, gleamed before his eyes, but he shook his head.

'I'll burn her myself, if you won't take her.'

Then, at last, he did reach out his hands and take the soft, plush bag, bulky with its precious cargo. He stared at it, unseeing.

'Sleep here.'

Her words were followed by a series of rustling noises, and the rattle of curtain rings, and he guessed she had gone into the bed alcove to join old Nonna. He stretched himself out on the sheepskins as instructed, his arms still holding the harp-bag. He stared at the banked fire. It was a long time before he slept.

CHAPTER FIFTY

Wulfgar woke alone.

His sponged and mended clothes were in a neat pile next to the harp and his saddlebags, beside the banked fire. A wooden bowl with a small loaf, a withered apple and a slice of hard cheese sat next to them. He went out to relieve himself in the yard, then came back in to rinse his face and hands in water from a pot by the hearth and dry them on the hem of his tunic, and to sit cross-legged looking at the food.

He had no appetite.

What had he thrown away?

After a while he got stiffly to his feet, wrapped the provisions in a bag and tucked them away for later.

He wondered where Gunnvor was. It was a relief to find her gone, and yet he felt he would have given his hopes of salvation to see her come in and raise her eyebrows at him as though the previous evening had never happened. Would he ever get the chance to explain himself? He had no idea what he would say, if he did.

Moving without conscious thought, he tidied the rugs he'd slept on, gathered up his possessions, found his cloak, and went back out into the daylight. Judging from the position of the sun, he had slept till almost noon.

The alleyway off the Gallowtree-gate was busy with folk. No one gave him a second glance as he walked, head down, through the houses and back towards St Margaret's Kirk. The mare he had brought from Gloucester had been tethered there somewhere, and he supposed she would still be there.

'Wulfgar!'

It was a cheerful shout. He turned to see young Alwin walking quickly towards him.

'Don't tell me the King wants me again?'

'No, no.'

'You look so much better than you did in York,' Wulfgar heard himself saying.

'Are you surprised?' Alwin frowned. 'I'd just been in my first battle, and my father not a month dead...' A darker shadow passed briefly across his face, but he shook it away like a dog shaking water from its fur. 'Come and have a cup of ale with me?'

Wulfgar could think of no reason to refuse. 'Not at the Wave-Serpent.'

Alwin shook his head. 'There's better at camp. Come on.' He took one of Wulfgar's bags. 'I was glad to see you,' the boy said, 'because we leave tonight.'

'Back to York?'

'Oh, no.' The boy's face took on a self-important expression. 'We march to war. But' – and he glanced from side to side – 'I mustn't tell you any more.'

'Against Wessex?'

'No, really. I mustn't say. Look, you sit here, and I'll bring you a cup.'

He was back in moments with two horn beakers. He had shown Wulfgar to a camp-fire – lately doused and still steaming – on the edge of the sea of tents, and pointed to a roughly-hewn round of wood. Wulfgar sat obediently, but he still wanted to know more.

'Are you attacking Mercia, then?'

'Sorry, Wulfgar!' For the first time Wulfgar could remember, the boy smiled. 'But you don't need to worry. I won't say anything else, but I'll say that. I owe you, after all.'

'You look like your father when you smile,' Wulfgar heard himself saying, remembering half against his will that last exchange of glances, that brief lightening of mood, before Alnoth of Brading had been hurried to the gallows.

The boy's smile deepened. 'Thank you. I'll remember that. I wish I could say you look like your brother, but I don't think I ever saw two men more different.' He looked worried for a moment. 'That's not an insult, to either of you. I mean, you're both in your own ways—'

Wulfgar held up his hands, half-laughing himself and wanting to cut through the boy's confusion. 'I don't suppose you saw Wystan at his best, at his trial,' he said, and wanted to bite his tongue. The last thing the boy needed was a reminder of that appalling day.

But Alwin was shaking his head. 'I wasn't at the trial,' he said. 'But I saw Wystan at Edric's hall often enough.'

'What?'

'In Amport.' Alwin looked wistful. 'They used to let me sit by the hearth with them when they were making their plans.' That horizontal frown had reappeared, bringing his black eyebrows together. 'Don't you wish Edric had kept his nerve? Then my Lord Seiriol would be King of Wessex already.'

There was a ringing in Wulfgar's ears. He found he was blinking very fast. It was hard to breathe. He tipped his head back, feeling the blood drain out of cheek and lip and chin.

'Are you all right?' Alwin's voice was full of concern. 'Put your head between your knees.'

'I'm all right,' Wulfgar forced himself to say. 'Could you – could you just say that again? About my brother?'

'That I used to see him when we came over from the Island? To Edric's house at Amport?' Alwin sounded puzzled.

'You're sure?'

'Of course. I told you, it was several times. It was only last winter, Wulfgar! I'm hardly likely to forget.'

'And you heard him plotting with your father and Edric of Amport to kill King Edward?' Wulfgar wanted it all laid out like a child's *abecedarium*, in the plainest and simplest of ways.

'Well, yes.' Alwin sounded puzzled. 'And my Lord King was there too. The Atheling, he was then.'

Wulfgar stared at the ranks of tents. Many of them were being struck and packed away, and between the bustling figures of men and horses, ox-carts and mules, he could see the King's tent quite clearly, still standing, with the fluttering banners and the carved tent poles. Once again, Seiriol had not lied to him. Had broken no promise. It was all in the words unspoken, the gaps between meanings. And in his own desperate desire to fill in those gaps. . .

'But my arm,' he said aloud.

'What?'

He looked down at his right arm. That painful and humiliating experience in Winchester Cathedral, had it then been a meaningless charade?

He shook his head.

A cleverer man might not have believed the Atheling's lies, but no one had ever called Wystan of Meon clever.

His heart broke for his poor, played-upon brother.

'Thanks, Alwin.' He handed his untouched beaker back to the boy. 'Good luck. I hope we meet again.'

He had a sudden longing to find Gunnvor, to tell her that she had been right all along.

To tell her many, many things. In law he was still her thrall, after all. 'I'll keep you,' she had said to him once, back in the spring, 'to sit at my feet and teach me English love-songs.' What he wouldn't give, now, to take her up on that offer.

But when he got back to the Wave-Serpent the only person he found was old Nonna, who looked at him suspiciously and told him that Gunnvor had left for Lincoln.

She didn't mention Toli Silkbeard, but his name floated in the air between them for all that.

He could bear this. He had borne so much already.

He walked slowly back once more to St Margaret's Church. For the last time, he told himself. The place was imbued with memories of Ronan, so powerful that it seemed impossible the priest could be dead, and indeed buried beneath the freshly turned sods only feet from where he was standing. He looked long and hard at the little painted image of St Margaret in her niche, in all her beauty and her defiance, wondering for the first time who had painted her, and whether the artist had had a real woman in mind.

Somewhere, not too far away, a drum began to beat.

A horn sounded, and then another.

A horse whinnied.

It sounded as though the army was on the march, and coming this way.

They were heading east, then.

Not Wessex, and not Mercia.

Not this time.

Wulfgar became aware of someone standing next to him, and he looked to his left to see Gerd, pale-faced and determined. She wasn't looking at him, and he took a moment to contemplate her plain, long-nosed profile, and to think that no man would guess how her smile transformed her. He knew she would be safe with Kevin's mother.

Had she really tried to revenge her father in Holy Wisdom by loosening the rope of the great polycandelon? He wondered whether he would ever have an answer to that question. Whether, indeed, he really wanted one.

The earth was shaking.

The army was in sight now, and getting closer.

Men on horses.

Something warm and insistent pressed against his hand, and he relaxed enough to let Gerd worm her bony, narrow hand into his and clasp his fingers tightly. There was the Atheling – *the King* – riding towards them.

And there was the Archbishop, on that lordly white mule, with its red caparison.

The vanguard had reached St Margaret's now, and they were riding past, and away up Gallowtree-gate, and out of Leicester's Danish quarter.

Would Gunnvor get to Lincoln before them? He wondered whether she were planning to warn Toli, or whether she came like one of the Spear's shield-maidens, as a harbinger of doom.

Line after line after line of marching men, and the ox-carts trundling heavily laden after them.

Wulfgar watched the army rumble into the distance. Only when the last of their thunder had died away did he look down, puzzled, to Gerd's hand still clutching his, and wonder what it was doing there.

HISTORICAL NOTE

GENERAL NOTE

A historical novel bears about as much relation to past events as a game of chess does to the politics, intrigues, power-plays and violence of a real medieval court. In other words, it is a highly stylised and simplified version of events. I have done my best, in *The Traitors' Pit*, to write nothing that *could not* have happened, but we know very little indeed about the minutiae of British politics in the years around 900 AD. Any attempt, therefore, at telling a story like this has to step almost immediately off the beaten track of chronicle and king-list, and start instead to hack its way through the uncharted jungle of personality and motive.

To take a single example, one of my major characters, King Knut of York, is only attested historically from his coinage. No contemporary chronicler ever recorded his existence. His coins, however, are extraordinary, as I hope this story conveys, and the Early Medieval Coins database lists 561 surviving examples, all silver. (The gold special issue is my invention. While Anglo-Saxon kings may have minted such coins there is no evidence that an Anglo-Danish one did.) If a king's coinage may be held to reflect the man in any way, Knut's certainly implies that he was no illiterate pagan barbarian warrior.

The Archbishop of York at this period is almost as invisible as the King. In the end, my portrait of Archbishop Lothward is a conflation of stray details that we know about several Archbishops of York in the late ninth and early tenth centuries, spiced with a good deal of imagination.

One fairly reliable fact, however, is that the rebel West Saxon Atheling, Athelwald, was accepted as King by the Danes in Northumbria: at least, the Anglo-Saxon Chronicle suggests that this happened, and there are three surviving coins minted in York at this period bearing the name *Alwaldus Rex*, a plausible Latin translation of King Athelwald. Of such fragile and ephemeral straws are my bricks made.

The Anglo-Saxon Chronicle also tells us that Athelwald abducted a nun at around the same time that he became King of the Northumbrian Danes. We do not know who she was, but if he had marriage in mind, it is plausible that she too was of royal descent. We know too little about the West Saxon royal family to be sure, one way or the other, but the laws of consanguinity promoted by the Church do not seem to have bothered the consciences of Anglo-Saxon kings particularly.

Another great mystery is the location of the Archbishop's quarter in York. Despite intensive archaeological research, no certain trace has yet been found of the pre-Norman Minster, nor of the church of Alma Sophia (Holy Wisdom) described so eloquently by the scholar Alcuin around a hundred years before my story starts. I took the executive decision to situate much of the Archbishop's palace within the footprint of the old Roman military headquarters of Eboracum: this provided Lothward with a suite of prestigious stone buildings while also suggesting a vaguely possible reason for the Archbishop's archaeological obscurity. In this scenario, some of his buildings might just look Roman when excavated, while others will have been destroyed, either when the Normans built their cathedral, or in later centuries. Where Holy Wisdom in particular is concerned I hope Dr Christopher Norton will forgive my having built such a glittering superstructure on his extremely cautious and scholarly foundations, published in the *Journal of the British Archaeological Association* (1998). My Holy Wisdom owes a little to surviving Anglo-Saxon churches at Deerhurst and Brixworth, but a great deal more to Charlemagne's palace chapel at Aachen.

Anglo-Saxon Winchester Cathedral, in contrast with York Minster, is well understood. Also known as the Old Minster, it was excavated forty years ago and the final publication of the results is expected to be in print by the end of 2012: the time lag there indicates both the amount of material and the high quality of the research. Edward's New Minster was indeed built immediately adjacent to the cathedral; the bodies of his royal ancestors were moved into the new church, and Grimbald of St Bertin was its first abbot. According to the Breviary of Hyde Abbey Grimbald was heart-broken when King Alfred died, and only agreed to stay in England if Edward made him abbot of the New Minster. Attentive readers will have noticed that my version of events is rather different.

The site of Godbegot House is still there, and still goes by that name, though the present building is late medieval: it was a pizzeria last time I was in Winchester. The name probably means Good Bargain, and it is recorded in royal ownership in the early eleventh century. The gold ring on which I based Wystan's was sold at Christie's auction house in 2010; Archbishop Lothward's gold and sapphire ring was found in a field near York in 2011 and is now in the Yorkshire Museum.

The execution cemetery at Harestock, just outside Winchester, is also real, and the name Harestock comes from *heafod-stocc* – almost certainly from the practice of decapitating some criminals and displaying their heads. Where this subject is concerned, I am very grateful for all the hard work of Andrew Reynolds, and particularly his *Anglo-Saxon Deviant Burial Customs* (Oxford University Press, 2009). Hanging seems to have been a standard means of execution, and this makes for some fascinating overlap with the death of Christ, as Wulfgar observes. Although Christ was of course crucified rather than hanged, there are several Biblical references to Him 'hanging on a tree'.

A NOTE ON ANGLO-SAXON LAW

Underlying the plot of *The Traitors' Pit* is a clause from a late tenth-century law-code (III Æthelred, 7-7.1), which makes it very clear how important the fate of a hanged man's body might be to his surviving family. This clause states that if anyone is related to an executed thief, and is convinced of his kinsman's innocence, he may put up a large sum of money and submit to the ordeal. If he comes through clean, he may take up his kinsman's body; if not he forfeits his stake and the dead man 'lies where he lay': *Gif he clæne beo æt þam ordale, nime upp his mæg; gif he þonne ful beo, licge þar he læg.* This reads like case law, based on a precedent established by a previous court decision. *The Traitors'*

Pit began with my wondering what sort of case might have given rise to such a clause being recorded.

The Anglo-Saxon and Norse legal systems were very different from their modern equivalents. An accused man was required to swear his innocence. Depending on the nature of the crime, he would have to produce a greater or lesser number of oath-swearers, all of good reputation, who would also attest his innocence. Failure to produce the required number was the equivalent of a confession of guilt, and if the court found the defendant guilty, his oath-swearers all shared in the shame – and the fine.

The Witan was never a formal assembly, more an informal body of advisors whom the king could summon at will. As far as I know, there was no convention that a poorly-attended assembly could not condemn a man to death: this is a plot device. But the ordeal was real enough, and it formed a major part of the Western European judicial system between around 800 and 1200 AD. Interesting work has been done on its psychosomatic aspects: the extent to which, if you perjured yourself and believed you had thereby damned yourself eternally, your body's ability to heal could be impaired. It is also clear that the ability to judge innocence or guilt lay in the hands of the priest administering the ordeal, and he might be taking into account information from many sources, not just from the physical damage inflicted by the hot water or the hot metal. All in all, it is likely that it was a more subtle diagnostic tool than it seems to us today. Like 'trial by oath-swearing', it may have worked effectively in these small, tightly-linked medieval communities, where people knew each other well by reputation, at the very least.

A NOTE ON NAMES
People

Anglo-Saxon names are exceptionally challenging for modern readers. There are numerous reasons for this. Very few male and even fewer female names from eleven hundred years ago are still used today, and those that are still familiar were popular in the nineteenth century, which means that Alfred, Edwin, Edith and Ethel tend to sound charmingly Victorian rather than robustly Anglo-Saxon. In their original spelling, Anglo-Saxon names are often dense with consonants and unfamiliar letters (Æþelðryð, anyone?), and it can be hard to know how to pronounce names such as Ecgberht or Osburh. By a series of unfortunate coincidences, many popular name elements sound inappropriate or funny to modern ears: Wigbald means Warrior-Bold and Sexburga means Blade-City, but it would be a brave parent who christened a child either of these in twenty-first-century Britain.

There are other problems, too. Particularly among the Anglo-Saxon aristocracy, there seems to have been a fairly small pool of popular name elements; and dynasties liked to give their offspring alliterating names. So for generation after generation everyone in a royal or noble family is called Athel- or Os- or Wulf- or Alf-something. It is hard enough for many historians to keep these people straight: it would be an unforgivable imposition on a novelist's readership. (Even so, I realise I have to apologise for lumbering you with Ketil, Kenelm, Knut and Kevin.)

I have taken a few liberties with names, therefore, in the interests of clarity. The most outrageous is with the Atheling. His mother was called Wulfthryth, and we have no reason to think she was anything but a West Saxon. However, to make Athelwald more distinctive, for the purposes of fiction I have decided she was Welsh, thus allowing me to give Athelwald a second, Welsh, name: Seiriol. This allows me to distinguish a little more easily between Athelwald the Atheling; his cousin Athelfled (Fleda) of Mercia, her husband, Athelred of Mercia; and her nephew and foster-son, Athelstan of Wessex.

I have modernised a few names. Kenelm would have been known to his contemporaries as Cynehelm, and Wystan as Wigstan (the *g* would have been pronounced more like a *y*). I have invented the name Lothward for my Archbishop of York, a plausible though unrecorded Anglo-Saxon name. Where the Anglo-Saxons would have used Æ/æ I have used either A/a or E/e. So Ælfflæd becomes Elfled. (I hope you're grateful.)

There was a Carolingian princess called Judith resident in Wessex from 856 to 860: she married first King Athelwulf, who died in 858, then his son, her stepson, King Athelbald, who died in 860. Then she went home. Judith in *The Traitors' Pit* is named after her: perhaps her mother was one of the first Judith's attendant women.

PLACES

Anglo-Saxon minster churches were usually established among the ruins of Roman settlements, which the English called *ceastras* (chesters, from Latin *castra*). This is why so many of the places in this story have similar-sounding endings: Winchester, Leicester, Gloucester, Worcester. I've tried to avoid writing sentences along the lines of *When Wulfgar got back from Leicester to Gloucester he met the Bishop of Worcester*, which teeter over the brink of parody. York is an exception. The English called it *Eoforwic*; the Danes turned this into *Jórvík*, which gives us the modern name York. If there had been no Scandinavian influence on the city, we would probably know it now as Everwich.

A NOTE ON MARRIAGE AND CELIBACY

At this period, around 900, marriage was not yet a religious sacrament. It was a contract between two individuals and two kindreds, requiring consent and witnessing. No priest was required. The married couple might then go and have their marriage blessed, but many would not. Thus Seiriol and Elfled are already married, by mutual consent, when they first appear in this story: they are asking the Archbishop of York for a public ratification and blessing of an existing contract, *not* actually to marry them.

Nor was celibacy yet mandated on parish priests in 900 AD, though some clerical thought was beginning to move in that direction. Senior clerics such as abbots and bishops would be expected to be celibate, but ordinary priests, and canons of collegiate churches, were often married. This is still very much the situation today in the Eastern Orthodox Church. Wulfgar is therefore not faced with a simple dilemma – be a priest or marry – but a rather more complex choice. He could leave the Church and marry; become an ordinary priest and marry; or stay true to his ambition and remain celibate.

GLOSSARY

Abecedarium – The full alphabet, written out as a teaching aid.

Ainkirk – Own-Church. This is a compound word I have made up, based on the German word *Eigenkirche*, which is a term commonly used by early medieval historians when writing about churches owned by laymen, outside the jurisdiction of a bishop. Although commonest in Germany they undoubtedly existed in England. There is, alas, no evidence that All Saints' Pavement in York (the model for Thorbjorn's All Hallows) was such a proprietary church, but it does contain a small gravestone from *c*.900 AD.

Alb – An alb is the long, white nightgown-like vestment worn by all clerical ranks to symbolise purity.

Aspergillum – This is used to sprinkle holy water. In the modern Western Church it is usually an instrument with a brush or a perforated ball on a handle, but in the Eastern Church branches of plants such as rosemary, basil or hyssop may be used. It's not clear what was in use in the tenth-century Anglo-Saxon church, but very probably a sprig from a suitable aromatic plant.

Bellwether – A castrated ram with a bell around his neck, which accompanied a flock of sheep, so the shepherd could keep track of them.

Bookland – Land which had been granted by the king by means of a written charter (*boc* in Old English).

Buskins – Buskins in this context are calf-length fabric boots embroidered with gold. We do not really know what footwear Anglo-Saxon kings wore on formal occasions, but Byzantine emperors wore purple buskins embroidered with gold eagles, and the buskin was also used as liturgical footwear (an 11th-century pair survives from the tomb of Pope Clement II in Bamberg Cathedral, in Germany).

Cartulary – A collection of charters.

Cathedra – A bishop's throne.

Censer – A small container hanging from a chain and containing charcoal and incense, also known as a thurible (< Greek *thus*, incense).

Chasuble – The outermost vestment worn by a priest, a chasuble is a large oval piece of cloth with a hole in the middle, often made of rich fabric and beautifully decorated.

Chrism oil – Consecrated oil used in a range of sacraments, including baptism, the ordination of new priests, and the anointing of the sick.

Dorter – Dorter is really a Middle English word, meaning sleeping-chamber or dormitory, especially in a monastic context.

Dreng – From Old Norse *drengr*. In this context, men of fighting age and rank. It gives us the Yorkshire place-name of Dringhouses.

Eldorman – This is from Old English *ealdorman*, which literally means 'older man', in an 'elders and betters' kind of way. By *c*.900 an ealdorman was a very senior aristocrat, analogous to the later earl. The modern English derivative from *ealdorman* is 'alderman', however, which sounds very civic and Town Hall-ish, and gives quite the wrong impression, so I came up with my own slight variant on the Old English word.

Ettling – From Old Norse *ætla*, meaning 'to aim, to intend', now confined to Northern English and Scots use.

Faldstool – A folding stool, widely used by people of authority in England from at least the seventh century, probably ultimately derived from a Roman general's campaign stool.

Fettle – 'To prepare, or attend to'. No longer found in Standard English.

Flyting – A ritual exchange of elaborate insults, either before battle or as a substitute for battle.

Frankish – French, only France hasn't quite been invented yet.

Garth – This is an Old Norse word for enclosure, cognate with 'yard' (from Old English *geard*).

Geld – Payment, tribute, tax. Very much the same word in Old

Norse (*gjald*) and Old English.

Gesta Alfredi – 'The Deeds of Alfred'.

Gíslar – Old Norse for 'hostages'. Again the Old English (*gislas*) and the Old Norse words are very similar.

Gjald – see Geld (above).

Godweb – This is an Old English word, literally meaning good-weave. It turns up unexplained in contexts where it probably refers to the most sumptuous of fabrics, whether ladies' dresses or churchmen's robes. Feel free to imagine heavy imported silks woven and embroidered in several colours, and including gold thread.

Gossip – From Old English *god-sib* (as in 'sibling') – someone to whom you are related through baptism, and with whom, presumably, you would want to exchange all the important news of the day.

Gralloch – *Grealach* is a Gaelic word meaning deer's intestines, which English transforms into a verb meaning 'to disembowel'. Although it's not recorded in English until the 19th century (probably as a result of the popularity of Victorian shooting estates in the Scottish Highlands), it seems the right sort of word for Ronan, with his Irish background, to use.

Habitaculum – Latin for 'small house'.

Hairst – A dialect word for harvest, which may come from loss of the 'v' in 'harvest' or (in Old Norse-influenced areas) from Old Norse *haust*.

Hearth-men – The king or lord's close followers.

Hide of land – The amount needed to sustain a family. Obviously the actual acreage would be different depending on whether an area had fertile or barren land.

House-carl – A word which in Old English and Old Norse can simply mean 'a household servant', but can have the more nuanced sense of 'an aristocratic retainer'. Modern historians use it in the latter sense.

Jarl – Norse title which gives us the word 'earl', broadly equivalent to the Old English *ealdorman*.

Johnsmas – The feast of the birthday of St John the Baptist, on 24 June.

League – About 5 kilometres (3 miles).

Lodestone – 'Leading-stone' – a naturally-magnetised mineral. Although the compound word isn't recorded in English until the sixteenth century, both elements ('lead' and 'stone') are much older, and the analogous 'lodestar' is attested in Old Norse (*leiðarstjarna*).

Lombardic – From Northern Italy, only Italy certainly hasn't been invented yet.

Matins – The first sung liturgical office of the day, before dawn.

Mediatrix – Female intercessor: a title of the Virgin Mary.

Midden – A word first recorded in Middle English meaning 'refuse heap', compounded from two Old Norse words meaning 'muck' and 'dung' (*myki-dyngja*).

Monasteriolum – Latin for 'little monastery'.

Nunnaminster – A convent founded in Winchester by King Edward and the Lady's mother. Historically, it was founded in 903 but I have brought back the foundation by a very few years.

Oath-swearer – In Anglo-Saxon law, the defendant was required to swear an oath, stating his innocence. Depending on the offence, a greater or lesser number of his more reputable kith and kin were also required to swear the same oath. Failure to produce the appropriate number of oath-swearers would result in a guilty verdict. If the defendant were found guilty (with or without the right number of oath-swearers), any fine to which he was liable would also be levied from the oath-swearers. A defendant with a bad reputation, whose guilt seemed probable, would find it very hard to muster the required number of supporters.

Oblate – A child in training to become a cleric.

Prestr – Old Norse for 'priest'.

Prime – Early morning prayer.

Quean – Harlot. The Old English word *cwéne* had a very wide range of meanings: 'king's wife', 'wife', 'woman' or 'harlot'. Nowadays 'queen' is the only modern word in common use, but 'quean' survived in English until the 18th century. ('Quine' is still commonly found in Scots, meaning 'girl' or 'woman'.)

Quernstone – One of a pair of thick, round stones about 60 centimetres (2 feet) across, used for grinding grain.

Reeve – A steward, estate manager, or official.

Sext – The liturgical office celebrated at noon.

Terce – Mid-morning prayer.

Thane – From an Old English word meaning, originally, servant, it came to mean a free retainer, one of a class of wealthy land-owners, broadly corresponding to the later gentry. A king's thane had special responsibilities and privileges.

Thole – From Old English *tholian*, meaning to suffer or endure. Still widely used in Scots.

Thrall – From the Old Norse word for 'slave'. 'Enthrall' comes from the same root.

Tunicle – A long, wide-sleeved, decorated tunic worn by sub-deacons at Mass and other services.

Vespers – Prayer at sunset.

Witan – The West Saxon senate, whose name literally means *The Wise*. A council of important laymen and clerics, whose role was to help choose and advise kings. An informal and often *ad hoc* assembly rather than any kind of formally-constituted council.